Praise for Boris Ak...

'One ... he most distinctive characters in historical crime fiction
... T... ..y years after his debut, Fandorin remains a thoroughly
engag... g hero' *Sunday Times*

"... rast Fandorin detective novels are always meaty, packed
...istorical detail, old-fashioned in the best sense and intricately
...d' *Daily Mail*

...most playful, ingenious historical thriller series in modern
...hing' *Guardian*

...pular hero to equal Sherlock Holmes and James Bond . . .
...in's finest creation and the star of his titles is Erast Fandorin –
...s, gentleman, polyglot, kickboxer, and all-round inordinately
...bloke' *The Times*

...n is an outstanding novelist . . . gloriously tongue-in-cheek but
...sly edge-of-your-seat at the same time' *Daily Express*

NOT SAYING GOODBYE

Boris Akunin is the pseudonym of Grigory Chkhartishvili. He has been compared to Gogol, Tolstoy and Arthur Conan Doyle, and his Erast Fandorin books have sold over forty million copies in Russia alone. He lives in London.

NOT SAYING GOODBYE

BORIS AKUNIN

*Translated from the Russian
by Andrew Bromfield*

WEIDENFELD & NICOLSON

First published in Russian by Zakharov Publications in 2018
First published in Great Britain in 2019 by Weidenfeld & Nicolson
This paperback edition published in 2020 by Weidenfeld & Nicolson
an imprint of the Orion Publishing Group Ltd
Carmelite House, 50 Victoria Embankment
London EC4Y 0DZ

An Hachette UK Company

1 3 5 7 9 10 8 6 4 2

Copyright © Boris Akunin 2018
English translation copyright © Andrew Bromfield 2019

The moral right of Boris Akunin to be identified as the author
of this work has been asserted in accordance with the
Copyright, Designs and Patents Act of 1988.

Andrew Bromfield has asserted his right to be identified as
the author of the English translation of the work.

A CIP catalogue record for this book is
available from the British Library.

ISBN (Mass Market Paperback) 978 1 4746 1099 5
ISBN (ebook) 978 1 4746 1100 8

Typeset by Input Data Services Ltd, Somerset

Printed in Great Britain by Clays Ltd, Elcograf S.p.A.

www.orionbooks.co.uk
www.weidenfeldandnicolson.co.uk

TABLE-TALK 1918

As the day drew to an end and twilight fell, the station suddenly came to life. A rumour had spread that there was going to be a train to Moscow. Two days previously, near the settlement of Ivashenkovo, locals had stopped an 'express' and robbed it after taking up a rail. Although it was only minor damage, there was no one to repair it – the line repairmen's trade union was holding a meeting.

And then suddenly – a train! Somehow or other it had been discovered that the Moscow train would take an alternative route along the Sergievsky Plant line and the carriages would arrive at Platform Three. People grabbed up their bundles, suitcases and little kiddies and went dashing off there.

In the year since the Empire's inglorious end, the Samara railway station, one of the finest in the nation, had deteriorated, like that baron in the play *The Lower Depths* by the proletarian writer Maxim Gorky, becoming more shabby and frayed, debased and decayed, until it hit rock bottom. They had stopped heating the premises back in December, and in the glacial winter season the two upper storeys stood empty – people ran up there to relieve themselves in whatever spot they could find: the station lavatories weren't working. The waiting rooms on the ground floor were not heated either, but it wasn't cold in there. People sat or lay on the benches, the windowsills and the buffet counters, or simply on the floor, and they warmed the air with their breathing, smoking, coughing and cursing.

And now approximately half of this grey-brown mass had roused itself and moved. The other half, which needed to travel in the opposite direction, stayed where it was.

The rumour proved to be true. Soon a train rolled up to the platform, panting out bluish smoke. It was not a long train, but neither was it merely a goods train, it had genuine passenger carriages: a blue first-class carriage at the front, followed by a yellow second-class carriage, and then three of the green, common or garden variety.

A crush immediately formed at the entrance to each of the carriages, and it was densest, of course, at the blue one. In the name of equality and brotherhood, all the tickets were identical, without place numbers and, naturally, without any classes – travel wherever you get a seat: if you can get a seat, that is.

The militiaman with a red ribbon on his sleeve and another on his cap struck the butt of his rifle against the platform.

'Form a queue, citizens! Show your tickets!'

But instead of a queue, everything happened in Charles Darwin style as the strongest and nimblest shoved the others out of the way or squeezed them aside. Right at the front of them all was an elderly, short Oriental with slanting eyes – a Chinaman, or perhaps a Kirghiz. Like a broom, the revolution had swept in all sorts of different people from Russia's peripheral territories, including some kinds that had never been seen before out here in the sticks. Everyone had suddenly started feeling miserable in their own places and a fine dust of humanity had gone flooding along the roads, halting in some places to eddy up into swirling dust devils.

'And where are you going, barging in with a great huge bundle like that?' the militiaman barked. He had a rifle and he liked being a boss, even if only a little one. In these new times, a man without a position and a weapon had become a nobody.

The presumptive Chinaman really did have a huge, long bundle wrapped in sheepskin thrown over his shoulder, but it couldn't be very heavy – the half-pint was holding it up quite easily.

'Don't go shoving that ticket at me, you foreign devil! There was a decree – no large items of luggage. One of the measures to counter profiteers and speculators.'

'I have two tickets, dear sir,' said the Oriental, bowing together with his burden. 'Two praces.'

He spoke Russian well, except for his pronunciation of the letter 'l'.

2

'That's not allowed, get out of here and don't block the citizens' way through! Who's next?'

The slow-witted Chinaman didn't move from the spot and his round face continued beaming in a broad smile.

'Two tickets, two praces, dear sir,' he repeated.

An immense hand with a blue anchor tattooed on it grabbed his shoulder from behind and a great hulk of a sailor, standing a whole head taller than the crowd, boomed at the obstinate nuisance:

'Are you plain deaf or just plain stupid? Didn't you hear what he said? Clear off now, before you get thrown under the carriage.'

The Oriental replied without turning around or stopping smiling:

'You crear off, you typhus rouse.'

He shifted his free elbow backwards gently and the sailor suddenly stopped being so tall as he doubled right over.

The Oriental told the militiaman:

'You're angry, comrade, because you're not feering werr. You need to take a rie-down.'

'A doctor, then, are you?' the militiaman snapped fiercely. 'Right then, show me your papers.'

'Yes, yes, I'm a doctor,' said the Oriental, nodding. 'You have a bad pain right here.'

He prodded the militiaman at some spot on his stomach. And it turned out that there was indeed a 'bad pain' at that very spot – the state official gasped, turned very pale, dropped his rifle and staggered.

'He's not feering werr,' the Chinaman explained to the other passengers, gently taking hold of the militiaman's collar. 'He's going to rie down for a rittur whire. Move over, citizens . . . Thank you very much.'

He laid the swooning servant of socialist law and order out on the platform, hoisted his own load a little bit higher on his shoulder and walked up the steps, taking his time. The others rushed after him.

Once inside, the passengers who were so eager to ride in first class discovered that they had backed the wrong horse. Some Ussurian Cossacks, who did not wish to be parted from their own horses, had recently travelled home from the front in this respectable carriage and, like the Samara station, it had fallen victim to the revolution. The sour odour of horses had irrevocably impregnated the walls, while the partitions, shelves, little tables and seats had all been consumed in a campfire that had left a blackened indentation in the floor at the centre of the devastated empty space. Only a single compartment at the end had survived, and the first people to burst in hurried towards it, although their movement could not really be described as 'hurrying'. No one dared to overtake the polite Chinaman with his cumbersome burden, and he moved staidly, without any fuss. It was only after the Oriental had looked around and taken his seat, setting his bundle in the seat beside the window in a vertical position, that the most combative of the other passengers started rushing into the compartment. The second person in was the gargantuan sailor, who had already recovered from the blow.

'Don't mind if I go up on top, do you?' he asked respectfully, and occupied a really sweet spot on one of the luggage shelves, where he could stretch out at full length.

Following that, the compartment was stormed by agile youngsters. Two railway station urchins, who cut profitable deals by occupying good seats and then relinquishing them for a substantial consideration, installed themselves: one, with flaxen hair, took a seat opposite the Chinese bundle, and the other, with ginger hair, took a place on the second luggage shelf. Another three people could now occupy seats down below. A girl, wrapped almost right up to her eyes in a vermilion shawl, plumped down beside the flaxen-haired brat. And lagging only very slightly behind her came a slim, panting youth in a grammar-school greatcoat and peaked cap.

'Hoop-lah, I got a seat!' the girl shouted joyfully. 'And I'm not getting up, not for all the tea in China.'

The grammar-school student said:

'*Veni, vidi, vici.* Ooph.'

The final place, the one beside the Oriental, went to an agile little priest, who had slipped through under the arm of some bungler.

'Hey, Father, that's not right,' said the bungler. 'I was in front of you!'

4

Unwinding a chunky, hand-knitted scarf and extracting a silver pectoral cross from under it, the reverend father declared:

'As it says in the Gospels, my son: "But many who are first will be last, and many who are last will be first." What right do we sinners have to complain about that? Would you like me to bless you thrice with the thrice-sacred benediction? Well now, that's your loss.'

And he jiggled about, settling in so thoroughly that it was immediately clear – this man wasn't going to get up either, not for all the tea in China.

The compartment was fully occupied, but the seating arrangements were not yet final.

'Who wants a lying place, a fine, rich one? And who wants the very best place by the window?' the urchins yelled.

'How much?' asked the bungler who had been overtaken by the priest. But when he heard the price – a hundred roubles – he spat and withdrew.

The place by the window was bought by a fat-cheeked woman in a short sheepskin coat, who haggled the price down to seventy Kerensky roubles and a boiled egg. The juvenile profiteer popped the spoils into his cap and disappeared.

But the second, ginger-haired urchin was unlucky. Instead of paying, a clean-shaven citizen in a short winter fur coat and a low, round astrakhan hat took the little lad by the scruff of his neck and flung him out through the door without saying a word.

'You some kind of contra, are you?' the pipsqueak screamed. 'I'll shiv you good!'

But the shaven-headed individual merely clicked his tongue obnoxiously and bared his teeth to reveal a glinting gold crown. The urchin disappeared in a flash.

* * *

In this way the aristocracy of the train was constituted by those who had installed themselves in the only compartment of the blue carriage. The other passengers settled down higgledy-piggledy along the walls and on the floor of the carriage's main section. Without any bells or announcements, in true revolutionary style, the steam locomotive jerked into motion, the carriages clattered against each other and the train set off.

'Too-too-oo!' droned the murky March twilight.

'May the Lord watch over travellers and wayfarers,' the priest droned in a sing-song voice. 'And may things be better for us at the end of the journey than at the beginning, otherwise what point is there in travelling?'

'That's for sure,' the man with the gold crown agreed, leaping up nimbly onto the upper shelf. 'This town's garbage. If it disappeared it would be no loss.'

'Oh, what are you saying? I've got a home and kin in Samara,' the woman said reproachfully, but amicably, without any malice.

Everyone was delighted that they had installed themselves so successfully.

The conductor peeped in – apparently there were still conductors to be found on trains.

'I'm not offering the others any,' he said, nodding offhandedly at the open area of the carriage, 'but if you like, I can let you have some kerosene. Eighty roubles a little bottle. Enough to light you all the way to Moscow, if you're careful how you burn it.'

Needless to say, there was no electricity on the train, and black holes were all that remained of the lamps, but there was a kerosene lantern, not yet lit, hanging from the ceiling.

The price was insane, but the passengers didn't want to travel in the dark, they could already hardly see each other as it was.

'Let's chip in ten apiece,' said the woman, clarifying the proposition for the Chinaman: 'You're sitting in two places, so you pay twenty.'

The Oriental bowed without arguing, but problems arose with the other occupants of the compartment.

'I haven't got any money at all,' the grammar-school student sighed. 'And anyway I can sleep in the dark, in fact it's better that way.'

The girl refused too:

'And I'm getting off at the first station. I'm from near Bezenchuk. Why should I pay for Moscow?'

The priest recited a verse of poetry:

> Not in the lamp's inefficacious glow
> Lies your defence against the dark,
> But in the strong shield bright faith will bestow
> When kindled by pure prayer's invigorating spark.

'Well, have it your own way,' the conductor said with a shrug.

But at that point the man with the crowned tooth leaned down from above and thrust a banknote at him with a grand flourish.

'Here, take a hundred, Peaked Cap. No change required. I'm paying for the entire agreeable company. That's Yasha Black for you.'

With the compartment illuminated by swaying, reddish light, the travellers were able to get a better look at each other. And travelling conversations started up – conversations specifically suited to revolutionary times, when people are cautious at first and don't mention their names. (The man with the crowned tooth didn't count – it was unlikely that he was called Yasha, let alone Black.)

The most talkative of them all was the reverend father. He told them that he served a parish in the Syzran district and had travelled to see the bishop in Samara, because he didn't have an archpriest to go to and his stipend hadn't been paid for a long time, but he had made the journey in vain, by God's will, and merely wasted his money, because the diocesan town residence was now occupied by a Poor Peasants' Committee. 'But never mind,' he said, 'we'll get by somehow even without a stipend, the Lord won't abandon us, and as the rector at the seminary always used to say: "A good priest will never go short."'

The girl had been living in town as a servant in the house of a 'legal advocate', but he had 'got beggared', because who needed the laws now, and the other gentlefolk had gone bust too, so there were no jobs to be had anywhere, but her father and mother were at home, and now eligible suitors had come back from the front.

The stout woman made a living by barter. She carried essential goods from Samara round the villages and returned with foodstuffs.

'So where are the goods?' doubting Yasha asked her. 'It looks to me like you're travelling empty-handed.'

The woman hesitated about whether to tell him, but she really wanted very badly to boast. She reached in under her skirt and plonked a little sack down on the table.

'There. A pound of needles. Out in the country the women have nothing to sew with. They give a sack of flour for a single needle.'

That was serious riches for revolutionary times and everyone was respectfully silent for a while. But Yasha still expressed doubt.

'They might give you it, but how will you transport that much back to the city? One cart won't be enough. You need horses and wagons. And they'll confiscate the flour at the tollhouse. And they could just bump you off as a speculator. Goods may come cheap, but shipping can be costly.'

The woman winked at him cunningly.

'The father of my godchild works in the Department of Railways. We've come to an arrangement. I give him half of the flour, and he gets it delivered, all present and correct.'

Well now, that made them respect her even more.

Then the grammar-school student made them all laugh.

'I'm going out into the country to barter for food too. In here . . .' – he slapped himself on the chest – '. . . I have a stamp album. I've collected stamps all my life, since the second class. Foreign stamps. Last summer I was offered a Swedish bicycle and an air rifle for them. So it seems like I did the right thing. And I won't let them go cheap.'

They laughed loud and long at him – the little priest putting his hand over his mouth, the women squealing and Yasha guffawing at the top of his voice. Especially when the youth batted his eyelids and babbled: 'I don't know what to take to barter with. This is my first trip.'

The only ones who didn't join in the mirth were the sailor, who had pulled his pea jacket up over his head as they set off and started snoring, and the Chinaman, who kept rearranging his bundle and probably didn't understand Russian very well anyway.

'And you, comrade, what necessity is it that has you travelling?' the woman asked Black, throwing her head back to look up and nudging the girl next to her in the side, since he couldn't see that from up there.

8

'I'm a traveller through the worldly elements,' the inhabitant of that exalted spot replied. 'An observer of life.'

'We know all about these observers, you just keep an eye on your little knick-knacks,' the speculator whispered to the girl, and put the precious little sack away, back under her skirt.

And then came the turn of the Oriental, whom they had all been glancing at curiously from the very beginning.

'And I suppose you're taking fabrics to barter, citizen Chinaman?' the irrepressible woman asked. 'If it's calico, that's always in demand. But if it's your Chinese silk, you need to know the right places. I can give you a few hints.'

'No,' the Chinaman replied curtly, unwrapping the upper section of his bundle for some reason.

'"No" what, begging your pardon?' the woman insisted, without waiting for him to continue.

'I'm not Chinese. I'm Japanese. And this isn't fabric.'

He folded back the edge of the sheepskin and parted a flannelette cloth, and a pale face with white hair and a neat little black moustache appeared in the gap. It was completely still and the eyelids were closed dolefully.

'A corpse!' the girl squealed, cringing on her seat in fright. The priest crossed himself, Yasha Black swore raucously and the woman screamed so loudly that the sailor woke up and jolted upright.

'This is not a corpse, it is my master. He is sreeping,' the Japanese said sternly, wiping the forehead of his strange travelling companion with a small handkerchief.

The grammar-school student whistled in admiration.

'Well, stone the crows. Lord Ruthven, straight up!'

* * *

Masa knew who Lord Ruthven was. A *kuetsuki* from an old English novel. A *kuetsuki* is a creature from the world beyond. He sleeps during the day and sucks human blood at night.

The boy didn't know how close his guess was to the truth: Masa's master really was sleeping. And today he really had dined on human blood.

The final portion of the nutritional mixture prepared according

9

to Professor Kirichevsky's prescription had run out the day before, and in the whole of Samara there had not been a single drop to be found of the basic ingredient, cod liver oil. And so Masa had fed his master with his own blood, after mixing a little flour into it.

The very first professor, back in the cursed city of Baku, had said: 'The injured man still has his swallowing reflex, which means that he won't die immediately. He'll live for another month or two. If that can be called living.'

On its way out the bullet had passed through the upper right section of the skull. Masa's master had been saved from death only by the fact that it was a small-calibre revolver. The killer had been given the gun by a woman who loved Masa's master. Masa simply could not understand whether this was karma's mercy or its malicious mockery. Perhaps it would have been better if that *akunin* had used his own usual forty-five and Masa's master had died immediately, and not tumbled into a black hole from which he could not be dragged back out.

'This is all quite astonishing,' the great luminary of neurosurgery, Kirichevsky, had said months later, in his Moscow clinic. 'Mr Fandorin is not dying, but he is not living either. Fortunately, modern-day science does not know much about the organisation of the brain.'

'Why "fortunatery"?' Masa had asked at the time.

And the *sensei*, the wise man, had replied:

'Because where there is no firm knowledge, one can still hope for a miracle. Concerning the brain we know that it lives according to certain laws of its own and is capable of spontaneously duplicating its own functional channels. New channels can be formed, bypassing the old ones. Apparently, the patient was a man of phenomenal brain and motor activity, was he not? People like that quite often emerge from a coma.' Only of course, after these encouraging words, the *sensei* had also added: 'But even in a case like that, such severe injury to the right frontal lobe usually results in the patient becoming an idiot when he regains consciousness.'

After that there had been many more professors. And they had said different things. The previous autumn, when the revolutions had made it really difficult to get hold of medicines, Masa had asked himself whether it was not time to stop tormenting a poor body in which no soul remained. A single pinch of his fingers, and it would all be over. The master himself would probably have demanded it if he could speak. But on the other hand, if the master could speak, why should Masa pinch his fingers together?

At the most bitter moment of Masa's torment, Kiri-*sensei* (that was what the Japanese called Professor Kirichevsky for the sake of brevity) had said that in the Volga city of Samara there was a certain Chinese healer by the name of Chang, who achieved incredible results by means of heating certain cunning little needles and jabbing them into the body. A colleague in the military hospital there had written to the professor, explaining how the Chinese healer had brought back to consciousness an injured man whose skull had been pierced through by shrapnel. Of course, all of the man's intellectual functions had been compromised, but he walked about, ate and reacted to simple commands.

Masa tried to picture his master reacting to simple commands, but he couldn't manage it. His master had never obeyed commands of any kind. Nonetheless, the Japanese had made his preparations and set out. The trains were still running at that time, and it was even possible to order a motor carriage with medical orderlies to get to the station.

In the five months he had spent in Samara, the country had fallen apart with incredible speed and a kind of reckless jauntiness, as if for a thousand years it had just been waiting for a chance to crumble into dust. Masa did not like the revolution, and for a very simple reason: in such times it had at first become difficult to support an invalid, and then absolutely impossible. Money was swiftly losing its value, goods and food, not to mention medicines, had all but disappeared, and there was no order left in anything. The most galling thing of all was that Chang-*sensei*'s treatment sessions had been producing results. Lord Ruthven? The boy should have seen Masa's master before Samara. He was as pale and fleshless as an Egyptian mummy. But the Chinese healer's needles and burning herbs had made him fill out and gain colour – a genuine Momotaro, the 'Peach Boy' from the Japanese folk tale. Sometimes he started moving his lips, as if he was talking to someone. Just a little bit longer, and perhaps he would have woken up. But Chang-*sensei* had said that he wouldn't stay in Russia any longer, because everyone here had gone insane. He had said there was a revolution in China too, but it was better to live among one's own madmen than among foreign ones. And he had set out for Nanking. Well, Masa couldn't detain him by force, could he?

'It's corred a "coma",' the Japanese explained to his travelling companions. 'A Greek word. It means "deep, deep sreep". My master has been in a deep, deep sreep for more than three years. He srept through the war and he srept through the revorution.'

'Lucky man,' the woman sighed. 'I wish I could have gone to bed in 1914 too and told everyone: "Wake me up, good people, when life sorts itself out again." That wouldn't be bad, eh? Everyone fighting each other, slaughtering and plundering, and he just keeps snoring away.'

'You foor!' Masa barked at the stupid woman. 'If my master hadn't forren into a deep, deep sreep in 1914, none of this would have happened – there wouldn't have been any war or any revorution. He wouldn't have ret it happen.'

His outcry set the woman blinking, and all the others went quiet.

They're all glancing at each other, thinking that my atama *is addled*, Masa told himself with a sigh. He hadn't used his native language for so long that he had started thinking in Russian, but sometimes he inserted Japanese words, in order not to forget *nippon-go* completely.

'Never mind. When my master awakes, then we'rr see,' the Japanese said threateningly, not addressing his travelling companions, but speaking into empty space.

'You need to place your trust in the Orthodox God and pray,' the priest advised him. 'In times of many horrors there are also many miracles. As the saying goes: "A simple prayer to God – and lo and behold! – you're cured."'

'I have prayed. To the Orthodox God and a non-Orthodox God, I've prayed to orr sorts of gods.'

'That means you did it wrong. I can tell you that as a professional,' said the priest, livening up. 'For the relief of the distressed in mind you should not appeal directly to the Lord, you have to appeal through the Blessed Virgin, the comforter of all who sorrow and pine. Let me show you how . . .' He raised his face to the smoke-stained ceiling and chanted soulfully, in a tearfully trembling voice: 'Immaculate Mother and Intercessor, intercede for me with your Most Holy Son for the healing of the mentally disturbed . . . what's his first name?'

'Erast.'

'The mentally disturbed Erast. Look down on him from on high and return his reason to him.'

'Amen,' said Masa with a sigh. He thought for a moment and crossed himself. It couldn't do any harm.

The sailor on the shelf looked down from on high.

'Pooh! You idle, good-for-nothing priests should be set to work. All you do is tell lies and gorge yourselves.'

'A bite to eat would be good all right,' said the man of God, not offended in the least. 'Shall we have supper, brothers and sisters?'

And they all began their supper, each of them eating what he or she had. The grammar-school student unwrapped a meat-rissole sandwich, the girl took out a thick slice of bread, sprinkled with salt, the sailor propagated a robust smell of herring through the air and Yasha Black munched on something crunchy up on his shelf.

The woman dined more substantially and abundantly than all the others. She took out some boiled eggs and about ten potatoes, and soon she had heaped up shells and peelings right across the little table.

'Isn't it a sin to guzzle meat or milk during Lent?' she asked the priest with her mouth full – he was feasting on neatly cut slices of sausage.

'It is permitted to consume meat and milk on a journey, if you don't have any Lenten fare,' the reverend father replied, 'but if you, my daughter, wish to treat me to some root vegetables, I shall refrain from the sin of pig's flesh.'

The woman merely snorted, but Masa sighed. He also had a lump of pig's flesh – a half-pound chunk of fatty bacon – lying close to his bosom, but he had to stretch it out as far as Moscow. Heh, if someone had told Masahiro Shibata in the time of his distant Yokohama youth that he would feed on the stale fat of a pig that had died long ago, he would have puked. But on a journey fatty bacon was more convenient than anything else. You couldn't eat a lot of that vile *kuso*, because it was disgusting, but it gave you strength. And after all, he would have to feed his master with blood once again, or perhaps even twice.

'It looks like we've skipped past Ivashenkovo,' the female speculator announced, gazing into the darkness outside the window, where not a single light was shining. 'If we can just keep rolling as far as Bezenchuk – after that they don't get up to any mischief.'

'Who gets up to mischief?' asked the sailor, also staring out into the pitch-blackness.

'The devil only knows. They put a log on the rails, and that means: stop right here! And then they walk through the carriages, robbing people.'

'And what if you don't stop? A log, so what? Crunch straight through it with the wheels, and it's anchors aweigh!'

'Then they'll start shooting at the locomotive. And you'll be lucky if they use rifles, they could use a machine gun,' the grammar-school student said with a nervous shudder. 'Last week near Syzran they killed the driver like that and the train flew off the rails on a bend. A lot of people were killed and injured. So you have to stop.'

The little priest crossed himself.

'The villains have gone totally berserk. Human life isn't worth a kopeck to them.'

The travelling observer of life also knew about the local problem.

'It's the peasants around here. The soldiers have come back from the front. I can understand them. Why sweat and strain? It's easier to earn a living with a rifle on the road. Clodhopping brutes.' He hung down and grinned at the female passengers. 'The first thing they do is rummage under the skirts of the women and girls. They know where your kind hide your loot.'

The girl wasn't frightened and she snickered.

'The only thing I've got to hide up there is girls' business.'

Yasha smacked his lips fruitily, the grammar-school student looked askance at the girl beside him, and the sailor chortled, but the woman became uneasy.

She pulled out her cherished bundle of needles again and started turning her head this way and that, wondering where she could hide it – and then she had an idea. She put it on the table and heaped potato peelings over it.

'If anything happens, God forbid, don't give me away.'

'Blessed are the poor in spirit, for they have nothing to hide,' the reverend father declared didactically. 'Therefore shall they know no fear when there is gnashing of teeth, the earth shudders and there are horrors on the road . . .'

He jinxed them.

Iron teeth suddenly started gnashing, the earth shuddered, the carriage lurched and the lamp jolted and went out. The train braked sharply, reducing speed. The passengers travelling facing backwards were pressed up against the wall. Those who were sitting or lying facing forwards were sent flying. Masa struck his chest against the little table, the sailor was flung off the luggage shelf and the little priest crashed into the girl.

The darkness was filled with cries of despair, women's shrieking and children's wailing. But then the train stopped dead. Outside two shots rang out one after the other.

'Well, here we are, a hold-up.' Yasha Black chuckled nervously. 'I've seen all sorts of things in my life, but I've never been robbed before.'

* * *

Probably the most surprising thing of all was the silence. On the other side of the carriage wall a baby started whimpering, but immediately fell silent again. No one said anything in the compartment either. Those who had fallen over went back to their places and rollicking Yasha clambered back up onto his shelf.

In the darkness nothing could be seen and nothing could be heard.

But then a match scraped, and a little flame flared up, illuminating a sullen and dissatisfied face with narrow eyes.

It was the Japanese, who had hoisted his sinister travelling companion back onto the seat and got up to light the extinguished lamp.

When there was light, it turned out that the passengers might not have been saying anything, but they had certainly not been sitting stiffly to attention either. Everyone was behaving rather strangely.

The grammar-school student had taken off his greatcoat, turned it inside out and put it back on. From the outside it had appeared quite respectable, but now it turned out not to have any lining and it had been transformed into some kind of grey sackcloth garment.

The girl leaned down, running her hand over the dirty floor, and then started rubbing that hand over her face.

The sailor crossed himself with rapid, sweeping movements, holding his peakless cap in his hands and moving his lips.

And the priest, for whom it might have seemed more appropriate to pray, stuffed the silver cross into his bosom, pulling out to replace it another cross of the same size, but made of iron, which he installed at the centre of his chest.

Yasha Black sat cross-legged up on his shelf, stuffing something under the tattered panelling of the ceiling.

'I'm hiding my wallet,' he said with a wink, noticing a glance from the Japanese. 'If they frisk me, I'm clean.'

The woman behaved in the most surprising way of all. She hoisted up her skirt and shoved a large dried perch in under her pink underwear.

Masa was particularly intrigued by this operation.

'Why are you shoving a dried fish into your drawers, citizen?'

'Didn't you hear? They reach in under your skirt first. If they don't find anything, they'll swear at me, or give me a beating. But at least this is some kind of booty. Maybe they'll leave me alone,' the woman explained in justification of her action. 'What are you doing just sitting there like that? Don't you have anything to hide?'

They heard a crude voice roaring outside the carriage, punctuating every phrase with obscene profanities:

'Don't get up! Just sit quietly! If anyone starts yelling his head off, I'll give him a bloody mug. If anyone budges . . . he gets a bullet in the forehead!'

The grammar-school student said in a whisper:

'I'll stick my head out and take a look.'

He opened the door a little and glanced out cautiously.

'Well! What's out there?' the girl asked after a minute, tugging on his coat-tail. 'How many of them are there?'

'One,' the boy announced, sitting back down in his place. 'With a sawn-off rifle. He's taking small items – watches and rings – and putting them in a sack.'

'Onry one?' Masa asked curiously. 'And they ret him take their things?'

'You just try not letting him take them,' the sailor boomed from up aloft. 'I dare say there are others waiting down by the embankment, with wagons.'

'I doubt that.' The Japanese scratched his round chin thoughtfully. 'Then he wouldn't just take smorr things. Perhaps the bandit is compretery arone. He put down a rog, stopped the rocomitive and now he's walking arong, robbing peopur.'

'Even if he is alone, he must be an absolute brute.' The sailor's teeth chattered. 'If he blasts you with a sawn-off, it's sweet repose with all the saints.'

Masa pondered philosophically: a wolf also sneaked into the fold on his own and chose which sheep to drag away, and the others stood there meekly and didn't even bleat. In truth, everyone decided who he was in life: a sheep, a wolf or a man.

'A-a-ah . . .' the female speculator suddenly cried out, but softly, as if she was uncertain. She slapped her hand down on the little table and howled, this time at the top of her voice. 'A-a-a-ah! They've gone! The needles have gone! Help! I've been robbed!'

The heap of peelings must have been scattered when the train braked so abruptly, and the little sack was not there under them.

'Look on the floor,' said the priest. 'Why start imagining sinful acts immediately?'

The woman plopped down onto all fours and groped around under the table.

'They're not there! Oh, Lord, they're not there! I'm finished! I bartered all my property for those needles! A wardrobe with a mirror, two feather beds, five poods of potatoes, a gold ring, a sewing machine. And I took a thousand roubles from the father of my godchild! Now I'm done for! Ooooh!'

She started howling again.

'Ai-ai-ai,' the reverend father said sympathetically. 'That's especially bad, about the father of your godchild. If he's a boss, it means he has resources. You wouldn't want to offend him. The only advice I can give to you, my daughter, is to pray.'

But Black grinned, baring his teeth:

'Neatly worked. I applaud the deed. Which of you is so nimble-fingered? I was up here on top, I didn't fall off the shelf.'

'That's a lie, you swindler!' the sailor flung at him. 'You jumped down too. The question is, what for?'

'Oh, God in heaven, oh, disaster! Oh, I'm done for!' the woman wailed shrilly, still crawling around on the floor. 'I might as well not go home!'

The door flew open with a crash.

'Who's bawling in here? I told you, no yelling!'

Everyone froze.

A terrifying man was standing in the opening, illuminated by the reddish kerosene light and framed in blackness. He was wearing a soldier's greatcoat and a city man's hat like a fur pie, evidently only just taken from someone. The bandit's lumpy face was bearded, his eyes were wild and he was holding a Mosin-Nagant rifle with the barrel and butt sawn off. He had a sack over his shoulder.

'Hey, you, on the floor! Sit down and shut up!'

The woman plopped down into her place. She carried on lamenting, but silently, weeping floods of tears.

'Travelling in a compartment,' the bandit declared with satisfaction. 'That means you have something to take. Will you hand it over, or shall I bump someone off as a warning? What have you got?' he asked, starting with the grammar-school student.

'There,' said the youth, showing him a little album. 'Stamps. I'm hoping to barter them for food. My father was killed in the war. My mother and I have been left alone. We're starving. But you take them, comrade. They're good stamps. There's even some from Madagascar.'

The bandit just cursed. He tore the album out of the student's hand, hit him over the head with it and flung it on the floor.

'What have you got?' he asked, leaning down to the girl.

'Mister, I'm from Kalinovka,' she said, raising her grimy face. 'Ten versts from Bezenchuk. Savel the blacksmith's daughter. Maybe you know him?'

'I've heard of him. Why are you all dirty like that?'

The girl immediately calmed down and her teeth glinted in a smile.

'I thought, what if it's strangers, so I smeared my face. So they wouldn't rape me. No need to be afraid of our own, though.'

The swashbuckling individual didn't like the idea of someone not being afraid of him. He raised his sawn-off rifle and fired into the ceiling. Debris rained down. The girl squealed and others in the carriage started wailing.

'Put everything valuable in the sack! Come on! Afterwards I'll search everyone. If I find anything on anyone, I'll kill them!'

And he clattered his breechblock.

After that the plundering went smoothly. First the sailor hung down from the shelf and handed over his watch. The priest hesitated briefly and pulled out the silver cross. Even Yasha, squinting at the rifle muzzle, swore and tugged two rings off his finger.

'What about you, you tough old bird?' the bearded man asked, taking aim at the crying woman.

She hoisted up her skirt and slapped the dried perch down on the table.

'There, that's the last thing I have, may you choke on it. I haven't got anything else. Someone else robbed me before you . . .'

She banged her head down on the table and her shoulders started shaking.

That only left the Japanese. At first he examined the bandit with interest, but soon started feeling bored and even yawned.

'Have you got anything, slanty-eyes? I know your kind. A quick frisk, and the gold comes pouring out.'

'Yes, I've got something,' Masa said with a nod, and yawned again. He was feeling drowsy. 'Ten-roubur gold pieces.'

The robber was amazed. He aimed his sawn-off rifle.

'Let me have them. Where have you hidden them?'

'Right here,' said Masa, slapping himself on the chest, where the last eight gold pieces were lying in a little silk bag. 'Take them yourserf, round-eyes.'

He hadn't decided yet whether to break the impolite *narazumono*'s wrist or simply dislocate it. But the *narazumono* surprised him by firing immediately, without any dilly-dallying, aiming at Masa's forehead.

Masa dodged the bullet, of course. Without even straightening up, he flung out his hand and grabbed the gun, swinging his feet round in a sweeping movement, and the bad man plonked down onto his knees. Since the bullet had landed somewhere very close to his master, Masa turned his head to look back – and froze in amazement.

Erast Petrovich was still sitting there as motionless as ever, but the bullet had flown by within a hair's breadth of his temple, leaving a long scorch mark.

Masa's eyes misted over in fury.

'*Bukkorosu dzoooo!*'[1] he roared, flinging the rifle aside.

Grabbing the blackguard who had disturbed his master's calm sleep by the throat with one hand, he drew his other hand back, clenched into a fist, intending to break the foul bridge of this villainous *akuto*'s nose.

A quiet, rasping voice exclaimed peevishly:

'*Sonnani sakebu na.*'[2]

Not believing his ears, Masa looked round.

His master's eyes were open slightly.

'*Damare, atama ga itai,*'[3] said Erast Petrovich, squinting at the light.

* * *

The first and most important duty in a man's life is gratitude. It comes before everything else.

1 I'll kill you!
2 Don't yell like that.
3 Shut up, my head hurts.

And therefore Masa set the bandit on his feet, handed him the silk bag of gold coins and bowed.

'Thank you, envoy of good karma . . . Where are you going? What about your rifur?'

These final words were addressed to the fleeing bandit's back.

Well, *Butsu* be with him.

Having performed his duty, Masa dashed back to his master, who was still saying something, but Masa couldn't make out the words, because the moment the bandit disappeared, the female speculator had started bawling her eyes out again.

'Quiet, you stupid woman!' the Japanese hissed, glancing round briefly.

The woman obediently started crying more quietly.

'Damn it, what bright light,' Masa's master complained, although the light was extremely dim. 'I can't see a thing, it's blinding. But I can hear a woman crying.'

He spoke hoarsely, as if his throat had grown rusty. Masa cautiously touched the mark left by the bullet. A mere trifle, there wouldn't even be a blister. Perhaps after all the sessions with Chang-*sensei* one more cauterisation was all that had been needed.

'I want to know why a woman is crying,' Masa's master said quietly but firmly.

'Is that the only thing you wish to know?' the Japanese asked cautiously, recalling Professor Kiri's warning about damage to intellectual functions.

Fandorin blinked and shook his head gently.

'No, I have many questions. Everything is somehow . . . strange. But first the woman must be helped. No doubt she has suffered some misfortune.'

'My life is ruined,' the woman said in a loud, flat voice. 'I'll hang myself, I swear, I'll hang myself.'

'Erast Petrovich Fandorin,' said Masa's master, introducing himself. 'I beg your pardon for remaining seated. For some reason I can't get up. And I can only see you indistinctly . . . What has happened to you, madam?'

'"Madam",' the sailor chuckled up above them. 'All the ladies and gentlemen have scarpered at this stage. The last . . .'

Masa showed him his fist without saying anything and the churlish ignoramus shut up. Thank God, Masa's master didn't seem to have heard what he had said, otherwise he would have started asking questions that it was still too soon to answer.

'I've been robbed,' the woman complained to this new man. 'One of these Judases in here.' She gestured, taking in everyone in the compartment.

Something snorted in the night and the carriage swayed and set off.

'We're on a train. In a compartment,' Masa's master said, and shook his head again. 'But there are too many people for a compartment.'

He started listing them, talking to himself.

'The two of us. The lady who has been robbed. A young lady with a dark complexion. Two men on the luggage shelves for some reason. A priest. And . . .' He peered into the opposite corner, where the philatelist was putting on the greatcoat that he had turned back the right way out. '. . . And an expelled grammar-school student.'

'What makes you think I was expelled?' the youth asked in surprise.

'You have no buttons in your buttonholes and no crest on your cap.'

'You've lost your mind. Who goes around wearing eagles nowadays?'

Masa showed the youth his fist too.

'Master, you have stopped stammering,' he said, coughing to clear his throat, which agitation had tightened. His heart had also started aching.

'That is because I am asleep. In my dreams I never stammer,' Fandorin explained. 'However, that is unimportant. Ladies must be helped, even in dreams. What has been purloined from you, madam?'

'Needles. Almost a whole pound! In a little sack! Oooh!'

The sailor hung down from the shelf.

'You should have kept a sharper lookout. Now stop snivelling.'

'Needles. A sailor instead of luggage,' Erast Petrovich stated without any surprise. 'What nonsense.' And he turned patiently towards the woman, no doubt regarding her as a vision in a dream. 'At night

22

I often dream of some absurd crime or other that I absolutely must solve. And I always solve it. You will stop weeping so loudly if the needles are found, will you not? What are they made of, iron?'

'What else?' the woman sniffled. 'Gold?'

'I don't know. Anything can happen in a dream. Did anyone leave the compartment?'

'Na-ah . . .' the female speculator wailed. 'You're right, comrade! We have to search them all! Let your Oriental friend here search them all.'

'Comrade?' Masa's master looked at him, as if expecting some kind of freakish antics from him too. Masa gazed wide-eyed at his master. Then suddenly he pinched himself hard on his fat cheek – perhaps he felt frightened that he might have fallen asleep and dreamed Fandorin's awakening.

Erast Petrovich nodded to himself, as if consenting to abide by the rules of this whimsical dream.

'We are not going to search anyone. We have not been granted the right to do that by any judicial authority. And in addition there are ladies present. But I trust that no one will object to a remote search?'

'Object to what?' the sailor asked suspiciously.

Yasha said:

'I'm not letting myself be frisked, no matter how. Without a warrant – screw that.'

Masa got up and cast hard glances at both of them. There were no more objections.

'Everyone agrees, master.'

'Excellent. I hope you have my ferroattractor with you?'

'Of course. I always have it with me,' Masa replied without hesitation, suddenly feeling very uneasy. He didn't have a clue what a ferro . . . tractor was, but he couldn't possibly sabotage the mentally unstable man's hopes.

'What's a ferroattractor?' the grammar-school student asked.

'An extremely powerful magnet. It is required in investigations when small metal objects have to be found at the scene – a pistol shell case, for instance. My assistant will now run the ferroattractor over the clothing of everyone who is present, without touching their bodies. If someone has concealed four hundred grammes of iron needles about their person, they will start jingling. Masa, show them how it works. Begin with me, so that no one will be offended.'

The gaze that the master fastened on the Japanese was somewhat hazy, but firm. Masa thought for a moment before triumphantly extracting from his bosom a little block the size of two matchboxes, carefully wrapped in a small piece of rag.

He raised it in the air, showed it to everyone and started moving his hand around Fandorin. Suddenly his hand seemed to jerk of its own accord and stick to the breast pocket of the warm jacket that could be seen through the gap in the parted sheepskin bedspread. The Japanese took out the metal comb with which he restored the parting in Fandorin's hair every day.

'And now you.'

The block first attached itself to Masa's chest; the Japanese took out a little baptismal cross and showed it to everyone, but especially to the priest.

'My baptismar name is servant of God Masair.'

And then the sensitive device moved downwards, towards his feet, and there proved to be a razor in his boot top. Masa used it to shave his master in the mornings and on one night, only just recently, he had used it to kill a man who foolishly attacked him in the street.

'Science,' the reverend father said respectfully. 'Right then, check me too.'

'Oh, what's that?' the grammar-school student suddenly exclaimed. 'Look here.'

He squatted down, dissolving into shadow – the light of the lamp did not reach down that far.

'What's that you're hiding with your shoe? Move your foot over,' the grammar-school student said to the girl, and then straightened up. He was holding a little sack full of needles in his hand.

'Mine! Mine!' the woman howled, bounding to her feet. 'They're all there, all of them, my little darlings! Ooooh!'

It was noteworthy that she didn't stop bawling, her wailing merely ceased being doleful and became joyful instead. And immediately, while she was still rejoicing, she gave the girl a heavy thump on the ear.

'Lousy bitch! Thief! Brazen hussy! You sat beside me, acting innocent!'

'I didn't take them! Honest to God, I swear! I didn't take them, missus!'

And she started crying too.

'Shame on you, young man,' Fandorin told the grammar-school student. He was still blinking at all the noise. 'You have all the habits of a professional thief. Not only did you steal the needles, now you're trying to shift the blame onto an innocent young lady. If this were not a dream, at the next stop I would hand you over to the station constable.'

'Co-constable?' the youth babbled. 'Station constable? My God, I'd ask for nothing more if only the constables came back. My God, going to the grammar school, instead of jolting about in these appalling trains, and no more sticking my hand into people's pockets . . .'

And he started crying too.

Why didn't I realise it myself? Masa reproached himself. *He's a professional* dorobo, *plying his trade on the trains. He said this was his first trip, but he knew where trains are robbed on the line and how. He said he was starving, but he has a white bread sandwich with a meat rissole.*

But all of this was absolutely unimportant.

'What happiness!' Masa sobbed, wiping away his tears and putting the chunk of fatty bacon back in his pocket. 'Master, you're not an idiot!'

Now half the compartment was weeping: the happy woman, the 'innocent young lady', the thief and Masa. The little priest was also sniffling compassionately and attempting to say something, but no one was looking at him.

'Thank you for that flattering assessment,' Erast Petrovich muttered. 'The needles have been found, but it still hasn't got any quieter. I'm fed up with this dream. I hope the next one will be better.'

And he closed his eyes, went limp and started breathing sleepily – not in the barely audible way he was breathing before, but with deep, regular breaths.

'There now, and you doubted,' the reverend father declared, finally managing to battle his way through the noise, 'but didn't I tell you that in times of many horrors there are also many miracles? You only need to know to whom to pray for what. Address prayers for the mentally distressed only to the Intercessor, the Virgin Mary. So will you persist in your lack of faith now, my son?'

THE BLACK TRUTH

Ku areba raku ari

Masa's master slept for a terribly long time – three and a half days, and for Masa they were more agonising than the previous three and a half years. Because the most terrible of the levels of *jigoku* is not the fiery level and not the icy level, but the one into which traitors fall after death: every day there begins with hope and ends with its collapse. Masa had never betrayed anyone, but he had supped this bitter torment in full measure. Sometimes the sleeping man's eyelids would start trembling but not open, sometimes the pale lips would suddenly stir, but not say anything, sometimes a faint spasm would run across the pale face – and then disappear, like a deceptive ripple on the water in a dead calm.

The swoon had become like a deep sleep, and yet it remained a swoon. When the sleeper would awake, and if he would awake at all, not even Kiri-*sensei* knew. 'Do not try to provoke the awakening, simply stay beside him and wait,' he had said. And then he had added with a sigh: 'Unfortunately, I cannot wait to the end with you. I am leaving tomorrow. I have no more strength to stay here in this madhouse that has been taken over by patients from the violent ward.' And he had left the sick country of Russia, just as the Chinese healer Chang had done.

After bringing his master home to Moscow, the Japanese had prepared himself to wait for as long as necessary. The sleeper must not find himself alone when he awoke.

In order not to absent himself even for a minute, Masa prepared rice balls, a bottle of diluted vodka and even a chamber pot, but he could neither eat nor drink, let alone relieve himself – he was too agitated.

So he didn't eat or drink or sleep, but what had come of that? On the third night his shameless *karada*-flesh eluded his control, betrayed him, and furtively dragged him down into a leaden, pitch-dark sleep.

Masa was awoken by something nudging his knee. He fluttered his eyelids and then squeezed his eyes shut. The room was flooded with spring sunlight.

A hoarse voice asked:

'Hey, are you unwell? You look awful. As if you had aged several years.'

Masa's master narrowed his eyes, blinked and rubbed his eyelashes with a feeble hand.

'Ah, forgive me!' he said. 'You were wounded . . . But since you can sit up, you must be feeling better, are you not?'

'I am feering better. I am feering much better,' Masa whispered, pressing his open hand hard against his chest, so that his heart would not leap out.

Masa did not shout, but whispered, because Kiri-*sensei* had forbidden him to traumatise his newly awoken master's psyche with a tempestuous display of feelings and told him to behave as if it was a perfectly ordinary awakening. 'Exude as much optimism as you can, do not communicate anything sad to the patient,' the professor had insisted. 'Otherwise the defensive reaction of the brain might plunge him into a new neural blockade.'

'But I seem to have fallen ill. My body feels as if it were not my own. I can barely even move my arms. And something's wrong with my eyesight.' Erast Petrovich attempted to lift himself up on his pillow but couldn't manage it. 'I've had some terribly strange dreams. The last one was simply idiotic. You and I were travelling in a train compartment with people packed into it like sardines in a can, and there . . . Never mind, it's all nonsense.'

Fandorin kept narrowing his eyes and squinting.

'Are we at home? Not in Baku? How is that possible?' He frowned and felt the back of his head very, very slowly. 'In a black, black city

'. . . Someone shot me. The sudden blow. I remember it . . . So I haven't been asleep, I've been unconscious? How long have I been laid out? And what has happened in that time?'

Only now did Masa finally believe that his master had really returned.

'You have been raid out for three years, eight months and twenty-eight days. What has happened in that time?' The Japanese moved on smoothly to the second question, remembering the weakened condition of his master's psyche. 'Orr the states are waging war, like the principarities in the *Sengoku-jidai* period. People are kirring each other by the mirrions. The Russian Empire no ronger exists, it has forren to pieces. But the sun stirr rises, winter has been forrowed by spring, and women are still as beautifur as ever,' he concluded buoyantly, on an optimistic note.

'I'm still asleep after all,' Erast Petrovich muttered. 'And it's another idiotic dream.'

He closed his eyes, but Masa didn't allow his master to sleep any more – he pinched him on the ear.

'Now very many peopur feer that they are having an idiotic dream. But this is not an idiotic dream, it is idiotic *genjitsu* – reality. Prepare yourserf to risten for a long time, master. Now I wirr terr you about everything in detair. Onry remember the words of the sage: "No matter what might occur in the vain worrd, the nobur man never rooses his equanimity."'

Then he spoke without stopping for an hour or even more, and his master failed to maintain his equanimity. In former times, when Masa told him about something, Erast Petrovich had been in the habit of asking questions to clarify the narrative as it went along. But now he merely repeated the same thing over and over again.

'What?'

'Wha-at?'

'Wha-a-at?'

And every successive 'what' was longer and shriller than the one before it, so that Fandorin's voice soon turned falsetto, after which he fell silent and listened without saying anything, only shaking his head occasionally.

No matter how hard Masa tried to inject a little enthusiasm, his story came out sadder than *The Tale of the House of Taira*. When he reached the events of the last few days (how the new Red government had capitulated to the Germans and fled from Petrograd to Moscow), the Japanese spread his hands guiltily:

'. . . No doubt there are certain positive aspects to the fact that you have rain like a rog since 1914, and in that time the worrd has forren apart, for the nature of existence is duar, but I beg your pardon, in this brackness of Yin, I cannot see even a weak grimmer of Yang.'

Fandorin said nothing for a minute or even two. Then he sighed.

'Oh, come now! Some good has come of it. You have finally learned to express yourself well in Russian. That is one. And, thanks to my injury, I seem to have shaken off my stammer. That is two. *Ku areba raku ari.*'

'You are right, master! Every croud has a sirver rining,' Masa exclaimed tearfully, failing to control his turbulent feelings after all. 'And the most important thing is that we are together and you are yourserf again! That outweighs everything erse!'

The ki plays hide-and-seek

Unfortunately, the Japanese was mistaken. Although he had awoken, Fandorin was not himself again. In fact little remained of the old Fandorin. The body had existed for too long in separation from the spirit and all the connections between them had disintegrated. It did not wish to submit to the will.

For the first few days Fandorin's vision was very poor, as if he had been afflicted by extreme short-sightedness. He coped with this trial by means of patient exercises. A certain little box proved useful: Erast Petrovich had inherited it from his father, a keeper and collector of family relics, many of incomprehensible significance – Fandorin had never taken an interest in the history of his family. The box contained a lock of ginger hair, wrapped in a piece of yellowed paper with 'Laura 1500' written on it. Fandorin had no idea who this Laura was, but he was delighted when he discovered that he could make out the letters and figures. Also in the box were several keepsakes from Erast Petrovich's own past. He examined with a feeling of sadness a portrait of his first wife, whom he could hardly remember, because their marriage had lasted only a few hours, and it had happened in a different age, in a different world, to a different Fandorin. But his sight gradually grew sharper and the pretty young face came to life and returned his gaze. A quiet voice spoke to him, asking: 'Have you lived your life happily, my darling? Do you remember your Liza at least sometimes?'

That voice helped the most of all. Erast Petrovich gazed into space with his eyes narrowed, and pictures of the past emerged from the thickening air, slowly acquiring clear focus. And together with the vision of his memory, his ordinary eyesight also grew stronger. On the second day the convalescent patient could already see the engravings on the walls, and on the third day he was able to read.

Things were not so good where his muscles were concerned. It was as if his body had been frozen on a glacier and did not wish to thaw out. Each movement was achieved only with a delay, only after the command from his brain was repeated – and with extreme reluctance. 'Pick up the cup,' his brain ordered his hand, but the hand seemed to hesitate, deciding whether to obey the command or not. And then it picked up the cup after all but went out of its way to spill the water.

His hands moved tolerably well horizontally and in a downward direction, but raising a cup to his lips was a far from simple task. It had once cost Fandorin less effort to lift a four-poods weight.

The state of his legs was a real disaster. They had to be given their orders three times. The first time Erast Petrovich crossed the kitchen independently (twenty steps), it took a little over two minutes. Then he repeated this straightforward route numerous times, achieving a certain increase in speed, but every time he reached the opposite wall, he sat down and took a rest.

Reasoning theoretically, the years of absolute immobility should have led to the accumulation in Fandorin's body of a devil of a lot of the *ki* energy that he had previously been able to distribute equally between his body's various parts or concentrate wherever he liked: in his fist for a blow, in his legs for running or jumping, in his loins for making love and so forth.

On the very first morning Erast Petrovich assumed the *zazen* pose with some difficulty, closed his eyes, brought his spirit into the condition of Great Calmness and conducted a wholesale interrogation of all the sections of his body by turn, asking: 'Is this where the *ki* is hiding?'

At this point Masa appeared with an enema bottle, bowed and announced:

'Nine o'crock, master. Time to do a *daiben*.'

And the Great Calmness immediately evaporated, ousted by the Great Fury. It was actually a good thing that the *ki* energy had not been located, otherwise the faithful vassal would have suffered at least moderately severe injury.

But the missing vital energy was not found either on the second, or the third, or even the tenth day. It had probably hidden away in such deep recesses of his being that it could never be dragged back out.

Nonetheless, Erast Petrovich performed his exercises all day, every day, and Masa watched compassionately, telling his master about events in the outside world.

And these events were absolutely incredible.

The Kaiser's forces had occupied almost all of Europe, from Pskov to the approaches to Paris; moreover they were bombarding the latter with a gigantic Jules Vernesque cannon that spat out hundred-kilogramme shells for more than a hundred kilometres. 'Do you remember the Church of Saint-Gervais in the Marais quarter?' Masa asked. 'In '99 we arrested "the Maniac from the Street of White Croaks" there. The German *daiho* smashed it to pieces with a direct hit and kirred all the people at prayer.' It was hard to imagine such a thing, but no harder than to imagine the landing at Murmansk of English soldiers, who intended to fight on Russian territory against the Germans and the Finns. For some reason Fandorin was surprised most of all by the fact that the Finns, those pacific dairy farmers and market gardeners, were also at war now.

'And in the accursed city of Baku there is more broody sraughter,' the Japanese informed him. 'The Turks used to sraughter the Armenians, now the Armenians are sraughtering the Turks. I hope they wirr sraughter that Turk whom I can never reach now. And in the Kuban,

White vorunteers are fighting with Red vorunteers. And Ukraine is now definitery a country, and everyone is fighting there too.'

There was also local, Moscow news that was no less amazing.

In the neighbouring houses they were 'consolidating' all the 'former people', Masa said, but the yard keeper, Lusha-*san*, a very beautiful and kind woman, was now 'chairwoman of the house committee', and in memory of their former love she was taking good care of Masa's interests.

Foodstuffs had long been 'issued on cards'. They used to give more, but now it was a terribly small amount, only a little bit of black bread. However, there was no need to worry about food, because Masa had found an excellent buyer for his collection of erotic *shunga* pictures and *netsuke* figurines. A very important man, the District Soviet Food Supply-*san*, he paid in gold ten-rouble pieces, and everything could be bought on the black market with those.

A 'Red Procession' had passed along Myasnitskaya Street – it was like a Procession of the Cross, but with red banners, and instead of chanting prayers, everyone sang revolutionary songs.

In the Zoological Gardens there had been a 'Freedom for Animals' meeting. They had released all the 'oppressed beasts' from their cages – all those that didn't eat people. Deer, yaks and llamas had gone running along the streets, and one pregnant *oku-san* had given birth prematurely right there on the pavement, because she ran into a South American armadillo on Presnya Street.

Erast Petrovich could not wait to see all these wonders with his own eyes.

On 10 April, after accomplishing a goal that had long eluded him – crossing the drawing room in half a minute – he wiped away his sweat contentedly and declared: 'That's it. Tomorrow I'm going out into the city.'

Masa was ready for this. He had constructed a means of transport – an armchair on little rubber wheels.

'The *isu*-vehicur is at your service, master, but for a start I'rr just wheer you arong our side street.'

'No,' Fandorin said firmly. 'This is an entirely different world, and I am an entirely different person. We need to get used to each other. I shall take my first steps without a nursemaid. Tomorrow I shall do my exercises and training until noon. And after that I shall set out on an excursion. Alone.'

The Japanese heaved a sigh, but he didn't try to argue. He knew that was how things would be.

'To make the *isu* go, you have to move this rever backwards and forwards. You can manage backwards and forwards, can't you? If you want to stop, press on this strut with your foot. Only not sharpry, or else you could toppur over . . .'

'Don't worry. I won't go until I have learned how to do it.'

'That is not what I am afraid of, master,' said Masa, rubbing his hand over his short brush of half-grey hair in a morose gesture. 'Moscow has become a dangerous city. You do not know it. You wirr feer rike Urashima Taro, who got rost in time. That is a bad feering. And that tayr ends badry.'

Urashima, a fisherman in a folk tale, spent several days on the bottom of the ocean as a guest of the king of the sea, but when he returned home it turned out that several centuries had passed by on the land and he did not even recognise his native village.

'Urashima ought not to have stuck his nose into the forbidden casket,' Fandorin replied nonchalantly, smiling at the thought that tomorrow the world would expand beyond the limits of this loathsome apartment. 'I shall not stick my nose into anything. I shall simply go for a ride.'

An amazing journey

The following day, 11 April, between two and three in the afternoon, Erast Petrovich muffled himself up in a warm coat with an astrakhan collar, but left his head uncovered, since it had to be kept cold, and trundled out through the gates. Masa saw him off with a ceremonial bow, recited a sutra of protection and crossed himself three times.

Pumping the lever, Fandorin slowly moved off along Lesser Uspensky (aka Cricket) Lane as far as Great Uspensky Lane, looking around him curiously.

He felt less like Urashima Taro than the hero of H. G. Wells' novel *The Sleeper Awakes*. Mr Graham awoke from a lethargic stupor in the year 2100 and failed to recognise good old England, because there was nothing left in it that was old, nothing that was good and very little that was English.

The decorous, aristocratic neighbourhood, formerly so neat and tidy, well swept and well tended, looked like a seashore after a tsunami, when the wave has already ebbed away, leaving the land strewn with mud, garbage, wreckage and the corpses of small animals. Right there on the pavement two rats were calmly gnawing the meat off a dead cat's bones as if they owned the area. *An excellent allegory of what has happened to Russia*, thought Erast Petrovich: *We have been nought, we shall be all!*

A miracle-tram rattled along Chistoprudny Boulevard, looking like a dish of grapes, the passengers were hanging so thickly from its platforms and steps, and even its buffers.

A platoon of soldiers tramped past with a waddling gait, holding all their rifles with the butts upwards for some reason, and they weren't speaking to each other in Russian. He thought they were Latvians. Strange.

From the boulevard Fandorin turned onto Pokrovka Street, across which red banners with sprawling white letters were hanging. Opposite the Church of the Assumption, that beautiful example of Naryshkin Baroque, a large strip of canvas was flapping in the wind, bearing the admonition: 'Careful, comrade! The priests are deceiving you!'

Erast Petrovich was unable to comprehend the next slogan, although he studied it for a long time: 'Maleprolet's RevGreets to 1st CongFreeFemLab'.

An icy wind tousled the grey hair of the time traveller and fine snowflakes fell on it, glittering silver but not melting. The temperature was definitely not above freezing. Raising his hand with difficulty, Fandorin pulled his white muffler tighter.

A lady in a Parisian coat and a crude peasant shawl said to her companion:

'Sweetheart, please, how many times do I have to tell you? Don't say "dear sir" in the street. You'll be the death of us! Only "dear citizen".'

Two old women minced past and one cried out excitedly to the other:

'Let's go over to the draymen's syndicate! They're giving out vouchers for galoshes!'

A certain individual, clearly a criminal to judge from his appearance, complained to his sidekick:

'Seven square metres of living space for an old convict like me! He's got to be a contra, no two ways about it!'

I need an interpreter, thought Erast Petrovich. He pumped the lever and set off with a creak along the chipped and cratered pavement.

The familiar Petrov's Restaurant had changed its old name for a new one: 'He who works, eats'. There was a mysterious notice on the door: 'Only members served on presentation'. Written below was the following: 'We do not accept tattered caps as pledges for spoons and bowls'. *So these same members must pilfer spoons and bowls, and therefore their headgear is demanded on entry*, Fandorin speculated. However, the notice on the menswear shop 'Paris and Vienna' resisted all his attempts to decipher it: 'All goods strictly barter. Do not offer money!' What did this mean – do not offer money in a shop?

In the course of his long period of unconsciousness, a multitude of fantastical visions had appeared to Erast Petrovich, sometimes in strikingly expressive and brilliant forms. The suspicion suddenly arose that all this was also a hallucination: an anti-Moscow Moscow, a tram carrying grape-people, absurd notices in the street.

The devil only knows, anything is possible. But the great Monzaemon wrote: 'Life is only a sad dream, seen in dream.' And apart from that, even in a dream the noble man does not betray his principles – what if the dream should turn out to be reality?

Suddenly passers-by started crossing quickly to the other side of the street. A man glanced round at the cripple in the wheelchair.

'Let me scoot you across, Grandad. The Cheka's coming.'

Three men with red armbands were walking towards them: one with a big wooden holster for a Mauser, two with rifles over their shoulders. The Cheka? Ah, yes. Masa had told him about it. 'Ch. K.' was some kind of abbreviation. The recently founded Red Guards' own Department for the Defence of Public Safety and Order – their Okhranka. Masa had said that the Red Guards' police were not too bad so far, at least they showed up with a warrant. But there were some other 'Black Guards', who plundered without any warrants, and sometimes out in the street, in broad daylight.

'No, no thank you,' Erast Petrovich told the Good Samaritan drily, shocked by that 'Grandad'. He felt curious and wanted to take a look at the representatives of the new authority. It called itself 'soviet', which meant a 'council' – but Masa hadn't really explained exactly what it was: was it based on advisory boards of some kind?

'Aha, the invalid ought to know,' the man with the Mauser said, walking up to Fandorin. 'You can't travel far away from home on a commode like that. Help me out, will you, Dad. Which building here is Axelrod's old place? See, we've got a decree.' He waved a piece of paper.

What is this, a conspiracy? Fandorin thought, the rage mounting inside him.

'I do not have any children, honourable sir.'

He tried to move away, but the Red gendarme grabbed the back of his chair.

'Who do you think you're talking to? Right, show me your documents!'

'Ah, come on, Korytov. Don't hassle a man who can't walk,' another man said. 'Forget about him. Let's go and ask that woman over there.'

The man with the Mauser roundly abused both Erast Petrovich and his mother but took his hand away. The Chekaists, or whatever it was they were called, moved on, taking their decree with them, and Fandorin shook his head as he watched them go. It was beyond him even to imagine a member of the Okhranka or the Gendarmes Corps swearing abusively in a public place.

If the Red Guards are 'not too bad so far', then what are the 'Black Guards' like?

The Heroes of Plevna

He did not have to wait long for the answer to that question. Five minutes later, having arrived at Maroseika Street, the explorer of revolutionary Moscow spotted a small knot of people ahead of him and heard an extremely unpleasant sound, one that had never failed to stir Fandorin's feelings: a woman choking on her own weeping. To pass on by without getting to the bottom of such an intense demonstration of grief was quite unthinkable.

'Mishenka, give me back my Mishenka!' the woman was wailing at the top of her voice – or rather, elderly lady, since the voice was cracked and the elocution was refined.

Masa had provided the invalid with a cane in case it was necessary to dismount and Fandorin supported himself with it as he elbowed his way forward.

An old man wearing a dove-grey greatcoat with crimson lapels and trousers with a general's red piping, but without any boots or even shoes – merely old, worn and patched felt slippers – was sitting on the pavement with his arms wrapped round his head and pressing one hand against it: blood was streaming copiously through his fingers. Behind him, a woman in a seriously dilapidated coat that had once been very decent was stepping from one foot to the other. She was small and skinny, with grey ringlets, and she kept gazing round helplessly, all the while repeating: 'Give him beck, give me beck my Mishenka! Give him beck! Oh, please! Where is my Mishenka?' The lady was clearly quite distraught. *She is like a little girl whose doll has been taken away, only a very old little girl*, thought Fandorin, wincing. It was a distressing sight.

He listened to the conversations of the people standing there, trying to understand what had happened.

People in the crowd were saying:

'It's the old man's own fault. He shouldn't go flaunting those general's stripes, the old regime's over and done with. Plus, if it's a requisition, then stand to attention. They could have wasted him on the spot for resisting. That's well within the norm for the "Blacks".'

'They took that Misha, is that it? And what did they smack the general with?' asked some people who had arrived later. The others answered them and the picture gradually became clear.

The old couple had been stopped by some Black Guard anarchist. He had seen that the woman had a medallion – gold, with diamonds

– and taken it. The general had tried to take it back – and received a pistol butt to the head.

Meanwhile the injured man had got up off the ground and put his arm round the weeping woman, but she pushed him away and kept shouting about her Mishenka. The old man was tall and aristocratic-looking with a little grey beard that had evidently once borne the proud name of 'imperial', but had now deteriorated to the status of a 'goatee' or a mere wispy clump.

'Gentlemen, in God's name!' the former general said. 'Run after them and entreat them! It's the only thing that Apollonaria has left. I'd go myself, but my head's spinning and my legs won't walk.'

'A diamond medallion? Oh sure, he'll give that back! Be thankful he didn't do you in,' he was told.

'It's not a matter of the medallion! Let him keep it! There's a photograph of our dead son and a lock of hair from his childhood in it.'

'See, they lost their little son,' a tender-hearted woman said, taking pity on the old man. 'Mister, why don't you run and overtake him? What does he want the photo for?'

'Aha, you run after him. I'm not sick of living yet,' the man she had spoken to retorted.

Everyone was already going on their way, having satisfied their curiosity. In and of itself the event was clearly an everyday occurrence.

Soon Erast Petrovich was the only one left beside the unfortunate couple.

'Sit the lady down,' he said. 'She's on the verge of fainting.'

'Yes, yes, thank you.'

The general gently led his wife across to the armchair and sat her down in it. She suddenly drooped and went limp. Then she sobbed and moved her lips for a little while before going quiet: she had either swooned or fallen asleep.

'Why are you so careless?' Fandorin asked. 'In a general's trousers, with piping. And a gold medallion in plain view.'

'The greatcoat and the stripes are because we're so poor. I have nothing else to wear.' The old man kept wiping away the blood with a handkerchief, but it didn't stop. 'All the rest of our clothes have been sold or bartered for food, but no one will take these things. As for the medallion . . . Well, you see, Misha was our only son, a very late child, we had already stopped hoping. He was Apollonaria's entire life. Misha was killed at Tannenberg.'

'Where?'

'In East Prussia, where all the Guards laid down their lives, remember? Misha had only just joined his regiment, and in the very first battle . . . Ever since then Apollonaria has been a little . . . more than a little unwell.' The general fingered one of the tips of his moustache in a delicate gesture. 'She put Misha's last photograph in the medallion, together with a lock of hair from his childhood. During the day she sits and looks at the photo, smiling and fingering the hair – and she is calm. At night she is never parted from it, she squeezes it tight in her fist. And recently she has started looking at it in the street too. I always take her out for a breath of air after lunch. And then this Black Guard showed up. He saw it and grabbed it . . .'

The old man suddenly checked himself.

'Please forgive me, I have not introduced myself. Alexander Ksenofontovich Chernyshev. A former professor of the Nikolaevsky Engineering Academy. I retired before the war, because of my age.'

Fandorin also introduced himself. They exchanged bows.

'Allow me to take a look at your wound, Count,' said Erast Petrovich. 'You are one of the Counts Chernyshev, are you not?'

'I have that misfortune,' the former professor said with a wry smile, removing the handkerchief from his wound. 'And therefore I am denied ration cards. The district soviet ruled that they should not be issued to the titled aristocracy. Former generals, by the way, are also not entitled to them, which makes me, as they say nowadays, a "double disenfranchisee". Something like a Jew born out of wedlock under the old regime.'

Fandorin examined the site of the injury.

'It was a strong blow but, thank goodness, tangential. There are blood vessels close by, hence all the bleeding. The skin is split open and, of course, there is concussion, but there is no need for sutures. It just needs to be disinfected and bandaged. You can consider yourself lucky.'

The general laughed drily.

'Lucky? You know, in 1913, when I retired, Apollonaria and I decided to celebrate that event with a round-the-world cruise. In San Francisco we missed the Shanghai steamship and it ran into a cargo vessel in the roadstead and sank, with all the passengers. We were absolutely astounded at being so lucky. But since then I've thought more than once what good fortune it would have been if we had just drowned in our wonderful first-class cabin and never seen anything of what came later . . .'

'Listen, I am a specialist in good luck. To be lucky means that you have been granted the best of all the existing possibilities. Of *the existing possibilities*, do you understand me?' Fandorin added severely, continuing in his own mind: *for instance, when someone shoots you in the back of the head at point-blank range, and after that you are merely left a cripple.* 'If that Black Guard, or whatever he is, had cracked your skull open for you, your wife would have been left all alone in the world. And what would have become of her?'

'She will die now in any case.' Chernyshev shuddered, looking at the sleeping woman. 'Apollonaria can't live without Misha's photo. She won't eat or drink. She'll just cry out all her tears and die. But you're quite right. I must be with her. You know, we have been together for forty-five years, and never parted. She even went to the Turkish War with me. She was at Plevna, in the field hospital, a nurse.'

'At Plevna?'

Fandorin tried to picture how the Chernyshevs would have looked forty years earlier, by the walls of the Turkish stronghold – he a young engineer, and she a frail, but no doubt resolute, young lady.

'Were you there too?' asked Alexander Ksenofontovich, looking at him with the gaze of a comrade from times long past. 'Oh Lord, why have we lived to see times like this?'

'You are asking the Lord God, are you not?' Fandorin asked with a shrug. 'Then let Him answer . . . And let us take the countess home. I assume you must live close by?'

'Very close, on Petroveritsky Lane. But you can hardly walk yourself. And it must be hard for you to stand, isn't it? What is wrong with your health?'

'The consequences of an injury. Never mind. If I hold on to something, I can walk.'

The two of them took hold of the back of the armchair – Chernyshev was also unsteady on his feet – and started pushing it along.

'You are right that in a certain sense Apollonaria's madness is a stroke of luck for her,' the general said in a low voice. 'In her state of stupefaction she is untroubled and, to all intents and purposes, even happy. At any rate, she was. But now the hell will begin . . .'

Catching a passer-by's sympathetic glance, Fandorin suddenly saw their threesome as if from the outside: two infirm old men slowly wheeling a half-dead old woman somewhere. And such, indeed, was the case.

But the old woman suddenly came to life. And she immediately started fumbling anxiously at her chest.

'Mishenka, where's Mishenka?'

'At home. We left him at home by mistake,' Chernyshev replied quickly, and whispered, 'I couldn't bear it if she started shouting in the street again.'

'Home, home!' the countess demanded.

The general shuddered and murmured:

'Lord, what will happen now . . .'

And only then did Erast Petrovich say what should have been said at the very beginning: 'I'll get your photograph and lock of hair back.' Then he corrected himself: 'I'll try to get them back.'

'But how? You are in a wheelchair. And where can one look for that scoundrel now?'

'What are his distinctive characteristics?'

The former general started listing them confusedly:

'Tall. In a black trench coat with a cape. A wide-brimmed hat, also black – you know, Garibaldi-style. In short – an anarchist.'

'I'll find him. With an appearance like that – I'll find him.'

The general's eyes turned moist.

'I know you are saying that out of pity. In order to console me. But thank you anyway. And if . . . if by some miracle you can manage to do it . . .' – a glint of hope appeared in his eyes. 'Don't see us any farther. I'll walk Apollonaria back home. And you make haste.

Our address is the former Chernyshev house on Petroveritsky Lane. The house committee allocated the caretaker's lodge to us. Get up, Apollonaria, let Mr Fandorin have his chair back.'

Erast Petrovich did not try to argue. He had to hurry, before the black Garibaldi dissolved into this city of a million people.

'But how will you find him now? At least twenty minutes has gone by! Give it up, it's impossible!' the former general shouted after the wheelchair as it rolled away.

There was no reply.

In actual fact picking up 'Garibaldi's' trail was entirely possible and potentially very easy. This individual was conspicuous and also dangerous. People not only noticed an individual like that, they also watched as he went on his way.

Following a trail was familiar and rather enjoyable work.

Erast Petrovich rode as far as Lubyansky Arcade – witnesses had told him that the robber went in that direction.

Stationed most conveniently at the crossroads between the Polytechnic Museum and the monument to the heroes of Plevna was a sentry with a rifle and a red armband – a Soviet policeman. The lower ranks of the police, no matter what they might be called and what authority they might serve, all operated in the same way: acting in a threatening manner with those who toadied to them and toadying to those who spoke to them in a threatening manner.

And therefore Fandorin did not ride out into the roadway, but shouted peremptorily:

'Hey, citizen, come over here.'

And he beckoned impatiently with his finger.

The policeman came over to him, but he looked displeased. This invalid in a white scarf didn't look like someone in authority.

'Get a move on, will you!' Erast Petrovich said to hurry him up a bit. 'How good are your powers of observation?'

'What?' the young fellow asked warily. In his peaked cap and short coat he looked like a factory hand. 'Who are you, comrade?'

'I am Fandorin,' Erast Petrovich said significantly. 'Did you receive the order to exercise revolutionary vigilance?'

'I did. What about it?'

'Did an anarchist with a beard wearing a black garment and a black hat pass by here about twenty minutes ago?'

'There was a man like that,' the policeman replied rapidly. 'Brazen, he was, the dog. He gave me a look and spat. When are they going to put those Black bastards in their place, Comrade Fandorin?'

'Soon. Which way did he go, did you see?'

'Why, of course. Down the slope.' The sentry pointed in the direction of Warsaw Square.

'Good man. Revolutionary gratitude to you.'

'I serve the working people!' the man responded. And then he asked Erast Petrovich's back: '. . . Comrade Fandorin, who are you?'

'A Hero of Plevna,' Erast Petrovich replied, nodding towards the monument.

Down the slope – that was good, excellent in fact. There were no turns all the way to the square, except into Lesser Spasoglinish-chevsky Lane, and that proved to be closed off by a barricade – no doubt it had still not been dismantled after the armed clashes in November (Masa had told him that army officers and cadets had fought the Bolsheviks for a long time).

On the corner, in front of All Saints Church, another promising tipster turned up – an urchin selling newspapers.

'*Deserters' Pravda!*' the young salesman bawled. '*Anarchy* newspaper! *Rabble-Rouser* magazine!'

Dealing with this individual proved very simple. Fandorin waved a ten-rouble banknote with bald-headed eagles (without crowns, that is) in the air – Masa had given him an entire wad of them – and the urchin immediately came running over.

'Do you have eyes in your head?' Erast Petrovich asked. 'Did a fop with a beard, wearing a black hat and a floppy black coat, pass this way, with a holster on his hip?'

'Uh-huh. Shall I tell you where he went?' the urchin asked and he snatched the note with his skinny little paw. 'He's in the "Red Rose". O-over there.'

He pointed to a two-storey building on the corner of Solyanka Street, where there used to be a flower shop, and even now there was a large sign outside with a rose on it.

44

'What's in there?'

'Well, that's no secret. Pay them and they'll pour you some lacquer vodka or neat spirit. They've got everything there, even trollops in the basement. Only you have to know the secret word. Throw in another tenner and I'll say it for you.'

Revolution or no revolution, life carries on regardless, including underground, black-market life, thought Fandorin. Where else would a den of vice be, if not in the vicinity of Khitrovka Square?

Well now, that pursuit didn't take long.

'Will you give me a tenner, then?' the youngster persisted.

'No, I won't.'

Erast Petrovich rode away.

'Aha, what would a feeble bastard like you want with trollops anyway?' the crude urchin shouted after him, but Fandorin had no time for feeling sad on that account. At that very second a tall, black figure stepped out of the abode of sin onto the pavement. The man, wearing a wide-brimmed hat and a trench coat with a cape (and yes, apparently with a beard) walked round the corner onto Solyanka Street and disappeared.

Erast Petrovich applied every ounce of his strength to the lever, accelerating to maximum speed. It was very good that 'Garibaldi' had only been in the dive for a few minutes. That meant he hadn't had enough time to exchange his booty for drink. But then another thought occurred to Erast Petrovich. *Once I catch up with the robber, what then? He's a massive hulk, with a pistol.* Previously Fandorin would have dealt with someone like that in a jiffy, even if he had three pistols, but how would things be now? *If he stands and waits for a moment or, even better, leans down, of course I could try to strike him with my fist, in a horizontal movement, because I can't strike upwards . . . Ah, damn it, just let me catch up with him!*

Enthralled by the thrill of the chase, Erast Petrovich shot out into Solyanka Street at full tilt, almost tumbling off the pavement, but somehow managing to brake and swing round.

The black figure was about a hundred metres away, with the skirt of his trench coat fluttering as he walked along. He was striding rapidly, in a hurry to get somewhere.

He disappeared again. He had turned towards the orphanage.

Worried in case his mark might disappear into some yard or entranceway, Fandorin sped up again, but this time he took the turn far more adroitly. Of course, the armchair lacked the manoeuvrability and speed of the motorcycle and sidecar on which Erast Petrovich had raced so dashingly through the streets of Baku, but the principle was essentially the same: watch the drift and use your body weight.

He was just in time to see 'Garibaldi' take another turn, this time to the left, into an avenue. *Where does it lead?* Fandorin wondered, trying to remember. *To the gates of the Banking Society, I believe. I don't think there is anything else there. At least, there didn't use to be . . .*

And so it was. The avenue, planted with beautiful bushes, led to a pair of gates standing wide open, behind which a courtyard and a pediment with columns could be seen. The building had once been a grand mansion, built after the Fire of 1812, and then it had housed the offices of the Association of Russian Banks. But what was here now? And where was 'Garibaldi'?

There he was, running up the wide steps. A door opened and slammed shut.

That seemed to be it. The chase was over.

Not everything is that simple

Fandorin realised what the place was when he read the inscription on the black strip of canvas decorating the fence: 'FREEDOM Individualist-Anarchist Artel'.

'Very interesting,' Erast Petrovich murmured. 'Well, let's take a look . . .'

A woman walked out briskly through the gates, looking anything but individualistic, let alone anarchistic – wrapped in a mousy shawl, with a paper bag under her arm and a paunchy bottle in her hand, and seeming very pleased about something.

'First time?' she asked. 'Don't be shy, servant of God. Ride across the yard, and then follow the wall round that way, behind the little wing there. Today they're giving out grain and sunflower-seed oil. Anarchy's only fierce with the bourgeoisie, but it helps the poor and needy like us. All simple and straightforward, no ration cards, not like with the Bolsheviks. Lots of people are frightened of anarchy and don't come, but they're wrong. These are good people, gentle, God grant them good health.'

In the courtyard Fandorin's eye was caught by two machine-gun nests constructed out of sacks of earth, and he saw the muzzle of a mountain gun protruding from the bushes. Gentle? Oh, yes indeed.

He didn't 'follow the wall round behind the little wing' but trundled straight up to the main entrance instead. A sentry with a black ribbon on his astrakhan hat was sitting on one of the steps, smoking.

'Well, look at you, bunkum on wheels,' he said, staring at the unusual armchair. 'You want to go into the artel, Grandad?'

'Yes. Can I go in?'

'You can do anything here. Freedom.'

The sentry yawned with a gaping, yellow-toothed grin and turned away. It was quite possible that he wasn't any kind of sentry after all, but simply a man who had sat down on a step for a smoke. There was no one at all in the machine-gun nests or beside the mountain gun.

Erast Petrovich had to part from his miraculous mobile armchair. He picked a black ribbon up off the ground, tied it in a bow and attached it to the back of his vehicle, trusting that no one would filch an ideological wheelchair.

Leaning on his stick, he walked slowly up the steps. The heavy door opened with no special effort – it was the same movement with which he moved the chair lever.

In the spacious vestibule black flags with slogans hung down from the ceiling.

'All power to anarchy,' Fandorin read. And then: 'Property is theft – P.-J. Proudhon'. 'The state must be destroyed – P. A. Kropotkin'. 'The individual is the soul of the revolution – Lev Chorny' (the devil only knew who that was).

There were people there too. At the centre of the oval space three individuals were talking loudly: a man with long hair and spectacles, wearing a student's greatcoat; a sailor with a machine-gun belt round his waist; and a small, creaky young woman. In his own mind Erast Petrovich called her 'creaky' because she kept gesticulating all the time, and every movement was accompanied by a light crunching sound. The girl's jacket was chrome leather, her trousers were shiny oilcloth, her shoes had gaiters and she also had a huge holster on her hip.

'. . . If you're my brother, then stop pestering me with your sexual question!' she exclaimed angrily in a thin, hoarse little voice. She had a smoking *papyrosa* dangling out of the corner of her mouth.

'That's bourgeois hypocrisy,' the man in spectacles protested with equal passion. 'Sexual self-expression is an essential attribute of the free individual. And there can only be one sexual question for a genuine anarchist. It doesn't matter who asks it, brother or sister. An honest question, answered honestly. "Do you want me, sister?" or "Do you want me, brother?"'

Fandorin hesitated, not so much intrigued by the incestuous topic of conversation as trying to weigh up how to proceed from here. Observing the inhabitants of this mansion was useful too. And the argument was tending in an ever more curious direction.

'And I think that until the revolution is completed, there's no time for the sexual question!' the young woman exclaimed. 'And no time for love.'

The sailor also put his word in.

'Concerning love, little sister, I couldn't say, but you can't fight nature – sometimes I could really fancy a bit of fraternal pushing and poking.'

He guffawed.

'You're a fool, Chubaty!' the creaky young woman shouted.

The man in spectacles reproached her.

'Go easy, Lynx. Rule number four.'

The young woman was actually embarrassed by this incomprehensible remark. 'I'm sorry, brother,' she told the sailor in a guilty voice.

He cautiously patted her shoulder with his massive paw.

'No, I'm sorry for the horseplay.'

Both the subject of the discussion and its tone seemed quite amazing to Fandorin, but he couldn't afford to waste any time.

'Listen . . . comrades,' he said, stumbling over this still unaccustomed form of address. 'A couple of minutes ago a man in a black hat and black trench coat, with a beard, came in . . . I'd like to have a word with him.'

The sailor looked round indifferently.

'The Bolsheviks have "comrades", we're all brothers – those of us that aren't sisters. There was someone who walked past. I didn't see who it was: he tramped off over that way.'

The sailor gestured in the direction of a corridor and turned away again – to carry on arguing.

'Thank you . . . brother,' Erast Petrovich said to him, and hobbled in the direction indicated, looking around attentively.

He was somewhat perplexed. The lair of thuggish anarchy did not look as expected. There were no disgraceful outrages taking place, the people were sober, the floor wasn't covered in spittle and there were no bottles lying about. Strange.

There were leather-upholstered doors along both sides of the corridor. Fandorin's mark could have gone in through any of them, or he could have gone on farther, to the flight of stairs that could be seen in the distance. If only Erast Petrovich could meet someone as polite as these three and ask who this 'Garibaldi' was and where he could be found.

One of the doors opened and a man came out wearing a white shirt with the collar unbuttoned, although the building was unheated and a cold draught was wandering along the corridor. He was rubbing his nose with a gesture that was familiar to Fandorin; that was what a seasoned cocaine-sniffer did immediately after a 'snort'.

Now that's the anarchist way, thought Erast Petrovich, *not all that 'brother', 'sister' and 'no time for love' business*. The reason for the unbuttoned shirt was clear too – the fierce white powder always made one feel hot.

'Happy snorting!' Fandorin said to the sniffer, using the normal greeting among individuals of that kind.

The reply was surprising.

'Bah, it's the gentleman playwright!' a deep, resonant voice exclaimed. 'What was your name . . . Fandorin? You haven't shown up for quite a while.'

The man took his hand away from his face and it seemed vaguely familiar. A second later a name also surfaced out of Fandorin's former theatrical and cinematographic life – Erast Petrovich had spent the three years before the war in that milieu, right up until the unpleasant incident in Baku.

The actor Gromov-Nevsky – that was who it was. A man of middling talent, who had never been accepted into first-class theatre companies – he was regarded as overplaying and striving too hard for his effects – but was enthusiastically invited to join private touring troupes to play romantic leads. He had a striking appearance and a booming voice, just the thing for the provinces.

Working his jaw muscles (cocaine induces cramp in the jaws), Gromov shook Fandorin's hand firmly. His pupils were dilated and his eyes glittered with unnatural energy.

'Where did you disappear to?'

'I have been ill.'

'So I see. You're walking with a stick. You've grown older.'

But Gromov wasn't interested in asking questions, that condition makes you want to do all the talking yourself. To tell the truth, the actor hadn't grown any younger either. His features had crumpled and sagged slightly, and his cheeks had yellowed.

'What a pity you weren't here. How brilliant I was last season and the season before! I earned five hundred for every entrance. The public went crazy. In 1916 I had three benefit performances. Just imagine, it became hard to walk along the street, with people asking for my autograph. They still recognise me even now, but the theatres aren't the same any more. There aren't any private companies and the repertory companies put on all sorts of nonsense – about various Pugachevs and the Paris Commune. Love is out of fashion these days.'

'I've heard that too,' Erast Petrovich said with a nod, thinking that this encounter was most opportune. Apparently Gromov was an insider here. He was certain to know 'Mr Garibaldi' too. Only he really was extremely garrulous . . .

'Well, to hell with the theatres,' Gromov exclaimed with a broad, sweeping gesture. 'Just look at the theatre all around us! These days all the world's a stage.'

That dictum is also familiar to me, thought Fandorin.

'But what are you doing here, with the anarchists?'

'I'm one of them. I like it here. What drama, what a company, what a stage setting!'

'And there is cocaine?'

Gromov looked round and lowered his voice.

'No, that there isn't. Don't give me away. Our impresario throws people out of the company for drugs and vodka. Out of the artel, that is.'

'Who throws you out?'

'The artel manager. The elected boss. A man of granite, not to be trifled with. Aron Liberty himself, the legend of anarchism. You've heard of him, of course.'

The imposing name (or pseudonym) meant nothing to Fandorin, but that was not surprising. The most resonant names in Russia in 1918 had never even been heard of in 1914. Five years earlier Erast Petrovich had once briefly glimpsed Lenin, the Bolshevik prime minister, but the other Soviet ministers, all those Trotskys, Sverdlovs, Dzerzhinskys (and whoever else Masa had mentioned) – God only knew where they had sprung from.

Aron Liberty, the legend of anarchism? It would be a good idea to find out a bit more about him and the local contingent here.

'I tell you what, Gromov . . .'

'Call me Nevsky,' the artiste corrected him. 'That revolutionary river, the Neva, is in favour nowadays. Think of me as the cruiser *Aurora*.'

And he broke into peals of laughter, although it wasn't clear what the joke was and what a cruiser had to do with anything.

He is right at the peak of his euphoria, Fandorin estimated. *I have to draw everything out of him before he starts coming down. Cocaine agitation lasts for half an hour at the most.*

'I tell you what, Nevsky,' Erast Petrovich continued, also in a jocular tone, but nonetheless firmly. 'Show me round this zoo of yours. I'm curious. Or else I'll give you away to your fearsome ataman.'

Nevsky gladly agreed. An audience of one is still an audience.

'Are you aware that Moscow today is bicoloured, Red and Black, and that there are two regimes, two powers, two sets of Guards – the Bolshevik Guards and the Anarchist Guards?' the actor began stentoriously. 'We overthrew the monarchy together with the Reds and we tolerate them for the time being, but it's already clear that they're not much better than the tsarist satraps. They want to replace one dictatorship with another. But Lenin and Trotsky won't get anywhere!' His powerful fist swung resolutely through the air. 'In Moscow alone there are fifty Black Guards communes, artels and brigades! "Hurricane", "Avant-Garde", "Whirlwind", "Lava", "Blizzard", "Stormy Petrel" and, of course, our own "Freedom"! The Bolshevik soviet, or council, sits on Tverskaya Street, and our "House of Anarchy" is five minutes' walk away, on Lesser Dmitrovka Street, in the old Merchants' Assembly building. The youth are almost all for us! And the workers too. Oh, what a speech I gave at the Tryokhgornaya Manufacturing Works! And how keenly they all listened, how well it was received! The Bolsheviks are the bookkeepers of the revolution, but we are its artists! The masses will follow us! Here, in the "Freedom" artel, we have a hundred and fifty brothers, and all of them truly fine fellows!'

It was time to divert the orator into a more constructive channel.

'A little while ago I saw a highly picturesque individual come in here, a genuine artist of the revolution. In a romantic black trench coat and a wide-brimmed hat. Do you know him?'

That made Nevsky suspend his exalted tone.

'Hang on now . . . They used to say that you weren't just a playwright, but a sleuth too.' The actor narrowed his eyes cunningly. 'Come on, let's have it. Are you investigating some crime or other? That could easily be the case round here. There are plenty of criminals in the artel. Give me a description of the person you're looking for.'

'I told you: bearded, a long black trench coat and a very conspicuous hat. He walked through the vestibule in this direction five minutes ago.'

Nevsky scratched his fleshy chin and chuckled.

'Come on. I'll show you something.'

He opened the door into a rather large room, crammed full of coat racks.

'This is our cloakroom, otherwise known as the wardrobe. Before the firewood ran out, when the place was still heated, our people left their outdoor clothing here. Come on, move a bit closer.'

Fandorin limped as far as the door and glanced in.

Identical black trench coats with capes hanging in a row. And lying above them, on the shelf for headwear, Garibaldi-style hats.

'The commune of anarchist tailors at the Tryokhgornaya Manufacturing Works had the idea of sewing a uniform for the Black Guards. They sent us a hundred sets as fraternal assistance. But Liberty said that a uniform was an attribute of compulsion. The trench coats and hats are still here. Anyone who has nothing to wear uses them. And we have plenty of guys with beards. Anarchists – what can you expect?' Gromov suddenly seemed to fade and deflate, like a punctured tyre. 'Okay, Fandorin, you stroll around on your own. Call into the "Temple of Reading". When we requisitioned the mansion, Liberty ordered us to fling all the financial literature out of the bank's library and we shipped in the anarchist classics instead . . . We've got all sorts of things here. You'll see . . .'

He gestured feebly with his hand and walked away. *His hit didn't last for very long*, Erast Petrovich thought. *Our romantic lead is a hardcore snorter.*

Fandorin moved on alone, leaning on his cane and sometimes holding on to the wall. Every twenty or thirty steps he had to take a breather. He spent most of his energy on preventing himself from becoming furious. *Since the* ki *energy has dried up, I'll have to accustom myself to managing without it*, Erast Petrovich tried to impress on himself. *For it has been said: 'The noble man despises infirmity of the body and regards what cannot be cured as good health.'*

He heard a triumphantly declaiming voice coming out through an open door.

'The fundamental principle of individualistic anarchism is the right of every individual to exercise free control over himself. This right belongs to every human being by virtue of their birth. The human being's right to choose is the supreme value and is respected under any circumstances. Any limitations on freedom can only be voluntary. Those who interpret such voluntary limitations in an identical fashion should reside together. The planet Earth is sufficiently large to provide space for all communities, with each of them adhering to its own rules, and those who do not want any limitations may live alone.'

A shaggy-haired young man who looked like a student was reading from a book, raising one finger in the air at the especially important places. He was being listened to by an audience of about twenty people – most of them young. They were all armed. Three were wearing identical black trench coats, and one of them was holding a familiar black hat on his knees – but his face was beardless and youthful.

Frowning, Erast Petrovich moved on. It seemed that the search would not be easy.

'. . . It is for this great goal that we shall organise the final and very greatest of revolutions!'

Someone started applauding behind Fandorin's back. Someone shouted out: 'Revolution now!'

In a large empty hall, where the floor was covered with mattresses, people were sleeping. Rifles stood against the wall in a row. Standing on the broad windowsill with its snout pointing out into the yard was a machine gun. *So part of the artel must constantly be confined to barracks*, Erast Petrovich surmised. *And since they sleep during the day, it means they're awake at night. Not such a very wild, free life, it turns out.*

He hobbled as far as a stairway leading to the first floor and hesitated, wondering whether to go up or not.

It was a damned difficult challenge. Which was precisely why Fandorin did not back down.

Taking hold of the banister, he set one foot on a step and pulled his reluctant body up. Another step. And another. A halt.

A snail climbing up Mount Fuji . . .

He gritted his teeth and surmounted another three steps. Then he rested a little.

Erast Petrovich had only one more 'route march' left to reach the next landing when someone called to him.

'Hey, who are you? What are you doing here?'

Standing by the banister higher up was a large-nosed man with black eyes that glittered menacingly. He was wearing a black trench coat with a cape and his hand was resting on a gun holster.

'I'm a free individual. I go wherever I want,' said Fandorin, peering at the stranger and wondering whether his stubble was long enough for the witnesses to have called it a beard. The dark-haired man had another distinguishing feature – a rather strong, guttural, Georgian accent. The general had not said anything about an accent, but perhaps the robber had taken the medallion without saying anything?

The Georgian bared his sharp, tobacco-stained teeth.

'They've sent a cripple, the smart-arses. Or are you just pretending?'

He slithered down the steps and took a firm hold of Erast Petrovich's elbow

'Will you walk yourself?'

And he dragged Fandorin upwards. With this uninvited helper the rate of ascent accelerated; Erast Petrovich only had to set one foot in front of the other.

He pondered whether he ought to poke this ruffian in the *mudo* point, but a paralysing jab required a good charge of *ki*, and there was nowhere he could get that from. And furthermore, it was written: 'If a storm drives your ship in the right direction, do not fight against it, but unfurl the sail wider.'

The artel manager Liberty

The storm dragged the ship along the first-floor corridor to a door with a plaque that said 'Reception'. And inside it there actually was an absolutely ordinary office space: filing cabinets, a desk with a telephone, a typewriter.

Sitting at the desk was a girl in black leather – the same girl that Erast Petrovich had seen in the vestibule, the creaky one. She looked up from a bookkeeping abacus, on which she was calculating something.

'Who have you brought me, Djiki?'

'Another spy,' said the Georgian. 'Someone reported he was walking around, looking at things.'

The girl (Fandorin remembered that she was called 'Lynx') wrinkled up her little snub nose.

'A bit old for a spy. And he doesn't walk too well, more like a wandering pilgrim.'

'Eh, they're cunning. I know these invalids. Once he kicks up his heels you'll never catch him. I'm taking him to Aron.'

'Go ahead,' the girl said. She clicked a bead on her abacus and noted something down. Then she bobbed her head in the direction of a beautiful door with moulding and a sign that said 'Chairman'.

Erast Petrovich's face darkened. The new life in which he found himself was full of grievances. In his former life young ladies did not lose interest in him so quickly: 'a bit old', 'a wandering pilgrim'.

'Go on, go on,' said the Georgian, nudging him in the back. 'The artel manager sees right through people. If you're a bastard, I'll kill you.'

Barely managing to stay on his uncertain feet after that nudge, Fandorin opened the door with his chest, and once inside the threshold he thrust his stick into the sumptuous carpet only just in time.

Someone in a black trench coat with an uncombed, half-grey beard was sitting on the edge of a huge polished table, dangling a shabby boot.

Raising his eyes from his book, he looked in calm amazement at the man who had come flying into the study, then looked at the Georgian.

'What is it, Djiki?'

The 'artel manager' had a rather strange appearance. His wide-set eyes possessed an unusual, quite distinctive quality. Their gaze seemed preoccupied, even drowsy, but at the same time a suppressed fire could be sensed in them, capable of blazing up at full force at any moment. The hue of his pale skin was also unusual, almost bluish, as if it had never seen the sun. *A rare specimen*, Erast Petrovich told himself. *Worth studying*.

'I told you, Aron, the Bolsheviks have got really brazen. This one's walking around quite openly. Where our machine guns are, where everything is, he's looking at all of it. We ought to bump him off and throw him out through the gates. As an example. Then they'll stop poking their noses in.'

'And what makes you think that he's a Bolshevik spy?'

'Who's responsible for security, you or me?' asked Djiki, getting angry. 'You do your job, and I'll do mine. If I say he's a spy, that means I know! Let me bump him off!'

The artel manager shrugged.

'Even if he is a Bolshevik, that means he has his own truth, simply a different one. That's no reason to kill him. Show him out of the gates, and there's an end of it.'

'I won't leave,' said Erast Petrovich. 'Not until I get what I came for.'

The inhabitant of the study looked at him again, this time with interest. He put down his book, got up and walked closer. The sparks in his eyes started glittering more brightly.

'You go, Djiki. I'll have a word with him.'

'E-eh!' the Georgian exclaimed, rolling his eyes up. 'We keep talking, talking. It's time for shooting! Making a revolution! The Bolsheviks won't talk for long!'

He walked out, slamming the door.

Aron Liberty examined Fandorin unceremoniously for quite a long time.

'An interesting combination. Lancelot, Seneca and Sleeping Beauty in the same binding.'

The final component of this triad made Erast Petrovich shudder. He asked in a cold voice, 'Why do you say that to me?'

'I always say what I think. Have I deciphered you correctly or not?'

I suppose so, Fandorin thought uncomfortably. *I really am wandering through this alien world like a sleepwalker.*

'Are you good at understanding people?'

'Only the interesting ones. With the uninteresting ones I sometimes make mistakes.'

'Always saying what you think must have caused you problems, has it not?' Erast Petrovich enquired.

'Of course. But what is life without problems? How would it differ from death? First I was expelled from grammar school. For speaking familiarly to the inspector. After that there were all sorts of things. In the Irkutsk transit prison I was once beaten so badly that I could hardly use my legs at all for six months. Worse than your case. The prison doctor didn't treat me, because I spoke familiarly to him too. Never mind, I recovered.'

He's telling the truth, isn't he? thought Erast Petrovich. *This man doesn't seem to know how to lie.*

'Well now, you have your rules and I have mine. I only speak in familiar terms to people very close to me. In fact, only to one person.'

'Probably your wife?' the artel manager asked with a crooked grimace. 'When a man cannot live on his own, he gets himself a crutch. What have you come here for? You don't look like a spy. Spies never look the way you do. Perhaps you wish to join the artel? I'll accept you, you're interesting.'

'I wish to understand who you are and what you are trying to achieve. What revolution is it that you propound? The revolution has already happened. Two revolutions, in fact, in February and in October.'

'A third is required,' Liberty asserted confidently. 'The first revolution was a bourgeois one – against tsarism. The second was a socialist revolution – against the bourgeoisie. The third will be an anarchist revolution – against the socialists. Russia will only become free after our victory. The dictatorship of the proletariat is still a dictatorship.' He spoke more and more excitedly and the fire in his eyes blazed brighter and brighter. 'Just look at how abominably this world is arranged. Children are born, and nine out of ten of them are doomed to back-breaking labour, to oppression and humiliation, and the tenth, supposedly the fortunate one, is doomed to feel that he is a parasite. No one has any choice. But a human being only differs from an animal in that he can choose who to become. Look how ugly this inequality makes humanity! How wretchedly and shamefully it lives! Look at the cities, these sooty, smoky graveyards of human destinies!'

'We cannot manage without cities,' Fandorin objected, not so much listening to the meaning of the words that were spoken as trying to gain some understanding of the man speaking them.

'We can! We have to. People were herded into these pens by force: it's easier to earn your daily bread here. All we have to do is remove the mediating link between labour and bread. All that is required is to crush the head of the hydra of the state, to strike a blow here, in Moscow – and people right across the country will arrange their own lives for themselves. Most will want to live on the land, breathe clean air and raise their children in open space and freedom. Tens of thousands of communes will self-organise and live by the dictates of their own intelligence, according to their own internal agreement. Like our artel. And the only people left in the cities will be those who want to work with machines or engage in science. And they will self-organise too. That is what a genuine revolution looks like!'

'You plan to overthrow the Soviet regime and you talk about it openly?'

'Conspiracies and intrigues are not our way. The revolution triumphs with its visor raised. We already have twenty-six strongpoints in the city. And there are more of them all the time. The people can see that the Bolsheviks only thirst for power, but the Black Guards live for an idea!'

'All of them without exception?' Erast Petrovich asked, in order to understand just how far this revolutionary dreamer was divorced from reality.

'Of course not,' said Liberty, actually surprised. 'We take anyone who wishes to join into our artel, we don't arrange interrogations. Because every individual is a priori worthy of respect and trust. Until such time as he forfeits them by doing something unworthy. The Freedom artel has a charter consisting of ten rules. Everyone who joins pledges to observe them.'

'And what rules are they?'

'The first is not to begrudge giving one's life for freedom. The second: to treat one's brothers and sisters with respect. The third: to help them always and in everything. The fourth: quarrelling with one's brothers and sisters is forbidden. The fifth: to fight only the enemies of the revolution. The sixth: all property is held in common, with the exception of personal items. The seventh: a strict prohibition on alcohol. The eighth: not to start a family until after the final victory of the revolution. The ninth: to carry out the military orders of the artel manager, without regarding them as a limitation of freedom. And finally, the tenth: if you have violated any of the rules, to accept the judgement of your brothers without complaint.'

'And how do you try people?'

'By a general vote. There are only two punishments. The lesser is expulsion from the artel. For that a simple majority is sufficient. And the supreme penalty is execution by firing squad. But this sentence requires a two-thirds majority. We apply the death penalty for grievous crimes: for murder, say. An individual is free in his decisions and actions, but at the same time he must bear full responsibility for them. Up to and including paying for them with his own life. Such is our anarchist Black Truth.'

'And have you ever executed members of your artel?'

'Twice. One brother got drunk and killed another brother with a knife. And on another occasion, when one of the criminals raped a grammar-school girl. You have seen Djiki, my assistant for combat matters. He is a former hold-up bandit himself and has lived a bleak, gruelling life. Djiki carries out the sentences: he has a firm hand.'

Fandorin made up his mind to speak out.

'If there are such strict laws in the Freedom artel, how would you deal with a brother who robbed a helpless old woman?'

And he told the artel manager about what had happened on Pokrovka Street.

Liberty heard him out with a frown.

'Yes, that is bad. I feel sorry for the old woman. But the rules of the artel have not been violated. The requisitioning of luxury items from members of the exploiting classes is in the order of things. We exchange the confiscated valuables for food, which we distribute to the needy without payment. If the hostile element resists, the use of force is permitted. He didn't kill that count, after all.'

'Keep the gold medallion. Give the photograph and lock of hair back to the unfortunate mother. That is all I want.'

The artel manager thought for a moment.

'I think we will return the medallion too, since it has only sentimental, not market, value. In that case, it is not a luxury item, but a personal one . . . What is your name?'

'Fandorin.'

'Come with me, Fandorin. The medallion should be in the repository where we keep the artel treasury. We'll find it now. Then I'll send one of the brothers with you. He can return it to the mother and take a receipt.'

Aron Liberty moved rapidly towards the door. Rather taken aback, Erast Petrovich hesitated for a moment before hobbling after him.

The artel manager was waiting for him in the reception office, listening to the creaky young lady.

She was saying:

'. . . And so we have a week's reserve of foodstuffs for a hundred and forty-seven fighters, plus surpluses. I reached an arrangement with the Bakunin Commune, and they have given us two Maxim machine guns in exchange for eight poods of flour and the canister of pure alcohol that we confiscated the day before yesterday – we don't need the alcohol anyway. Over and above that we still have ten poods of flour, thirty pounds of sugar, twelve sacks of potatoes, as well as vegetable oil, for distribution to the general public. Shall I distribute them?'

'Of course. Well done for making the arrangement about the machine guns. We'll be needing them soon.'

Liberty gave the girl an affectionate slap on the shoulder and her fresh little face turned pink with pleasure.

'Come on, let's go,' said the artel manager, hurrying Fandorin along and taking him firmly by the arm. 'Is it easier to walk like this?'

'Yes, thank you,' Erast Petrovich said morosely, hating his own rubbery legs.

'That little sister's worth her weight in gold,' Liberty said in the corridor. 'I don't really know who is more valuable to the artel, Djiki or her. By the way, in Georgian "Djiki" means "panther", and the girl is called Lynx. So both my assistants are from the cat family, which is only right. The cat is the most freedom-loving of animals, the Romans were right to seat it at the feet of the goddess Libertas. Everything here hinges on Lynx, she is like our chief of staff. A genuine Russian girl, one of those who live for an idea. Girls like her used to fire at governors and ministers, and die in prison hunger strikes. Last year Lynx enrolled in the Women's Battalion of Death and set out for the front. Not out of any so-called patriotism, but in the name of women's rights. What a girl!' The artel manager laughed admiringly. 'She got a bullet in the chest and barely survived. And now, as you see, she's right back at the forefront of events.'

The corridor took two turns and ended at a metal door with a padlock. There was a sentry beside it, but his rifle was lying on the floor and he was finishing a drawing on the wall – a huge naked woman, depicted in charcoal with the greatest possible naturalism.

'What are you doing, Kozlov?'

The young man looked round. His appearance was gipsyish, with a black beard, but was wearing a soldier's greatcoat, not a trench coat.

'Can't you see? I'm drawing. You said yourself that a free individual should . . . how was it? . . . develop the artistic impulse in himself. So I'm developing it, it's boring just standing here. Good, isn't she?'

'Nothing good about it,' the artel manager said angrily. 'Lewdness like that demeans the female sex!'

Kozlov took offence.

'Then I'm damned if I'll vote for you today. And I'll tell the lads too.'

'To hell with you then, don't vote for me,' Liberty muttered, taking out a key. 'At least I'll get a bit of rest . . .' Having opened the door, he reached his hand inside and found a switch. 'Go in, Fandorin. All the confiscated property that hasn't been exchanged for foodstuffs is kept in there. Lynx is in command here. She keeps everything in good order.'

In the small, windowless room with its walls completely covered by wooden shelves and cupboards, neatly sorted valuables were laid out on a table – separate sections of silver tableware and candlesticks, stacks of gold coins, cigarette cases, tsarist medals, earrings, necklaces and rings. There were medallions too, but not one with diamonds.

'What, is it not here? Perhaps the brother who confiscated the medallion has not returned yet?'

'He has. Half an hour ago.'

Liberty's lower jaw seemed to turn to stone.

'According to the rules every fighter who has carried out a requisition must hand in the confiscated items to the treasury immediately on his return. If he doesn't, then he is a thief. He has stolen from his brothers! For that he must be tried. Could you identify him?'

'I haven't seen his face, but I know his distinctive features.'

'Excellent. Now you will see everybody.' The leader of the anarchists drummed his fingers on the table angrily. 'Did you hear what the sentry said about voting? We have elections for the artel manager once a week. That's our custom. Every Thursday, at five in the afternoon, a general meeting. Today happens to be Thursday, and the time . . .' – he glanced at his watch – '. . . is half past four. Come on, you can show me the scoundrel.'

A free choice

The meeting of the artel took place in the rear courtyard – no doubt there was no space in the building large enough to hold the entire brigade. About a hundred and fifty people were standing in the asphalt square that was squeezed in between the main building, the wings and the fence – almost exclusively 'brothers', as Fandorin noticed immediately. The number of 'sisters', including the already familiar Lynx, probably did not amount to as many as ten. The anarchist ladies were no less picturesque than the men, but at this particular moment Erast Petrovich was not interested in them.

It was good that they had all gathered outside, in the cold. It meant that they were wearing their outer garments and – what was particularly helpful – their hats. Fandorin counted the items of Garibaldi-style headgear (twenty-seven), rejected those men who were not wearing a trench coat with a cape, which left eleven, and from this remainder he selected the tall men with black beards. That left only three.

One of them had a prominent Adam's apple, with a wispy beard, and was very young, but at the same time stubborn-looking, with his lower lip thrust out provocatively. He was standing with his hands in his pockets, spitting every now and then.

The second was swarthy, with a rapid, flashing glance, and he kept stepping from one foot to the other, as if he was ready to go shooting off at any moment. Clearly a dashing criminal type.

The third, on the contrary, was completely static, with a stony face, overgrown almost right up to the eyes with a thick beard.

It was easy to picture any of the three in the role of a street thief.

The meeting was conducted by the rather sinister Panther-Djiki. And it was easy to see why – these wild freemen were clearly a little bit afraid of the fierce Caucasian.

Djiki was a hopeless orator.

'Right, then,' he said with his hands on his hips. 'Not the first time, is it? So off you go, Aron. You're on.'

That was his entire introduction.

No doubt, as the acting artel manager, it was Liberty's obligation to address the meeting with an election speech.

But the speech was not overlong either.

Liberty walked up onto the porch, ran his ardent gaze round the courtyard and began in a quiet voice:

'Thank you for re-electing me time after time. You're probably sick of hearing the same old things every week. So I'll keep it brief. About the most important thing. About our Black Truth. Why is it called black?'

They listened to him attentively. *A crowd can sense genuine, unalloyed obsession very clearly*, thought Fandorin. *It gets a charge from it, and even becomes infected by it.*

'. . . Because we don't whitewash man or paint him in bright colours. We like him black. Just the way he is. I love all of you: the angry, the resentful, the syphilitics, the execrated, the unwanted, the sinners, the criminals – every kind. And do you know why? Because you are here, in the Freedom artel, which means that, for you, freedom is the most important thing of all. You are the same as I am. You are my brothers and sisters. Like me, you will begrudge nothing and nobody for the sake of freedom. And I will begrudge nothing and nobody, including myself, for your sake, and you know it. That's all, I've finished. You are free people, decide.'

They didn't clap him, they didn't shout out in approval, but the silence was more eloquent than any applause.

That is what a leader should be like. At all events in a Russia in the throes of revolution, Erast Petrovich told himself, and sighed – to begrudge nothing and nobody – that was too high a price. Even for freedom.

But Liberty stood beside him and whispered, as if he hadn't just pronounced those exalted words:

'Well, can you see the villain?'

'Three men match the distinctive features,' Fandorin replied in an equally quiet voice. And he explained who they were.

'Spartacus, Hatchet, Zhokhov . . .' Liberty hissed through his teeth, narrowing his eyes ominously. 'Okay. When the election's over, we'll get to the bottom of things.'

Meanwhile the meeting continued.

When Djiki asked whether the artel was ready to vote or whether anyone else wanted to address the meeting, a hand was raised.

'We've had enough of Aron!' a man in a peaked cap shouted. 'With that kind of Liberty, there is no liberty! Brothers, let's make the actor the artel manager! We want Nevsky!'

Gromov-Nevsky was right there, wearing a trench coat over his shirt, pale-faced but smiling. He waved to everyone, bowing facetiously, and a sumptuous lock of hair flopped down across his forehead.

'That's our artiste,' said Liberty. 'A celebrity. He speaks magnificently at meetings and in general has contributed a great deal to the propagation of our ideas.'

Erast Petrovich could not detect any hostility or envy in these words.

The crowd livened up. Someone laughed and someone shouted out: 'Go on, Nevsky! Make a speech!'

The actor walked lightly up the steps, threw off his trench coat and tossed back his thick thatch of hair. He spoke with effective pauses, in an excellently trained baritone.

'Dear brothers and even dearer sisters, I shall also be brief. Unlike the previous speaker, I can't stand the sight of any of you. Because you're monsters. Half of you are bandits and half of you are weirdos, like yours truly. Instead of sitting at home drinking tea, you risk your backsides seeking adventures.' The audience laughed. 'But I hang about in this dive for the same reason as you do. What they have out there . . .' – Nevsky gestured with his hand at the world outside the fence – '. . . is boredom, but in here we have fun. Mind you, we could have a bit more fun. My election programme includes only one point. Instead of prohibition, let's have positive encouragement. The seventh rule should be rewritten to read: "If anyone can't hold his drink and allows vodka or cocaine to transform him into a swine, he must be booted out, but let everyone else get hammered to their heart's content." That's it, I'm finished. You're free people, decide,' the actor said in a very good imitation of Liberty's rather dull voice, and bowed.

The crowd in the courtyard clapped and laughed.

'They'll depose you now,' Fandorin said in alarm. That would render his business more complicated, just when it had seemed to be moving to its conclusion.

'Let them,' Liberty commented indifferently. 'People have a free choice. If they want to carouse, that's their business. It's all right, in a week they'll realise it's not the right thing to do and elect me again, and they'll restore the prohibition on alcohol. Don't you worry. No one will abrogate the other rules, so we'll unmask the thief in any case.'

Djiki announced the voting.

'First raise your hands if you're for Aron,' he said, and flung his own fist up first of all.

To Fandorin's surprise almost the entire crowd followed the Georgian's example, including even Nevsky. Catching Erast Petrovich's eye, the actor winked. It was clear that general attention and applause were all that the 'romantic lead' required.

The victor didn't deliver an acceptance speech.

'All of you on duty, back to your places!' he shouted. 'And the others, don't go too far away. Zhokhov, Hatchet and Spartacus, come to see me in five minutes.'

The best of the worst

'What do you intend to do? Search them?'

Fandorin could not keep up with the gloomy artel manager. Liberty stopped and waited for a moment.

'No. A search is humiliating. And in any case the thief could have hidden his booty somewhere. I'll have a talk with them. I told you that I have a good eye for people. And I'm sure that you have a good understanding of them too. I deliberately didn't tell them to come immediately. I'll explain briefly about each of them for you. Spartacus, the youngest, used to be an apprentice telegraph operator, but last February he got drawn into the revolution. He came to us from the Wantons.'

'Who are they?'

'The most extreme of the anarchists. They believe that all members of the exploiting class are criminals and should be annihilated. The Wantons have planted bombs in first-class railway carriages, burned down expensive dachas and fired at the windows of rich houses. All without any real rationale, hence their name, the Wantons. Spartacus is an intemperate, even cruel, young man. I think it's his youthful maximalism. But he is not a bad person. During the November battles we stormed the headquarters of the Provisional Government's militia, and they have kennels there. Well, there was a fire and the dogs were howling because they couldn't get out. And Spartacus dashed straight into the flames and dragged out a bloodhound. He risked his own life. I don't think it was him who robbed the old couple. That is, he could have taken the medallion, but it's not like him to hide it.'

Erast Petrovich didn't try to argue, although in his time he had seen all sorts of 'youthful maximalists', including hard-core criminals.

'What do you have to say about the swarthy, jumpy one?'

'Hatchet. Did you see that he has a short-handled hatchet in his belt? Hence the nickname. He handles that crude instrument like a surgeon handles his scalpel, using it for opening a door, or trimming his nails, or breaking a skull.'

'A hold-up man,' Fandorin said with a nod. He had guessed the second man's trade correctly, and it had not been difficult.

'A criminal element,' Liberty confirmed. 'We have a lot of them, as I told you. That's natural. A bandit instinctively rejects an exploitative society and its laws. There have always been people like Hatchet in Russia. They got up to mischief in the forests and on the roads, and slaughtered noblemen with Stenka Razin and Emelyan Pugachev. Anarchy is a special kind of magnet. It attracts the very best and the very worst. Or rather, the very best of the best and the very best of the worst,' he corrected himself. 'I don't think I can vouch for Hatchet. A leopard and his spots . . .'

'And the third man? The immobile one?'

'He only looks immobile: Zhokhov. He moves fast when he needs to. A war hero, with a full ribbon of St George. A reconnaissance scout. He used to creep through the front lines and bring back prisoners for interrogation. Single-handedly. He's generally taciturn, but he opened up to me once. He said that behind the German lines he used to kill one or two men "to warm up" at first, and only then take someone alive. He is one of those men in whom the war roused the wild beast. I can't say anything about him. An interesting individual, but entirely unpredictable.'

They finally reached the reception office, where Lynx was setting out folders of some kind on shelves in the little box room.

'Congratulations on being re-elected!' she said, poking her head out.

'If only it meant something,' Liberty growled. 'Three men will come to see me now. Let them through.'

'I know, I heard. Spartacus, Hatchet and that nightmarish Zhokhov. I can't bear to look at him, brrrr. He smells like a corpse.'

'Don't lie. What corpse?' Liberty asked in surprise – he obviously had not read Chekhov. 'I have a good sense of smell, I would have sensed that. Anyway, show them in to me.'

Before even a minute had gone by there was a knock at the door. The suspects came in one after another: first the criminal 'surgeon', then the 'Wanton', and finally the war hero, strolling at a leisurely pace.

'Greetings, brothers,' said Liberty.

Wearing identical trench coats and hats, with their faces overgrown with black hair, they really did look like three brothers – youngest, middle and eldest.

'What have you called us in for, boss?' asked the impatient Hatchet. 'What's the matter? I haven't slept since yesterday. I was going to go to the mattress room and hit the hay.'

Liberty looked at him with his glittering eyes, as if shining a light right through him. Then he examined the others in the same unhurried manner. Spartacus took no notice at all of this, just staring into empty space and sniffing. Zhokhov bore the piercing gaze with absolute imperturbability. But Hatchet didn't like this examination. The corner of his mouth twitched and there was a hysterical note in his voice when he spoke.

'Why are you eyeing me like that, like you were drilling a hole right through me? Tell me what you want!'

The artel manager asked in a quiet voice:

'Did any of you carry out a requisition today?'

'Not me,' Hatchet replied quickly. 'What about it?'

'Eh?' asked the young lad, who hadn't heard immediately. 'No, I was dealing with business of my own.'

Zhokhov shook his head.

Liberty turned absolutely sombre. He must have been hoping that the medallion would be handed in after all.

'Let there be no more requisitions. A violent period is about to begin. There's going to be a clash with the Bolsheviks.'

Zhokhov nodded.

Hatchet said:

'We'll spill the Reds' mucky red gunk for them.'

'Eh?' Spartacus repeated.

'Starting tomorrow I'm putting the entire artel on a combat footing. And I'm asking you three to go on stand-by duty immediately. I need you, brothers. Hatchet, I'm assigning you to check the sentries. Make sure they stay alert. They've started making idle chatter and counting crows. The machine-gun nests in the yard are unmanned. And instead of guarding the treasury, the sentry's drawing a woman on the wall.'

'Understood,' said the former bandit. 'They'll be standing to attention on guard.'

'Spartacus, you go to the telegraph room. You haven't forgotten what you learned, have you? In the commanders' meeting at Central HQ we agreed not to use telephone connections for secret conversations any longer. The exchange is occupied by the Bolsheviks and they listen in.'

'I can't,' Spartacus said with a frown. 'Not today, I just can't. I've got business to deal with.'

'What kind of business is that?'

Spartacus blushed.

'Personal . . .'

'Personal business after the victory of the revolution!' Liberty exclaimed furiously. 'Quick march to the telegraph room! Do you remember the ninth rule?'

The youth nodded with a miserable air.

'Now you, Zhokhov. Lynx has done a barter and got us two new Maxims. Check their condition. If there's anything wrong, fix it. You're the only one I trust, you're a master of all trades.'

The taciturn man inclined his head and parted his lips for the first time to ask in a hoarse voice:

'Is that all? Then I'll be off.'

The others followed him.

'Which one, do you think?' Liberty asked.

'Any of them. Including the boy. He wouldn't have taken a golden trinket for himself, but he's in love, isn't he? I know that vacant look very well. Perhaps he has some Cleopatra who demands expensive gifts.'

The artel manager sighed.

'Yes. I keep forgetting about that factor. All right. This is what we'll do next . . .'

The door swung open and Djiki burst into the room.

'The Latvians are setting up a machine gun in the attic of the next building!' he announced excitedly in his guttural accent. 'What do we do, Aron? Let's show them they can't play games with us.'

'Calm down, Djiki, calm down.' Liberty took hold of the Georgian by the shoulders. 'Cool off a bit. It's too soon to start shooting at the Bolsheviks. Take some of the lads and go up into the attic. Show the Latvians out politely. Requisition the machine gun. Let them give Aron Liberty's greetings and our thanks for the donation of arms to Comrade Dzerzhinsky. Do you understand me? Po-lite-ly.'

The Caucasian chuckled. 'Why wouldn't I understand? Politely. I'll leave the machine gun in place, only with a squad of our men.'

'That's right. Now go.'

They were left alone again.

'You started telling me what you intend to do next,' Erast Petrovich reminded him.

'Not I, but we . . .' Liberty stood with his back to the door, rubbing the bridge of his nose intently. 'Perhaps this vile story is all for the best. The decisive confrontation between the Black Truth and the Red one will take place any day now. The trial of a thief will shake the brothers up. And throwing the scoundrel out won't be enough. I shall demand the supreme penalty. We have to tighten up revolutionary discipline before the great events.'

'How will you determine which of them is the thief?' asked Fandorin, not particularly convinced by the anarchist leader's deductive capabilities.

'Very simply. We'll pay a visit to your count now and ask him to describe the robber's appearance in greater detail. That's all. You know the address, don't you?'

'Yes, it's only ten minutes' walk from here. Petroveritsky Lane. The former Chernyshev building. They live in the caretaker's lodge.'

Apparently Liberty was anything but simple after all. He had given the suspects instructions that meant they couldn't go away anywhere – in effect, he had placed them under house arrest. And soon, in half an hour at the most, the guilty party would be unmasked.

'Let's take a walk,' said Liberty, putting on his hat.

'Some will walk, and some will ride,' Erast Petrovich said, sighing.

The quirks of good luck

No one had touched Fandorin's 'vehicle', protected by its black ribbon. Tired from all his walking, Fandorin lowered himself into the armchair with a feeling of relief and took hold of the lever.

They set off.

'Listen,' said Erast Petrovich, squinting sideways at his companion, 'you're an intelligent man and no longer young, you've seen a lot of things. Do you really believe in all this?'

'In all this what?'

'In your "Black Truth". That people, just as they are, are capable of "self-organising"? That our vast, illiterate country, where everyone lives according to the principles "every man for himself" and "it's not my funeral", will be transformed into a brotherhood of anarchist communes?'

'"Every man for himself" and "it's not my funeral" express correct, innate instincts,' Liberty replied calmly. 'In fact they express the entire essence of individualistic anarchism. All kinds of "statists", including the Bolsheviks, hate human nature, they violate it. They force people to live for the sake of some invented ideals, whether it's the Third Rome, Faith, Tsar and Fatherland or the Dictatorship of the Proletariat. But all that is useless for a human being. He wants to live for his own sake and the sake of his dear ones, to help those he knows and loves, to work for himself and not for someone else's uncle. That is what is called freedom. And it is not any kind of utopia. Our country consists nine-tenths of peasants, and they are all natural anarchists. They don't need any regime over them. They know how to impose order in their own commune and defend themselves against outsiders. The state machine is not necessary for transforming grain and meat into industrial goods. The worker and the peasant will come to an excellent arrangement. In 1916 I was in a cell with a certain Ukrainian. An extremely simple young man – Nestor Makhno was his name. He and I talked about this a lot. And now he writes to me from Ukraine. They have set up a peasant commune in their district and they live according to the anarchist truth. It works excellently – without any police or any bureaucrats, or any money. That is how the new world will be born. If we don't blunder here in Moscow, of course. The Bolsheviks are powerful opponents . . .'

As he listened to these considerations, Fandorin glanced round every now and then. Eventually he interrupted.

'We're being tailed. And quite intensively. They've been there ever since the gates. They're trying to remain inconspicuous, but they're working clumsily.'

'Agents of the Extraordinary Commission, the Cheka,' Liberty explained offhandedly. 'They've become more active just recently. When I go out, they always tag along behind. They want to know where I've been, what I did, who I met. I told you: Bolshevism is no better than autocracy, they can't manage without secret police. Take no notice. They haven't got the guts to touch me. All hell would break loose!'

And he didn't even look round.

In the thickening twilight they proceeded slowly up the incline of Kosmodemiansky Lane until they only had to turn the corner to reach the Chernyshev building. At Fandorin's speed the journey had taken a full twenty minutes instead of ten.

'That yellow mansion over there,' said Fandorin, pointing. 'Hey, my good man, where's the caretaker's lodge here?' he called to a small, extremely drunk individual who had wandered out of the gateway.

The proletarian gave him a dark look.

'All the "good men" have had their guts ripped out . . .' He shifted his gaze to Liberty in his black trench coat, with a Mauser on his belt, and took fright. 'The caretaker's lodge? It's in the yard, on the right. The steps are steep, mind you, don't slip.'

The steps down into the semi-basement really were steep. Erast Petrovich looked at them doubtfully – there was no chance he could get down them.

'Wait here. I'll have a word with them. It will only take a minute or two,' said Liberty.

He ran down the steps, pushed the door and went in.

'Hey, master of the house!' Fandorin heard his voice call from below.

And then silence fell for a long time. Not just two minutes, but five, then ten. Fifteen.

Fandorin's brows started rising. He shouted:

'Mr Liberty! What's taking so long?'

No reply.

He would have to go down after all.

Getting up out of the chair, Erast Petrovich took hold of the wall and propped his stick against a step, trying to judge where to set his foot. His *ki* energy, that base traitor, observed his titanic efforts spitefully.

'*Chikusyo!*' Fandorin swore in Japanese, so that it would understand him better. He was on the third step, with four still to go, when the door opened. Liberty was standing below him. His face was trembling strangely.

'The old man and woman are dead. Murdered. There's blood everywhere. Absolutely fresh. It's still pouring out of them . . . That is, it was pouring out, when I went in. It has stopped now . . . I don't know how long I stood there . . .'

'For a revolutionary, you're too sensitive,' Erast Petrovich said angrily. 'Move aside. Let me through.'

He negotiated the second half of the stairway with short, clumsy little hops, relying more on his stick than his legs. He pushed the anarchist aside and walked into the tiny, dark little apartment.

The former general and his wife were lying on their backs on the floor. The general had his arm across his wife, as if trying to protect her.

They were both killed with a metal object, most probably a knuckleduster, Erast Petrovich noted by force of professional habit, squatting down with a struggle. *He was struck on the forehead, and she on the temple, and the blows were struck by a man of considerable physical strength.* An expression of fright had frozen on the general's face. He had guessed what was about to happen. Most likely he had recognised the murderer. In contrast, the old woman's features were calm and relaxed. She had probably looked like that before she lost her reason. And yes, the murder had happened very recently, no more than twenty minutes ago. And from that it followed . . .

'Our conversation in the study was overheard,' Liberty said in a hollow voice. 'You mentioned the address, didn't you? The villain realised that he was bound to be exposed and ran here. And while we were on our way, he made sure no one would ever find him.'

But Fandorin, having concluded his examination of the scene, permitted himself a thought about a different, inconsequential little matter.

There was no longer any need to return the photo and the lock of hair. Those items no longer had any value for anyone in the world. And in effect the count and countess had been lucky, they had lived together a long time, although not always happily, but they had died on the same day, almost even in the same instant. Apparently good luck could even be something like this . . .

'But it's not possible,' said the artel manager, continuing to deduce what was already clear to Erast Petrovich. 'Lynx was behind the door all the time. She wouldn't have allowed anyone else to eavesdrop . . . Lynx? But how? Why?'

He swung round and ran out of the basement, forgetting about Fandorin.

The end of the investigation

On his four wheels Erast Petrovich bowled along quite briskly, having achieved a substantial mastery of daredevil wheelchair driving, but he tottered at a snail's pace along the corridors and up the steps in the artel, so that he missed the overture.

He heard Liberty's loud voice shouting in the reception office.

'Answer me! Which one of them did you blab to? Hatchet? Zhokhov? Spartacus? Which one? Well, why are you putting on an air of insulted innocence? No one else could have eavesdropped except for you. And now two people have been murdered. Their blood is on your hands! Why don't you say anything? How could you?'

Fandorin opened the door.

The artel manager was hovering over his assistant, shaking his fist in front of her nose. Lynx was standing in front of him, pale-faced, biting her lip and looking up with wet eyes. She wiped a tear away furiously.

'How could you?' she shouted back. 'How can you say that? To me!' She choked. 'I didn't eavesdrop on anything. Ah, you . . .'

She turned away abruptly.

Liberty grabbed her by her thin shoulders and swung her back round.

'Miracles don't happen. Fandorin and I were talking face-to-face, alone. Standing close to the door. Let's suppose that you didn't deliberately eavesdrop, but you couldn't have helped hearing. The address was mentioned. And the murderer got there ahead of us. How can you explain that?'

'I'm not going to explain anything to you . . . Think whatever you like.'

The girl lowered her head stubbornly. Her chin was trembling.

Erast Petrovich decided that it was time to intervene.

'Young lady,' he said, moving closer. 'Do you mean to say that you were not here?'

She nodded without speaking.

'Where did you go out to?' asked Liberty. He was breathing heavily.

'I didn't go out anywhere,' Lynx growled. 'I'm not going to explain anything to you.'

She wasn't in the reception office, but she didn't go out anywhere? Fandorin looked round.

'You were in there?'

He pointed to the half-open door of the box room, where the shelves of folders were.

Lynx nodded again

'But if someone came into the reception office, you must have known. The door would have creaked, you would have heard steps. Was someone here?'

She nodded again. Her shoulders started shaking.

'Did you see who it was?' Liberty shouted.

She shook her head once, abruptly.

'It is hard to believe, young lady, that you didn't glance out to see who had come in,' Fandorin said gently. 'That is not like you.'

'I was standing on a chair. Getting the personnel list down off the top shelf. He . . .' – Lynx jabbed her finger hostilely at the artel manager – '. . . told me to check and report to him on income and expenditure. But I called to him and he answered.'

'Who did you call to? The man who came in?'

'Yes. "Hey," I said, "who's there? Wait a moment, I'll be out right away." And he said to me: "Don't hurry, little sister. I'll wait."'

'Who was it?' Liberty asked furiously. 'Could you tell from his voice?'

The girl didn't deign to answer him.

'Who was it?' said Erast Petrovich, repeating the question, and she told him:

'Zhokhov.'

'Are you sure?'

'His voice is impossible to confuse with anyone else's. Hoarse. And he named himself. "It's me, Zhokhov." But he didn't wait, and when I got back, he was already gone . . .'

Fandorin and Liberty exchanged silent glances.

'How could you, how could you think that about me?' Lynx complained bitterly to the artel manager. 'That I eavesdropped and then gossiped to someone? Is that like me?'

'But what was I supposed to think?' Liberty mumbled. 'And why didn't you say straight away that it was Zhokhov?'

'You attacked me so furiously! You'd already decided I was guilty! I'll never forgive you . . . For your sake, I . . .'

Her face crumpled up and she started crying desperately.

'Oh, come on now, come on,' said Liberty, stroking her shoulder awkwardly. 'I admit that it was bad of me . . .'

Fandorin intervened unceremoniously in this touching clarification of feelings.

'Mr Liberty, let us set about dealing with the murderer.'

'How will we find him? His trail must be completely cold by now.'

'I don't think so. Or why did he do away with the witnesses? No, he's here somewhere.'

They set out to search. Liberty asked everyone they met on their way whether they had seen Zhokhov.

'He was downstairs,' the fifth or sixth person they met told them. 'Chatting with the actor, Nevsky.'

They went down. On the stairway Liberty impatiently tugged his sluggish companion along by the elbow.

'Hey, Nevsky!' he shouted, letting go of Fandorin's arm and running down. 'Come here, will you!'

The actor walked over, casting curious glances at Erast Petrovich. He chuckled.

'I see you've become inseparable. Like Don Quixote . . . and another Don Quixote.'

'Where's Zhokhov? You were talking to him. How long since he left?'

'About five minutes. Maybe ten. He said he was going to the treasury to hand in some confiscated property or other. Why?'

'To the treasury?'

Liberty went dashing back up the stairs to the first floor. Fandorin also swung round and invented a new way of climbing up. First he thrust the cane into one of his button loops, in order to free his hand. Then he took hold of the banister and shifted both feet together in a single jerk, then threw his hands up higher and jumped again. It was quicker that way.

Nevsky walked beside him.

'What's wrong with our Bakunin? I've never seen him like this before.'

Erast Petrovich could not answer; his teeth were tightly clenched.

He set off down the long corridor at a genuine gallop, putting one arm round Nevsky's shoulder and leaning on his stick with his other hand.

They turned the corner.

Liberty was standing there, clutching his head in his hands. A man was lying in a pool of blood on the floor below the drawing of a woman. It was the sentry, Kozlov. *Exactly the same kind of blow as at Petroveritsky Lane*, Fandorin determined while still some distance away.

The door was half open and the smashed-off padlock was lying to one side.

'Oh, what slaughter is this!' the actor exclaimed, quoting the words of Prince Fortinbras as he abandoned the invalid and ran forward. 'Have we really been robbed? Have the expropriators been expropriated? How very neat!'

The three of them entered the treasury together. The silver tableware and other bulky items were still in place, but the small items of jewellery had disappeared.

White-faced in his fury, Liberty jerked his Mauser out of its holster and started blazing away at the ceiling.

*

A minute later the room and corridor were full of people who had come running at the sound of shots. Djiki pushed his way through to the front.

'Cordon off the entire perimeter,' the artel manager ordered. 'We're looking for Zhokhov.'

Everyone started droning: 'Zhokhov, where's Zhokhov, who's seen Zhokhov?'

'Zhokhov went out into the rear yard,' someone said, and the entire crowd ran off in that direction.

The yard in which the meeting had taken place was dark and empty. An asphalt surface with a manhole cover at its centre, the iron bars of the fence – and nothing more.

'He got away, the bastard!' said Djiki, turning to the artel manager. 'Climbed over and got away. We'll never find him now.'

While everyone clamoured loudly, discussing what had happened, Erast Petrovich walked across the yard and stood by the fence, then squatted down by the iron manhole cover.

He came back.

'Order this man to be searched,' he told the artel manager, pointing to the actor. 'You gave yourself away, Nevsky. We only know that Zhokhov was going to the treasury from what you told us. Why would he have told you about that, if he was planning to commit a robbery?'

It went very quiet.

'Have you gone gaga, you old cripple?' Nevsky exclaimed, stunned. 'Aron, he's a provocateur. He wants to start us squabbling with each other. Do you know what he did in the tsar's time? He's a detective, a police sleuth.'

'Hey, hang on a moment,' said Djiki, turning towards him. 'You told me he was a Bolshevik sleuth.'

Nevsky opened his mouth – and didn't say anything.

'That's a terrible accusation,' said Liberty, looking Fandorin in the eye. 'Do you have any proof?'

'Search him and you'll find it.'

'He is my brother. I will not humiliate him by searching him without adequate evidence.'

'The evidence is there,' said Erast Petrovich, pointing to the manhole cover. 'Zhokhov's body. I saw several drops of blood on the asphalt. I'm sure the murder method will prove to be the same – a blow with a knuckleduster. Mr Djiki, keep an eye on Mr Nevsky, so that he doesn't run away.'

Liberty nodded to the Georgian, who put his arm halfway round the actor's waist.

'If Zhokhov's not there, I'll stuff the invalid in the manhole myself, I promise,' he said to reassure Nevsky.

The actor, however, was not reassured by these words. He licked his dry lips and glanced round. The anarchists were standing in a dense crowd behind him.

'Yes! There's someone lying down there!' someone shouted from the middle of the yard, shining a torch down into the manhole.

'Search him!' the artel manager ordered.

From out of Nevsky's pockets they took gold brooches, earrings and several rings with precious stones. A knuckleduster. And a false beard.

'You vermin,' said Liberty. 'We'll try you right here and now. In our fraternal court.'

The fraternal court

Not entirely convinced of the acumen of the 'jurors', Erast Petrovich repeated the basic propositions of his address for the prosecution once again, this time in brief.

'Nevsky is a drug addict, with a severe addiction to cocaine. That is one. That powder costs stratospheric amounts of money, and that is why Nevsky joined the Freedom artel – so that he could rob people in the street with impunity, under cover of the Black Truth. That is two. Since his face is known to many Muscovites, he put on a false beard – probably taken from a theatre dressing room. That is three. Nevsky took the medallion he confiscated from the old Chernyshev couple straight to the Red Rose tavern and exchanged it for cocaine. That is four. I was incautious enough to tell him who I was looking for and describe the suspect's distinctive characteristics. Knowing my past, Nevsky immediately realised that I was on his trail. That is five. He tried to get rid of me by lying to Djiki, saying that I was a Red spy. Then, at the meeting, he saw me standing beside Liberty as he told three men who fitted the description I had given him to come to his study. That is six. Nevsky became alarmed and went there to find out what was happening. He was lucky, because Lynx was not in her usual place. He is an actor, and it was easy for him to imitate Zhokhov's voice. After hearing that Liberty and I were going to Petroveritsky Lane, he realised that he was in danger. That is seven. He got there before us and did away with both witnesses, not showing any pity, even for a mad old woman. That is eight. Then he decided to kill two birds with one stone: rob the artel treasury and put the blame on Zhokhov . . .'

Erast Petrovich looked at the chairman of the court – Aron Liberty – and summed up:

'The motives for the crime are evident, the chain of events has been reconstructed in full and we have the material evidence.'

The artel manager turned to the jurors:

'Is that clear?'

'What's not clear about it? He's a bastard! Waste him!' the yard exclaimed in a multitude of voices. It was filled with faces that were either white or black, depending on how the light fell from the windows – the lights were on in all the rooms in order to illuminate the yard. All the members of the artel's brigade were members of the jury.

'We offer the floor to the defence,' the chairman announced. 'Brother Nevsky, if you have anything to say, say it now.'

The actor, who had heard out the accusation sitting on a step of the porch, got to his feet. He wrapped his trench coat round himself picturesquely, no doubt imagining that he was on stage, facing a full house.

'Do you think you're anarchists?' his resonant voice thundered. 'Do you think he's an anarchist?' he asked, pointing his finger at Liberty in a dramatic gesture. 'No, you're petty bourgeois philistines. And this dismal wimp that you keep lumbering yourselves with time after time is twice as bad as the rest of you! He spouted his drivel about the Black Truth to you, and you listened with your mouths hanging open. Let me explain to you what the genuine Black Truth is. It's like a black, starless night. It's like the endless cosmos!' He jabbed his finger up triumphantly towards the sky, which truly was impenetrably black. 'The truth lies in genuine freedom! And genuine freedom is not freedom from the state or freedom from society, it is inner freedom! You decide for yourself what you are entitled to and what you aren't. You decide for yourself – not under the tyranny of a morality invented by someone else. The worst form of slavery is moral slavery, the shackles of other people's conceptions of good and evil! To hell with morality! To hell with the eunuch Aron! Brothers, let us live in a different way! With no limits, in unrestrained joy and delight! It will be such a sweet life that afterwards we won't be afraid of dying! Why on earth should you try me? I'm one of you, I'm the same as you are! I *am* the Black Truth. Elect me – no, not as your artel manager, we are not boat haulers, we are not carpenters – elect me as your ataman! I promise you that life with me will not be boring. Everyone in favour raise their hands!'

The echo bounced about between the main building and the wings and then faded away. The meeting was buzzing. The passionate speech had made an impression.

'I'm not clinging to my place!' Liberty shouted above all the noise. 'If you want to elect someone else – go ahead. Right now, if you like. There's no need to wait for a week. But one step at a time. First, we vote on the sentence. If the accused is acquitted, then we'll proceed with an election. Agreed?'

The artel started murmuring in approval.

'There's only one thing I want to say. An anarchist needs morality more than absolutely anyone else. Without firm rules, without authority over himself, a man turns into a wild beast. And now we vote. All those who think brother Nevsky is guilty, raise your hands. And remember that the penalty for this crime is death. A two-thirds majority of the votes is required for a conviction.'

To Fandorin's surprise, so many hands were raised that there was no need to count them. Everyone, or almost everyone, was in favour of the supreme penalty. Apparently their understanding of the Black Truth was different from Nevsky's.

The actor jumped to his feet and howled in the voice of King Lear abandoned by everyone:

'Brothers! Come to your senses! Are you anarchists or sheep? Brothers!'

Djiki swung his hand and gave Nevsky a resounding thump on the ear.

'Shut your mouth! You're not our brother any longer. Come on! I'll finish you off in the basement.'

He grabbed the condemned man by the collar and dragged him into the building.

Liberty waved his hand, appealing for silence.

'Quiet, brothers and sisters! The trial is over, but I have an important announcement. The artel is switching to combat-ready status. All leave of absence is cancelled. Lieutenants, gather your squads of men. Check the weapons. Lynx will let you know who should station themselves where. The hour of the third revolution is approaching. We overthrew the tsar, we overthrew the Provisional Government, and now we will overthrow the dictatorship of the Bolsheviks! Tomorrow the House of Anarchy will become the headquarters of the Black Revolution! We will smash the cage of the state to pieces. We will set the people free! Freedom now!'

'Freedom now!' a hundred and fifty voices roared.

And at that very moment the night exploded in a recitative of malevolent fury: ta-ta-ta-ta-ta-ta. The first-floor windows burst, shards of glass showered down and lumps of plaster went flying. A long, stuttering burst of machine-gun fire, right above their heads.

Then there was a resounding silence, but it didn't last for long.

A booming voice, amplified by a megaphone, shouted out of the darkness, from the direction of the fence.

'Citizen anarchists! You are surrounded. We have a battalion of Red Guards here, with twelve machine guns! In the name of the Soviet authorities I offer you a chance to surrender. Tonight the Extraordinary Commission for Combating Counter-Revolution is disarming the Black Guards right across Moscow! Do you hear me?'

The sound of shooting was heard in the distance, from various directions. Somewhere a cannon thundered, and then thundered again.

'We will release all who lay down their arms! But those who offer resistance will be annihilated. You have five minutes to make up your minds. After that you must accept the consequences of your decision. I repeat: five minutes.'

Found it!

Even before the voice had fallen silent, Liberty yelled furiously:

'Everyone to their places! Take up defensive positions!'

The yard came to life. Some ran to the central porch, some went dashing to the wings of the building. There must have been pre-defined positions in case of an unexpected attack.

But the Reds didn't wait for five minutes, and this time the machine gun opened fire directly at the crowd.

Erast Petrovich saw people collapsing with blood-curdling howls or pressing themselves back against the walls.

There could be no doubt about the outcome of the battle. The anarchists had been caught unawares, and they were doomed.

In a situation like this the most important thing is not to lose your head. Especially if you cannot rely on your legs. Therefore, Fandorin first figured out how the machine-gunner was working (zigzagging from left to right, then back in the opposite direction). When the line of bullets started moving away from him, Erast Petrovich climbed slowly up the steps, stepping over the bodies, and vanished into the building.

It was not safe inside either. The building was being pummelled from all sides. Everything was rumbling and cracking, crashing and shuddering. Some of the bullets came in through windows and doors and ricocheted along corridors.

Return fire started up from the building, but it was sparse and uncoordinated.

The machine guns suddenly fell silent. The same voice, muffled by distance, shouted:

'The final warning! Come out with your hands raised! Or we'll slaughter the lot of you, right down to the last lousy rat!'

'Commence firing!' Liberty cried from somewhere, apparently on the first floor.

The shooting started up again.

I must get out of this unwholesome situation somehow, Fandorin thought, crossing exposed sections of space with all the speed he could muster and slowing down in the more sheltered spots. The Reds were battling with the Blacks, and that was fine, let them: *aku va aku-o kuu* – one evil was devouring another. But what could a noble man do when he had been abandoned by his *ki* energy? Of course, that still left the intellectual energy of *chinoo*, which gave him the only correct advice: withdraw to where the bullets were not flying and wait until this *Sekigahara* ended. It would not go on for long. The Black Guards were firing blindly into the night, and that was like trying to hit a kopeck in the darkness, while the artel was aglow with lights and presented an excellent target. In all the turmoil no one had thought of turning off the electric power. There were bodies lying across the floor. Fandorin stopped beside one of them with a frown.

It was Djiki. His shirt was torn open on his chest and his gun holster was empty. His head was twisted to one side and there was a bright crimson, vertical indentation on the back of it. Someone had grabbed the Caucasian by the throat and smashed his skull against the floor. It was not difficult to guess who. No doubt the Georgian had been distracted by the sound of shooting and the condemned man had been quick to take his chance . . .

Mr Nevsky chose the wrong theatrical speciality, Erast Petrovich thought morosely. He ought not to have acted romantic leads, but *hualiens*, the jugglers and tumblers of the Chinese theatre. But still, there was no way that even a *hualien* could get out of this building while it was being raked right through by gunfire. If his own brothers saw him, they would shoot him, and the Reds would not spare him either. *Akuma be with him, let us leave this artful dodger to his own karma.*

Upstairs it was crowded: the main body of the fighters had gathered here, having withdrawn from the ground floor. To judge from the shooting and shouting, the Reds had already gained entry down there, and in several places at once.

Liberty was moving from room to room, speaking to the gunmen: 'Goodbye, brothers! Remember, it is better to die on your feet than live on your knees. Goodbye . . . Remember . . . Goodbye . . . Remember . . .'

In his long trench coat, with his half-grey beard, he looked like the ghost of Hamlet's father. *And he's saying the same thing*, thought Erast Petrovich: '*Farewell and remember me . . .*'

Little Lynx devotedly followed the lanky, skinny Liberty.

'Keep your head down, Aron, keep your head down!' she kept repeating as he passed by each window.

'He's so rash. He doesn't think about himself at all,' she said when she caught Fandorin's eye. 'You know, I've always dreamed about this. That he and I would be together to the very end.'

'You love him,' Erast Petrovich said in amazement (although he could actually have deduced that earlier).

The girl replied simply:

'Yes, I do.'

'But you said now isn't the time for love.'

'He needs me. He doesn't know it himself, but he needs me very badly. Without me he'll be lost,' Lynx replied, as if she was making excuses.

Fandorin was perhaps not very well versed in female psychology, but he had an excellent understanding of men. Still, he didn't tell the girl that men like Liberty do not need anyone. That they are eternal loners.

For some reason Erast Petrovich carried on following the artel manager and his companion. Perhaps because they were moving slowly and he didn't fall behind with his stick. A bullet shattered a door panel, spraying chips of wood over him and Lynx. The girl wiped her cheek absent-mindedly.

'Do you know how old Aron is?'

'I assume he is over fifty.'

'Thirty-seven. And he has spent seventeen years of that time in prison, exile and hard labour, where people age twice as fast. Can you imagine it? He's the freest man in the world and he has been kept in a cage for half his life.'

The intense onslaught of fire suddenly ceased.

'Surrender, anarchy!' This time the blaring voice was declaiming from somewhere below them. 'It's all up with you! The ground

86

floor is ours! We only want Aron Liberty! We won't touch the rest of you!'

Various replies were shouted from the first floor. In some places it was 'Go to hell!' and in others it was: 'We surrender, we surrender, don't shoot!'

Liberty turned back towards Lynx.

'I won't compel anyone. Everyone decides for himself. If anyone wants to live on his knees – let him live. But they won't put me back in a cage again. I'm going up into the attic. I'll keep on firing as long as my cartridges last!'

He tugged his Mauser out of its holster and ran towards the stairs.

'I'm with you!' Lynx exclaimed, dashing after him.

In the other rooms survivors were arguing keenly about whether to fight or not. No one was firing.

'Hey, wait!'

Erast Petrovich also set off towards the stairs, but now the other two were moving too quickly for him to catch up with them.

Striding over two steps at a time, Liberty climbed up to the landing between floors and glanced back at Lynx hurrying after him.

'Wait!' Fandorin called to them. 'There's absolutely no need . . .'

His words were drowned out by rumbling and crashing. Someone had opened fire after all, and the building was pummelled once again by abrupt bursts of machine-gun fire and volleys of rifle fire.

Something small and black fell from above, landed right at the artel manager's feet, and bounced. A hand grenade! So the attic had been taken by the Reds. They had probably scrambled up the fire escape on the outside of the building.

After that everything happened in a split second.

Lynx grabbed Liberty by the arm and pushed him with such un-womanly strength that he lost his footing and went tumbling down the steps. The girl lost her balance too and started falling, but she never touched the floor. The explosion picked up her little body, tossed it aside and slammed it into the wall, which was instantly splattered with blood.

Fandorin helped Liberty, who had been stunned by his fall, to get to his feet, and dragged him away from the stairs. The Reds were in no hurry to come down. They tossed another grenade, but that one bounced down the steps and exploded harmlessly.

Walking on stiff legs, the artel manager kept looking back.

'A pity. She was a genuine fighter . . . But it doesn't matter. We'll all be killed now.'

'Not all of us. Do you hear?'

Now men were shouting out right across the first floor:

'We surrender! We surrender!'

'Well then, I'm alone.' Liberty shook his Mauser. 'And I won't shoot myself. I won't give the Bolsheviks that satisfaction. Let them kill Aron Liberty themselves!'

'There's absolutely no need for you to die. Make your way out into the yard. It's dark outside. Perhaps you can get away.'

'And what then? You heard, they're killing our people right across the city. Where will I go? I don't know Moscow. I don't know anyone here.'

'If you can break out, go to Pokrovka Street, to Lesser Uspensky Lane. Ask for Cricket Lane, that's what it's usually called. You'll see a yard behind a fence, and a small house with columns at the back of it. Knock. A Japanese man will open the door to you. Show him this. Give me your hand.'

Fandorin took out an indelible pencil, licked it and wrote on the artel manager's hand in Japanese: 'Help him'.

'What is that scribble?'

'A magical spell that will save you . . . Run to the corner study. A drainpipe runs past the window there. Will you be able to climb down it?'

'In 1911 I escaped from the Yakutsk Central Prison down a rope from the roof. But what about you?'

'I can't manage the pipe,' Erast Petrovich sighed. 'Never mind. I'll be all right. Run.'

The artel manager dropped his trench coat on the floor and ran.

Downstairs someone yelled through a megaphone:

'Come out one at a time, you Black rats! Hands up, faces down. Don't be afraid, we won't kill you! We'll just give you a bit of a drubbing and kick you out of the gates!'

That prospect did not suit Fandorin. It was better to wait until everything quietened down. And he went back to his original plan.

To reach the repository he had to go to the very end of the corridor. As he walked along, pale, disoriented men came thronging out of doors towards him, many of them covered in blood and some barely able to walk. *The Red Truth has proved stronger than the Black*, Erast Petrovich thought. *Which is only natural, since in a direct clash between individualism and collectivism, the former has no chance of victory.*

Round the corner, already in the wing of the building, the corridor was dark and empty. The buxom anarchist Venus spread her legs wide on the wall at the foot of which the artist-sentry had died. Fandorin walked into the dark room, closed the door firmly behind him and started feeling along the wall to find the switch. He thought it was somewhere on the right. Ah, there it was.

The light flashed on.

A voice behind his back exclaimed in delighted amazement:

'Well, look who's come to visit!'

Sitting cross-legged on the table, squinting against the bright light, was Nevsky.

'Great minds think alike. So you also realised that the bullets won't come flying in here? Would you believe it, what good fortune! Here I am, sitting quietly and waiting, and my enemy's corpse just drifts in of its own accord!'

The actor jumped down onto the floor, flung his arms wide apart buffoonishly, as if in the prelude to an embrace, and declaimed:

> How sweet is revenge, oh ye judging gods!
> Like honey it does sweeten my soul!

At the phrase 'good fortune', Fandorin frowned. The giddy goddess had become rather too free with her betrayals.

Nevsky smiled rapaciously.

'Finished showing off, have you? Played your little game of tribunals? Now I'll be the judge. And I declare my verdict immediately, with no prevarication. "Worthy of death are you, spawn of Beelzebub!"' He raised his hand majestically and turned the thumb down.

'With what shall I do you to death, Monsieur Fandorin? I should like to choose something striking.'

He picked a silver candlestick up off the table, turned it over in his hands and put it down again.

'No, that is trivial . . . Now, there's the very thing! The instrument of God's wrath.' He picked up a heavy, eight-pointed Orthodox crucifix. 'I guarantee instantaneous absolution of all your sins. Or perhaps something else? I honestly just don't know. Such an embarrassment of riches.'

Nevsky continued with his playacting, simulating pensiveness and dragging out the pause.

'No! It is decided! You are a noble hidalgo and you are entitled to die by the sword!'

He picked up an Order of St George presentation sword with a gold hilt and bared its blade. Spots of light glinted on the polished steel.

> Oh sacred sword, my damascene blood brother,
> Dispatch the malefactor to the lowest pit of hell!

Fandorin wondered whether he could try to reach the jester with his cane. No, it was not worth even trying. It wouldn't be a strong, rapid blow, and he didn't want to appear pitiful. Better to accept death without any fuss.

Nevsky had clearly studied stage swordplay. He performed some elegant, fanciful loops in the air with the sword and then made a lunge – Erast Petrovich instinctively recoiled, otherwise the point of the blade would have pierced his chest. He backed away and bumped into a cupboard.

The actor smiled malevolently.

'Aha, so you're not made of stone after all. You don't wish to die. But you must, it cannot be helped. Now I shall take pleasure in slowly pinning you to the wood. Like a butterfly in a collection, with a pin through its little belly.'

He lowered the blade slightly, to Fandorin's abdomen. And pressed on it.

A sharp pain transfixed Fandorin's body, and Nevsky also twisted the sword hilt slightly, widening the small wound.

'We're not going to hurry, are we? This is so enjoyable!'

I can't reach him with my fist, thought Fandorin. *I could reach him with my foot, but I can't lift it. I have to stand still and not move. The important thing is not to groan or cry out. Surmounting pain is one of the joys of a samurai.*

But it was not only painful. In his belly, in the very depths of his body, there was something else happening; he felt a strange, tickling sensation, as if a butterfly was fluttering its little wings. Erast Petrovich stopped listening to the *xiaoren's* idle babbling and started focusing intently on his own body.

Is it really possible . . . Is that really it? So that's where it was hiding!

But of course, where else would it be? The hara *is the receptacle of vital energy. When a samurai wishes to let it out, he cuts open his belly. The stab of the steel has aroused the* ki *energy. It is awakening!*

The current flowed from deep within him, growing stronger with every instant. There was no more pain, only an intensely resonant vibration, filling his entire being.

With a joyful laugh, Fandorin grabbed hold of the blade. The edge of it was not sharp – who ever sharpens a decorative sword?

Nevsky shut up and raised his eyebrows in amazement. He tried to force in the sword – it didn't budge an iota. He tried to pull it back towards himself – that didn't work either.

'What kind of hocus-pocus . . .' he muttered.

And suddenly he let go of the hilt and sprang back to the opposite wall, also covered with cupboards from top to bottom. He pulled out his pistol.

'Damn you! Die simply then, from a bullet!'

It seemed to Erast Petrovich that his enemy's movements were strangely retarded: Nevsky moved away somehow very smoothly and took a long, long time pulling the Browning out of his pocket – it got snagged on the cloth and freed itself only slowly. He could easily have knocked the pistol out of the blockhead's hand or knocked him off his feet. But he didn't feel like hurrying. His body had missed the feeling of speed and it craved strong sensations.

There, now Nevsky had pointed the barrel, aiming directly at his forehead. Fandorin didn't stir a muscle, he just smiled. A ticklish trickle of blood ran down his belly under his shirt and it felt pleasant. His entire *karada* was sparkling with life, like freshly poured champagne sparkling with little bubbles.

The Browning spat out a dart of flame. Fandorin's head swayed to one side, as if of its own accord. The bullet bit into the wood with a crunch.

His hands also acted without any command, in swift co-ordination.

The left hand turned the sword so that its hilt was towards him and tossed it up. The right hand caught it and flung it in a crisp, precise throw.

Another shot rang out. The second bullet passed within a millimetre of Fandorin's ear.

And the pistol dropped to the floor.

Nevsky squinted downwards, as if trying to make something out, but couldn't. There certainly was something to contemplate: the sword had pierced right through the actor's throat and sunk into the door of a cupboard to half of its length.

'Now which one of us is a b-butterfly?' Erast Petrovich asked.

The dying man's hands seized the hilt of the sword – and fell away. His eyes closed. His body went limp, but remained hanging against the cupboard.

Fandorin was no longer looking at the dead man. He clenched and unclenched his fingers. Then he squatted down and jumped up into the air, not very high at first, and then again, a metre and a half into the air. He slammed his fist down on the edge of the table. The table's legs splayed apart, the tabletop slumped over to one side and the goblets, candlesticks and other glittering nonsense slid off it in a jingling cascade.

'That's more like it,' Erast Petrovich told his *ki* energy. 'Now don't p-play the fool any more.'

I've started stammering again, he suddenly realised. *Must I always have some kind of disability? Well all right, better to stammer and have* ki *energy than trill like a nightingale from a wheelchair.*

He glanced at the door and listened.

In the distance someone was issuing commands:

'Search all the rooms. Where do they keep the stuff they stole? Post sentries! Has Liberty been found?'

Stepping lightly and soundlessly, Fandorin walked along the corridor and peeped round the corner.

The commands were being given by a little half-pint with a sumptuous moustache, dressed in a leather jacket with a red star on it. There were men everywhere – picking up abandoned weapons, dragging dead bodies along, checking rooms. In a minute or two they would reach the wing.

Erast Petrovich didn't wait for them.

He walked in through the first door, swung the window wide open and, without the slightest hesitation, vaulted over the windowsill, out into the darkness.

How good that felt!

THE RED TRUTH

'Cheka' and 'Chekvalap'

The 'cabservicelabourer', as old-style cabbies were now known, pulled up in front of the large aristocratic manor house on Povarskaya Street. He turned towards his passenger and crossed himself.

'There it is, the former house of Count Sologub. God Almighty, I didn't expect to get here alive.'

'Yes, you folks have a lively old time of it here in Moscow,' said the passenger, a young military man, as he jumped down onto the pavement.

It was twilight, round about the hour of dawn, but the city had not slept during the preceding night. There had been intense firing in several places at once, trucks carrying armed men had careered along the streets, and when they were driving through the Samotyoka district a burst of machine-gun fire had rattled along the surface of the road.

'Here. As we agreed.'

The military man thrust a banknote at the driver without looking at him. The driver examined his passenger closely, fixing his eyes on the marks left on his coat where shoulder straps had been unstitched.

'You need to throw in another hundred roubles. For all the scare's I've been put through.'

'Uh-huh. And my trousers and boots too. A deal is a deal.'

The young man – he was tall, light-haired and well set up – took his travelling bag down off the seat.

'Look here, Your Honour,' said the driver, narrowing his eyes.

'You know what's in this place now? The Cheka' – he nodded towards the sentry at the gates, which were standing open. 'I'll tell him you've been passing hostile remarks. And I'm a proletarian, I have the authorities' trust.'

'You're a piece of shit, not a proletarian. You're not getting anything at all.'

The fair-haired man stuck the banknote back in his pocket.

The cabby opened his mouth to yell, but after looking for a little longer, he changed his mind. There was something hard to make out in the young man's face, an alarming kind of contradiction. The look in the bright, cornflower-blue eyes seemed cheerful enough, but he had a firm, sullen fold running down beside his mouth, a white scar on his temple and the tip of another jagged scar peeping out from under his collar. This military man might easily not be so very young after all.

Whispering a foul oath, the 'cabservicelabourer' lashed at his old nag. The passenger put on his peaked cap, which he been holding in his hand so far, and it turned out that he wasn't any kind of 'Your Honour' at all, but a Red Commander, or Redcom – there was a crimson fabric star on the cap-band. He walked over to the sentry and asked in a harsh voice accustomed to commanding:

'Where can I find Comrade Orlov here?'

'Go on through. They'll tell you inside.'

'And you're not going to ask for my documents?'

'What for?' The sentry yawned. 'We don't get outsiders coming in here.'

With a shake of his head, the 'Redcom' set off across the broad courtyard, hemmed in on both sides by the wings of the mansion. Men with rifles suddenly came pouring out of one of the wings and the man at the front, no doubt the officer, turned back and shouted:

'There aren't any more trucks, comrades! We'll have to run there! Now move those feet, bugger it!'

They went tramping past him, all their faces sombre and weary.

'Somehow I don't see Natasha Rostova here,' the light-haired man murmured as he watched them go. His Russian literature teacher at grammar school had told him that the manor house on Povarskaya Street was the house of the Counts Rostov in Tolstoy's novel *War and Peace*. But now there was a piece of plywood nailed crookedly to the door, with words daubed on it, also crookedly, in white paint: 'All-Russian Extraordinary Commission for Combating Counter-Revolution, Speculation and Sabotage' – the Cheka.

Once inside the entrance hall, the visitor frowned. There was no order in here either. There was just a crowd huddled round a table with a sign that said 'Duty Officer', and everyone was talking across everyone else while a tormented man in an unbuttoned field jacket fended them off as he shouted into a telephone in a hoarse, strained voice.

'Reinforcements? They were sent half an hour ago ... How should I know where they are?'

It was clear that nothing could be achieved here.

Patience was not one of the light-haired man's virtues. He knitted his flaxen brows together even more angrily and turned his head, trying to spot someone suitable – and with a swift, precise movement he grabbed the elbow of an orderly who was running by with some documents.

'Comrade, where is Orlov around here?'

Without turning round, the orderly jerked his arm, but failed to free it, and only then looked back.

'What do you want with Comrade Orlov? Who are you?' And just like the cabby, he fixed his eyes on the military man's shoulders.

'I'm someone Orlov needs to see. And as for why, I'll tell him that. Take me to him, comrade, if you would be so kind.'

The stranger's fingers had a grip of iron, and although his voice was quiet, it was somehow very persuasive. The Cheka man immediately became polite.

'Come with me. He's on the first floor.'

They walked up a stairway.

'Why do you have shooting all over the city?' the Redcom asked. 'There was a three-inch gun hammering away somewhere.'

'We're finishing off the Black Guards. We're sick of those trouble-makers ... Hey, Kriukov, this comrade here is for Orlov!' the orderly shouted from the doorway of a secretary's office, but there was no one inside. 'He's gone out somewhere ...' The orderly listened to a voice coming from behind another door. 'Wait here, and when

Comrade Orlov is finished on the phone, go on in.'

Then he suddenly checked himself, realising he had no idea who he had brought to see his commanding officer.

'What's your name? Where are you from?'

'Romanov. I was summoned from the Pskov front by telegram,' the light-haired man replied. '"Report to Orlov at the Cheka." I didn't have a clue what the Cheka was. But an order's an order. So here I am.'

The educational work being conducted behind the door at that moment concerned precisely that – what exactly the Cheka, or All-Russian Extraordinary Commission, was.

The inhabitant of the office, a man of about forty with a short little beard, wearing a soldier's blouse under a leather jacket, rubbed his eyelids as he drove home his message to the commissar of the central telephone exchange.

'Kriushkin, how much longer are your operators going to confuse the Cheka with the Chekvalap? We've got an emergency here, all hands to the pumps, and every second call I get they ask me: "Is that Chekvalap, the Extraordinary Commission for the Supply of Felt Boots and Bast Shoes?" Gather your foolish women together and hammer into their heads what the Cheka is . . . I know myself that a lot of new institutions have moved down here from Peter and no one is used to their names yet. But make sure they don't confuse our institution with the others. One more call about felt boots and I'll stuff your head into a felt boot, have you got that?'

He slammed down the receiver, laughed and stroked his little beard.

The phone rang again. This time there was no mistake, it was a call from the commander of the detachment sent to liquidate the 'Freedom' anarchist artel, the second-most important stronghold of the Black Guards.

'He got awa-ay, he got awa-ay! Treachery!' the telephone receiver howled and throbbed furiously. 'You've got a traitor in the Cheka, Orlov!'

'Calm down, Šileikis, drop the dramatic effects. What's wrong? Who got away? Have you disarmed the artel or not?'

Orlov suppressed a yawn. He had spent two sleepless nights in a row: from the tenth to the eleventh they had been working out the plan of liquidation at the collegium, and last night there had been even less time for resting.

'We disarmed the artel all right, our casualties are small, only six wounded, but Aron Liberty got away!' Šileikis shouted, his voice breaking into a croak. He was an old Party man – very reliable, only rather highly strung. 'We turned everything inside out, and Liberty's not there! I put a cordon of your men, all Chekists, round the place in advance. And some snake let him through! Orlov, you've got a traitor!'

Keeping hold of the receiver, the occupant of the office leaned down over a map of the city, on which the Black Guards' bases were marked with twenty-six black circles, and drew a red cross over one more of them. Now there were only three still to be crossed out.

'Calm down, Šileikis. Your Latvians have done their job. My congratulations to them. And I don't have any traitors. I gave orders for Liberty not to be detained.'

'What?' the receiver gasped.

'Think about it. Say we did bump off that crackpot Aron. The entire international anarchist movement would have raised a stink about it. And putting him on trial would be even worse. Let him go wherever he likes. He's not dangerous without the artel . . . Anyway, Šileikis, it's like this. I know your lads are tired, but help is needed on Dmitrovka Street. We're already pounding them with a cannon – but they won't surrender. Get over there and help out. That's all, now go to it.'

He cut off the call and shouted:

'Kriukov!'

The door opened, but instead of the man's assistant, the dashing commander in an officer's greatcoat without shoulder straps walked in and was greatly surprised.

'Nail, is that you?'

The harsh, mocking face of the man with the little beard softened. Orlov was not taken aback by the sight of his visitor, in fact he seemed very pleased to see him.

'Yes, yes, it's me. Come in, Staff Captain.'

They embraced each other.

'Wait, so Orlov is you?' said Romanov, still unable to gather his wits. 'I just couldn't figure out who it was that had summoned me . . . But why have you become Orlov?'

'The times require it. Under Nikolashka I used to take my aliases from small birds – flitting this way as Rook, flitting that way as Thrush or Woodpecker. Under the Provisional Government I became Nail, because they had to be nailed down hard. But now we have the power, and we rule the sky like eagles, and so, taking my cue from "oryol", the eagle, I've become Orlov. The entire sky is ours, I can fly wherever I like . . .'

They stood there, examining each other with delight.

'It's marvellous that you've come, Romanov. I need you really, really badly.' Orlov ran the edge of his hand across his throat emphatically. 'But first, Commander, tell me about how you fought the Germans.'

'I fought them lousily,' the new arrival said with a dismissive gesture. 'Our Red Guards are no damned good for anything! How can there be any Guards, when there isn't any army? You know yourself that all the regulars have been demobilised. The soldiers have all gone home . . . What stupid nonsense. We'll have to fight the Germans anyway, the Brest-Litovsk treaty is worthless. We need a real Russian army.'

'There aren't any Germans and Russians, there are only those who are for us and those who are against us.' Orlov prodded his old acquaintance in the forehead with his finger. 'Hammer that into your officer's head once and for all. The German workers are our people. And soon they'll be fighting alongside us. And we'll have a normal army. A Red Army. There's been an order about that from our Soviet of People's Commissars, the Sovnarkom. Everything in its own good time. We're only just getting started.'

He laughed and stretched.

'What are you so pleased about?' Romanov asked in bewilderment. 'The front has collapsed, there's fighting in Moscow, you've got bedlam in your commission, and you're grinning.'

'I'm pleased, Alyosha, because I'm happy. There's only one thing

I'm afraid of – waking up in the morning to find that it's all a dream. Our revolution, our victory, all of it. What a great elephant, what a huge mammoth, we brought down, didn't we! History has never seen the like of it! You know, I never understood how people could find life boring. I always found things interesting. But not nearly as interesting as now. Chernyshevsky and Vera Pavlovna's dream. Jules Verne and *From the Earth to the Moon*!' Orlov laughed again, with his strong white teeth glinting. 'You don't look like someone who's bored either. So will you wait awhile this time before you shoot yourself? Remember how it was in summer, at Smarhon? I only just managed to grab your hand in time. And after that I didn't let you leave my side for two days.'

Romanov's face seemed to turn to stone, but not for long, just a second or two. He replied with a joke.

'Now when he had said these things, he cried with a loud voice, saying, "Lazarus, come forth!" And I did rise and did walk.'

Orlov gave him a very serious look and nodded to himself.

'I see. You've taken the question of "to be or not to be" off the agenda. And that's right. And if you ever get tired of living – why go to all that trouble yourself? There are any number of others eager to help you out with that. Just last night, for instance, we knocked the anarchist fellow travellers down off their high horse. And after that, my intuition tells me it will be the Social Revolutionaries' turn. The revolution is a skittish kind of mare, she won't carry more than one rider. And it's not certain that even one will stay in the saddle. That's what I want to talk to you about, Staff Captain. Sit down and take the weight off your feet.'

Romanov sat down and made ready to listen. Not a drop of joviality was left in the occupant of the office now, he was all serious concern.

'The anarchists and the SRs – okay, we'll sort them out. The Germans don't have any time for us right now, the Entente and the Americans are finishing them off. But the bad thing is that our Red power isn't firmly established yet. Why did we move the government from Peter to Moscow? Because the city of Petrograd is hostile to us. Nobles, merchants, government officials and other elements of the "respectable public" make up almost a quarter of the population. In October we caught them on the hop, but the place is like a slumbering volcano. In Moscow the ratio's better, but things are far from simple here too. There are believed to be at least forty thousand former officers here alone. And most of them, of course, are just dreaming of ripping our guts out. Now just imagine that some resolute, single-minded element succeeds in organising all these people who are hostile to us into a united striking force. A single strike from them would leave us pulverised. Do you know how many of us there are in the Cheka? Only a hundred and twenty. And experienced men, who know how to unmask conspiracies? Zero. There are plenty of underground conspirators, like me, but what are we used to doing? Not seeking, but hiding, not pursuing, but fleeing. Now do you understand why I summoned you from the front?'

'Because I served in counter-intelligence. But I used to catch German and Austrian spies, not conspirators. That's a different speciality. Conspirators were the Okhranka's business.'

'Well, I'm sorry,' Orlov said with a shrug. 'No one from the Okhranka works for me. Are you refusing, then?'

Romanov sighed.

'I told you that time back at Smarhon, and I'll repeat it now. I've made my choice. I'm with the revolution. So tell me, what exactly does the revolution want from me?'

'You won't like this kind of work,' Orlov warned him.

'Don't worry, I'm a young lady with a serious past. Do you think I liked it in counter-intelligence? It's bloody business, dirty.'

A swarthy, broad-faced man wearing criss-cross belts shambled into the office without knocking.

'It's all over at Dmitrovka. They've surrendered, the vermin,' he said. 'That's it, Comrade Orlov. You can make your report.'

'Uh-huh,' Orlov said, and winked. 'Look who's here.'

'Kriukov. So you're here as well?'

Romanov shook the swarthy man's hand.

'Where else would I be? Wherever he goes, I go.'

'And you're no longer a lance corporal.' The former staff captain looked at the former lance corporal curiously – he had changed greatly. 'And by the way, Orlov, what's *your* rank now?'

'We don't have ranks. I'm a member of the collegium of the Cheka, and Kriukov is my assistant.'

'And who will I be?'

'A contra – a counter-revolutionary. According to our information, an officers' conspiracy already exists and is expanding rapidly. We need to plant our own man in the underground organisation. An officer, of course. Now do you understand what is being asked of you?'

Romanov frowned and a harsh furrow appeared across his forehead.

'No. I won't play the police spy. I was fighting side by side with these men yesterday. How can I worm my way into their confidence and then inform on them?'

'I told you he'd refuse,' Kriukov said with a sour grimace. 'Once an officer, always an officer.'

'Keep quiet, Timofei,' said Orlov, calling his assistant to order. 'Alyosha, tell me – do you believe in God?'

The question was so unexpected that Romanov blinked a few times before answering.

'No. But what has that got to do with anything?'

'Then here's a second question. Do you like the way the world is arranged?'

'Who could possibly like it?'

'Well then, if the world is so bad and there is no God, who's going to set the world to rights?'

Romanov started getting angry.

'Why are you talking to me like a teacher with a kindergarten child? Speak plainly.'

'I am. I couldn't possibly speak more plainly. Let me start with myself. I tell you honestly: I didn't get involved in the revolution in order to put the world right, but because I am who I am. Ever since I was a child, I've wanted to turn everything topsy-turvy. Mingle-mangle it all, tip everything arse over elbow. Or go places where no one has ever been before. "Eh," I used to think when I was a kid, "if only I'd lived three hundred years ago – I'd have discovered new continents. Or on the contrary, if only I'd lived a hundred years later, I could have flown to other planets." Then one day, when I was already almost a young man, it suddenly hit me. A world that is arranged humanely – that was something no one had ever seen and where no one had ever been. That would be the very greatest of discoveries and the very greatest of adventures. To arrange the world so that it was not only for people like us, who were lucky enough to be born in a clean, decent family, but for *all* the people. Take a look at Kriukov here. From his earliest childhood he lived in hunger, filth and swinishness. If not for the revolution, he would have died in that dung heap. But we have more than a hundred million Kriukovs. And now they are all going to live according to the effort that each one of them makes. Whoever is intelligent and capable will cease to be nothing and become everything.'

Orlov's assistant listened with his eyes gleaming. And Orlov worked himself up more and more, rapping out his words.

'Of course, we won't build heaven on earth here, in our poor, wild, backward country. But we will at least put an end to hunger, illiteracy and humiliation. And for the sake of this great, this unprecedented goal, it's worth twisting yourself out of shape a bit, begrudging neither sweat, nor blood, nor life . . . You fought alongside officers at the front, I spent time in jail with anarchists and escaped from hard labour. But last night we stabbed the comrades with whom we made the revolution in the back! We killed very many of them, and those who survived will curse us and hate us to the end of their days. But for the sake of this great goal of ours, we even resorted to that! And he . . . he wants to demonstrate his cultured sensitivity to me, this great melancholy sentimentalist . . . He feels embarrassed, you see, in front of the gentlemen officers!'

The member of the Cheka's collegium choked on his own frenzy, unable to carry on speaking. He had become terrifying.

But Romanov wasn't frightened by him. He merely tugged on his collar and scratched the bullet scar on his neck.

'All right, all right, stop shooting fire out of your eyes. You've convinced me. I'll manage without any sentimentality. Only let me tell you this. I'm not prepared to regard myself as a scoundrel. If I'd sat in jail with someone, as you did, or escaped from hard labour with them, then I'd look out for my old comrade somehow or other. So

I warn you straight away: I won't do anything that goes against my heart. Is that clear?'

Orlov no longer seemed to be in a raging fury. He winked at Kriukov again, merrily.

'What is clear, Comrade Romanov, is that you have not yet matured sufficiently to accept the tenets of class morality. Why look, your very name is suspicious. Never mind, Alyosha: Kriukov and I will gradually re-educate you. But right now, this very day, I want you to go on a fishing trip.'

'What kind of fishing trip?'

'A free and easy boat ride. Out into the open sea. There are sharks swimming around out there, but we don't know exactly where. I can't give you a net, or a harpoon, or any bait. We only know that an officers' conspiracy exists, the entire city is whispering about it, but as for where the conspirators can be caught – that's for you to figure out. You're a professional, after all.'

With a bare hook

In counter-intelligence parlance, the kind of assignment received by Alexei Romanov was called 'fishing with a bare hook', meaning that there is reliable information concerning the existence of a hostile spy network, but there are no names, or descriptions, or addresses – nothing at all, in fact. In a normally functioning counter-intelligence establishment, a system of 'markers' or 'jingle bells' is set up – that is, guidelines are issued to departmental subdivisions, police stations, railways stations and cab stands and sent to venues of potential interest to the enemy: keep a record of any kind of suspicious activity within such and such parameters. Sooner or later one of the fish will be sighted, a little bell will jingle, and after that it's a matter of skill and technique.

Never before had Romanov had to cast a single line with a bare hook in order to catch such an immense shoal of fish. But on the other hand, the assignment could not really be called extremely difficult, since there were three circumstances that simplified it greatly.

Firstly, he would not be dealing with professional intelligence operatives, but with amateurs who were unlikely to possess any conspiratorial skills.

Secondly, unlike a spy organisation, this military conspiracy had to constantly expand its ranks – after all, its goal was to take control of a city with a population of two million.

Thirdly, and finally, the contingent from which the conspirators recruited their new members was known – it consisted of former officers, such as Staff Captain Romanov.

So he just had to bait the hook with himself and select the right spot for his fishing expedition. That was all there was to it.

Having concluded his lengthy logical cogitation, Romanov mentally wound time backwards, imagining himself as he used to be before the pivotal events of that summer. Or rather, before a certain event of which Orlov had abruptly reminded him. Alexei himself had sequestered this particular plot of his memory behind a blank fence and he tried never even to glance back in that direction. And even now he didn't really look back. He simply told himself: *I am a front-line officer who understands damn all about politics, but has been embittered by the revolution, which has destroyed the state and the army. I am insulted by the insolent loutishness of the unbridled soldiery, I regard the Bolsheviks as German agents, an infernal force, the wreckers of Russia, and I hate them so much it makes me grind my teeth in fury.*

Orlov and Kriukov sat there quietly, observing Romanov after he fell silent and then suddenly squeezed his eyes shut.

That was Alexei working his way into character. When he opened his eyes again, the world seemed to have changed its colours. The beautiful aristocratic palace where Natasha Rostova once lived was now occupied and controlled by coarse, spiteful, hostile men. Not only had they seized the Rostov house, they had desecrated this entire ancient, beautiful city. *What an ugly mug*, Romanov thought, looking at Kriukov with loathing. *A vile brute, sprawled out in an Empire-style armchair.*

'Pick up that cigarette end, you wretched scum. That parquet is a hundred and fifty years old, and you've burned a hole in it.'

'What's that you said? What's that!' Kriukov started blinking and squirming under that vehement gaze.

But Orlov laughed.

'Excellent. Off you go, Your Excellency, and save Russia from the vulgar louts.'

And Romanov went.

Outside the door, though, he stopped and said to himself: 'Right then, I'm not a Red commander, but an ordinary demobilised officer. I don't have any ration cards, or money, or roof over my head, or relatives in Moscow. Where would I go?'

The answer was obvious. A military man accustomed to being looked after by the state, just as a dog is accustomed to finding food in its bowl, would make his way to the headquarters of the district military command. After all, a state did exist, even if it was a Bolshevik one.

Where was the district headquarters in Moscow?

Leafing through the telephone directory on the secretary's desk, he found it. Prechistenka Street. Not far away.

He stood in front of a black-spotted mirror (someone had stubbed cigarette ends out on that too) and examined himself carefully. It would probably be enough to unstitch the star from his cap and pin onto his tunic the decorations that an officer was expected to wear constantly.

Forward march, Staff Captain.

The red rag hanging on the large public building bore the words 'Military Inventory Administration of the RKKA'. Romanov stopped in front of the entrance with a perplexed frown – as any officer would have done at the sight of that incomprehensible abbreviation.

The door kept banging as men walked in and out.

Another man just like Alexei stood beside him – wearing an officer's cap without a badge and high boots with spurs. The yellow piping on his uniform indicated that he was a dragoon. He started panting.

'What's the "RKKA", do you know?' Romanov asked.

'The Workers' and Peasants' Red Army. I was thinking of perhaps enrolling . . . They give you rations.' The dragoon sighed. 'You have to live somehow . . . Argh, I'll go in.'

Alexei followed him. A lot of men were jostling about in a long corridor – they all appeared to be former officers. Clear enough.

After demobilisation the lower ranks had simply gone back home and returned to their former lives, but where could the professional soldiers go?

Alexei started slowly striding to and fro, looking and listening. Conversations in low, dismal voices: nothing to live on; rations, rations, rations; look how low we've sunk; Russia's finished; the English are in Arkhangelsk, the Germans are advancing on Paris.

Men looked at Romanov too. Or rather, at his chest. He had unfastened his greatcoat and his military decorations were clearly visible: a Soldier's Order of St George and an Officer's Order of St George, an Order of St Vladimir with crossed swords.

'Take them off,' an elderly artilleryman advised him. 'Just recently a commissar yelled at a man with a St George and tore his cross off. Why go asking for trouble?'

The only thing he was wearing on his uniform was his academy badge, all that remained of his medals were little holes.

'They might not tear them off, but you certainly won't get an assignment,' another man said.

'I haven't been paid for three months! Just let them give me my pay! I don't want any assignment from them!' Romanov said in a loud voice, not like the other men. 'The highest authority in Moscow now is the German ambassador Mirbach, the Bolsheviks do what he tells them to do. What, then, am I going to serve the Germans, who killed my comrades?'

'I can see you definitely don't have a family,' the artilleryman said, and sighed sadly. 'But I've got three children. Yes indeed.'

The other man whispered:

'Better to have Mirbach running things than Lenin and Trotsky . . .'

'Gentlemen, gentlemen, be more careful,' a third man hissed. 'Haven't you heard about the Cheka? They could easily be walking around here, listening.'

Everyone fell silent, glancing round.

Romanov spotted a rather elderly, handsome gentleman in a long cavalry greatcoat, with a greyish goatee beard, who really had stopped and was listening. He didn't look anything like a Chekist agent, and indeed, if Orlov could be believed, the Cheka didn't have any agents.

As the cavalryman walked past, Alexei muttered contemptuously, especially for him.

'Call themselves fucking officers! Pah! A herd of sheep . . .'

Then he repeated similar things in the same vein in another two places, all the while watching the elderly man out of the corner of his eye. The man didn't actually approach him, but he didn't fall behind either. Could he really have taken the bait, at the very first cast?

'Ah, to hell with this Red Army of yours! It can go choke on my pay!' Romanov finally declared in a thunderous voice, and set off towards the exit.

Was the man behind him or not? He mustn't look back.

Someone was following him, following and keeping pace with him!

Outside in the street Alexei stopped to light a *papyrosa*. The footsteps behind him immediately fell silent. And when he moved on, they resumed.

He felt an almost-forgotten sensation, the thrill of the hunt – and then suddenly he felt ashamed. *Good God, you're not hunting strangers, but your own people, Russians, with whom you were fighting side by side only yesterday.* But now men were divided into 'us' and 'them' according to different tokens. And in general, Orlov was right: to hell with these melancholy vapours!

Romanov employed an elementary secret-agent trick – he pretended to adjust his cap. He had a little mirror hidden in his palm, so that he could look back without turning his head.

Hoop-lah! The 'tail' wasn't the elderly man he had seen, but some skinny little squirt in a Finnish ski jacket. Standing there, pretending to study a poster on an advertisement pillar, but squinting sideways. But maybe Romanov was mistaken? The squirt was really very young, no more than a boy.

To check, Alexei used another little trick, also primitive: after he set off, he grazed a person coming towards him lightly with his shoulder and turned back to apologise.

The boy gave himself away completely by darting behind the pillar.

That's all fairly clear, then. Not like Conan Doyle's Adventure of the Dancing Men. *The elderly cavalryman wanders along the corridor of the military inventory administration, picking out officers who look promising to him, and then gives a signal to the young lad, who obviously hangs about not far from the entrance. And now the boy will dog this stranger's footsteps to check where he goes, who he meets, where he lives and so on. I could play this simple little game for a while, of course, but I don't want to waste any time.*

And so Alexei did something simpler than that. He turned into an entranceway, concealing himself in the dense shadow, waited until the 'tail' stuck his head in to follow him, and grabbed the boy firmly by the scruff of the neck. Seen from close up he turned out to be a completely green specimen, about seventeen, or maybe even younger, with white skin, a scrawny neck and fluff on his upper lip. When he matured, he would be a handsome man, but he was still an ugly duckling.

'Still wet behind the ears, and already spying!' Romanov hissed. 'You Chekist pimple!'

The lad wasn't frightened, only offended.

'I'm not what you've taken me for at all! And I'm not wet behind the ears, I'm a Junker. Talk of pimples is degrading!' he exclaimed in a muffled, squeaky voice. His forehead really was speckled with pink pimples – that was why he had taken offence.

Alexei kept his fingers tightly clenched and even jerked his hand higher, lifting the boy up onto the tips of his toes.

'What are you tailing me for, if you're a Junker?'

'I'm not tailing you . . . I mean, I am tailing you, but not the way you mean . . . Let me go, I'm choking. Let me go, will you! I'm from people who think the same way as you do.'

'And what exactly do they think about?' Romanov asked suspiciously, but he let go of the boy's collar. 'Speak more clearly.'

'I'm Kopeishchikov. Venya . . . I mean, Veniamin Kopeishchikov. A Junker at the Alexandrovsky Academy. That is, a former Junker. And you're an officer, I know that. Just tell me, are you a patriot?'

'Seeing as you've introduced yourself . . . I'm Staff Captain Romanov, Alexei Parisovich. What strange sort of question is that, about being a patriot? I'm a Russian officer, and that tells you everything.'

'I'm not asking out of simple curiosity . . .' The young lad blinked, trying to get something clear in his mind. Then he decided. 'Come along with me. We'll go somewhere where someone will talk to you.'

'Who? And what about?'

'A patriot just like you. Let's go, Alexei Borisovich, it's not far from here.'

Simple and straightforward, thought Romanov. Not much like German intelligence or even the Austrians. They invite the first man they come across to a secret rendezvous.

'Firstly, it's not "Borisovich", but "Parisovich". And secondly, if you're a Junker, then address a senior officer in the appropriate manner.'

'I beg your pardon, Mr Staff Captain, sir!' said Venya Kopeish-chikov, drawing himself up to attention. 'I wasn't a Junker for very long, I didn't have time to get used to it. Let's go, you won't regret it!'

'All right,' growled Romanov. The thrill of the hunt had got completely lost somewhere, all that remained was a mournful sense of frustration. 'I've got nowhere to go anyway. I don't know anyone in Moscow . . .'

The meeting place

It really wasn't far to walk, only about ten minutes – along Arbat Street and across Sobachya Square into some side street or other (Romanov read what it was called on the nameplate – Trubnikovsky Lane). Along the way Venya didn't shut his mouth for a second, managing to impart a whole heap of information: that he had only been accepted into the academy in October, when he turned sixteen; that he didn't get a chance to swear the oath of loyalty, because the 'fracas' had broken out immediately – and then he had been on a barricade, firing a gun, but he didn't know if he had hit anyone or not, and didn't want to lie about it; that he had only been in the 'organisation' for a short time and was still in his probationary period.

But when Alexei asked what kind of organisation it was, the Junker hesitated.

'Ivan Klimentievich will tell you that. I mean, the lieutenant colonel will tell you. I'm not supposed to. And please, don't tell him that I let slip about the organisation.'

'I won't.'

Young Veniamin livened up again and carried on babbling.

It turned out that the 'rendezvous' was actually the apartment in which he lived with his sister Zinaida. She was wonderful, although she was already getting on a bit – nine years older than him. She was also a genuine patriot, Alexei didn't need to hide anything from her. Her surname wasn't Kopeishchikova, but Gruzintseva, after her husband. Vladimir Gruzintsev was a very fine man and, by the way, he was a General Staff officer. He had been killed in the Carpathians, and Venya felt terribly sorry for him.

Romanov stopped listening to this nonsense. It occurred to him that a conspiracy which could set up an 'organisation' like this could not possibly pose any danger. The usual Russian dilettantism. Orlov had been wrong to be concerned. The very fact that rumours about an officers' conspiracy were doing the rounds in the city was a sure sign that it wasn't a serious undertaking. He should just take a look at the man in charge and have a chat with him, man to man, about not playing games with the Soviet regime and not leading people up the garden path and into trouble. It could end badly – these were uncertain times.

The building to which the loquacious Junker led him was relatively new, built not long before the war. They walked into the entrance hall through the back door (the main door had been boarded up in winter and left like that, Young Veniamin explained). Then they walked up to the first floor.

The boy rang the bell in a special way: two long rings and three short ones. He declared gravely:

'That means it's one of us.'

Conspirators, Romanov said to himself, sighing as he readied himself to meet the female 'patriot', no doubt some rapturous idiot.

The door was opened by a young lady in a grey dress with a white collar. She was tall, with a girlish plait hanging down over her shoulder, but it was immediately clear that she was a lady and not some young damsel. Alexei would have realised that, even if the boy had not told him about her husband being killed. Young damsels did not have that intent, slow gaze and those creases alongside the mouth.

He clicked his heels together and announced his name, without giving any explanations – there was no need for them in any case.

'He's one of us,' Venya blurted out. 'Another one. You give him some tea, Zina, and I'll run to get Ivan Klimentievich.'

He was about to run off straight away, but the young woman stopped him by holding on to his sleeve.

'Zinaida Andreevna Gruzintseva,' she said to their visitor. 'Veniamin, you're not running off anywhere until you put on your cap and take your gloves. I didn't check in the morning, and you're just delighted about it. The thermometer says eight degrees.'

'Oh Lord, Zina, what am I, a little child?'

The boy cast an embarrassed glance at Romanov, but he took the cap and the gloves, then dashed off down the stairs two steps at a time.

'Please, come in.' Gruzintseva stepped aside to allow her visitor to enter. 'Take your coat off and go through into the sitting room. I can tell you've come straight from the station. You still have the smell of a locomotive. That's good.'

'Why is it good?' Alexei asked, thinking: *What a keen glance she has. And she's neither rapturous nor an idiot.*

'It means you have only just arrived. Which means you're not a Chekist agent. I'm always afraid that Veniamin will bring some kind of impostor.'

And you're right to be afraid, Romanov replied in his own mind.

'Then why do you allow him to . . . deal with such matters?' he asked out loud, gesturing vaguely. 'It really could end very badly. How could anyone tell who I am? Forbid him to do it. I can see that he does as you say.'

'Yes, he is used to obeying me. He was only twelve when we were left without our parents and he had no one but me. But Veniamin isn't a child any longer. And in times like these, boys have to become men early. What could I tell him? "Let everything go to hell, and you just sit still and keep quiet, you'll be safer like that"? That's not the way boys become men. Although, of course, I'm terribly afraid for him . . . Do sit down, I'll just be a moment.'

And she walked out of the room.

He looked around. An ordinary sitting room, just like any other, but there were two unusual features. In one corner there was something like an icon case, but instead of icons it contained photographs, illuminated by an icon lamp. A man and a woman (they must be her parents) and a military man with an academy badge on his uniform coat. No doubt he was her late husband, although he looked perhaps a little too old for Zinaida Andreevna. The second unusual feature was a typewriter with piles of paper stacked up beside it. Romanov walked over to it and read an unfinished line of typing: 'MARAT: For every tear that you spill, poor working woman, the aristocrats will pay a drop, no, a barrel of blood! You have suffered enough. The time of the people's consolation and reckoning has arrived!'

'I earn money by typing for theatres,' Gruzintseva's voice said behind him. She had come in so quietly that Romanov had not heard her. The lady of the house was holding a tray in her hands: a cup of tea, a few slices of bread, butter. Not too bad for these hungry times. 'For the most part now they stage all sorts of revolutionary nonsense, but on the other hand they provide a work ration and even pay a little something in addition. I've learned to type well, without any corrections. That's how we live.'

I expect you do everything well, without any corrections, Alexei thought. He liked this lady very much, and that had finally ruined his mood.

He really was feeling extremely hungry, but he tried to take the smallest bites he could possibly manage and chew slowly, calculating that he would eat three slices and leave the fourth one.

'Don't be embarrassed. There is plenty of bread,' said Zinaida Andreevna, glancing at her visitor from time to time, but not asking any questions.

'Perhaps I ought to tell you about myself?'

'When Ivan Klimentievich comes, you can tell him.'

'But . . . who is he – Ivan Klimentievich? Your brother didn't explain.'

Gruzintseva said nothing for quite a long time, and Romanov already regretted that he had asked the question.

'A squad leader,' she replied eventually, evidently having taken some decision in her own mind. 'But drink your tea. I think that I am embarrassing you.'

And she left him on his own – no doubt to avoid any more questions.

A quarter of an hour later he heard the doorbell ring in the corridor: brrrrrr-brrrrrr-brr-brr-brr. Romanov got up and walked out into the hallway. In a situation like this it was important to assume the positional advantage: an individual who finds himself in a new space has not yet got his bearings or adapted his eyesight to a different level of lighting, and while he is still squinting and blinking, you can form your first impression of him – the most important one.

Of course, the individual by the name of Ivan Klimentievich proved to be that same man in a cavalryman's greatcoat, with a goatee beard. Alexei's secret-agent intuition had not let him down.

'Hang on a moment,' he said, speaking first, while the new arrival was still squinting at him. 'I've seen you before somewhere . . . Ah, in the administration building, just a little while ago.'

'Lieutenant Colonel Zotov,' the cavalryman introduced himself. 'I'm afraid the young man has misled you concerning . . .' he gestured aimlessly, casting a sideways glance at Venya Kopeishchikov, who was standing there with his head lowered guiltily. 'The young man is fond of fantasising.'

Romanov guessed that the Junker had received a dressing-down for his haste. And his first impression of the 'squad leader' was this: a typical career-minded army man, undoubtedly conscientious and efficient: the only strange thing was that at his age (about forty-eight, or even fifty) he was still only a lieutenant colonel.

'The staff captain can be trusted,' Gruzintseva suddenly said in a quiet voice. 'And in any case, it's too late to be secretive.'

'Really?' Zotov exclaimed in relief. 'I have grown accustomed to trusting your judgements, dear Zinaida Andreevna. Well then, that's excellent. What's this, are you taking tea? I wouldn't mind joining you.'

*

The lieutenant colonel turned out to be not much more experienced as a conspirator than Venya the Junker. Instead of interrogating the stranger properly, he told the stranger about himself. The mystery of the discrepancy between his age and his rank was easily explained. Ivan Klimentievich Zotov, a career soldier, had been taken prisoner at the very start of the war, in August 1914, and so he had not been promoted through the ranks. He had returned from Germany only two weeks earlier, and 'had not been able to recognise the Motherland'.

'What monstrous stupidity, what a terrible mistake the Bolsheviks have made in signing an ignominious peace!' he exclaimed passionately. 'I saw Germany from the inside, it is completely exhausted. We only had to hold out for a few months, and that would have been it – victory! We should have retreated, but not surrendered. Even if we had to yield the capital, like Kutuzov! But now what? National disgrace, the scorn of the allies. And of course, no share in the division of the spoils. The only salvation for Russia is to overthrow the Soviets and rejoin the Entente. The moment I got back home, I threw all my energy into searching for men who understand this and are ready to take action. And I found them. Quickly. There are a great many of us, Romanov, and more every day.'

'Zinaida Andreevna said that you were a squad leader. What does that mean?'

Only then did the lieutenant colonel check himself.

'Hang on for a moment. First you tell me where you served and what you were awarded such honourable decorations for.' He nodded at Romanov's uniform tunic.

At the mention of counter-intelligence, the lieutenant colonel frowned. In the old, pre-war times that kind of service was regarded as none too honourable for an officer. But he was mollified somewhat on hearing that the Soldier's Cross of St George had been awarded for an attack.

'So you can do more than just shuffle papers around. Well then, I'd be glad to accept you into my squad. You see, the organisation has the following system. Each new man, regardless of his rank and age, is enrolled as a private, but is granted the right to enlist other officers, taking personal responsibility for them. As soon as you have gathered three men, you become a squad leader. When the three men become nine, you become a platoon commander. For instance, thanks to you (you are the last man I need) I shall soon be promoted.' Zotov laughed. 'After that I shall rise to be a company commander and then, perhaps, a battalion commander; that is, I shall reach my former rank – before the war I commanded a cavalry battalion. In our organisation careers are made rapidly.'

'And do you – that is, we – have a name of any kind?'

Romanov realised that the conspiracy was not so very stupidly arranged after all. Of course, such a lax system of recruitment made it easy to fall foul of an informer or simply a blabbermouth, but the chain could be snapped off with the same ease. And at the same time, with each rank-and-file member of the organisation as a recruiter in a Moscow that was teeming with officers, their membership must be growing by leaps and bounds.

'"The Union for the Defence of the Motherland". A good title that reconciles all political viewpoints – except, of course, for the views of the Bolsheviks. And don't think that we have no units larger than a battalion. We have regiments and brigades, and even a division,' said Zotov, lowering his voice significantly and glancing round at the door, although the only people who could be eavesdropping on him were the lady of the house and her brother – they had tactfully left the officers alone together.

'Even a division?'

Romanov performed a rapid multiplication in his head, and it came to more than two thousand men. Oho!

'And perhaps even more than one. But then, I don't know exactly. I can't see that far from my low perch. But I can assure you that this business is managed by extremely serious people. When the hour strikes, we shall instantly seize all the key points in the capital and paralyse the Soviet regime. One blow will be enough for us, as it was enough for them in Petrograd six months ago. At that time they took the bridges, the communications hubs, the government residence – and suddenly they had all of Russia's vast expanses in their grasp. We shall do the same, only in a more precisely organised manner, like officers.'

No, this is by no means an amateur undertaking, Romanov told himself. *The very idea of a mass organisation with thousands of members, consisting of easily replaced dilettantes, but expertly managed, from a single centre, is quite brilliant in its audacity and efficiency. You can go chasing after the tentacles of this octopus for as long as you wish and snap them off, but you still won't reach the head, and while you are trying to do that, new tentacles will keep sprouting.*

'I've come straight from the train and I don't know anyone in Moscow,' Alexei said out loud. 'I need to find somewhere to stay, and then I'll be ready to carry out any orders.'

Venya the Junker proved to be not so very tactful after all. The door opened a crack and a clear voice exclaimed:

'Mr Staff Captain, stay here with us for a while! He can, can't he, Zina? Vladimir Ivanovich's study is empty in any case.'

'Yes, of course,' Gruzintseva replied in the corridor after a pause.

Before evening Alexei had caught up on his sleep – for his nervous days at the front and his onerous journey all at once. When he woke and sat up on the sofa, he saw that the table was laid: a snow-white napkin, symmetrically arranged cutlery, salami sandwiches on a china plate, biscuits and a thermos flask of tea. A genuine sight for sore eyes. And a note in small but firm and very elegant handwriting: 'We have hot water'.

He ate and then got washed in a genuine bath, with a gas geyser – a long-forgotten luxury. And then he lingered for a long time over shaving, taking pleasure in it, then trimmed his moustache and his fingernails. For the first time in many months he felt like a member of civilised society.

On returning to his room – the study of a General Staff officer killed in the war – he started walking up and down the line of bookcases, filled mostly with military and historical volumes. He was trying to work out what to do next. It was too soon to report back. And what would be the point? In any case, Orlov had nobody except men with rifles, and they would only be required at the final stage. The first thing that had to be determined was who to seize and where. The 'octopus constitution' was certainly convenient as far as security was concerned, but at the same time it did have a weak point. Of course, it was impossible to identify and arrest several thousand conspirators. But that was not necessary. If you could simply locate the head of the octopus and strike a blow against it, you would have no need to be concerned about the tentacles. Without directions and any means of communication, they would be rendered helpless and cease to represent any danger.

It was very quiet in the study. The thick carpet muffled his steps and the carved clock wasn't ticking. Alexei wondered whether he ought to wind it up – in his childhood he had been very fond of winding up his father's old Moser with its little bronze key. But no, it was better not to. If the clock of such a diligent housekeeper was not working, there must be some reason for it. A clear reason. The inhabitant of the study had died, and time had stopped.

Suddenly, having recalled Zinaida Andreevna's diligence, he realised that he had not cleared away his shaving tackle.

In just his socks, so as not to make any noise, he walked out into the corridor and listened. Not a sound from anywhere. The hour was already late.

Damn, and he had forgotten to turn off the light in the bathroom too!

He opened the door slightly and froze.

Zinaida Gruzintseva was standing at the washbasin with her eyes squeezed shut, holding the shaving brush up to her nose. What for?

'Oh, I beg your pardon, do forgive me,' Romanov said. 'I'll wash it straight away.'

Her eyes opened and he saw embarrassment in them.

'No, I beg your pardon,' Gruzintseva murmured. 'I . . . I had grown completely unused to this smell. The smell of a man. Venya doesn't shave yet . . .'

Alexei stopped looking at her, in order not to embarrass her even more.

'You must find it unpleasant that I have moved into your husband's study. I'll move out as soon as Colonel Zotov finds something. He promised . . .'

'I thought I would find it unpleasant, but somehow . . . Somehow it feels good to have a man living in the house again.' Gruzintseva turned on the tap and started washing the shaving brush slowly and thoroughly. She wasn't looking at Romanov any more either. 'You know, Vladimir Ivanovich and I didn't live together for very long, I didn't even have time to come to love him properly, although he was a very good man. A friend of my father's. When our father and mother were suddenly . . . Venya has probably told you, I suppose?'

'No.'

'We had an estate on the Volga, and in winter we always went there for Christmas. The last winter before the war was very warm, do you remember? They fell through the ice on the Volga, together with the sleigh and the horse. Disappeared, as if they had never existed . . . It sometimes seems to me now that the whole of Russia, the entirety of my former life, has slid down into that blackness under the ice, and . . .' She shuddered. 'I was twenty-one, Venya was twelve. I don't know how we could have survived, if not for Vladimir Ivanovich. He was there with us all the time. It seemed such a natural thing to marry him. And everything would have been fine for us, I'm certain of that. But we got married in April, and the war began in August. After that he came back once on leave – and that was all . . .'

Romanov sighed as he listened. How many young widows like this were there in Russia? And how many more were still to appear?

'I seem to have turned sentimental, it's not like me,' said Gruzint-seva, clearing her throat. 'It's the smell that's to blame. You stay with us as long as you need to, Alexei Parisovich. Don't worry, I won't torment you with any more sentimental conversations. Goodnight.'

In effect, she had ruined Romanov's attempts at operational planning. When he returned to his room, he was no longer thinking about practical matters. He was wondering only how it could have come about that Orlov and Kriukov were now his kind of people, and Zinaida Gruzintseva, Zotov and Venya were alien to him. It was absurd, insane.

An endless shaggy dog story

'The Army Supply seal here is genuine. And it is here too . . .' Orlov put down the pass and picked up the warrant granting the right to travel on the railways. 'The bastards have their own people in the

Soviet of Defence and the People's Commissariat of Railways. A rotten state of affairs, Kriukov.'

His assistant examined the document against the light.

'Fuck it! The forms are genuine too. They were only printed with the watermark crest just last week!'

Romanov, standing beside the window, breathed out a stream of smoke through the small open pane. Orlov had a vicious cold and the smell of tobacco smoke set him coughing. It was more than halfway through April, but it wasn't getting any warmer yet.

'As the joke has it, you don't know everything yet, Your Honour,' said Alexei, wafting the bluish cloud out with his hand. 'What did I learn from Zotov this week? That the Union for the Defence has agents everywhere. The Soviet authorities take anyone who comes along into their institutions, without checking them. The Soviet administration and the Red Army command staffs are all thoroughly worm-eaten. How many former officers and functionaries have you taken on? Five thousand? Ten? I dare say you don't even know yourself. And you know even less about which of them are enemies and which aren't. When the revolt begins, the conflagration will break out in a hundred different places at once.'

'What do you suggest?' Orlov asked morosely.

A new feature had appeared in his office: an iron bedstead by the wall, covered with a soldier's blanket. The member of the collegium was now quartered at his place of work.

Alexei explained the gist of his idea, concluding with these words:

'To sum up, we have to find their headquarters. It's hard for me to do that alone, I need assistants.'

Orlov coughed hoarsely. 'Akha, akha,' he croaked, clearing his throat. 'We're not wasting any time on that either. We've set up an intelligence section for surveillance and gathering operational data. It has fifteen members already, so you'll have your assistants.'

'Your clueless chumps are no use to me. They'll only blow their cover and ruin the whole business. Zotov told me that the Union for the Defence has a special agency that handles security. It's called the Security Sector. And the men in it are professionals – former members of the police, the gendarmes and the Okhranka. The closer you get to the headquarters, the stricter the security measures become. I don't need surveillance, I need assistants on the inside.'

'How do you mean?'

'It's like this. I'm one of their active members now. You can see the kind of job they've arranged for me – a Special Representative of the Soviet of Workers' and Peasants' Defence for Supplying the Red Army. A "Specrepsovarmsup",' said Romanov, stumbling over the official Russian abbreviation for his new position. 'I'll be a liaison agent, that's what the warrant is for. But there's more to it than that. I've been granted the right to recruit my own department of two men. From inside the three of us will be able to do more than your green "agents". Can you find any former officers among your more competent colleagues?'

'There's Schwartz,' Kriukov recalled. 'With the big nose, the student. He was a warrant officer under Kerensky.'

'That's right, Osip's a bright lad. But where can we find another one?' Orlov tugged on his beard. 'There aren't any more officers.'

'Let me have Kriukov,' Alexei suggested. 'I'll say I've met an old comrade-in-arms, we fought together. He's not an officer, of course, but I'll say I vouch for him. If they decide to check, it's all true. We were together at the front.'

Orlov broke into a hacking cough again and slapped himself on the chest.

'You swine, Alyosha. You're taking advantage of my weakness. Depriving a sick man of the last thing he has . . . What do you think, Kriukov?'

'I'm not a wench, you don't have to ask me,' the former corporal replied. 'Just don't, you know, forget to eat without me. Don't go roaming round the streets unless you really have to. And take that powder the doctor prescribed.'

'Oh, take this damned man away from me!' Orlov exclaimed with a wave of his hand. 'At least I'll get a bit of rest without a nanny.'

However, nothing came of the plan for Romanov's assistants. Zotov asked what Warrant Officer Schwartz's full name was and, on hearing that it was Iosif Samuilovich Schwartz, immediately declared that Jews were not accepted into the organisation. He turned down

Corporal Kriukov too – there was no place for lower ranks in the 'Union' either. That was the rule.

'I wanted to build my career rapidly, but I've failed,' Alexei joked ruefully. 'I'll never be a squad leader.'

His first idea had to be abandoned – he would just have to work on his own. That didn't alter the strategy, but it dragged the whole business out a lot.

The strategy had been prompted by the structure of the 'Union' itself. Follow the chain cautiously, link by link, from squad leader to platoon commander, from platoon commander to company commander, from company commander to battalion commander, and so on all the way right up to the very top – just making sure not to give the game away.

Zotov didn't even have to be tracked down. He already regarded the Staff Captain Romanov as one of his own and told him the address at which he could be found if necessary. He even let slip that twice a week, on Tuesdays and Fridays, he met with his platoon commander to report to him and receive his orders.

The following Friday Alexei simply tailed the lieutenant colonel from his home. At Patriarch Ponds Zotov sat on a bench for ten minutes with some Mr Handlebar Moustache or other, and from there Romanov tailed the new mark. This individual travelled by tram to Crimea Square and went into the Provisions Depots building, signing the register at the security gate in the lobby. From his signature the Chekists established that he was the accounting clerk Khristofor Petrovich Bakshaev, who lived on Greater Ushakov Lane. Aha, a bookkeeper – with a bearing like that.

Romanov followed the 'bookkeeper's' trail for three days, since his position as a 'specrepsovarmsup' fortunately did not require him to attend any place of work. Bakshaev met with another two men who, from their appearance, were clearly also officers, but Alexei didn't waste any time on them. When Romanov had taken courses in counter-intelligence work, he had attended several lectures on visual deduction, an extremely useful instrument for surveillance. Without even hearing what people were talking about, a great deal can be determined with the help of 'psychogestures', that is, from their movements and facial expressions. Such as the approximate topic of conversation and the balance of power. These two stood lower in the hierarchy than Bakshaev. They were squad leaders of the same kind as Zotov – that much was clear. But on Sunday, in the tearoom of the Medical and Sanitary Workers' Trade Union, Handlebar Moustache sat at the same table as Horseshoe Moustache and conducted himself in a behaviourally unambiguous fashion: first he spoke in a tense manner, looking into the other man's eyes (he was reporting), and then he listened in an equally tense manner (he was receiving his orders).

Horseshoe Moustache turned out to be Dr Kirillov from the nearby military hospital, a former physician with the Life Guards of the Cuirassier Regiment. An enormous amount of time was wasted on this damned Aesculapian, and all because of Alexei's own stupidity. Kirillov did not contact anyone who looked like a member of the underground command. It was only on the seventh day, and purely by chance, that Alexei overheard a fragment of a quiet conversation in a doorway, in which the doctor said to his own medical assistant: 'As you command, Karl Petrovich.' Moreover, Romanov had seen this medical assistant at close quarters every day, and he had not been called 'Karl Petrovich' at all, but 'Prokhor Ivanich'. So quite clearly *he* was the battalion commander.

However, Romanov had a stroke of luck with the next link in the chain. That very same day the bogus 'Prokhor Ivanich' paid a visit to the Khamovnichesky Barracks and strolled along the fence with the commander of the Paris Commune Regiment, Comrade Stadnis. At the conclusion of the conversation he received an encouraging slap on the shoulder, from which it followed that Stadnis commanded a regiment not only for the Reds, but also for the conspirators.

Romanov was starting to become thoroughly fed up with this entire never-ending shaggy dog story, especially since in his official capacity Stadnis constantly met with various direct and indirect superiors, so that each one of them who had previously been an officer had to be checked afterwards. But they all turned out to be above board.

It was not until the May Day demonstration that Alexei finally got his sighting of a brigade commander. While the Paris Commune Regiment was lined up in front of the Historical Museum, waiting for its turn to enter Red Square, its commander suddenly walked over to get a light from a street knife-grinder. The knife-grinder looked the very living epitome of Liberated Labour as he swished a little knife along the edge of his stone wheel, saluting the proletarian festival with a fountain of sparks, and he had a red calico armband on his blue smock. But as the regimental commander lit his *papyrosa* from the crude hand-rolled cigarette, he moved his lips for a really long time, and the knife-grinder replied briefly and abruptly, following which Stadnis nodded guiltily.

And Alexei immediately stopped feeling bored. He was very warm now, in fact positively hot! This was the brigade commander. The flame was very close!

He knew from Zotov that the highest level of the conspiracy consisted of a 'division', so there was only more step left to climb.

Immediately after the fascinating ritual of lighting-up, the interesting knife-grinder stopped scattering sparks and fled from the scene of red-bannered rejoicing via Theatre Square, after which he continued on his way through the courtyards and back alleys. After the first gateway Romanov came across the abandoned lathe. The red armband was lying beside it. Sticking his head round the corner he saw the man walking ahead of him throw off his smock to reveal a respectable shantung-silk suit beneath it.

'Ah, now I have you, my little bird, you won't slip through the net. I won't part from you for anything in the world,' the hunter crooned quietly to himself as he darted in rapid, soundless spurts from one hiding place to the next. The 'brigade commander' looked back every now and then, but in an unprofessional manner: a second before the movement it was clear from his shoulders and neck that he was about to turn his head.

On Kuznetsky Most Street the mark hailed a 'cabservicelabourer' with badge number 578, crying out to him: 'I pay for speed!' The carriage clattered off at a spanking pace in the direction of Trubnaya Square, but that was all right. A competent undercover agent would certainly have changed his means of transport before he reached his destination, but subtleties like that could not be expected from such woeful conspirators as these.

And indeed, Badge Number 578 later told the Chekists that he had taken his generous passenger to the corner house on Semyonovska-ya Street and seen him say hello to the yard keeper there.

'The former Lieutenant Colonel Gushchin, living under his own name,' Orlov announced that evening. 'A Muscovite, he was absent for a long time and returned home at the end of March. It's quite possible that he was sent here from the Don. The yard keeper has heard Gushchin say something to his wife about Novocherkassk. This is a big fish now, Alyosha. There's only one level left until we reach their command staff. I implore you – don't let them slip off the hook.'

'Don't butt in where you're not needed, and they won't. But there is one complication,' Romanov said in a preoccupied tone of voice. He had been able to get away to Povarskaya Street only late in the evening, and for a good reason. 'They're sending me on an assign-ment to Kazan, as a courier. With an important message for the branch there.'

'What branch?' asked Kriukov.

'I had a conversation with Zotov today. A lousy one.' Alexei sighed. 'It turns out that the Union has branches in several cities. On the appointed day the uprising will begin simultaneously in all of them. That's why they send couriers out from Moscow. I was chosen because I'm a former counter-intelligence man and I have experience of clandestine activity. In Kazan I have to stand under the railway station clock every day from nine to nine-fifteen. Sooner or later someone will come up to me and give me the password. And how many couriers are travelling to other cities, and to which ones, Zotov doesn't know.'

Orlov frowned.

'Where's the message?'

'Here.' Romanov held out a little cardboard box. 'It's written on the bottom, under the matches.'

The member of the collegium and his assistant stared at the se-quence of numbers with their heads close together.

'It's in code, fucking damn it!' Kriukov swore.

'And what did you expect?'

Alexei wanted to torment them for a little longer, while he

released smoke rings into the air with great relish, but Orlov quickly saw through his game.

'From that smug-looking mug, I'd say you've already broken the spell of this gibberish. Well?'

'That's why I was stuck at home until so late. I hadn't expected such sophistication from the Union for the Defence. It's a mathematical cipher based on Chase's system, the English use it. In 1916 I worked with them on the case of a German submarine, that was the only reason I could understand it. I had to tinker about for a while, but I figured it out.'

'What does it say?'

'There are just three words. "First of June".'

Kriukov swore again, and there was an ominous pause.

'Romanov, give me a *papyrosa*, will you?' Orlov said.

'You mustn't smoke, you'll start coughing again,' his assistant told him.

At that the member of the collegium swore too.

'There's only a month left, and we still haven't located their centre! And you're going away! What are we going to do? Work on Gushchin without you?'

'Under no circumstances. Better send someone to Kazan under my name. It's a simple enough business. He just has to hand over the box.'

'No, we can't do that . . .' Orlov ruffled up his hair furiously. 'You're needed there too. The republic's gold reserves are stored in Kazan. If there's a revolt and the gold is seized by our enemies, it will be a disaster. You go, Alyosha. As well as delivering the matchbox you'll have to get a hook on their organisation. The Kazan comrades will finish the job without you, but you set them on the trail. And get back here quick. We won't go interfering with Gushchin without you. My word on it.'

And Romanov went to Kazan. He stayed there until the twelfth of May and managed to do a great deal more than simply 'get a hook' on the Union's local organisation. He reached the very top of the conspiracy. It was not arranged as cautiously as in Moscow, and all the threads led to the army garrison command. Alexei identified one of the leaders, and all that remained was to determine the others, but on the twelfth of the month an express telegram arrived from Orlov, ordering him to return immediately.

Romanov travelled back to the capital like a People's Commissar – in a special train with just one carriage and no other passengers. Trains travelling in the same direction and even troop trains made way for him, and his train stopped only to take on coal. On both occasions Romanov had to send a telegram: 'Have passed Ibresi', 'Have passed Murom'.

He arrived in Moscow on the afternoon of the thirteenth. He was met by Orlov in person, with a car, in which they talked.

The collegium member immediately cut short Romanov's complaints about not being allowed to unravel the Kazan ball of thread all the way to the end.

'The comrades can pick up the ones they know, and to hell with the rest of them. There's no time for Kazan. We don't know which way to turn here.'

He didn't laugh or crack any jokes and in general he wasn't like his usual self.

'Information about the Union for the Defence of the Motherland is coming in from all sides. Not only in Moscow, but also in Kaluga, Yaroslavl and Tula, we're picking up all sorts of counter-revolutionary riff-raff – some who wag their tongues too freely, some who get caught through sheer stupidity. And every time the thread snaps off. This means that the Union is setting up more and more branches. And how many cities are there that we know nothing about? We're sitting on a barrel of dynamite, Alyosha. We have to yank out the fuse as quickly as possible, and that's here in Moscow. So get on with it, finish the job with Gushchin.'

Romanov stretched and leaned back in the soft seat. He had slept all the way from Murom to Moscow and still not woken up completely.

'Never mind, we still have some time until the first of June.' He yawned. 'No point in getting flustered. The worst thing of all will be if they get wind of our surveillance. Then they might strike ahead of time. And after that things will explode in the other cities on their own. Don't rush things, Orlov. A good jockey never winds up his horse's nerves before the off. I'll just call back home and have some tea, then enter the racetrack and win you the prize.'

Orlov calmed down a little bit.

'It's a good thing you're so cheerful. There are two sorts of cheerful people – the intelligent kind and the fools. Do you know how to tell the first kind from the second?'

'How?' Alexei asked with a smile.

'The intelligent ones ride in cars, and the fools tramp about on their own two feet. Get out of this car.'

But of course – he couldn't drive into Trubnikovsky Lane in the Cheka's Packard.

'Just a moment, Venya! I'll put my dressing gown on,' Gruzintseva shouted somewhere in the depths of the apartment when Romanov gave the prearranged ring on the doorbell.

The little chain jingled.

Zinaida Gruzintseva's head was wrapped in a towel. There was a note of fright, or perhaps confusion, in her voice.

'You?'

Alexei couldn't help his glance sliding down of its own accord to the spot where fine drops of water glistened on the skin in the opening of the dressing gown. Embarrassed, he lowered his glance all the way down to the floor, where it encountered the white feet below the dressing gown, and he had to raise his head after all. He caught the smell of a woman's freshly washed hair and something else sweet that disturbed the rhythm of his breathing.

'Well, I'm back . . .' he said, unable to think of anything more substantial.

In all the time since that first conversation, Alexei and his landlady had never once found themselves so close to each other. Gruzintseva had seemed to be avoiding her lodger. She must have sensed how awkward he felt in her company. And of course, Romanov was almost never in the apartment, he used to disappear for days at a time, in pursuit of his shaggy dog. When he returned, his supper was waiting for him on the table, covered with a napkin. In the morning, no matter how early he might rise, he had always heard the tapping of the typewriter coming from the sitting room. He took breakfast in the kitchen, alone, or, if he was unlucky, with the

Junker. Romanov didn't like being with this boy whose fate had already been decided, but unlike his sister, Venya was not particularly sensitive, in fact he was absolutely delighted when they found themselves sharing a table. He immediately started sharing the events of his enthralling underground life. He had finally been accepted as a fully fledged member of a squad of three! He had been given a very important assignment, a top-secret one, but he could tell the staff captain about it! He had taken a trip out of town to a rifle range and scored forty-two points out of fifty!

All in all, the Junker had had a very bad effect on Romanov's mood. But when Alexei encountered Zinaida Andreevna, the conversation had always been brief: Hello – I feel so awkward about you washing my things – Oh, don't feel like that, I'm used to it – Take a week's worth of ration cards – Really, there's no need, we have enough of everything. And that was the end of the conversation.

Which only made the silent pause that hung in the air between them now all the more surprising. Zinaida stood there, blocking the doorway, looking straight into his eyes, with her slightly parted lips quivering.

'I thought I would never see you again,' she said, and her voice quivered too. 'You suddenly just disappeared. And Colonel Zotov stopped calling round. Venya doesn't know anything. At first I was offended: how could he do that, without even saying goodbye? Then I saw that some of your things were still here. My God, I thought, something has happened to him! Eleven days!'

'I was given an urgent assignment by the colonel, that's why he didn't come round either – he knew I wasn't here. And I didn't say goodbye when I left because there was no one at home. I couldn't leave a note, the rules of secrecy don't allow it. Please forgive me,' Romanov exclaimed in confusion, noticing the tears in her eyes. 'I didn't realise that you would be upset by my disappearance . . .'

'No, please, it is you who must forgive me,' said Zinaida Andreevna, suddenly recovering her wits. 'I'm keeping you on the doorstep. And look at the state I'm in. I've completely let myself go without a man in the house.'

She pulled her dressing gown more tightly round her, concealing her breasts. She tried to say something else, but sobbed instead, unable to help herself, and gestured angrily.

She set off along the corridor but looked back after a few steps.

'You have a strange effect on me, Alexei Parisovich. Like raw onions. And I rarely cry.'

She brushed away a teardrop, at the same time trying to smile, and stood there for a few moments, as if waiting to see whether he would answer.

Romanov didn't say anything. He didn't even go into the bathroom, which must have been drenched with disarming aromas after Zinaida Andreevna's presence. He didn't even eat. He simply dropped off his travelling bag and went to Semyonovskaya Street. And he promised himself that from now on he would stay at Trubnikovsky Lane even less often. The operation was approaching the stage when total concentration and diligence were essential. This was no time to be tormented by pangs of conscience.

A surprise

The only job that Romanov entrusted to the Moscow Chekists was preparing a 'hide', also known as a 'blind'. These terms, used in hunting a wild boar or a wolf, were what counter-intelligence agents called a stationary surveillance point. Orlov told him that an apartment with a telephone had been rented opposite the building in which the 'brigade commander' Gushchin lived. A bicycle had been made ready in case the mark should take a cab, as on the previous occasion.

Alexei was satisfied with the apartment. Not only did it have a good view of Gushchin's entryway, it even allowed him to peep into the windows. In the kitchen there was a supply of *papyrosas* and food – bread, sausage and a tin box of tea.

However, you didn't sit in a 'hide' alone. A partner was needed, or else you couldn't even have a wash or visit the toilet.

He phoned Povarskaya Street.

'Orlov, send that warrant officer of yours over to me here at Semyonovskaya Street. What's his name, Schmidt?'

'Schwartz. Aha, so you've turned to the collective work ethic after all, you solitary artisan.'

A warrant officer, even one from the 'Kerensky levy', must at least have completed a basic officer's course. So at the very least he had been trained to draw up charts, keep accounting records and use a pair of binoculars properly. And then he was a student, not a proletarian with whom you couldn't even have a decent conversation. The devil only knew how long they'd be stuck sitting on their hands in here.

Schwartz showed up an hour later and his very appearance made Alexei feel depressed. A proletarian would have been better than this exaggerated Jew from a Black Hundred gang anti-Semitic caricature: a large nose and thick lips, with a mop of fine, black curls, and even wearing a pince-nez. At least he rolled his 'r's properly, but he drawled his vowels, especially the 'a's, in a Moscow manner that grated on a St Petersburg ear.

'So you're the celebrated master sleuth, then?' Alexei's new assistant asked, looking him over sceptically. 'Pleased to meet you.'

'We'll see in a while whether you're pleased or not,' Romanov replied, ignoring the hand held out to him.

He knew this intelligentsia breed very well. If you started spouting airs and graces, they would take advantage, striving to demonstrate what unique and brilliant individuals they were. On the other hand, if you rubbed them up the wrong way, they would turn sulky, but at least they would make a real effort.

He explained briefly and drily what would have to be done and what the rules of observation were.

Schwartz heard him out fastidiously and murmured under his breath:

'A crass boor and anti-Semite. So to hell with him.'

'What?' Alexei asked in amazement.

His partner politely explained:

'Take no notice. I'm just talking to myself. A habit.'

And so it became clear that there really wouldn't be any dull moments with Agent Schwartz.

However, he conducted surveillance quite irreproachably. He stood at one side of the window, in the shade. He made little holes in the net curtains for the lenses of the binoculars. He didn't turn his head away and wasn't distracted by anything. Only he kept singing all the time in a rather repulsive falsetto, as if there was no one else in the room. The songs had strange, lingering melodies and the subject matter was utterly incomprehensible.

'What language is that?' asked Romanov, who for lack of anything else to do had decided to dismantle and lubricate his Nagant revolver.

'Ancient Hebrew. I'm a Jew, did you not notice?' Schwartz replied caustically, keeping his eyes glued to the binoculars. 'And by the way, whether you are interested or not, a light has come on in the hallway. I can see a man putting on a bowler hat. He's preparing to go out.'

Alexei assembled his revolver in ten seconds and dashed to the door.

'Don't be distracted by anything! Write down everyone who comes to visit.'

He tumbled down the stairs and glanced cautiously out of the front door.

Gushchin was just coming out. He raised his collar and gave a little shiver (there was a light drizzle sprinkling down from the sky), then set off in the direction of Taganka Square.

Romanov followed him until the evening. Gushchin had three meetings, all of them brief: two with unfamiliar individuals and one with Stadnis again. From the psychogestures it was clear that Gushchin was senior to all three of them, which meant they were regimental commanders. Not what Alexei was looking for.

When Alexei finally made his way back, his partner was still sitting at the window with the binoculars: he glanced round briefly and frowned, but didn't say anything.

A piece of paper was lying beside him. Romanov glanced at it.

16.45 – The yard keeper. Stayed for 4 min.

17.12 – A postman. Genuine. 1 min.

18.50 – A courier. The usual one. About 6 feet tall, thin, limps slightly on left leg. 1 min.

'I can guess how you realised that the postman was genuine. He obviously delivered mail to other apartments too. But what made you think that the man with a limp was a courier, and the usual one, at that?'

'He went in with a newspaper and came out without it,' Schwartz muttered gruffly. 'A newspaper is convenient for camouflaging an encrypted message. He kissed the hand of the lady of the house, spoke briefly and left immediately. So it wasn't his first visit.'

'It seems I have been lucky with my partner.' Romanov smiled and sang a line that he had remembered from one of Schwartz's songs: 'Shaalu shalom, shaalu shalom. Yerushalayim.'

Schwartz looked round again, this time with interest.

'Not a crass boor, and apparently not an anti-Semite. Well then, shall we introduce ourselves? I'm Osip.'

Conversation made the work go more cheerfully.

Iosif Schwartz had been a student at the Moscow Technical College. He hadn't fought in the war prior to 1917, because he had an exemption certificate, or 'white ticket'.

'Why should I die for the Russian tsar? We Jews have never had much to thank Russia and the Romanovs for, quite the opposite in fact. I was a Zionist. I thought I'd get my diploma and go away to Palestine. Let the Russians live as they like, but we Jews had to build our own state. But since the February Revolution everything has changed. I look around and I like what I see. Eh, I think, if there's no more Pale of Settlement and discrimination, why leave? When I can make a difference right here at home.'

'Why did you join the army?'

'I joined the army because of Mirkin.'

'Because of whom?'

'You don't know who Mirkin is?' Schwartz asked in amazement. 'I thought everyone knew Mirkin. Although of course, until quite recently, for me "everyone" meant "every Jew". Lev Mirkin is the chairman of the "Union of Jewish Soldiers". A hussar who earned a full Order of St George in the field, but until the February Revolution had remained a volunteer, because Jews were never made officers. But in 1917, after the prohibition was lifted, he reached the rank of cavalry captain in a few months. Last spring, he addressed the Zionist youth and exhorted them not to leave; he said: "Our motherland is Russia, and one does not abandon one's motherland in hard times."

He spoke well. Anyway, I threw away my white ticket, graduated from college and ended up at the front. But in the trenches they soon put my head straight. When you're all close together and any one of you could be killed or crippled at any moment, you soon understand that it doesn't matter who's a Jew and who isn't. The important thing is who's brave and who's a coward, who you can rely on and who you can't.'

Romanov nodded. He knew the way things went. And then sooner or later you met your Orlov and he explained to you where the truth lay – if you hadn't already understood that by then.

'So what was the main thing I realised? Mirkin might be a hero, but he was mistaken. A man's motherland isn't Russia, and it isn't Israel, but the entire world. And until a good life is established throughout the world, there won't be any good life in Russia, or in Israel either. That is the most important truth. So I became a Bolshevik internationalist,' Schwartz concluded pompously.

'But even so you remained a Jew. You sing songs and root out anti-Semites.'

'Can a duck really stop being a duck because it's a bird?' the former warrant officer asked with a shrug. 'It's excellent that I'm a Jew. The world revolution needs Jews. Because we are there in every country. We are like the cement that binds everything together. Or rather, we are the electric wires that the current runs through, so that the light will come on everywhere. Oh, now they've put the light out. They're going to bed. Maybe we should get some rest too? It's after two in the morning.'

'I'll take a rest, no doubt I'll have to go running all over the city again tomorrow. You stay here and keep watch.'

Alexei felt as if he had only just closed his eyes when something flicked across his forehead. He sat up abruptly on the trestle bed, and another crumpled piece of paper flew into his face.

Dawn was seeping in through the window.

'Rise and shine,' Schwartz said in a quiet voice, tearing his eyes away from the binoculars. 'There's a light on in the hallway. The mark is putting his hat on.'

Romanov was already pulling on his boots.

'What time is it?'

'Twenty minutes past four.'

Where could Gushchin be going at such an early hour? There had to be a good reason for it.

'You can hit the hay while I'm gone,' Romanov shouted back from the corridor.

The mark behaved differently from the day before, gazing around every ten steps, so he was clearly on important business. Yesterday he had met his subordinates, today he was going to see his superior – that would only be logical.

Alexei was getting very, very warm!

Of course, Gushchin's laughable precautions were no problem for Alexei. In an empty street he could fall back to a safe distance and move in dashes, from one point of cover to the next.

Advancing like this, they reached Taganka Square, where Romanov was unlucky at first. What a terrible thing to happen! A cabby suddenly appeared completely out of the blue, shooting out from behind a corner at this godforsaken hour. Gushchin waved his hand and got into the cab. Romanov could really have done with his bicycle now.

But then fortune had a sudden change of heart. In a booming voice that could be heard at a distance in the stillness of dawn the cabby exclaimed:

'Strastnoi Boulevard? We'll get you there!'

The cab set off downhill along Zemlyanoi Val Street.

About five minutes later Romanov also found a cabby. He didn't want to take a passenger – his shift was already over – and since Alexei didn't have an official document, he showed his Nagant instead. This persuasive argument proved effective.

They shot off at top speed and along a shorter route – across the Yauza River and along the boulevards – so that Romanov reached the square in front of the Strastnoi Monastery ahead of his quarry and spent several minutes hiding behind the statue of solitary, morose Pushkin until the familiar carriage halted on the corner of the Sytin Printing Works.

And for quite a long time after that Gushchin meandered through side streets, constantly looking round. Romanov slid along after him like a silent shadow.

The mark halted opposite a large apartment building and started waiting for something or someone. The time was 4.52.

At precisely five a man as erect and stiff as a pikestaff, wearing a check peaked cap, walked out of an entranceway. Gushchin stepped towards him, raising his bowler hat. The stranger merely nodded and held out his hand. The divisional commander, no doubt about it.

Romanov almost broke into song.

The conspirators set off at a slow walk in Alexei's direction. He hid in a gateway and merged into the wall.

They walked by, no more than five steps away.

'. . . The numbers are growing, but the sum allocated remains the same,' Gushchin was saying hastily. 'It doesn't affect Stadnis, all his men are on Soviet pay, but Berdnikov and Tyshkevich are in great difficulties.'

'Very well. I'll raise the question of finances with the command staff. Immediately.'

The divisional commander's profile was as clearly defined as if it had been forged out of cast iron, with a moustache shaved into a narrow strip. Romanov didn't have time to make out anything else.

He decided to count to twenty before venturing out to follow – God forbid that jumpy Gushchin should happen to glance round and spot him. Then he decided it would be safer to count to thirty.

Fate had protected him – there was no doubt about it.

At the count of twenty-seven someone in a grey coat and a grey cloth cap glided soundlessly past Romanov's hiding place.

What sort of development was this?

Romanov peeped out cautiously, just a little – and hid again.

The man in grey jerked his hand up to his eyes, as if to glance at his watch, but slightly higher than necessary for that. A familiar gesture. That was how secret agents were taught to check whether they were being trailed. Their watches were fitted with mirror glass.

There weren't any smart alecks like that in the Cheka. The

conclusion? The divisional commander was being followed by a well-trained personal bodyguard.

The pursuit was becoming risky. Sooner or later a professional would spot him.

A surprise. And a highly unpleasant one.

All or nothing

Nonetheless Alexei decided to keep following this interesting three-some until the narrow side streets came to an end. On a wide street or a square, of course, he would have to let them go. Ah, what a shame!

About five minutes later the divisional commander and Gush-chin parted company. After that the man with the cast-iron profile continued on his way alone – if you didn't count the 'shadow' accompanying him at a distance. The bodyguard kept about twenty metres behind on the opposite pavement, constantly looking around and not forgetting to check his rear, sometimes glancing at his watch, sometimes looking into a shop window.

Romanov wanted desperately not to let a catch like this slip away. A certain idea did occur to him, but it was so audacious that at first Romanov dismissed it as raving nonsense. However, the little idea only returned, scrabbling at the door even more insistently.

The man with the cast-iron face had told Gushchin: 'I'll raise the question of finances with the command staff. Immediately.'

That meant he was on his way to a meeting of the command staff – whose command staff was clear enough. This was a chance to discover where the entire leadership of the Union met, and perhaps to identify its membership.

Of course, the risk was great. But if he succeeded, the prize would also be great.

Up ahead a wide gap appeared between the buildings – some large street or other. The pursuit would end there.

It had to be now, it was all or nothing.

Act one: a comedy with a costume change.

Alexei stopped concealing himself and instead ran straight at the man in grey with loud, long strides. It was an excellent moment – the division commander had already turned the corner, but the bodyguard was still in the side street.

Naturally, the man in grey looked back and cast a rapid glance over the approaching man, following the routine familiar to every professional: face, hands, shoes. A 'tail' could often be identified from his footwear. In order not to attract attention a 'shadow' often changed his hat or turned his outer garment inside out, but changing your shoes is more difficult. If a factory hand suddenly turns out to be wearing decent half-boots, it's clearly a masquerade.

A former Okhranka man, not from the Gendarmes Corps, Alexei concluded (as he ran he had also – of course – conducted a top-to-bottom inspection). From closer up he could see that the man in grey had a distinctive bear-like gait; the gendarmes wouldn't have taken him with flat feet like that.

'Do you have a watch? What time is it, mate?' Romanov shouted, as if he intended to go running on by. 'Damn it, I overslept, missed my shift!'

The bodyguard hadn't spotted anything suspicious about the hurrying man and he raised the arm with his watch on the wrist.

Romanov grabbed it, twisted it behind the man's back, clamped his left elbow round the sucker's neck, pressed on his carotid artery and held up the body when it went limp.

Everything seemed quiet on all sides.

There was no one behind him. No one was peeping out of the windows.

He dragged the unconscious body as far as the nearest entryway, pulled off the grey coat and put it on, then jammed the peaked cap on his own head. For good measure he struck the bodyguard on the temple – so that he wouldn't wake up too soon.

And now to catch up with his quarry.

The divisional commander had not moved on very far, only about a hundred metres. To be on the safe side Alexei increased the distance between them to the maximum and pulled the peak of the cap down over his face.

A couple of times, first on Nikitsky Gates Square and then on the boulevard, beside the seated stone Gogol, Alexei's mark looked back briefly, but he didn't seem to have noticed the substitution.

Alexei did not know Russia's old capital – which was now, of course, its new one – very well, but the place to which the boulevard led was famous: it was the site of the Cathedral of Christ the Saviour, with its massive dome. In the middle of the square the mark halted, as if he had recalled something. Then he suddenly turned and beckoned Romanov with an imperious gesture.

It was time for the second act: a comedy of errors.

As the distance shortened, with every step the expression on the severe, cast-iron face changed: from mild surprise to puzzlement to alarm.

'I don't know you,' the divisional commander said, and his hand slipped into his pocket.

'I haven't been in the organisation long,' Romanov replied in a quiet voice. 'The Security Sector is expanding too.'

Since they had a 'Security Sector', it was reasonable to assume that it was responsible for the safety of the leadership.

The hand abandoned the pocket and hung poised in mid-air.

'And where has Rychkov got to?'

'I was ordered to relieve him.'

The open hand reached forward.

'Colonel Merkurov.'

'I know who you are,' Alexei said with a quiet chuckle, respectfully accepting the offer to shake hands. 'My name is Romanov. Why did you call me over to you? The instructions don't allow it. People are watching.'

The first beggars were already sitting on the porch of the church, although there was still a long time to go until the dawn service.

'I know. I have an urgent assignment for you. I shall be in the clinic for a long time. Rather than hanging about outside with nothing to do, go back to my place and take a blue notebook from my wife. I left it behind in the hallway. You know the password, my wife is called . . .'

'I know that too,' Romanov interrupted. 'It will be done.'

And he didn't move from the spot.

'Well then, do it.'

'After I have escorted you all the way.'

'What kind of distance is there left?' asked Merkurov, nodding his head in the direction of Ostozhenka Street. 'I can walk the rest of the way on my own. I'm not a young lady. And I shall need the notebook.'

'I'm a military man. Orders are orders.'

Merkurov didn't try to argue, he merely swore. *So their Security Sector operates independently*, Alexei concluded. *It's not subordinate to a divisional commander.*

'Then let's walk together. What point is there in playing the fool now?'

They set off.

'Are you also a former agent of the Okhranka, like Rychkov?'

Alexei cleared his throat resentfully.

'I'm from military counter-intelligence.'

'I beg your pardon,' said Merkurov, slightly embarrassed. 'Are you an officer?'

'A staff captain.'

'So Vasily Vasilievich values me that highly. That's flattering . . .' Alexei's companion murmured absent-mindedly, and fell silent for a long time, pondering on thoughts of his own. Romanov dropped back half a step and started monitoring the three zones: the left, the right, the rear; the left, the right, the rear.

They passed a small monastery with a red wall and came out at a small square with a park.

'Damn it, I'm the last,' said Merkurov. 'Everybody's here already.'

Sitting and walking about in the square were one, two, three, four, five men, all dressed differently, but they all turned to look and then turned away in exactly the same manner. At the same time each of them held himself apart from the others, as if he had nothing to do with them.

Also bodyguards, no doubt about that, Romanov concluded.

'That's all, Staff Captain. You've got me here, now dash back and get that notebook. Try to get a cab. And I'll go and take a spot of treatment.'

Merkurov set off towards a one-and-a-half-storey detached building with a sign that said 'Outpatient Clinic'. *Very convenient for secret meetings*, Romanov concluded. *Anyone at all can come here without arousing any suspicion.*

He strolled a short distance along the pavement, feeling the rapid, probing glances of the other men on him. Meeting their gaze, he screwed up his eyes slightly, as secret service men do when they wish to greet each other imperceptibly.

And then, after swearing quietly and even striking himself on the forehead, he set off quickly towards the porch of the building. Let them think that he intended to overtake Merkurov.

In the reception hall there were chairs for visitors standing along the wall and a 'Sister of Mercy' sitting at a desk below posters about lice and syphilis. She was late middle-aged, with ferocious features that looked far from merciful, and a little linen cap with a red cross on it.

Two doors – one on the left, the other on the right.

'Who do you wish to see? Dr Ananiev or Dr Zass?'

One doctor is surely for camouflage, he receives the ordinary visitors, and the other is the one I need, thought Romanov. *But which one is he?*

'Don't ask stupid questions,' he said angrily. 'Who could I come to see at six o'clock in the morning? I'm with Merkurov.'

She swayed her head to the left without speaking.

A corridor. One door at the end of it. The sound of voices behind the door.

Romanov took a deep breath. He knocked loudly. The voices fell silent.

And now for act three: all or nothing.

Quarantine

A doctor's office like any other: glass cupboards, a framed diploma, a washbasin with a mirror. Six men inside. One, probably the doctor himself (Ananiev or Zass?), sitting at a desk; four, including Merkurov, sitting on chairs along the walls; and someone else standing behind the putative doctor. There was no time to examine them.

'What is it?' asked Merkurov. He turned abruptly and explained to the others. 'This is my bodyguard, Staff Captain Romanov.'

The one standing behind the 'doctor' swayed slightly and the fingers of his left hand slipped into his right sleeve. In his state of intense concentration, Alexei immediately registered this smooth but rapid movement. The man was short and thickset, with a completely bald or shaved head and a fleshy face. Following his secret agent's habit of giving a nickname to individuals whose names were unknown, Romanov mentally dubbed him 'the Tolstoyan' (the bald man was wearing a 'Tolstoy smock' under his jacket).

Left-handed, with superb reaction speed. What has he got in his sleeve – a small Steyr six-shooter attached to his wrist? And why is the 'Tolstoyan' standing, when everyone else is sitting?

'That is correct, gentlemen, I am Staff Captain Romanov, but I am not a bodyguard.'

Alexei looked at the 'doctor', who was undoubtedly the most important person here.

A bald patch and high forehead, bags under his eyes, a keen and at the same time very calm glance (not a good combination). Soiled cuffs on his shirt, a button missing on his jacket (an eternal loner, sets no store by his appearance). Hands clasped together on the desk, slim fingers with dirty nails stirring slightly (no, not a doctor; very intense inner energy, but total control over his emotions).

Instead of asking: 'Then who are you, if not a bodyguard?' the 'non-doctor' merely narrowed his eyes, waiting for what would come next. A serious individual, very serious.

'I am a rank-and-file member of the Union,' Alexei continued, still looking only at the most important man present, but following the 'Tolstoyan's' hands with his peripheral vision. 'In the organisation for five weeks. Formerly a counter-intelligence agent. I served with General Zhukovsky and Prince Kozlovsky. One of my specialities is protecting especially important individuals. At one time I was even attached to His Majesty's train. And I, gentlemen, find it quite intolerable to observe the shambolic system that you have here! Conspiratorial organisations that operate like this are doomed to fail! The only reason all of us have not yet been snatched by the Chekists is their own lack of professionalism! But they will snatch us, you may depend on it. And I decided to prove to you how easily it can be done.'

He spoke forcefully and very rapidly, constantly increasing the volume of his voice, in order not to lose the initiative for an instant.

'As easily as multiplying two by two, by means of elementary surveillance work. I have followed the entire length of your farcical little chain. From a squad leader to a platoon commander, then to a company commander, a battalion commander, a regimental commander and a brigade commander. And he did an excellent job of leading me to Mr Merkurov.' Romanov nodded at his charge, who was listening with his jaw hanging open. 'Yes, in your organisation a divisional commander has a bodyguard – a "shadow" in our professional jargon – but I'm sorry, that is simply not good enough. I neutralised him easily and took his place – and now here I am at a meeting of the General Staff . . .'

The 'Tolstoyan' finally revealed what he had in his sleeve – a narrow, stiletto-like knife.

'What has happened to Rychkov? I'll kill you!' he shouted, moving the hand holding the knife down and back. It was a throwing knife.

'. . . And if it was a Chekist in my place, he wouldn't have presented himself here alone!' Romanov concluded, preparing to dodge if necessary.

The 'non-doctor' clicked his tongue gently.

'Stay, Vasily Vasilievich. These jibes are directed at your area. And Staff Captain Romanov's "appearance before the people" demonstrates the correctness of his criticism.'

The bald man breathed in hard, put his knife away and squeezed his hands into fists.

Now Alexei could allow himself to relax a little, and he cast a glance over the other men.

So, not counting Merkurov, there were three of them.

Two of them were typical field officers, or even generals: one with plump cheeks, a 'French crop' like a beaver's fur and a walrus moustache ('the Walrus'), and a long, lanky one with gingerish hair ('the Cockroach'). They both had strong faces – it was clear immediately that they had not made their careers sitting in staff offices, but facing bullets. The third man did not look like a professional soldier. A dandy in an exquisitely pressed morning coat with mother-of-pearl cufflinks and lively, aquiline features with a sarcastic mouth, twirling an elegant, silver cigarette case in his hands. Alexei dubbed him 'the Phantom'.

The cursory inspection did not prevent him from speaking.

'Your Rychkov is unharmed,' he bluntly informed the 'Tolstoyan', Vasily Vasilievich. 'After he lies down for an hour or two, he'll be as good as new. So you're the "Security Sector", are you? You work poorly. I get no sense of experience. Who were you before? A police constable at a crossroads?'

And then, not allowing any time for a reply, he addressed the 'non-doctor'.

'Why did I take the risk of bursting in like this? The security system requires urgent reorganisation. Otherwise we might not live to see the first of June.'

'How does he know about the first of June, Victor Borisovich?' Vasily Vasilievich asked rapidly. 'Rank-and-file members aren't supposed to know that! Not even the battalion commanders know it!'

'I was sent to Kazan with a dispatch. I'm not an idiot, I guessed what the words "first of June" meant.'

The 'Tolstoyan' smiled menacingly.

'A slight inconsistency. The dispatch was encrypted.'

'To a counter-intelligence man, your outdated Chase is chicken feed,' Romanov snorted derisively. 'I think they know that system even in the Cheka.'

'In-ter-est-ing,' Victor Borisovich drawled.

He bored into Alexei with his puffy eyes – a habit often encountered among major criminals who regard the world as a place for hunting and people as a flock of sheep – they are always choosing the next victim to grab in their jaws.

'You acted correctly, Staff Captain. Do you have a weapon?'

Alexei started at this unexpected question.

'A Nagant.'

'Surrender it to Vasily Vasilievich.'

'Why?'

'Because I order you to.' The keen glance flashed with a steely glint, but the voice remained soft. 'After all, as a counter-intelligence agent, you understand that we have to check you. You can stay in quarantine for a while. If everything you have told us about yourself is true – then you will assist Vasily Vasilievich. And if you are not the man you have presented yourself as being, our relationship will . . . take a different turn.' He gave a quiet chuckle. 'Vasily Vasilievich, please take the staff captain away and we, gentlemen, can get back to our work. We have a large agenda today.'

Romanov's guard led him out through the rear door into a dark little corridor and frisked him deftly. He took the revolver out of Romanov's pocket and located the knife attached to his ankle by a small strap. Vasily Vasilievich examined it curiously, clicked the little button and winced at the blade that leapt out.

'Naughty, naughty!'

He took Alexei's watch too. And then he said:

'Bend your head down.' And he tied a large handkerchief over Alexei's eyes.

'What's that for?'

'To keep things secret. Careful, there are steps here.'

He led Alexei along by the arm – for a long time. Romanov counted seven turns and three stairways – they walked down, then climbed up and walked down again. There was no way that spaces as large as this could be contained in this detached building – his escort was deliberately confusing him, leading him through the same places several times.

Another descent. The air turned colder and it smelled of mould. A basement.

A screech of iron. A nudge in his back.

'Well, now we're home. You can take off the handkerchief. And meanwhile I'll arrange some lighting.'

A small, windowless room with a low ceiling. A folding bed, covered with a soldier's greatcoat. A bucket in the corner, under a lid.

Vasily Vasilievich set down a kerosene lamp on a stool.

'There now, that's a bit cosier. Later on they'll bring you something to eat and everything will be just splendid. Make yourself at home, Mr Critic.'

He went out and clanged the door shut. A little window immediately opened in it.

'You have a genuine prison cell here,' said Romanov.

'It's needed sometimes. For quarantine, for instance. And not only for that. I'll leave the window open, for ventilation.'

My, my, how considerate, thought Alexei. *He can glance in through the window at any moment without being seen.*

The bald patch on Vasily Vasilievich's round head glinted in the opening.

'It's fine for you idling around in here, but I've got extra work to do because of you. Okay, then, enjoy yourself.'

The head disappeared.

'Hurry up, eh?' Romanov shouted after it.

He wasn't afraid of the check, the only question was how long it would go on for. If he disappeared for a long time, they might decide in the Cheka that their infiltrated agent had been exposed and terminated. He just hoped that Orlov wouldn't be too hasty and mess things up.

But then, didn't the philosophers assert that it was pointless to worry about matters that you were unable to influence? After taking comfort in this thought, Alexei recalled another piece of wisdom – soldier's wisdom: if you have nothing to occupy yourself with, lie down and take a nap. Army service had taught him the useful skill of catching up on his sleep in advance.

The prisoner of the dungeon stretched, yawned sweetly and started settling down.

The footballers

'Arise, oh most innocent of babes.'

The first things that Romanov saw when he opened his eyes as he lay there on his side were his Nagant revolver and knife lying on a stool. Which meant that everything was fine.

He lowered his legs off the bed and looked up at Vasily Vasilievich's smiling face.

'So you've done the check? Now what?'

'Now we'll shake hands, embrace each other and be as thick as thieves. I'm Vasily Vasilievich Polkanov.'

Alexei got up and shook the joker's hand. Polkanov jerked Romanov's hand towards himself, swung the sleepy newcomer round and caught him in a very expert chokehold. A knifepoint was aimed straight into Alexei's eye – he couldn't stir a muscle.

But it didn't last for long. After a couple of seconds Polkanov gave Alexei a gentle shove in the back and laughed good-naturedly.

'I'm joking. That was just to make you wake up more smartly.'

And to immediately establish the hierarchy in the dog pack, Romanov thought.

'What time is it?' he asked morosely, rubbing his crushed throat. 'I get the hint.'

Polkanov returned the confiscated watch. Alexei dropped it.

'Damn, my fingers have gone numb. That's some tight grip you have . . .'

He squatted down and performed an elementary manoeuvre called 'bull in a china shop', striking the standing man in the groin with his forehead, while simultaneously tugging hard on his ankles. Polkanov crash-landed on his backside with a howl. Romanov had his own ways of establishing the hierarchy in a dog pack.

'A joke for a joke,' he said. 'My name is Alexei Parisovich, but I only talk on such familiar terms with officers. You are clearly not among their number.'

Polkanov got up, holding his bruised coccyx. He smiled without any malice.

'So the score is one–one, as they say in football.'

'Do you play football?' Romanov asked in surprise.

'I'm a fan. How about you?'

'Before the war I was in the St Petersburg University team.'

'Hang on . . .' Polkanov gasped. 'Are you the goalkeeper Romanov? I still remember the way you saved that penalty in the match with Sparta!' He reached out to shake hands again, this time without any tricks. 'I'm pleased to meet you. Well, one footballer can always get along with another. Because they understand the meaning of the word "team".'

'Is it morning now or evening?'

Alexei's watch showed half past ten.

'Morning.'

'Have I really been stretched out for more than twenty-four hours? I feel as if I could still sleep a bit more.'

'No, it's still the same beautiful morning,' Polkanov replied with a cunning smile. 'We're not such total chumps as you think, Alexei Parisovich. We do know how to do a few things. All the General Staff's documents, including the archive of the Second Department of the Quartermaster-General, which included counter-intelligence, are now in the Red Army headquarters in Moscow. All we needed to do was send a little note to our man there. He passed on your service record to us. And everything's in order, including the photo in your file. There's only one little question. The last entry is for June 1917: transferred to the army in the field. What happened after that? What have you been doing?'

There was nothing to be afraid of here. After the October revolution the military bureaucratic machine had stopped dead in its tracks. No paper trail of his move to the Red Guards could have been left in his old records.

'I've been building up my rage.'

'Rage is a useful kind of thing. I've always had a lot of it in me, like a hungry dog.' Polkanov bared his teeth jokingly and even growled. 'Only I didn't immediately find the right outlet for my rage. Victor Borisovich opened my eyes.'

'And who is he?'

'Well, would you ever!' Polkanov exclaimed in surprise. 'You a counter-intelligence agent, and you didn't recognise Victor Savvin!'

Ah, that was who he meant! Alexei had heard about Savvin, of course. In the tsar's time, he had been the most famous of the underground terrorists, the head of the Socialist Revolutionaries' combat organisation, ubiquitous and elusive. After the February revolution, under Kerensky, he had become a deputy minister of war, the most energetic member of the Provisional Government. Now it was clear why the 'Union' was such a formidable force.

'I dealt with spies, not political activists. Unlike you. You are from the Okhranka, aren't you? I recognise the training.'

'Detective, first-class. I was outstandingly good at my trade, I loved that work. I liked being the authorities' guard dog and watching over the sheep. Tearing at the wolves with my teeth and snapping at the sheep to make them feel afraid.'

'But how did you come to be with Savvin?'

'By the will of Providence. I don't believe in God, of course, but some kind of miracle from Him must have been involved . . .' Polkanov smiled at his recollection. 'One day I start tailing a certain suspicious individual. Suddenly I realise that it's Dragon – our code name for Savvin. Well, I start trembling with joy. What a stroke of luck! Five thousand roubles' reward! Eh, I thought, I'll take him myself: I was ambitious and overconfident. We weren't allowed to carry firearms, but I had my little knife. I go strolling along towards Dragon, whistling and looking around. And when I draw level, snap – I grab him. I had this move that had never let me down: I grab their private parts with one hand down below and put my blade to their throats. "Shut your trap!" I say. "Freeze!" And I squeeze my fist tight.'

Polkanov shook his head, as if he was still surprised even now.

'Anybody else would have yelled out in pain or shuddered. But this guy didn't stir a muscle. "Oho," he says, "such an intimate approach." Then slowly and calmly he takes hold of the knife with his bare hand. "Smart lad, good for you. And bold. Not afraid to take me on his own." And he squeezes the blade tight. The blood's running down over my wrist, straight into my sleeve, but Savvin couldn't care less! He's actually smiling! "Aren't you sick," he asks, "of running to the sound of your master's whistle like a little mutt? Come along with me to saunter through the woods like a free wolf." He looked straight into my eyes, point-blank, and that gaze of his – well, you've seen it yourself. And something came over me. I followed him and never once regretted it afterwards.'

'Why did you go?' Romanov asked curiously.

'Because I sensed that this was my man, and my life. A genuine life. How can I tell you . . . Beside someone like that you become a greater man yourself. Of course, I don't have any great illusions about myself. If Victor Savvin is like Peter the Great, then beside him I'm not Menshikov, or even Yaguzhinsky, just Alexander Rumiantsev, maybe. But that's enough for me. Do you know who Rumiantsev was?'

'Well, *I* do, of course,' Alexei replied in surprise.

You didn't expect that kind of erudition from a former police spy. Captain Rumiantsev was the first Russian master of secret operations. He had distinguished himself by kidnapping Mazepa's nephew and heir, Voinarovsky, and then brought the fugitive tsarevich Alexei back from Italy.

Polkanov chuckled.

'I used to be a thickhead in the old days, all right. I wasn't interested in anything except beer and cards, but in thirteen years with Savvin, I must have read a thousand books. When you fly after an eagle, you rise high. All right, let's get down to business. Since you're such an expert in security, Alexei Parisovich, come on, tell me how our team ought to play, in order not to let in a goal.'

'I told you I only talk on informal terms with officers . . .' said Romanov, smiling broadly. 'But that's not quite right. I do the same with footballers too. You can't stand on ceremony during a game.'

They shook hands again, for the third time, firmly and wholeheartedly.

'First of all, Vasily, I have to have the full picture. After all, I broke through to the goalposts along the edge of the pitch.'

'You might have broken through, but you wouldn't have scored a goal. The closer you get to my goalposts, the denser the defence gets.'

'Let's take a look at that. The first question. How often does the command staff meet?'

Will he answer or not? Alexei felt himself tense up inside.

'They used to meet once a week, if there was nothing urgent. Now it's three times. During the last week before the first of June they'll meet every day.'

'That's a weak point.' Romanov frowned disapprovingly. 'A single strike, and they'll all be taken at once.'

Polkanov winked at him.

'It's not all that simple. But for the time being, carry on asking your questions.'

What does he mean? In what way is it 'not all that simple'?

'All right. The second vulnerable point is the head of the Union, Savvin. Where does he live, how is he guarded?'

'He's well guarded. He always has two of my finest lads with him. But I can't tell you where he lives. I don't know that myself. Savvin is like a fox. He doesn't spend the night in the same place twice. An old habit from way back. Not even the Okhranka was able to find him.'

'All right. The third shortcoming in the system is the divisional commanders. And you can't reassure me on this, I've seen for myself that they are guarded lousily. The Chekists only have to latch on to one, the way I did with Merkurov, and nab him – and there is no more division. Who are the other three?'

Polkanov paused for a moment and then told him.

'Divcom-1 is Zhbanov. The one who looks like a beaver.'

Walrus, Romanov concluded.

'The long, skinny one is Colonel Scherer, Divcom-2. Divcom-3, Merkurov, you already know . . . And the smart, handsome man with dark hair is Captain Mirkin of the cavalry group.'

'Do . . . we' (he had almost blurted out 'you') 'even have a cavalry group?'

'Why, naturally. A hundred officers enrolled in the Red Cavalry squadrons and the Red Army's cavalry school. On the first of June they'll form up into several flying columns. Rapid strikes, with their own signal service. It's a huge city, there has to be cavalry.'

'Hang on . . .' Romanov exclaimed, remembering his conversation with Schwartz the day before. 'That Captain Mirkin? From the "Jewish Soldiers"?'

'Uh-huh. A good man. As Savvin says: "Mirkin might be a Jew, but he's a soldier."'

'But how can that be? I wanted to enrol my comrade, Warrant Officer Schwartz, in the Union, but my squad leader told me: "We don't take Jews!"'

'Mirkin is Mirkin. Even the Jew-baiter Scherer respects him. And Mirkin is our treasurer too. He manages all our finances. As Savvin says: "Mirkin might be a soldier, but he's a Jew."'

After swiftly reviewing his options, Romanov chose the most promising approach.

'I'd like to take a close look at each of them. Their characters and habits. So far I only know Merkurov. I think it will be enough to hold a solid briefing on operational security with him. But I would like to follow the others for a while and observe. Individual security measures are only effective if they conform to the habits and psychological characteristics of the subject. Let me have their addresses.'

'What do you want their addresses for?' Polkanov responded evasively. 'Come along with me and you can observe to your heart's content right now. And while we're at it I'll tell you about their psychological characteristics.'

'Where are we going?'

'The meeting isn't over yet. Savvin has twenty-three points on the agenda.'

'Can we do that?'

'The Security Sector can do anything. If it's careful about it,' Polkanov said with a wink. 'Come on, Alexei, let's go.'

They walked up out of the basement into a small, very spick-and-span room.

'My monastic cell,' said Polkanov. 'This is where I while away my eremitic days.'

He walked over to a wall, slid up a shutter of some kind and put one finger to his lips.

Romanov heard voices.

He could now see the familiar doctor's office through a square pane of glass.

Vasily whispered:

'From that side this is the mirror above the washbasin.'

'. . . Approximately what per cent of the total complement is that, General?' Savvin's clear, slightly hoarse voice enquired.

The chess players

'As you yourself understand, Victor Borisovich, under the present system of recruiting, it is not possible to determine the total complement of a division. For security reasons listings are not kept, and membership at the rank-and-file level is provisional: if a man has joined the Union, it doesn't mean that we can definitely rely on him,' said Divcom-1, General Zhbanov. 'In theory a division consists of about two thousand fighting men, not all of whom, however, should be regarded as "real soldiers". As I have already said, my provisional assessment indicates that we shall do well if a thousand men report at the assembly points on the first of June. You can see what percentage that is. Fifty at the most.'

'I have the same figures,' Merkurov put in.

Divcom-2, Scherer, simply nodded.

'But my men will all come, I'm sure of them,' Mirkin declared cheerfully. 'Cavalrymen can't be compared with foot soldiers.'

'It's just that you have fewer men, Lev Abramovich, and the line of communications is shorter: from you to the platoon commanders, and that's all,' Zhbanov remarked.

Polkanov seriously hindered Alexei's attempts to listen by commenting straight into his ear.

'Zhbanov's the easiest of all to deal with. He understands the requirements of security and doesn't break the rules . . .'

Savvin started speaking again and the head of the Security Sector respectfully fell silent.

'I can go farther than that, gentlemen. Fifty per cent will not show up on the first of June. Not even twenty-five per cent will show up. They're all flesh and blood, and they're all frightened. It's one thing to rise up into the attack out of the trenches, shoulder to shoulder, but every one of our men lives at home, many of them surrounded by their families. They are uncertain. And afraid. The same thing that happens to any revolution will happen to us . . . Don't pull a wry face, Colonel, we are all precisely that – revolutionaries – if the word revolution is understood in its original meaning: an overthrow of power. At the first stage it is always only the boldest and most dynamic individuals who put themselves forward. If they can hold their ground or, even better, achieve some degree of success, those of average boldness join them, and the others only join in after that. And when victory is already in sight everyone else, who never intended to revolt, rises up too. Therefore it will be perfectly satisfactory if on the first of the month every division can assemble at least ten per cent of its complement. Several hundred valiant men are enough to throw the Soviet regime in Moscow into total confusion and, with any luck, in the other key cities too. For this reason, gentlemen, a "plan of priorities" has been drawn up. If too few men have shown up, a division focuses its strike exclusively on target number one. If there are more men, two targets are attacked; if there are even more, three, and so on.'

He turned to Scherer.

'Let's take your case, Anton Alfredovich. Assuming you see that on the morning of the first of June you only have a hundred men at your disposal, how do you act?'

Divcom-2 replied confidently.

'I gather the men into a concentrated striking force and strike at target number one, which is . . .'

Polkanov stuck his oar in again:

'Scherer's a real disaster. He drives his bodyguards away. He says: "I'll take care of myself." And at the same time he's rash and unobservant.'

Alexei barely managed to make out through the whisper what was 'target number one' for Scherer's division – the Central Committee of the Bolshevik Party.

'. . . The first of June happens to be a Saturday, and on Saturdays they gather in their Sanhedrin, as if they were going to the synagogue to pray. We shall gain entry via the Borovitskaya Tower, where one of our men will be in the guard. In five minutes we'll be in place and we'll slaughter all the little Yids, along with all their Shabbos goys.'

'Colonel Scherer, if you wouldn't mind,' said Savvin, casting a glance at Mirkin.

The colonel was embarrassed.

'I beg your pardon, Lev Abramovich . . . I don't mean it like that. But you know yourself that their organisation is thick with Jews, piled one on top of another . . .'

'If your precious Father-Tsar had treated the Jews differently, they wouldn't have joined the revolution. Who knows, there might not even have been any revolution,' the dapper cavalry captain replied. 'Really and truly, Colonel, sometimes I listen to you and wonder whether I ought not to defect to the Reds.'

'Don't think that I am an anti-Semite,' said Scherer, still trying to make excuses. 'You know what high esteem I hold you in. And I do believe it is possible to find worthy representatives of your nation.'

Mirkin nodded ironically.

'You speak exactly like my acquaintance Izya Schiffer. "You can fling rags at me, but sometimes you do come across decent people even among the goys."'

Everyone except Scherer laughed, and Savvin said:

'On that note I propose that we conclude this profound discussion and get back to business. Provided, of course, that Colonel Schiffer – that is, Scherer – has no objections.'

The colonel put on such a long face that the laughter became loud guffawing. The imperturbable Savvin also chuckled, from which it was clear that his slip of the tongue had not been accidental. Eventually even Scherer started sniggering:

'Ah, to hell with all off you!'

Romanov caught himself smiling too. His old commander, Lieutenant Colonel Kozlovsky, had also given the impression of being a genuine Neanderthal and double-dyed anti-Semitic reactionary when he launched into discussing politics, but at the same time he was a splendid comrade and a very magnanimous man in general. Ah, where was he now? It was obvious enough *who* he was with. With *these* men, of course.

'All right, Anton Alfredovich,' said Savvin, continuing the serious conversation. 'Let us assume that you don't have a hundred men, but a hundred and fifty, or two hundred.'

'I separate out a second detachment for target number two. The Central Telegraph Office. According to the plan, the detachment advances . . .'

'Mirkin's a problem too,' Polkanov whispered. 'He doesn't argue or get obstinate, but when he wants to, he just breaks away from his security detail and disappears.'

He stopped talking and Savvin stood up at the desk.

'Gentlemen, I'm no great hand at making speeches. I'm not a man of words, but of action. Nonetheless, I would like to tell you this. All of us in the Union for the Defence of the Motherland are different, we have all the animals two by two. But we all have a common cause – to build the ark on which we shall save our world from the flood. And when we have saved it, that's when we shall argue about what the new Russia will be like – monarchist, republican, socialist, federative, or whatever else. Afterwards, when our ark sails to the shore.'

Mirkin mimed applause.

'Bravo, Victor Borisovich. A most apt political allegory. Thank you for not mentioning the Hill of Golgotha or the Garden of Gethsemane, I would have taken that as yet another attack on the Jews. But Noah's Ark is excellent. It is recognised by Christians and Jews alike.'

Everyone laughed again.

Jolly fellows, thought Romanov, feeling concerned. *So what is their plan for seizing the Central Telegraph Office? How can we expose the traitor in the Kremlin garrison? And what are the priority targets of the other divisions?*

'It is already eleven, gentlemen,' Savvin announced, looking at his old pocket watch. 'We have convened as indefatigably as the Provisional Government under the unforgettable Kerensky. We meet again on Friday.'

Everybody stood up.

'Lev Abramovich, please stay for a while. I would like your report on income and expenditure.'

Romanov would have been glad to listen to something about financial matters too, but Polkanov slid down the hatch cover.

'So now you have taken a look, what observations do you have?'

He doesn't completely trust me, thought Alexei.

'As for General Zhbanov, as you said, everything is fine. With Merkurov, it's enough to replace his bodyguard with someone more experienced and also have a serious talk with him. As for Scherer, he is jumpy, quick-tempered and vain. The best thing would be to attach a secret security detail to him. Since he's not observant, he won't notice it.'

'You're talking sense,' Polkanov agreed. 'I ought to have twigged that for myself. But what do we do about Mirkin? The main problem is that he doesn't complain, he agrees to everything and cracks jokes about it. But if he wants to, it's "hey presto" and he vanishes into thin air.'

'I'll think about Mirkin. He's not such a simple individual.'

'Uh-huh, let's try thinking about him together. We've got all the time in the world. I'll accommodate you here, just behind the wall, it's a good little room. You'll like it.'

'All right. I'll just go and get my things.'

'Ah, you don't need anything,' Polkanov declared amicably. 'I'll share my smalls and suchlike with you. From now on, Alyosha, you don't set foot outside of here. You'll be here in the outpatient clinic all the time. It will be more cheerful for me that way too. We'll talk football to our hearts' content.'

'What?'

'Well, what did you expect? That I'd let you go wandering around the city after what you've seen and heard?' Polkanov shook his head reproachfully. 'No, brother: when you listed off our weak points – Victor Borisovich, the General Staff, the unit commanders – there was one Achilles heel you forgot. Me. As head of the Security Sector, I know more about the organisation than anyone else. If I'm picked up by the Chekists, it's a disaster.

'That's why I never go out anywhere. I stay put in here, like a spider, weaving my web from my own snug little corner. And now you're exactly the same. You know too much. Until the first of June, consider that you and I are under house arrest.'

Alexei hadn't been prepared for this turn of events. How could he pass on all the information that he had gathered to Orlov? Climb out through the window during the night? He couldn't do that. If his absence was spotted, the game would be up! Damn!

'Never mind,' Polkanov consoled him. 'It's not exactly solitary confinement, is it? This is a big building, wander around wherever you like. And there are people calling in all the time too. People come in off the street to see Dr Zass, and our people come to see Dr Ananiev. That's me, by the way, Dr Ananiev. If you need treatment for the clap, I'm your man.'

'Thanks, I think I'd rather keep it for a while.'

They laughed.

'You'll get to know the lads from the Sector, they often drop in. And make friends with our Maria Lvovna, who sits in the reception hall. Sitting there as quiet as a speckled hen, a sweet little forget-me-not,' Polkanov said with an affectionate smile. 'You should have seen how the three of us – Savvin, Maria and me – blew up a general of gendarmes in 1907.'

He led Alexei into the next room, or rather a storage closet with a window so narrow that it would be impossible to squeeze out through, no matter how much Alexei might try.

'Not a luxury apartment, but at least it is safe. I'll go and get a mattress and a blanket, and you take a stroll around.'

The recommendation to make friends with Maria Lvovna was a good one. The woman sat there like Cerberus beside the way out, and there was no way to slip past her. It would be good to find the way to her heart.

He went to the reception hall. There were no visitors, but Mirkin was leaning down over the Sister of Mercy and telling her something in a jolly voice. So he had already made his report to the chairman.

'Ah, and here he is, D'Artagnan,' said the cavalry captain, turning round. 'I was just describing to Maria Lvovna your spectacular appearance in front of the General Staff. "The pendants have been purloined, Your Majesty!" We haven't been introduced. Lev Mirkin.'

First of all, following the rules of courtesy, Romanov introduced himself to the lady, even clicking his heels as he did so, but she responded with a severe, mistrustful look.

Well, to hell with the old frump. She could wait. Mirkin was of greater interest right now. If Alexei could just catch him with the Union's cash box . . .

'I know who you are, Captain. May I have a brief word?'

They went out into the corridor.

'I am Vasily Vasilievich's assistant now. He complains that you run away from your bodyguards.'

Mirkin put on a guilty expression.

'I won't do it again. I swear on Christ the Lord!'

'A fine promise from the lips of a Jew,' Alexei reproached him. 'When you have no "shadow", you're taking a great risk. You won't notice if anyone picks up your trail and tails you all the way home – and you have the money and, what is even worse, all the records and reports.'

'No.'

'What do you mean, "no"?'

'I don't have anything. No records and no reports. It's all in here.' Mirkin tapped himself on the forehead. 'That's why I was appointed treasurer. I have a mathematical memory. You see, I'm a chess player.'

'I studied in the physics and maths faculty too. And I also play chess.'

The cavalry captain livened up at that.

'Really? And can you play without a board?'

'Yes, I can.'

'Let's check that. Bagsy I'll be white,' said Lev Abramovich, rubbing his hands together. 'Right then, let's say we start with the English opening, shall we? I go C4.'

This isn't a conspiracy, it's a sports club, thought Romanov, trying to work out how he could extract Mirkin's home address from him.

'All right. C5.'

'I go G3.'

'Right, G6.'

Neither of them named the pieces – the piece in question is quite clear to a good player in any case.

'Well, naturally, G2. Where did you see action?'

'I reply G7. If we only count the front line, in 1914 I was in East Prussia. Wounded in the arm.'

'And I got a lance stuck in my thigh there.'

'In 1916 I was in the Brusilov Offensive.'

'I picked up a piece of shrapnel there.'

'Last summer I was at Smarhon.'

'No, at that time I was in hospital. Smarhon – is that where the women's battalion went into the attack? That's something that should be remembered for ever.'

Alexei frowned for an instant; he could picture so clearly the event that had split his life into two parts.

'. . . But I would prefer to forget it.'

Mirkin replied in a quiet voice.

'No. We won't forget anything. And then perhaps the bad things will never be repeated . . . I'll go C3.'

Romanov had already taken himself in hand. He chuckled.

'Generally speaking, I prefer to play on a real board. When you take a queen, it's like slipping your arm round a young lady's waist. And taking a rook is like hugging a woman round the thighs.'

The cavalry captain snorted.

'You paint a seductive picture. I can tell that chess isn't your only passion. Nor mine, either. You know what, Romanov. Come round to my place sometime. We'll play on a board. I live not far away, on Sivtsev Vrazhek Lane.'

'Whereabouts on Sivtsev?' Alexei asked absent-mindedly. He didn't have a clue where Sivtsev Vrazhek Lane was. 'To A4, I think.'

'Tut-tut-tut. Are you violating the canon? You want me to open up, so that you can play a dirty trick on me?'

'I swear on the Torah and the Talmud that my intentions are honourable.'

Mirkin laughed.

'I like you, D'Artagnan. I have the feeling that we'll be friends. Come round to my place today. After ten. Sivtsev Vrazhek Lane, house number eight, the first floor. It's a pity you're not a cavalry-man. If you can stay in the saddle, why don't you join my squadron, instead of rusting away in the Security Sector? We'll have a dashing time of it.'

I like you too, thought Romanov, *but what was the reply that D'Art-agnan gave to Cardinal Richelieu? 'Through some fatal eventuality, all of my enemies are here, and all of my friends are there, so that I should be poorly received here, and poorly regarded there.'* Alexei felt absolutely no satisfaction in having hooked Mirkin. It's easy to obtain information when a man trusts you.

These useless thoughts were replaced by a different, more useful one. Get him to open up and then play a dirty trick? Well, now . . .

'I beg your pardon, Lev Abramovich, but I have just remembered an urgent piece of business. We'll finish the game some time later.'

And he dashed back to Polkanov at the double.

He flew into the room without knocking and stopped. Savvin was there with Polkanov.

'I beg your pardon . . .'

'I am just leaving.'

The head of the conspiracy shook Polkanov's hand, then stopped in front of Alexei and looked into his eyes for a long time.

Try X-raying men with weak nerves, Romanov chuckled to himself, pretending to be embarrassed. An interesting idea occurred to him:

Why not bump off these two right now? That would put a quick end to the conspiracy!

No, not an end. The divisional commanders very likely associate with each other outside of General Staff gatherings. They would hold a meeting even without Savvin and Polkanov.

'Well, we're agreed,' said Savvin, concluding some conversation or other and taking leave of his deputy.

'Why did you come bursting in as if the house was on fire?' Polkanov asked. 'Important business?'

'I've realised what the main problem is with the system of security.'

'What is it?'

'It's like in football. If all you do is defend your own goalposts, you can't expect to win. You have to attack and let the opposing team do the defending.'

Polkanov gazed expectantly at his assistant.

'Let's hear it without the football. Plain and simple.'

Alexei started explaining. At first the other man listened doubtfully, then with narrowed eyes, very attentively, and finally he became excited too and started interrupting with questions.

Having received all the answers, he said:

'It's brazen, but tempting. And you know what I value most of all, Alexei? You didn't try to flaunt your plumage in front of Savvin but waited until we were left alone. That's the right way, the team way.'

Savvin is brighter than you are, he wouldn't have swallowed the bait, Romanov replied in his own mind. *But you swallow it, because you imagine that you're a wolf, when you're really only a guard dog.*

Polkanov hesitated for a minute or two and then asked with a pensive smile, 'Shall we really do it, for old times' sake?. . .'

The jokers

'. . . Stretch my legs a bit, play a game of cops and robbers? I've got stale, sitting in the office.' Orlov smiled in exactly the same way as Polkanov – with nostalgia. 'Of course, the part you're offering me is a rotten one. I'm used to being on the other side of the gun sight.'

'What gun sight?' Kriukov asked. He had gone out to pass on

instructions and missed the most interesting part.

'Alyosha will tell you about the gun sight. Report first, he's feeling anxious.'

'Well then, it's like this . . .' Kriukov started listing off the facts for Alexei. 'I did everything as you ordered. Schwartz will take up position to observe Mirkin's apartment. I gave him Vorobyov as a partner, he's a meticulous lad, he won't mess things up. Kulik and Antoshkin will keep watch on Merkurov's apartment. I gave them your piece of paper and ordered them to learn it off by heart. The windows, times of departure and arrival, not to tail him when he goes out, and all the rest of it.'

'I trust Schwartz, and I'll take a look at the others,' said Romanov. 'Well then, the picture we have is as follows – I'm summing up especially for you, Timofei. Firstly: we can't pick up Savvin. Secondly, we won't be able to take the command staff with a single strike either.'

'But wasn't Polkanov lying to you when he said they had the place dynamited?'

'No, he wasn't. Try to storm the outpatients' clinic, and all you'll get is a heap of rubble.'

'Ah, who gives a shit? So okay!'

'Thanks, Timofei, for not giving a shit about me either,' Alexei said with a bow. 'Of course, I'm willing to be blown up together with the enemies of the revolution, but you Chekists are the only ones who would be blown up, and the command staff would escape unharmed. There's some kind of underground passage in the basement. Polkanov won't tell me exactly where.'

'I didn't hear about any underground passage,' said Kriukov, making excuses. 'I'd already gone out when you mentioned it.'

Orlov hissed at him.

'Well then, don't interrupt. Carry on, Alyosha.'

'So what do we have? We can't hack off the head of the conspiracy. But we can lop off all four of the wolf's feet.'

'Take out the three divisional commanders and Mirkin,' Orlov explained for his assistant. 'Without them communication between Savvin and the organisation will be broken off.'

Kriukov nodded.

'That's clear enough. We know where two "feet" – Merkurov and

Mirkin – are. But we don't have the addresses of Scherer and Zhbanov. Even with just two divisions, Savvin will create such mayhem in Moscow, there's no knowing how it will end. All the officers and the Junkers, and the entire anti-Soviet element, will come crawling out of every nook and cranny. Romanov, can you really not drag the other addresses out of Polkanov?'

'He's a cunning customer, cautious. He tells me some things, but not others. He doesn't trust me overmuch. So I had this idea . . .'

Orlov picked up the thread.

'The idea of "Operation Trust", the point being that Polkanov comes to trust our Alyosha like his own brother. And that, dear Comrade Kriukov, leads us back to the aforementioned gun sight.'

'Speak plainly, eh?' said Kriukov, shifting his glance from one of them to the other. 'Just what have you thought up?'

'I tell Polkanov that the best form of defence is attack. "What's the most important thing for us right now?" I ask him. "To make sure that the Cheka doesn't expose us at the very last moment. And the Cheka is first and foremost one member of that vile collegium of theirs – Orlov, who's in charge of all their surveillance work. A terribly dangerous bastard – cunning and energetic, with a keen nose."'

'Hey, hey, ease off a bit,' said Orlov, shaking his fist at him.

Kriukov grinned.

'Nah. The way Romanov describes you is right. Well?'

'Polkanov says: "I've heard about Orlov. A serious gentleman."'

'There, you see,' said Orlov, raising his finger. 'People respect me.'

'You wait with your little jokes,' said Kriukov, jostling him with his elbow. 'Then what?'

'I say: "We have to liquidate this Orlov. Without him the Cheka will start scurrying about like a headless chicken. We'll gain time – before Dzerzhinsky can find a competent replacement for Orlov, the first of June will be here."'

'Romanov wants to get me in his sights, understand?' Orlov said with a devil-may-care smile. 'And bump off his senior comrade in person, with his own hand. And why not? I like the idea.'

Kriukov blinked.

'There's something I don't understand here . . . How's that again – bump you off?'

'That's what Polkanov asks me too: How? I told him: I'll arrange that for myself. It's my profession. So I sketched out the details for him. He pondered it for a while, then pondered some more, and agreed. And that's why I've been let out of the clinic: to lay the ground for a terrorist attack against a Cheka sleuth.'

'But what about Savvin?' Orlov asked in a low voice. 'Has he approved this?'

'Polkanov didn't inform him. He said: "Savvin and Orlov used to be together, supposing Savvin turns sentimental? I decide," he says, "on my own authority."'

'Mmm, yes, a tricky business, life.' Orlov sighed. 'If anyone had told me before the revolution that Victor Savvin and I would be hunting each other . . . After all, the two of us are peas from the same pod, almost twins. But our roads have parted. And if Savvin tries to get in my way, so much the worse for Savvin. A pity, but it can't be helped.'

And he sighed again. Alexei understood him very well. The same old problem of former friends, now on opposite sides.

'Just don't go all sentimental on us,' Kriukov said. 'But just how, Romanov, do you intend to kill Comrade Orlov? That's what I don't understand here.'

'In the street, in full public view. I'll shoot him from a window or maybe an attic. In counter-intelligence we once invented this special little sphere of fine gum elastic for fake shooting tricks. It was filled with red dye. Bang! The man grabs at his chest and blood oozes out through his fingers. *Pravda* writes: "Comrade Orlov, member of the collegium of the Cheka, falls heroically in the fatal conflict". And they print a beautiful portrait in a black frame. After that I'll enjoy the absolute trust of the Union for the Defence of the Motherland.'

'Very cunning, very neat,' Kriukov said approvingly. 'Well done, Romanov.'

Orlov got up, walked over to the window and pretended to be taking aim with a rifle.

'Cunning and neat, all right, but still not neat enough. In the first place, if I get bumped off, then I have to hide away, assume clandestine status, don't I? I can't do that, I'm up to my eyes in work. And in the second place, Alyosha, you're a professional, of course, but I know a thing or two about these matters as well. I have sometimes shot geese in an ambush too. What are you going to shoot me with? A blank cartridge?'

'Well, not a live one.'

'Then let me tell you this. I personally can always distinguish the sound of a live shot from a blank one. Your Polkanov is no fool, he's bound to send someone to watch the boss of the Cheka get killed. And as likely as not, that someone will be experienced. If he realises you fired a blank, instead of "Operation Trust", we'll have "Operation Fiasco".'

Alexei frowned. Orlov was right.

'Are you suggesting I fire a live round and miss?'

'That's risky too. The bullet will ricochet off the surface of the road or something else and strike a spark, and that could be noticed. No, Alyosha. We need you to shoot me for real. Only not to kill me, just wound me. That will be enough to inspire trust, and I won't have to go underground afterwards.'

'Wound you? You mean actually wound you?' Romanov asked incredulously.

'Well, yes. Just slightly. How good a shot are you?'

'I'm a decent shot, and Polkanov has promised to let me have a Mauser with an optical sight. With a support and a butt stock, I can easily shoot a hole in a kopeck at fifty metres, but . . . Are you sure?'

'Timofei, is your Mauser's sight well adjusted? Let him have it.'

'Now what have you thought up?' Kriukov asked, taking his large pistol out of its wooden holster.

'Come here,' said Orlov, beckoning Alexei over to the window. 'Look, there's our office manager, Comrade Yagoda, on his way back from the canteen.'

Down below in the courtyard a dapperly dressed man was walking along with a bowl of hot soup, holding it out in front of him.

'Now we'll check what sort of William Tell you are. Yagoda shouldn't eat that *shchi*. It's tasteless muck, I've tried it.'

Kriukov chuckled and nudged Alexei on the shoulder.

'Go on, Romanov. Look, he's wearing a general's tunic.'

Weighing the Mauser in his hand, Alexei declared sadly:

'Serious people, the backbone of the state. Hooligans!'

He waited until the man walking by was sideways-on to them before raising his hand with a dashing flourish. And then, as if he hadn't even taken aim (he had, of course, only very quickly), he fired.

The bullet punched through the bowl and it came alive, jumping out of the hands of the victim of this experiment, and the office manager let out a howl and almost jumped out of his skin.

He turned towards Orlov and Kriukov, who were chortling in the window (Alexei had judiciously hidden behind the curtain).

Comrade Yagoda's tunic was covered in steaming cabbage.

'You're an idiot, Orlov, and your jokes are idiotic! I'll write a report to Dzerzhinsky! You've ruined my tunic! And these boots are kidskin!'

'It wasn't me, it was Kriukov,' Orlov declared, pointing his finger. 'He didn't mean to. He was just cleaning his Mauser.'

He backed away from the window, laughing quietly.

'And by the way, about those kidskin boots. Next week we'll receive ten pairs as rewards for colleagues who have especially distinguished themselves. If you just put a neat little hole in me, Alyosha – one pair is yours. But if you shoot cack-handed and kill me, you can forget it . . . Stop grunting like a pig, Kriukov. He's reporting you in writing to the chairman of the Cheka, and you just stand there, guffawing.'

'Operation Trust'

The deputy head of the Security Sector and the Cheka special agent spent several days preparing for the operation, each in his own way. In the former capacity, Staff Captain Romanov devoted hours to studying the routine behaviour and usual routes of his 'target' and diligently getting his hand in using a Mauser C-96 with a handmade, but superlatively crafted, optical sight. Polkanov excused his assistant from all other duties.

The Chekist agent Romanov didn't waste any time either. He personally devised for Orlov both a routine and a route appropriatefortheterroristattack,andthengroomedhis'target'forthe performance.

At number 11, Bolshaya Lubyanka Street, work was approaching its end on refurbishing the former building of the Anchor Insurance Company as the headquarters of the Cheka. The town house on Po-varskaya Street had become too cramped for the rapidly expanding institution; it didn't have enough offices and there wasn't enough space to set up a prison for important suspects. Large numbers of such individuals were expected in the near future, and for that reason a three-storey building with an enclosed courtyard, a large number of convenient rooms and an extensive basement had been selected. At this moment in time they were breaking down old par-titions and putting in new ones, shipping in furniture, building in safes, replacing doors and so forth, and all the work was under the personal supervision of collegium member Comrade Orlov. Every day, at precisely ten o'clock, like clockwork, he arrived at the Luby-anka and walked into the entrance hall.

It was an ideal spot. Directly opposite it was an empty building with an attic that had a dormer window. The distance for a direct shot was only twenty-five metres – too close to miss, even without an optical sight.

They agreed that Orlov would get out of his car and hold still for a couple of seconds, leaning against the car door, supposedly giving instructions to the driver. Alexei intended to shoot at his collar, in order to scratch his neck. A wound like that looked serious and there was a lot of blood, but it would heal up quickly. It required an exqui-sitely precise shot, of course, but Alexei was sure that he wouldn't miss. He filled the rounds himself by hand, using a chemical balance, so that the powder charges were identical to within a milligram. He trained at exactly the same distance, and soon he could notch the edge of the head of a nail hammered into the wall with his bullet.

When everything had been got ready and all the calculations made, he reported to Polkanov that it was time. Polkanov insisted that he arrange a rehearsal.

In the morning the two of them went up into the attic and watched as the Packard rolled up to the future headquarters of the

Cheka and Orlov climbed out energetically, followed by the awkward Kriukov.

'I fire and run that way,' said Romanov, pointing to the roof of the adjacent building. 'I climb down the back stairs, then make my way through the courtyards and side streets to Kuznetsky Most Street, where you're waiting in a cab.'

Polkanov scrutinised everything very thoroughly.

'It's a workable plan, but there's one bad point. The Chekists will come running to the windows at the sound of a shot. They'll see a man running across the roof opposite and open fire. There's nowhere to take cover here.'

'My trail will be cold long before they can figure out which way to look.'

'Okay, tomorrow we'll snip off a Chekist and score a goal against the Soviets.' Polkanov smiled sweetly. 'It will be a beautiful operation. As good as when we bumped off that tsarist minister Plehve. They'll write about it in all the textbooks.'

In the morning three of them drove out: Polkanov's man in front, posing as a cabby, with Alexei and Polkanov behind. They stopped on Kuznetsky Most Street, in front of the smashed, gaping windows of the former 'Muir and Mirrielees' branch. 'Wait for us here, Kolya,' said Polkanov. 'As soon as we dart out of that gateway over there, start moving. We'll jump in as you drive by.'

He picked up something long, wrapped in a piece of cloth, off the floor and climbed down onto the pavement.

'Where are you going?' asked Romanov. 'What's that you've got there?'

Polkanov ducked into an archway without saying anything and parted the cloth slightly to reveal a glint of black metal.

'One rod is good, but two is better. A beast like this has to be put away for certain.'

Alexei's throat constricted in panic. Everything was falling apart. He had to pull out of the operation. But how?

'That's not what we agreed. What the hell do I need you for? You'll only get in the way!'

Polkanov looked at him with a sly smile.

'I started feeling a bit jealous somehow, Alexei. I want to get into the textbooks too. Come on now, don't be stingy. We'll pass the ball to and fro.'

What can I do? What can I do? What can I do?

Stun him with a blow to the bridge of the nose and nab him? That's easy enough, but then what? Polkanov's a tough customer, he won't give me the other addresses. I can't torture him, can I? Seize the clinic? There's no one there but Maria Lvovna, and she's as tough as nails too. Well, we could arrest Merkurov and Mirkin. But we can't be certain they stay at home during the day, and by evening they'll already know Polkanov has been arrested.

'Why are you creeping along like a snail?' asked Polkanov, looking round. 'Nerves playing up?'

'There's no need to hurry. I've got everything calculated down to the last second.'

Still not having decided anything, he followed Polkanov up the stairs.

In the attic Polkanov took out a compact Nagant carbine, an ideal weapon for shooting from a short distance.

'Ah, Alyosha, you should have seen how elegantly I took out an entire guard detail, four riders, in the operation in 1912. Like little partridges.'

He took off his jacket and arranged it neatly on the windowsill. Then he lowered his braces, rolled up his sleeves and pressed his cheek against the carbine, aiming at the opposite wall.

'Let's stand close, like a dancing couple. We'll lash the ball into the goal at the count of three. Why have you frozen up like that? It's five minutes to ten already.'

Romanov took up position beside him. He knew now what he was going to do, and he didn't like it one little bit.

The Packard appeared.

'Exactly ten o'clock,' Polkanov whispered, shifting his gun barrel. 'The politeness of kings. Ready? I'm counting.'

The car stopped.

'One . . .'

Orlov climbed out and leaned against the door. Kriukov clambered out of the front seat.

'Two . . .'

Alexei fired. Orlov collapsed as if his legs had been scythed from under him.

'What have you done?' Polkanov asked, swinging round in fury. 'I said at the count of three!'

'I don't want to share the glory,' Romanov said with a crooked grin.

'You idiot, you only wounded him!' Polkanov hissed, looking down, and set his eye to the sight again.

Orlov was trying to get up, while Kriukov fussed over him, glancing round at the attic.

He must have spotted the gun barrel, because he collapsed directly onto his boss, shielding him with his own body. A shot rang out at the same moment and Alexei saw it send tatters flying from Kriukov's jacket, in the middle of his back.

'They've spotted us! Let's run for it!'

He grabbed Polkanov by the elbow and dragged him away from the window.

In the building opposite, men were already shouting:

'In the attic! In the attic!'

'Hang on.'

Polkanov calmly adjusted his braces and put his jacket on.

They ran out onto the roof.

Romanov looked back.

Orlov was stirring feebly under the motionless Kriukov.

This was bad, very bad.

They started firing from the windows opposite. One bullet clattered ominously against the tin plate of the roof, and then another.

'Move your feet!' exclaimed Polkanov, looking round.

Alexei raised his Mauser and shot the running man in the back, just above the shoulder blade. Polkanov gasped and fell.

'Did you catch a bullet?' asked Romanov, leaning down over him.

'I ran out of luck . . .'

The air hummed and crackled as the firing from the windows grew more intense.

'Come on, get up! They'll kill us!'

'I can't . . . You run for it . . . Report back . . . I'm finished . . .'

Alexei grabbed the heavy body under the arms and dragged it onto a slope of the roof where the bullets couldn't reach them.

'You'll never drag me all the way,' Polkanov mumbled. 'You'll only get hit yourself . . . Run for it!'

'Shut up! I don't abandon my own.'

They went down the back stairs with their arms round each other. Polkanov bit his lip against the pain, but he didn't cry out.

They stumbled across the courtyard on four unsteady legs.

'. . . I didn't want to trust you . . . I thought there was something . . . Forgive me, Alexei . . .' Polkanov babbled, constantly trying to collapse onto his side.

'God will forgive you. Get a move on, damn it! There's not far to go now!'

Sloppy sentimentalities

The wounded man was operated on right there in the outpatient clinic by Dr Zass, a quiet man who tried with all his might to pretend that he had no idea what his neighbours did. Even now Zass didn't ask how it was that 'Dr Ananiev' had managed to acquire a hole in his back in broad daylight and why they hadn't taken him to a genuine hospital.

'I have removed the bullet and treated the entrance wound, but the apex of the lung has been punctured. He needs to be transferred to an inpatient facility,' the doctor told Savvin and Romanov, without looking into their eyes.

'Oh, these intelligentsia types,' said the most dangerous man in Russia, shaking his head as he watched the doctor walk away. 'An absurd species. Under the tsar they helped the revolutionaries but pretended not to have the faintest idea about the bombs and the blood. Now they help the counter-revolutionaries, but still pretend to be fluffy little dandelions. So no one trusts the intelligentsia – neither the old regime nor the new one. And if we win, we won't love them either. For it is said: "I shall eject you from My mouth, since you are neither cold nor hot."'

'What shall we do with Polkanov?' asked Romanov, looking at

the waxen face with closed eyes. 'Perhaps we should send him to hospital, as Zass says? He could have been shot by robbers.'

And in the hospital the Cheka will pick him up, he thought. But Savvin said:

'Don't worry about that. Like you, I don't abandon my comrades-in-arms. Polkanov and I have eaten more than one bushel of salt together. We'll send him to a place where the care will be good and no sleuth will ever sniff him out. Ah, what a pity, to be left without a deputy like him at precisely the most fraught time. It's like having my right arm cut off.'

'I'm to blame. It was my idea,' Alexei said dejectedly.

'A good idea. And it's a good thing that Orlov wasn't killed, but only wounded. We'll put him on trial. We'll condemn him to death, and then pardon him, for former services. I wonder if he would pardon me for former services?' Savvin asked himself thoughtfully. 'That's not important. The important thing, Staff Captain, is that the Security Sector is all yours now. Polkanov vouched for you before the anaesthetic. I'll present you to the command staff tomorrow, then you can take the reins and familiarise yourself with all our secrets. But be quick about it, we can't waste any time getting you into harness.'

Soon Romanov knew everything about the Union for the Defence of the Motherland.

It had an approximate membership of five thousand men in Moscow alone. Most of them were simply waiting for the order to show up at the assembly point at the appointed hour, where they would be given their weapons and combat assignments. There were branches of the Union in Kazan, Yaroslavl, Rybinsk, Ryazan, Chelyabinsk, Kaluga, Murom and Tula (Alexei gave the names and addresses of the leaders to be passed on to the local Chekists).

Now he also knew the addresses of all the divisional commanders, and from them he ascertained – supposedly in order to strengthen security – the locations of all nine brigade commanders and twenty-seven regimental commanders. The only thing that remained a secret was where Savvin himself hid, but for the operational plan that the Cheka was preparing that no longer had any importance.

Alexei decided that he wouldn't live in the outpatient clinic – in an unguarded apartment he would be less restricted in his movements – and he went back to Trubnikovsky Lane on the very first evening. He happened to arrive just in time for dinner.

Venya Kopeishchikov dashed to shake his hand and invited him to the table, but Zinaida Gruzintseva was not delighted by her wandering lodger's unexpected appearance. She sat there without speaking, looking down at the tablecloth.

However, there were no awkward pauses. The Junker wagged his tongue incessantly, sharing news of the conspiratorial life.

'It's such a pity that I have to go away,' he kept repeating. 'Right now, of all times. But a mission is a mission.' And he subsided into suggestive silence for a second or two.

Eventually, of course, he couldn't help himself and, after first lowering his voice, announced with pride that he was involved in a highly responsible undertaking: transferring weapons to a secret regimental depot.

Alexei knew the locations of all the arms depots, and so he advised the boy to keep mum. Venya flushed, said goodnight in a huff and left the room.

The two of them were left alone, in an oppressive silence.

'I can see that you find my return disagreeable,' Romanov said with a sigh. 'You haven't said a single word all evening and you haven't even looked at me once. Spare yourself the trouble, Zinaida Andreevna, I understand everything. I'll collect my things and leave straight away. I shan't bother you again.'

He got up.

'Sit down,' said Gruzintseva, raising her eyes. They were glinting brightly. 'You see nothing and you understand nothing. All this time I have had only one thought: he won't come back again. And I felt as if my life was over . . . I realise that I don't know you at all. I have invented you for myself. But one thing I can tell for certain. I can see it. You are exactly the same kind of wounded bird as I am. You are lonely, just as I am. And you want to be cured of that cruel illness as badly as I do. Please don't interrupt me,' she told him. 'I am afraid in any case that I shall not finish saying what I have to say . . . All the rules of propriety have been abrogated now. Terrible times have arrived. Death is on the rampage everywhere. Everything could come to an end at any moment. And so every day, every hour, is especially precious. Love has so little chance against death . . .'

She got up.

'Please. Don't say a word. Put your arms around me. Simply embrace me – and that is all. Only slowly. Or else my heart will break . . .'

She closed her eyes and held out her arms expectantly.

Alexei also got up abruptly – his chair flew back with a screech.

'Your feeling was correct, Zinaida Andreevna. Almost correct . . . I am a wounded bird too. I also suffer from loneliness. But you were wrong about one thing. I do not wish to be cured. It is incurable. Forgive me, please forgive me . . .'

He turned away quickly, in order not to see her contorted face, and walked out, clattering his heels. He hastily flung his things into his travelling bag. Outside the door, already on the stairs, he clutched at the left side of his chest. His heart was cramped so tight that he couldn't breathe.

'Never mind,' Romanov said out loud. 'I'll stay at the clinic for a while. In fact it's better that way.'

The day and the time had already been set – the thirty-first of May, nine in the morning. That was when the final meeting before the revolt would take place. Romanov had thought of a way to solve the problem of the dynamite and the underground passage. No one would escape arrest, including Savvin himself.

But even so something was amiss. Romanov's beloved boss Kozlovsky had once taught the young, green Alyosha that the success of any large counter-intelligence operation required the correct psychological condition, which consisted of two elements: intellectual excitation and emotional calm. As far as Romanov's intellect was concerned, the excitation was about as extreme as it could be – because of it Romanov didn't sleep a single minute on the night of the thirtieth of May. But the situation was not nearly so good as far as psychological calm was concerned. And as the appointed hour drew nearer the inner discomposure become ever more acute.

At dawn Alexei stopped tossing and turning on his bed and set about solving this problem.

He failed to creep unnoticed through the reception hall, where Maria Lvovna was sleeping as lightly as a guard dog. The damned woman immediately opened one eye and stuck her hand under her pillow, but she calmed down when she saw that it was Romanov. If one of her bosses was going somewhere at the crack of dawn, he must have a good reason for it.

Romanov walked through the empty coolness of sleeping Moscow as far as Trubnikovsky Lane and started throwing stones at the window of Venya's room. After the sixth hit, a tousled head appeared behind the pane of glass.

Alexei pressed a finger to his lips and beckoned: come here and don't wake your sister.

'Disaster, Junker,' he said morosely when the boy came down. 'The conspiracy has been exposed. Today there will be wholesale arrests. Leave this place immediately and take your sister with you. It doesn't matter where, just as far away from Moscow as possible. Here is some money, and here are your documents.'

Polkanov had a hoard of forms and false seals at the clinic – for every possible Soviet institution and every possible situation.

Of course, the young lad started showering him with questions, but Romanov cut him short.

'There's no time. I still have to warn the others. Take care of your sister. And that's all. You're a soldier, and that's an order. Carry it out!'

The Cheka had learned from Alexei himself the entire chain of command from divisional commander Merkurov down to Zotov's squad, in which Venya was registered. They would have taken him, and Zinaida too.

But now they wouldn't be taken.

He felt a bit better. But there was one more piece of sentimentality left.

He felt no regret about the members of the counter-revolutionary command staff, except for one. In recent days Alexei had paid two visits to Cavalry Captain Mirkin at his home, hoping to worm the sources of financing out of him in conversation. He hadn't succeeded. But he had developed a liking for Mirkin. They had played chess, chatted about all sorts of things and laughed a lot. It was unfortunate that Mirkin was a dedicated enemy of Bolshevism, but he was a truly fine, rare individual. Alexei did not want to condemn him to certain death.

'We have received intelligence information that the Chekists will make a surprise attack during today's meeting. First several agents pretending to be ordinary patients will take seats in the reception hall to see Dr Zass. And then the main forces will arrive. I have only just learned about this from a reliable man. I won't go back to the clinic, it's too risky, so I'm warning the members of the command at their home addresses. As soon as I find a new place for staff headquarters, I'll let you know. Here is your new address. It is known only to me. Wait for a signal. And now I beg your pardon, but I still have to go and see Scherer and Zhbanov.'

'What about Savvin?' Mirkin shouted after him. 'And Zass?'

'Zass doesn't know any secrets, and Savvin has been informed, of course. An emergency channel of communication was provided for an eventuality such as this. Don't waste time, get away from here!'

Outside in the street, Alexei stopped pretending to be in a hurry and allowed himself to light up a *papyrosa*.

Well, now his emotional state was simply ideal.

He even managed to call back in to Povarskaya Street, where preparations were proceeding apace.

The charm of the operation lay in the fact that it did not require many men. A few physically strong fellows and a firing squad of armed men, who had no idea why they had been assembled beside trucks so early in the morning.

The arrest group was commanded by Schwartz, who was nervous and pale-faced at his responsibility.

'Don't get jittery, Osip,' Alexei told him. 'Everything will go off like clockwork. Do you want to go over the plan one more time?'

'Yes, let's.'

'At half past seven the members of the command staff will assemble in the clinic. Savvin will arrive last, as usual. I shall be there from eight o'clock. As soon as I know that everyone's there, I'll phone here and say what we agreed: "Bogdan Ivanovich, send us some syringes". Maria Lvovna won't suspect anything, because Bogdan Ivanovich is a clerk at the Red Army stores, who steals weapons for the conspiracy . . .'

'There's no need for all this detail. Why are you treating me like an idiot?'

Schwartz smiled slightly, which was already good.

'After that it's simple. You send the armed squad to the clinic, and then shoot round to Butikovsky Lane with the group. The trucks make a lot of noise as they approach the clinic. Did you tell them to sound their horns?'

'I repeated it three times.'

'Good. They mustn't take the bodyguards in the square by surprise or else they'll take fright and start shooting. We don't want that. Let them go running into the building to warn everyone. Following the plan of emergency evacuation, everyone will go down into the basement and enter the underground passage one by one. I'll stay behind to light the detonation fuse – supposedly. Well, you know where they'll emerge from the passage. You'll receive them graciously there, at Butikovsky Lane, also one by one.'

Alexei himself was highly pleased by these operational dispositions. It wasn't an operation, but an artistic masterpiece. Now *this* was certain to end up in the textbooks.

'Romanov, you're a genius,' said Schwartz, who had finally calmed down. 'Perhaps you're a Jew, at least on your mother's side?'

'I'm a Jew from the side of life,' Romanov replied. 'All right, I have to run. It's seven twenty-five already.'

The first thing that struck him as strange, but didn't alarm him yet, was that there weren't any bodyguards in the little square in front of the clinic. Not a single one. Were the members of the command staff late?

Then Alexei saw Zass hurrying down the steps with a leather bag in each hand.

'Where are you going, Doctor? What about your patients?'

Zass stared at Romanov in amazement.

'I'm sorry, but I don't understand anything about your riddles . . .

A quarter of an hour ago Mr Mirkin came running up, in a very agitated state. First he shouted: "Maria Lvovna, Doctor, I've come for you! I realised that Romanov hadn't warned you! Leave immediately!" Maria Lvovna asked him: "What do you mean, leave? Why leave? Everybody has only just arrived." And then everybody started running about and shouting: "The Chekists, the Chekists will be here soon." And in less than a minute, I was left all on my own. Nobody explained a thing to me! I collected together the bare essentials, here they are . . . perhaps at least you will tell me what to do?'

Alexei stood there, absolutely stunned.

You wanted emotional calm, you sloppy sentimentalist. Shooting's too good for you . . .

He pushed the doctor aside and darted into the clinic, to the phone.

Zass paused for a moment and ran off in the opposite direction.

'Don't get dejected, Alyosha. The job can't be graded "excellent" or even "good". The best mark it can be given is "satisfactory plus", but the exam has been passed anyway. The important thing is that there won't be any revolt.'

Orlov was still in hospital, but as of today he had taken the management of business back into his own hands. He had been provided with a telephone in his ward and people were bringing him reports and information. A list of people who had been arrested was lying on the locker beside his bed, weighted down by an ashtray with a heap of cigarette ends.

'We let Savvin and the members of the command staff get away, of course. But almost all of the brigade commanders and most of the regimental commanders have been arrested, and we're also seizing the arms depots, one by one.'

There was a knock and a liaison officer walked in, holding out a piece of paper. Orlov turned awkwardly, took it and started reading.

'Good news. We raided their cavalry detachment's arms depot and our "Jewish soldier" Mirkin was there.'

'Was he taken?' Romanov asked with a sombre shudder.

'As a cold corpse. He pulled out a pistol, so the lads cut him down. A pity. They haven't learned how to take anyone alive yet. Now we'll never know who was supplying the Union with money.'

He peered intently at Alexei.

'Hey, why so long-faced? You should be proud. What a job you've pulled off! You smashed a conspiracy against the republic. And with almost no losses on our side. We only lost one man, and that wasn't today, but earlier on. Timofei Kriukov. May his memory live for ever. What a fine comrade he was!'

Orlov's face turned sad. But the member of the collegium didn't surrender to mourning for long – he wasn't that kind of man. The gaze directed at Romanov began beaming with its usual mischievous glow.

'And another victim of the Cheka's heroic operation is my splintered shin. You turned out to be a lousy shot, Alyosha, after all your boasting.'

'I explained that to you! I had to wing you so that you would fall. Otherwise Polkanov would have downed you permanently. I had no other option!'

'I don't know anything about that. But you won't get any kidskin boots as a reward. You haven't earned anything better than a pair of tarpaulin ones. And I can't put on any kind of boot.' Orlov pointed to his leg, suspended in mid-air.

Alexei was in no mood for joking. He plucked up his courage and said:

'You know, it was me who wrecked the operation . . .'

And he explained about Mirkin, concluding his confession as follows:

'Knowing him, I ought to have realised that he would go dashing to the clinic to save Zass. If not for my sloppy sentimentality, everything would have turned out differently. And now these contras that we didn't finish off will be scattered in all directions, like dragons' teeth. And the conflagration will break out in a hundred different places . . . I ought to be court-martialled.'

Orlov peered at Alexei from under his knitted brows.

'Eh,' he said with a sigh, 'then I should be court-martialled too. You know, I can't forgive myself either, for letting the anarchists get away in April. Now Aron Liberty is fouling things up for us in the Ukraine, and we'll see a lot more trouble from him. And the others too . . . The hardest thing of all is liquidating those who were your friends only just yesterday. We have to keep studying the revolutionary Red Truth, studying it over and over again. And it's harsh. Your friend is anyone who's a friend of the revolution, and anyone who is its enemy is your enemy too. We have to learn to be ruthless, without that there won't be any victory. That's why the Red Truth is red, brother, because it's watered with blood.'

THE GREEN TRUTH

Mona's enigmatic smile

'All that is not mourning is celebration. All that is not pain is joy.'
Mona had lived in the world with this motto to the respectable age
of thirty-four years, and it had never once led her astray. Of course,
all sorts of things had happened. You couldn't really take much joy
in an aching tooth or a broken heart. But the dentist or the best
healer (that's right – time) did his job, the pain and the mourning
came to an end, and once again it was possible to celebrate each day
and night, because a reason could always be found – both by day
and by night. Simply look at the world through blue eyes instead of
black ones – and Mona's eyes were a quite exceptional shade of blue,
out-and-out aquamarine in fact.

And a reason was found even now, in circumstances that were, to
put it mildly, far from brilliant.

In the dirty waiting room at the dirty railway station, Mona
reached out her flask to the tea urn to get some boiling water and a
furious woman who was also thrusting a bowl of crumbled bread in
under the tap, to mix up her 'soup', barked at her:

'Don't touch that, you noseless bitch! Where do you think you're
sticking your foul paw! You shameless slut!'

'Slut yourself,' Mona replied with a nasal twang. 'I'll spit in your
bread soup in a moment.'

And she raised the bandage across her face, revealing the beautiful
sight beneath it: instead of a nose, a blue and crimson horror with
two little drops of pus (wax, natural colours, Italian resin). When

she got off the train, Mona had withdrawn into the bushes and constructed her camouflage, painstakingly depicting the tertiary stage of syphilis, and tied a piece of cloth over it. Judging from the way the shrewish woman recoiled from this highly artistic canvas, Mona had done a truly excellent job. How could she possibly not rejoice in that?

Feeling proud of herself, Mona filled her flask and scratched her forehead, on which the pinpoint rash (gouache with a sprinkling of sand) had not yet dried completely.

'I used to be a seamstress, before I was an actress . . .' Mona sang quietly, delighting in the putrid tone of her voice, which was produced by the two little clumps of cotton wool stuffed into her nostrils.

And now to set out. The railway stage of the 'Exodus' was behind her now, and although it had been far from sweet, the real adventures were only just beginning. The trains didn't run any farther than Belgorod, because the authority of the Soviets more or less came to an end here. Ahead lay no-man's-land, and there was no way to cross it except on foot. But what did a syphilitic beggar woman have to fear? Who would be interested in such a wretched creature?

Encouraging herself with this thought, Mona set off along the dusty street that led south from the station (the afternoon sun was shining into her right ear). Somewhere in that direction the Kharkov high road should begin. No one really knew who was in power now in Kharkov – still the Reds, or the Whites, or no one at all? The month of May 1919 was a mischievous prankster and sorcerer, sweeping its broad fan this way and that, setting everything eddying and swirling, so that there was no damn way to make sense of any of it.

Mona's outfit for a tourist expedition across the Wild Steppe was excellent, planned with all the thoroughness that was so typical of her.

Looked at from the outside, it was a ghastly collection of old cast-offs. A formless sack of a robe with crooked patches (an alpine coat pulled inside out, with sackcloth sewn over it), a pair of battered, flaking ruins on her feet (stout Swiss shoes after appropriate processing) and a tattered sack over her shoulder

– anyone who started rummaging in there would soon think better of it.

At the guard post on the way out of town, she faced her first examination. Suspecting that Mona was a speculator, the sentry promptly stuck his hand in the sack. Then he cursed abruptly and pulled it out again – his fingers were covered in something brown and sticky.

'What you got in there?'

'Old rags, for wiping away the pus,' Mona replied in a mournful, nasal voice, and demonstrated her remarkable nose again. In actual fact the stain was liquid carmine, a make-up foundation that didn't dry out – an absolutely indispensable item in her work: it lent the wax a lifelike shimmer, like genuine skin.

The soldier didn't grope any deeper, so he didn't dig down as far as the little 'Bulldog' pistol hidden at the bottom of the sack, but he didn't leave her alone either. A pig-headed character. Patting down Mona's sides, he detected the little bag of ironmongery in the inside pocket under the shapeless robe and exclaimed delightedly:

'Aha! Get it out! Show me!'

He prodded his finger disappointedly at the tiny little spools and screws.

'What's this?'

'I'm a seamstress, dear sir. I picked up a few supplies in town, to mend my machine. The cursed thing's broken down.'

But the Red Army man didn't back off, even now.

'Have you got any documents? Maybe you're a Cadet spy?'

Documents – Mona had one of those, certainly. The form had cost her two dried Caspian perch, and she had manufactured the seal herself – mere child's play for an artist.

'Hop it,' said the sentry, and Mona hopped it. Past the boom and out of Sovietland.

So now she had another reason to celebrate – an exam passed with an 'excellent' grade.

Looking at the undulating plain, traversed by gullies and ravines, she recalled a quotation from *The Lay of the Host of Igor* that she had once learned off by heart at grammar school: 'And let us mount up, brothers, our swift steeds, and behold the blue Don!'

Right then, let's mount up and behold.

Life is lavish in its gifts to an individual attuned only to good things. Before Mona had even covered two versts in her remarkable shoes, she was overtaken by an empty wagon and a young peasant lad on it shouted: 'Get on, missus, I'll give you a ride. I don't like it on my own, it's boring.' *Now this, of course, is a fine piece of encouragement from destiny*, Mona decided.

It was quicker and more comfortable to travel on wheels, lying on soft hay, and on taking a closer look at her driver, Mona saw that he was good-looking. A cheerful character, a bright daisy with white teeth, long golden eyelashes and unshaven cheeks that glinted gold too. A genuine faun, only without a reed pipe.

For shame, Turusova, she told herself, *and you such a cultured woman.*

At that point the faun blew his nose into his fingers, then wiped them on his orange-peel stubble, and her unseemly mood evaporated.

Mona chatted cheerfully with the lad about all sorts of nonsense (about town prices, about an unprecedented flash flood, about who was worse – the Reds or the Whites). It didn't hinder her train of thought in the least.

What's the real trouble with men? she ruminated. *You want to talk to the clever ones and cuddle the sexy ones, but as a general rule a sexy man isn't intelligent and an intelligent man isn't sexy. And even if one thing does coincide with the other (it's rare, but it happens) that's a problem too. You meet some type who's breathtakingly handsome and infernally intelligent as well. And you think: this is it, I'm done for now. I could gobble him up like a juicy rissole. But then the handsome devil says something intellectually subtle or paradoxically precise, and it sets you pondering. Those lively flies start buzzing around in your head, the mental processes switch on, and when your head switches on, female concerns immediately switch off. You can love someone with your mind or your body, but not with both at the same time – there's just no way.*

As a rather intelligent individual, Mona realised, of course, that the problem lay, not in the men, but in herself. Whose fault was it if, as her father would have expressed it, she had a deviant libidinal orientation? So she had lived her life like this, in the vice-like grip of this insoluble dilemma, keeping the flies and the rissoles apart. No husband, no children . . .

She sighed, swinging her legs as they dangled over the edge of the wagon, and laughed at her own humbug.

She had never wanted to get married, and as for having children – brrrrrrr, she wanted that even less. Reproducing was for those who had nothing more interesting to do.

It was a pity, of course, that her already long life had not contained very many amorous adventures, but she had only herself to blame. She was inordinately choosy. There had been plenty of candidates, she certainly couldn't grumble about that. But since the absolute ideal was unattainable, Mona had always fallen in love with men of exactly the same type: sexy (that is, tall, with good figures, handsome and – most importantly – capable of organising a good time) but not excessively intelligent. Fools, of course, were out of the question, they were no use at all to anyone, but Lobachevskys were not required either.

However, in 1914 all the handsome, good-time men had gone away to the front, and after 1917 they had disappeared completely – at least in Sovietland – and that was another reason, although not the main one, why Mona Turusova had set out on her 'Exodus'. The main reason was that her lovingly constructed world had been devoured by rats.

'Everyone's on the move now, they just can't stay put,' sighed the wagon driver, who was called Yerosha. 'It's like all of Russia's had turps smeared under its tail, and it's just gone wild. Take you, missus, you ain't from our parts, I can hear that from the way you talk. Where are you rushing off to? Why can't you stay put at home? Going to get your disease treated, are you?'

'You're smart, Yerosha, you guessed first time. They can't cure my ailment at home,' said Mona, flattering him.

'Yes, I'm smart,' the lad agreed. 'That's what my ma tells me too: "You've got a good head on your shoulders, Yerosha."'

But what Mona's mother used to tell her was: 'Don't live with your head. Don't repeat my mistakes. Live with what's most important in you. The most important thing in me is my heart, but I tried to live with my head. That's why I neglected love at first.

And then I got married, because that seemed the smart thing to do. Then I got divorced, because intelligence on its own doesn't get you very far. And it was only the third time around that I more or less got the right fit. Your father is a wonderful man and we have a very sound family.' But confessions of this kind always concluded with a sigh.

Mona's father really was wonderful. Now, there was someone with a vast repository of intelligence. Dr Turusov, a professional explorer of the human psyche, explained family life as follows: 'The most stable of all unions are those in which one partner is a plant and the other is a plant pot. As long as the soil in the pot remains rich in nutrients and is kept sufficiently moist, the plant will do what it is supposed to do – blossom – and the pot will admire it. Both of them benefit.'

The most important and best thing about Mona was her fingers. They were absolute magicians – they could feel all the little bumps and hollows of existence, and then reproduce them in the form of perfect copies.

In her youth Mona had lived in Paris and studied sculpture for a while with the great, insane Camille Claudel, who was also fond of talking about what was most important. In her view, the most important thing in life was the correct choice of material. Mona had tried different materials – plaster of Paris, stone and various metals – but they all had an odour of dead flesh about them, and she wanted to catch life and hold it. In her disillusionment, she even took up photography, but it only irritated her with its two-dimensional nature and it offered nothing for her fingers.

At the age of twenty-five, she finally found her ideal material. She started making wax figures that were exactly like live ones. Better than live ones. She painted them with colours that she invented herself. And she sewed the clothes for her dolls.

In pre-war Peter, Turusova's 'wax characters' had started becoming fashionable. A three-dimensional portrait was far from cheap, and Mona did not take on just any old client. First, she sat the person in an armchair and felt their face with her fingers, which told her more than her eyes did. If subjects were interesting, she sculpted them. If not, she refused.

And in addition, just for herself, she had gradually transformed her studio into a fairy-tale kingdom, populated by little wax figures one tenth of life size. The inhabitants of this kingdom were all the people who had ever attracted Mona's close attention for one reason or other. And each one of them had ended up in the right place for him or her.

That hateful tormentor of Mona's childhood, the grammar-school inspector Izvolskaya, now herded pigs in a little meadow. Mona's 'first kiss', the Junker Keller, remained an eternally enchanted prince. A lover from whom Mona had parted painfully lay in a little glass coffin, transfixed by an aspen stake. But there were also six other lovers, from whom she had parted with no hard feelings. In her ideal world she had rewarded each of them in accordance with his own desserts.

Gallant soldiers marched along a diminutive street, while a languid young lady peered out of a little window. A wise alchemist, the spitting image of Dr Turusov, tried to conjure up the philosopher's stone.

There were lots and lots of things in the kingdom of wax. Mona became so attached to it that she didn't even leave the doomed city of Petrograd while it was still possible.

But hadn't her wise papa said in the autumn of 1917 that the Russian soil was exhausted, and it was time for the plant and the pot to move to the good, black earth of different regions? 'Psychiatrists are only needed in those places where the psychologically healthy isolate the psychologically sick from society, but there's nothing for me to do in a country where the insane incarcerate the healthy.' And he had carried off Mona's weeping mama to Finland, and from there through Sweden and France to Switzerland. In Geneva he had been made a university head of department and he wrote Mona letters, asking her to come. But then letters from abroad had stopped getting through, and it had become impossible to leave Russia.

In any case Mona had no intention of abandoning her wax subjects. She managed to get by, selling off her furniture little by little. She learned to be a speculator, exchanging things for food. However, the population of her kingdom stopped increasing, because she couldn't get any wax anywhere. A month earlier, in April, she had found out that a certain 'candle commune' had started working near Pskov, and the communards there were short of wicks. She got hold of some wicks, took them there and exchanged them for a pood of very decent wax. After a week away, she returned home feeling very pleased – and her kingdom was gone. In the starving city the rats, who had nothing to eat, even on the rubbish heaps, had started creeping into apartments. And they had gobbled up the entire fairy-tale population: ladies and their suitors, yard keepers, grammar-school students, kind and unkind lovers. Nothing at all was left of that wonderful world, except for pellets of rat excrement.

Mona bawled her eyes out for a whole day, the way she used to do as a child before she formulated her excellent motto for life. And she started readying herself for her 'Exodus': back to her childhood, to her father and mother.

But since the time of her parents' departure, the proletarian republic had slammed shut all the escape hatches that led out. In winter it had still been possible, although it was risky, to cross the border with Finland across the ice, but during the warm part of the year, only a roundabout route remained: to the south, into White Russia, and from there by sea, around Europe.

A long way? Yes. Difficult? Dangerous? To put it mildly. But what else could she do? She couldn't stay in a country of victorious rats, could she?

For Mona the distance from decision to action had always been short.

She gathered herself. And she set out.

The journey from Peter to Moscow turned out to be easy, except that she had to hang about in Bologoye for two days and nights, because all the passenger trains had been mobilised for the requirements of the front. There had been more adventures on the journey from Moscow to Belgorod, during which she had been put off the train three times, and it had been shelled twice – she didn't know by whom – and then not far from Kursk the locomotive had 'croaked', and everyone had had to shove the train along the line for seventeen versts. But never mind, she had got here.

And now the most difficult part had begun: crossing the 'twilight lands', where there was Red power in the small number of towns, and 'Green power' – that is, no authority at all – all around them. And glimmering somewhere in the distance, beyond the steppe, was the light of 'White power'. Many people tried to get through to it, and not everyone succeeded.

But Mona, naturally, would succeed – of that she had no doubt.

The splendid Yerosha drove his travelling companion to his own destination of Maslova Pristan and told her about a woman who had a sewing machine.

Mona had worked out a simple and brilliant plan for obtaining provisions on her journey. There was no point in taking them with her, you couldn't carry a large enough supply for the whole way, but an intelligent person could always find herself food to eat and a roof to shelter under.

Here in Maslova Pristan she put her idea to the test.

She knocked.

'Lady of the house, does your sewing machine need mending?'

Well, naturally, it turned out that it did. In recent years there hadn't been anywhere to get German technology repaired, especially in such a remote spot.

While preparing for her journey, Mona had obtained large numbers of spare parts by barter and mastered the skills of mechanical repair work – this unsophisticated art had proved easy for her nimble hands.

The lady of the house was so delighted that she fed Mona, gave her a bed to sleep in, packed up some food for her journey and, most importantly of all – gave her some priceless advice. When she heard that the handywoman was making her way south, she said:

'Why wear out the soles of your shoes? Just look what spring's like this time round. The Donets has overflowed its banks far and wide and they're floating rafts all the way up here. Ask to join the raftsmen and sail on your way like a lady. Can you find something to pay them with?'

'I can,' Mona replied, finally convinced that fortune was on her side. Travel along the river – that was brilliant!

In the morning she found the Northern Donets, which was swollen with meltwater and eddying with whirlpools.

And true enough, her luck did not let her down. There was a small raft swaying at the quayside, with an open launch tied on behind. A short little individual with thick lips and long shins had just jumped down onto the logs, holding a loaf of bread and a jug of milk in his hands. No doubt he had just run to the market.

Mona called to him.

The young lad was a simple person and pleasantly shy, but at the same time garrulous. He told her that he was helping his Uncle Stas float timber for log houses to the south, to the 'Cossacks', because those parts were bare and there wasn't any good timber and, war or no war, they still had to build houses.

'Take me with you,' said Mona. 'Here, look what I'll pay you with.' She showed him a gold watch that she took out from under her armpit, where there was a secret pocket. 'A good watch, a gentleman's.'

'I'd take you anyway, lady, why wouldn't I? A raft's not a horse, I reckon, it doesn't care. But I can't do it without the boss's say-so. And Uncle Stas is sleeping, see. He'll start swearing if I wake him up.'

There were four feet protruding from a little straw cabin at the far end of the raft: two wearing boots of old Russia leather and two wearing galoshes over foot wrappings.

'And who's the other one there?'

'A wandering pilgrim latched on to us, a man of God.'

'Well, where there's a male pilgrim, why not a female one too? Push off. If your Stas wakes up and starts swearing, I'll climb off onto the bank.'

And she convinced him.

They pushed off from the mooring with two poles and set off.

How good this is, thought Mona, lying on an armful of hay with her hands under her head, looking up at the little white clouds.

The waves swayed her gently to and fro, the May breeze ruffled a ginger strand of her hair and it slithered ticklishly across her forehead, but she felt too lazy to take a hand out from under her head.

And she fell asleep like that, lulled by the river.

A strange pilgrim

She woke up with her mouth full of saliva. There was a smell of rich fish soup in the air: even through the bandage her nose had caught the wonderful smell before her brain woke up.

The warm sunshine was gentle and caressing, and the raft was still swaying in the same way. Opening her eyes slightly, Mona saw the rocky cliff of the right bank slipping past, embellished with the light green foliage of bushes.

'So you didn't save your soul, then, Grandad?' a hoarse voice enquired lazily. 'You didn't manage to hide away from the world?'

A different, slightly muffled voice replied, stammering slightly:

'There's no hiding from it. It came calling on m-me itself.'

'And jammed a knee up your backside, did it?' The first voice laughed. 'It's good at doing that, all right. Eat your soup.'

Spoons clattered in plates. Mona opened both eyes, but carried on lying there quietly, in order to work out who was there and what was happening.

A small campfire was burning out on a sheet of steel. Standing beside it, on a support made of three bricks, was a steaming cooking pot. There were three eaters. Mona didn't bother to look at the young lad she already knew, who was slurping down his soup noisily. The other two were a broad, unshaven man with a copper-coloured face (he had to be Uncle Stas) and a grey-haired old man wearing a monk's skullcap and a cassock, belted round with a length of rope. He was sitting in quarter-profile towards her, so that she could only make out one lean cheekbone, overgrown by a white beard, and half a moustache – not grey, but black.

The smell grew even more delicious – that was the fish, being finished off on the hot coals. Mona was terribly hungry, but she hadn't yet decided whether it was time for her to wake up officially or not. She sensed something alarming in the copper-faced raftsman and the rhythm of his voracious movements. Mona was good at divining such things. How greedily he gnawed the flesh off one, two, three little perch! How unpleasantly he licked his fingers.

Suddenly the 'boss' turned round, and Mona barely managed to lower her eyelashes in time.

'Eh, a fish to cook and a woman to fuck,' he said with a satisfied belch. 'Wake up your ugly freak, won't you, Foma. I fancy having my way with her.'

There was no point in pretending any longer. Mona sat up abruptly.

'I said I would pay,' she said quickly. 'And if you don't want me to, I'll get off. Just pull over to the bank.'

'You're going to pay right now.'

Stas came over to her with his galoshes squeaking and unfastened the belt of his trousers. From below he looked huge.

'Have you lost your mind?' Mona shouted. 'My nose is rotten, you'll get infected.'

She lifted the bandage to illustrate her point.

But the 'boss' wasn't frightened.

'Ah, I'm the same way meself. We'll take pity on each other, wench. Two sick folk together. You just cover your ugly mug with the hem of your skirt, it's a foul sight.'

She jerked the sack over to her and fumbled for the little revolver among the rags, but was too panicked to find it.

'Foma, will you go second?' Stas asked the young lad.

'Nah, Unc, I've still got to wed.'

The reply was spoken feebly. There'd be no help coming from that quarter.

'Well, please yourself. Maybe you'll take a fancy to it afterwards. How about you, Grandad? Or don't you want to any longer?'

'I don't want to,' the monk replied disdainfully. He had turned away completely.

After failing to locate the 'Bulldog', Mona decided to jump into the river. She was an excellent swimmer, and it wasn't far to the bank.

She ran three strides and then fell, without immediately under-standing why – until Stas, and then Foma, burst out laughing.

While Mona was sleeping, someone had tied a rope to her leg. There was no time to untangle the knot, that repulsive copper mug was already hovering over her.

Her hand slid back into the sack, and this time it found the ridged handle immediately.

'Get away!' Mona shouted, aiming the twitching barrel at the raftsman. 'I'll shoot!'

For a second, or perhaps two, the mug stopped scowling. Then it bared its teeth again in a grin.

'Nah, you won't shoot. You haven't got the guts.'

A massive paw tore the gun out of her hand, and another thumped her very deftly and painfully on the head.

'Lay yourself out!' the 'boss' ordered her. 'And if you start kicking up, I'll trample you. Well?'

One of those moments in life was approaching in which there is nothing to celebrate or rejoice at. In black moments like that, there is only one thing left to do – scream. And Mona screamed, desperately and hopelessly

'Aaaaaaaaah!'

'Yell all you want, that's all right.'

Stas bent down and grabbed the edge of the shapeless robe. Mona choked and fell silent.

'She doesn't want to. I think that's obvious,' she heard the old man say. 'Leave her in p-peace.'

The raftsman swung round.

'Don't butt in, Grandad. I'll toss you in the river.'

The monk or pilgrim – God only knew who he was – got to his feet with surprising agility for his age.

'I repeat for the last time: get away from her.'

Foma jumped on the unexpected intercessor from behind, wrapping his arms round his throat. The old man made a strange kind of movement, sending the lad's legs flying up in the air so that he swung over and smashed his head hard against a log. He went still.

The 'boss' growled: 'I'll kill you!'

He flung up his massive hand, in which the little revolver looked like a ludicrous toy.

The crack of a shot rang out. It was impossible to miss from ten paces away, but the old man squatted down with a speed almost too great for the eye to follow and, seemingly in continuation of the same movement, grabbed up the cast-iron pot of fish soup.

The second shot didn't hit the old man either – he swayed to the side. And the cooking pot, flung with erocious force, flashed through the air and struck Stas a resounding blow on the forehead.

The raftsman threw up his hands, dropped the gun and tumbled into the water with a splash.

With her mouth gaping open, Mona looked to see whether he would surface.

He didn't.

Another splash. That was Foma, who had woken up and jumped off the raft into the water. He swam to the bank with frantic over-arm strokes.

Mona's hands were trembling.

'Has that man . . . drowned?'

'It serves him right,' the pilgrim growled gruffly. 'He doesn't de-serve your pity. Now the cooking pot – that's a real shame. It would have come in useful.'

'I didn't mean it like that,' Mona said quickly. The last thing she wanted to do was reproach her unexpected rescuer. 'I'm not sorry for him. He was an appalling creature. How neatly you caught him right on the forehead!'

'I was lucky . . .' The strange pilgrim squatted down and untied the rope. 'He hit you. Turn your head and I'll take a look . . . It won't leave a bruise.'

'You're not a monk,' said Mona, looking at him. The old man's face was not entirely old: there was only one crease in his forehead, a vertical one; his eyes were blue, and not faded by age; his long hair and beard were grey, but the moustache was still entirely black. If she could just feel the texture of his cheeks and chin, it would be clear to her what kind of man he was. 'You're an educated man, I can tell that from your speech. Why this masquerade: the beard, the cassock, the little cap?'

'I haven't cut my hair or shaved for a year. I was living in a mon-astery in the north. Hence the clothes. Monks have good reasons for dressing in this way. It's c-convenient in the open air. And for travelling round the country in present circumstances too.' He examined the stage scenery on Mona's face sceptically. 'Your ulcers have got smeared, madam. What are those yellow drops – Italian resin?'

Mona grabbed hold of her nose.

'I'll wash it off straight away . . . What's your name?'

'For the last year I've been called "Brother Sergius". Or "Father Sergius", depending on who was addressing me.'

If you don't want to tell me your name, then don't, Mona thought, and replied in the same tone of voice.

'And in my documents, I'm the seamstress Fedosya Kukushkina.'

He nodded indifferently and moved away.

Mona knelt down at the edge of the raft and spent a long time washing off the make-up, casting sideways glances at this 'father-brother'. He was probably also making his way south, but what for? Who was he? An officer? It was quite possible. An erect bearing and precise movements. It was clear from his way of speaking that he was accustomed to commanding. If he was a military man, then he was probably a general, that fitted with his age. Although for a military man, his movements seemed exceptionally unconstrained – there was no sign of any restriction by a uniform. Interesting.

This incomprehensible man turned over in his hands the 'Bulldog' that he had picked up off the logs, and suddenly tossed it into the river.

'Hey, Brother Sergius, what do you think you're doing?' Mona exclaimed indignantly.

'You won't kill a dangerous man with that piece of garbage, you won't even wound him seriously, only infuriate him.'

As he answered, he looked at her again. His eyebrows (also not grey, but black) shot up in surprise.

'Why, you're young. And . . .' He didn't finish the sentence, but Mona guessed the ending: '. . . and beautiful.'

'For you I think I'm more like "Father Sergius".'

She immediately stopped feeling angry with him. To hell with the 'Bulldog'. This travelling lady had at least acquired a protector of sorts. Better travel with a knight of advanced age than without any knight at all.

'What are we going to do?' she asked, to check how the 'father' would react to the first-person plural pronoun and the suggestion that now they were going to do something together.

The question was received as something quite natural – Sergius started pondering. At that point Mona finally realised that the incident with the excessively amorous raftsman was yet another of fate's gifts, and not at all what it had seemed at first.

'We'll have to abandon the raft. It has to be punted off the shallows all the time. I can't stand duty constantly on my own without a break, and you won't have the strength for it. Let's move into the launch.'

He took a sack on a strap out of the little straw cabin. Mona picked up her own sack and followed the old knight. Let him get used to caring for a lady and taking decisions. The wise Dr Turusov had taught his daughter: 'Being a woman has great advantages. When it's convenient – you're weak. When you need to be – you're strong. Exploit men's arrogance and muscular strength, they are easily manipulated. And in general, the world ought to be run by women. For the greater part of its history humankind lived under a matriarchy, and it worked magnificently. The problems started when men took charge of society.'

The launch was old, but sturdy, with a mast, a motor and oars. Continuing to play the part of a timid maiden, Mona sat down on the bench, folded her hands helplessly on her knees and started watching Father Sergius fiddling with the motor.

'A single-cylinder Evinrude, with a built-in magneto and silencer. It could have been worse,' the old man murmured. The motor started up with a snort and the launch sailed round the deserted raft and shot off briskly down the river.

'Do you know about complicated mechanisms like this?' Mona enquired respectfully, although the mechanism was not particularly complicated. She would have worked it out herself. Only perhaps not as quickly.

'I have an engineering diploma in propulsion systems.'

I can imagine what propulsion systems were like a hundred years ago, when you received your diploma, she thought. *Steam engines with whistles.*

'And where did you earn it?' she asked, cautiously continuing the line of small talk.

'At the M-Massachusetts Institute of Technology.'

'In America?' she asked in genuine amazement.

Sergius switched off the motor and the boat slowed down.

'Why are we stopping?'

'We're not stopping. We'll simply drift at the speed of the current and save petrol for situations when we need to move fast. See, there's only one reserve canister of fuel.'

But Mona had got interested in America now.

'I suppose you've done a lot of travelling?'

'Yes, I have always been a wandering pilgrim. Only I didn't wear a cassock. When we reach parts that are even moderately calm, I shall part with it. And with the name "Sergius".'

Without the bandage across her face, Mona felt like a beautiful woman, and she untied her kerchief too, exposing her wonderfully thick, bronze hair to the sunshine. The old man glanced at it from time to time. No doubt it glinted rather attractively.

'Why "Father Sergius" in particular? In honour of Leo Tolstoy's character?'

'The monks of the forest monastery where I lived have not read C-Count Tolstoy. It's in the Northern Vologda district, a remote area. A solitary bear had started paying them visits and made their life impossible. I had a talk with him on the very first day and Mishka the bear went away. So the brothers dubbed me Sergius, in memory of St Sergius of Radonezh, the tamer of bears.'

'How do you mean, you "had a talk" with him?'

'I looked into his eyes. Predators are easy to manage. They only attack in three instances. If they are very hungry and regard you as edible. If they are frightened. And also depending on their sex.'

'Their sex?' asked Mona, growing even more interested.

'Why, yes. A female defending her children. A male trying to impress a female. The bear had no argument with me about anything. From my behaviour, he realised that I was not food. And I didn't do anything to frighten him. There was no female nearby either. So he went away.'

'But how did you end up in a northern monastery anyway?'

The launch crept along more slowly than a man walking. Ahead lay absolute uncertainty and Mona knew almost nothing about her companion, but she was enjoying all of this immensely: the leisurely river, and the green banks, and the blue sky and – most of all – talking to an intelligent man who had lived an interesting life, with whom she didn't need to think about womanly matters, because he was already beyond that age.

'In spring last year a friend and I decided to behave in an oriental fashion. Two thousand years ago a certain sage said: "If you have ceased liking the world and you cannot change it, leave the world to its own k-karma and withdraw from it." So we withdrew.'

'Its own what?'

'Karma – it is almost the same thing as "fate", only without the overtones of fatalism. The Japanese believe that fate is not preordained by anyone, it can be changed. You see, my friend is Japanese. He said: "We'll find a quiet *o-tera* somewhere (that's something like a hermitage) and we'll live there until *satori* comes to us." *Satori* is . . .' Father Sergius thought for a moment and gestured dismissively. 'It will take too long to explain that, it doesn't matter. I know the Northern Vologda district quite well. We secluded ourselves in the most remote monastery there and passed an entire year quite excellently. Sometimes news from the world outside – each time worse than the time before – found its way into our backwater, but we simply lived our lives, waiting for *satori* . . . Well then, that is a state in which everything suddenly becomes completely clear to you,' the narrator explained after all, although rather vaguely, but Mona didn't try to delve any deeper. She wanted to know what had happened next.

'A month ago, when the river ice started moving, everything became completely clear. Without any *satori*. A brigade of SPUs or "Special Purposes Units" – I swear to God, I have no idea what that actually means – sailed up the river to us and started throwing the monks out, because "a special camp for hostile elements" had to be installed in the monastery. I requested the hegumen's b-blessing to talk with these SPUs in my own manner, but His Reverence would not permit it. We had to leave.'

'Where did you go?'

'First we went home. To see what had become of Moscow. And I saw that it had become impossible to live there, in my own native city. Not because of the Red Terror, but because nobody was opposing it. People are simply living their lives, waiting to see how everything turns out in the end. They work for their rations, go to the cinematograph, talk about p-politics in a whisper, play cards . . . You know, I have no complaints about bad people. Their position is clear enough: they are on the side of Evil. But I can't bear the sight of good people who are unintelligent or weak. In the course of my long life I have come to the conclusion that Evil has better luck with its representatives than Good. And the deserters from the army of Good are far more numerous. This is clear even from the physical point of view. It is easier to fall than to rise up and submission is easier than resistance. I left because of the universal impotence.'

Mona nodded – that feeling was familiar to her. In former, more complicated days, these deliberations on Good and Evil would have made her wince, but in the present dichromatic, black and white, or rather, Red and White age, they seemed entirely apposite to her.

They fell silent, both thinking their own thoughts.

Things carried on like this until an alarming thought occurred to Mona. How long would this comfortingly calm man stay with her? He wasn't tiresome either: he answered questions and didn't ask about anything himself.

'So you have left Red Moscow,' she said. 'And where are you going now? To the Whites?'

And suddenly she felt worried – generally speaking, it wasn't done to ask about that kind of thing.

But Father Sergius answered as if there was nothing special about the question.

'I'm not interested in the Whites. They wish to go back to yesterday, and you can never do that. The revolution happened because yesterday Russia was in a bad way. Yes, I do intend to find my way into White territory. But only in order to get out of a country that wishes to exchange a bad past for an appalling future. I can't change anything, and I don't care to watch this process.'

He heaved a sigh. But Mona was quite overjoyed.

'That's really good! I also want to reach a White port, in order to sail abroad from it. I don't care which one it is. Where are you going to – Yalta, Sebastopol or Novorossiisk?'

'To Sebastopol. The friend I have already mentioned will be waiting for me there. But I shan't enter the Crimea immediately. First I have to call in somewhere else.'

'Where's that?'

'You see, my friend and I had a falling-out. As I have already said, he is Japanese, but he has lived in Russia for many years. And in Moscow, he said to me: "We have two homelands, mine and yours. I have lived in yours for forty years, but it no longer exists. Now it is your turn to live in my homeland for forty years. We will sail from Sebastopol to Port Said, and from there to Yokohama."'

'And why did you have a falling-out?'

'I said that first I had to be certain that Russia had only two roads, the Red or the White. And Masa – that is my Japanese friend's name – declared that that was not fair, that I was simply stalling for time. And our ways parted. He went to Sebastopol and is waiting for me "to stop rummaging in the b-belly of a dead tiger". And I promised him that my trip would not take long.'

'What trip? Where to?'

'You see, when I got back to my Moscow apartment, there was an interesting letter waiting for me there. From an old acquaintance.'

Father Sergius fell silent, gazing absent-mindedly at the glittering water. Mona waited for a little while, then touched his sleeve impatiently.

'You were talking about a letter from an old acquaintance.'

'Eh? Yes. I'm sorry. He is a convinced anarchist, a proponent of the so-called "Black Truth". His name is Aron Liberty, and he has now based himself in the Ukraine. They have something like an anarchist republic there. He has invited me to take a look at it for myself. He writes: "Do come, you won't regret it". I am almost certain that it is all n-nonsense, a utopia, but nonetheless I decided to pay him a visit, by way of an excursion, in order to purge my conscience. Who knows, what if . . . It's a beautiful letter, and he is a serious man.' Father Sergius sighed once again. 'I'll take a look, make certain that it's all raving nonsense – and go on to Sebastopol, to join Masa.'

Mona feverishly tried to work out what would be better – to be left alone again or to impose herself on this outlandish tourist as his travelling companion. Couldn't that turn out to be safer?

'Where is this anarchist republic? Is it far away?'

'In Pryazovia. There's a little district town there by the name of Gulyaypolye.'

'Do you mean Bat'ko Makhno's republic?' Mona shrieked. She had heard a lot of talk about the steppe ataman and his Gulyaypolye brigands in the Belgorod train, when she was trying to decide what route to follow to the south.

In the 'twilight zone' between the Reds and the Whites, dozens of steppe republics had sprung up, each with its own 'bat'ko': the 'Chyhyryn Commune' of Bat'ko Kotsura, the 'Holodnoyarsk Council' of Bat'ko Chuchupak, the 'New Camp' of Bat'ko Bozhko, the 'Knightly Cossack Host' of Bat'ko Angel and a certain 'Green School Directorate', but the 'bat'ko' most talked about had been the Gulyaypolye ataman Makhno.

No thank you, she didn't fancy any excursions of that kind. It couldn't be helped: she would have to part company with Father Sergius.

'I intend to travel down the Donets as far as Izium,' the false knight declared, concluding his tale. 'You can sail farther on your own. It's easy to steer the launch, just move the rudder. And I'll teach you how to use the motor.'

'This Japanese of yours is a fine friend.' In her frustration Mona wanted to say something nasty. 'Letting an elderly man go on such a dangerous journey alone.'

'What makes it so dangerous?' Father Sergius asked in surprise. 'It isn't dangerous at all by Masa's and my standards. I'll just drop in to see someone I kn-know. If I don't like it there, I'll be in the Crimea a few days later. And if, contrary to my expectations, I do like it – I'll invite Masa to join me.'

Mona turned away. Of course, it was very pleasant to feel that she was under someone's protection, but it was best not to get used to it. You were only truly free when you weren't dependent on anyone.

Shove off, then, go to your Gulyaypolye, and good riddance!

Down along the river

She decided that she wasn't going to get used to Father Sergius, in case she might grow too fond of him. She was grateful to have been rescued, of course, and overall, he was a rather worthy individual, attractive in his own way (not in *that* way, but as a personality), but their journey together would not last long, and it would be better if no one was saddened by the parting. They'd done a bit of talking, and that was enough.

The whole business was simplified by the fact that Father Sergius was not desperately keen to pass the time with his travelling companion either. He sat in the stern, steering as solemnly as if he was directing the course of a dreadnought.

What a preening peacock, Mona thought to herself, rather piqued by this total absence of interest in a relatively young and rather beautiful woman.

The 'pilgrim' had taken off his idiotic skullcap, and the cassock too. In a shirt and trousers he looked almost like a normal man. 'Almost' – because the grey hair and beard still transformed him into Nekrasov's character Grandad Mazai.

They carried on like that, drifting slowly past the fields, meadows and small woods and using the motor to travel fast past the villages. Who knew what the local people had on their minds, and who was in authority there? It was best not to take any risks. But anyway, nothing ominous happened.

At the jetties women washed laundry and young urchins watered horses. The village folk glanced indifferently at the stuttering boat, taking no interest. The only reminder that there was a war going on was a cavalry detail. It was impossible to tell which side it was from, but to be on the safe side Father Sergius moored the launch by the bank, under a cliff, and they waited there for it to pass.

The only time the travellers exchanged a couple of words was when Mona took the food that she had earned in Maslova Pristan out of her sack. She politely offered him some, and he politely refused.

Mona ate lunch and dozed off. She woke as lightly as she had fallen asleep, and when she opened her eyes, she caught her travelling companion's glance on her.

He said calmly, without any embarrassment:

'Forgive me. You were smiling so sweetly in your sleep. I haven't seen any young, beautiful women for a long time. There weren't any in the monastery, of course, but there weren't any after that either. As if they had all fled from Russian to foreign lands. As a certain ancient author said: "In dishonourable times the b-beauty of women is more striking."'

The holy hermit is apparently paying me compliments, Mona thought in cheerful surprise. But he immediately spoiled everything by adding pensively:

'A very accurate observation. One could add, more precisely: "even moderate b-beauty".'

'The moderate beauty . . . of a woman who is not very young?' she put in.

Now that did make him embarrassed.

'I'm sorry, I wasn't thinking of you at all. It was an abstract reflection . . . And on the matter of age, I will take the liberty of observing that middle-aged women in fact have the most interesting faces. You can still see the little girl of yesterday in them, and already see the old woman of t-tomorrow . . . Oh, Lord,' Father Sergius exclaimed, becoming totally embarrassed. 'What kind of nonsense am I babbling? I've become a wild savage! For heaven's sake, I didn't mean you. On my word of honour.'

She couldn't help herself and chuckled – he was so ludicrous now. And after that their relationship seemed to settle into the right channel of its own accord. Sometimes a long conversation would start up and sometimes a long silence would set in: it was no longer tense, however, but natural.

On several occasions Father Sergius took up the oars and rowed incredibly powerfully, without getting tired. Later on the river emerged onto a plain, spreading out across a wider expanse and straightening out, and he put up the sail.

Mona was in a glorious mood. She liked her travelling companion – and most of all because she felt at ease with him. At ease as a woman. It must have been the excessively romantic situation that

made her feel awkward at first: a fair maiden and a noble hero –
that was fraught with possible complications. It was just like in the
cinematograph. Or in that story her mother loved to tell her.

But, on having got to know the 'noble hero' better, Mona was
convinced that he was unsuited for her on every account. Firstly, he
was intelligent. Secondly, he was mirthless. Well, and, of course, he
was terribly old.

Good!

'It's good, all right, but too fast,' Father Sergius suddenly said:
catching her astonished glance, he smiled. His smile was a little awkward and strained. As if it had become rusty. It was obvious straight
away that this man only rarely smiled. 'I'm sorry. I've become accustomed to talking out loud. I told you I had become a savage. I meant
the sail. It's good that we have a following wind, but we are moving
too quickly because of it.'

'How's that?'

'The raftsman Stas (I cannot say "God bless his soul") told me
about the journey down the river. We shall cut across the territory
of a certain "Kozolupinsky Republic". This free state supplements
its b-budget by robbing those who sail through it, and therefore that
stretch of river is best traversed at night, without any lights and very
quietly. We shall have to put in to the bank and wait for twilight.'

He steered the launch towards the bank, which was thickly
overgrown with half-submerged bushes. It was an excellent spot.
Concealed under the branches, the boat could not be seen, either
from the river or from the land.

He himself did not lie down, however, but seated himself in the
stern and started sorting out the contents of his traveller's sack.
Mona watched surreptitiously.

First the old man took out a pair of field binoculars and started
polishing their lenses thoroughly with a velvet cloth. That was a
long, boring business. Mona yawned and wondered whether perhaps she should really get some sleep. But the next item extracted
from the sack was interesting – a small ornamental wooden box.
Father Sergius took some kind of yellowed parchment out of it and
unfolded it carefully.

'What's that?'

'That's what I would like to understand. It was in a casket of relics of my ancestors. My late father collected them and I never had time to sort them out. I decided that if I was leaving my homeland for ever, I would take at least this with me. I keep studying it, over and over, but so far quite f-fruitlessly.'

She sat up and glanced over his shoulder. The ancient scrawl was impossible to make out.

'I can read "This remembrance" at the beginning, but after that, not a thing . . . And the end is legible again: "Corne . . ." then some other word, and "s-set his hand to this". The founder of our family, who arrived in Moscow in Tsar Alexei Mikhailovich's time, was called Cornelius. Perhaps it's him?'

He started moving his lips.

The theme of family antiquities failed to rouse Mona's interest, but now she had stopped feeling sleepy.

She decided to stretch her legs.

She walked to the edge of the bushes, beyond which there was a vast, open field. She parted the branches and squatted down in fright.

About three hundred metres away there was a column of soldiers, enveloped in dust and extending along a road, with no end to it in sight.

At the head of it, moving along slowly under a furled banner, was a group of riders, ten or fifteen men.

Mona ran back and told Father Sergius. He put his palimpsest away and got up, taking his binoculars. 'Let me look too!' she demanded.

They stood shoulder to shoulder. He looked through the right cylinder and Mona looked into the left one, but soon moved away. Firstly, because his beard tickled her cheek, and secondly, because she couldn't see very much. The binoculars were too powerful. In the little white circle peaked caps and astrakhan hats swayed to and fro, and a horse's muzzle with bared teeth edged into view too.

'Reds,' Father Sergius concluded. 'A brigade of them at least . . . Staff officers riding up ahead. Probably reinforcements for the Kharkov front line.'

'Look!' she cried, touching his sleeve.

A passenger automobile was hurtling along the road towards the column, trailing a fox's brush of dust behind it.

The car stopped in front of the head of the column and three agile little figures jumped out of it – one at the front and two others behind it.

'Something urgent,' said Father Sergius. 'Well, never mind them. What business is it of ours? They won't stick their noses in here.'

The riders started dismounting and surrounded the men who had climbed out of the automobile.

Suddenly a shot rang out. The group of men immediately started moving. One man on horseback broke away from it, followed by another, and both of them set off at a gallop across the field – towards the bushes. It seemed to Mona that they were riding straight at her.

Shots were fired after the galloping men. The horse under the one at the back stumbled and collapsed. Mona cried out at the sight of the rider rolling across the ground.

The man in front reared his horse up on its hind legs and jerked on the bridle to turn his steed round, firing all the time with a revolver.

The second man ran up to him, limping slightly. He jumped up and perched on the horse's crupper behind the rider. They started galloping again.

'Good for him, he didn't abandon his c-comrade,' remarked Father Sergius. 'But in general, I don't like the look of this.'

'Why?'

'Because they'll lead that entire horde straight to us. Quick. We're casting off.'

And he ran towards the bank. But Mona stayed behind, enthralled by the drama. In a hail of bullets, the two fugitives dashed towards the thickets of bushes, no doubt hoping to hide in them, but not knowing that there was a river behind them. They were doomed! But if they were fleeing from the 'comrades' and shooting at them, that meant they must be decent people.

'Quick, what are you doing?' Father Sergius shouted from the water. Over there the motor started roaring, starting at the third jerk – trrr, trrrrr, trrrrrrrrrr . . .

The riders jumped down off their horses in front of the bushes about forty metres to Mona's right.

She stuck her head out and started waving her hand:

'Gentlemen, gentlemen, this way! We have a boat!'

The tall one jerked on the arm of the other one, who was small and had a rucksack on his back, and pointed at Mona.

They dived into the thickets, disappearing from view. But they were running towards her – the crackling sounds were coming closer.

The Reds in the field had stopped firing and were mounting up. They would come galloping this way soon.

'Follow me, follow me!' Mona shouted, looking round as she ran.

Now they were right beside her. A well set-up, handsome, light-haired man and a skinny, short man with dark hair, who was also quite good-looking. The incredible thing was that in these desperate circumstances they were quarrelling and swearing at each other.

'Comcodsec, you're a cretin! Now what have you done?' the dark-haired man yelled.

The light-haired man replied just as furiously.

'I saved you from arrest! That's Kandyba, the head of the Special Section!'

Absorbed in their own incomprehensible argument, they barely even glanced at Mona. Comcodsec (what a name!) merely asked:

'Where's the boat?' And then, hearing the motor, he nodded: 'Aha' – then turned back to his companion and asked:

'Is your uncle really Gai-Gaievsky? How did Kandyba ferret that out?'

'There's no need to ferret it out. It says in my résumé: "Mother; Gai-Gaievskaya, Antonina Zenonovna. A rare surname and a rare patronymic. What of it? Divcom-3 commander Makhrov has a brother who commands a division in Wrangel's army, and this is only an uncle! They would have got things straight and let me go!'

The only thing Mona understood was that the dark-haired man was apparently the nephew of General Gai-Gaievsky, the commander of the White Guards' Volunteer Army. They often wrote about him in the Soviet newspapers, and even printed cartoons: a fat man in a pince-nez, with a gallows in one hand and a whip in the other.

'Gentlemen, you can finish your argument later! Quick!'

'Yes, yes,' growled the terribly angry nephew, overtaking her and jumping into the boat first.

The light-haired man hoisted Mona into her seat from behind (decisively, but civilly), clambered over the edge of the boat and shouted:

'Come on, Grandad, full speed ahead!'

Father Sergius cast an unfriendly glance at him and turned a lever.

The launch jerked up its bow, flung out a fountain of spray from under its stern and shot off.

Three Men in a Boat (to Say Nothing of the Dog)

Amazingly enough, the pair carried on squabbling in the boat, without even thanking her for rescuing them.

'I'm not to blame for anything,' the dark-haired man ranted. 'Who asked you to fire, Comcodsec? I would have explained everything!'

'Who to? Kandyba? He would have had you shot without thinking twice about it. Ah, you! I saved your life, and you just bite my head off! Bugger off back to your Reds, Comrade Depcombrigstaff . . . whatever your name is . . . Shtukin!'

'Skukin, my name is Skukin,' the dark-haired man corrected him angrily. 'And who are you, anyway? Why did you interfere? All I know about you is that you're the commander of the code section . . . Kaganovich, isn't it?'

'Kantorovich.'

Mona realised that these two did not know each other at all.

'Everybody get down,' Father Sergius said curtly. 'They'll start shooting now.'

Looking back, Mona saw men on the bank. They were readying their rifles. The launch had travelled quite a long way from the bank, and she wasn't afraid, but even so she quickly flung herself down into the bottom of the boat, clashing elbows with Depcom-whatev-er-it-was Skukin.

'I beg your pardon,' he apologised, wincing at the screech of the bullets. One of them clanged against an iron oarlock. Mona shrieked.

'It's all right,' said a calm voice from the stern. 'We'll turn the b-bend in a moment, and they won't be able to see us any more.'

The launch listed slightly and the shooting really did break off.

Mona and the two others sat up.

'Who are you?' Father Sergius asked morosely.

The first to reply was Kantorovich.

'I'm an officer, a staff captain. I enlisted with the Reds in order to get to the front and desert to our people. I was waiting for the right moment. And when Kandyba jumped on you and yelled: "Surrender your weapon, contra!"' he continued, turning to Skukin, 'I thought you were one of us too. So I took him down.'

'Who is this Kandyba?' Father Sergius interjected.

'The head of the Eighth Army's Special Section,' Skukin explained. 'Our division was only formed a week ago. He was assigned to the Eighth, and the Special Section probably started checking the résumés of the military specialists. They saw that General Gai-Gaievsky is my uncle and wanted to get things straight. But this bright spark . . .' – he nodded at Kantorovich – 'blew away the top Chekist. So now, if you please, I'm a traitor and an enemy of Soviet power.'

This mournful monologue concluded with a robust word.

'There's a lady present,' Father Sergius rebuked him

The dark-haired man looked at Mona a bit more closely.

'I beg your pardon, madam. From the way you're dressed, I thought you were simply a country wench. Allow me to introduce myself. Arkady Sergeevich Skukin, lieutenant colonel of the General Staff. Formerly, of course. Conscripted into the Red Army and appointed Deputy Commander of Brigade Headquarters Staff – not such a bad appointment, by the way. Thanks to this cretin Kantorovich I have been transformed into a state criminal.'

'Listen, K-Kantorovich,' Father Sergius said to the light-haired man, 'couldn't you have taken a more plausible name for yourself?'

The staff captain replied in a dignified tone of voice.

'Firstly, for your information, Jews also sometimes have blond hair. And secondly, I wasn't able to obtain any other documents . . . I've fired all my cartridges,' he growled, looking at the open cylinder of his revolver and shaking the empty cartridge cases out of it. One of them hit the side of the boat, bounced off and struck the helmsman on the knee. '*Mille pardons*, venerable elder. And who are you?' the pseudo-Kantorovich asked.

The helmsman picked up the cartridge case, tossed it into the water and replied drily:

'I am a venerable elder.'

'. . . Father Sergius,' Mona put in. She felt embarrassed by his impoliteness.

What was he so angry about? Surely not because two young men had appeared in the launch?

She was in a simply excellent mood.

Having rested a little and calmed down, the rescued men became more talkative.

The staff captain (Mona decided that he could remain Kantorovich, since he didn't give any other name) told them that he had been in the Moscow underground, and when the arrests began, he had enlisted in the army of 'comrades'. Since in the past he had been a student of mathematics and a chess player, they had taken him into the code section.

'I didn't leave empty-handed,' Kantorovich boasted. 'I took all the codes. I think the Whites will be glad to see me.'

Skukin, having cooled off a bit and, evidently, thought things over, was no longer feeling angry about this sudden twist of fate.

'The same goes for me, only even more so. I expect my uncle will find a good place for me. If I had happened to be in the south, naturally I would have gone to the Whites, but I'm from Petrograd, so I had no choice. Back in military college a clairvoyant forecast that I would be a general. I thought I was going to be a Red one, but a White one is even better. Especially since things are going quite well for them, and worse and worse for the Reds.'

The final phrase made it quite clear that in his own mind Skukin had already crossed the line of the front. Catching Mona's searching glance, he said defiantly:

'Yes, madam. I'm a pragmatist. And an ambitious careerist. And I never make myself out to be better than I really am.'

Both of the officers were fascinating characters and Mona would have gladly palpated their faces to gain deeper insight, but she had to be content with the faculty of sight.

Among the other essential things that she had with her for the journey was a 'carver' – a small, curved knife for carving wood. Wood was a boring material, but where could she get any wax?

When they had travelled a good distance away from that bad spot, they put in to the bank again in order to wait for darkness, and the entire company got out onto dry land. Mona amused herself by carving. It didn't prevent her from keeping an eye on things and, in addition, no one would ask a person engrossed in artistic work to perform tedious womanly duties, and such tasks did exist. While still in the launch Kantorovich had caught plenty of fish very deftly and rapidly with breadcrumbs, and now they had to be fried. Venerable Sergius and Skukin busied themselves with making a campfire while the staff captain gutted his catch and Mona, instead of playing the agreeable hostess, transformed a piece of wood into a gryphon – and everyone looked at her artwork respectfully.

'What's your first name?' she asked Kantorovich.

'I'm Shaya Mordechaievich,' he replied cheerfully. 'My "comrades" called me Shaika, but you can call me Shaenka.'

'And I'm Fedosya Kukushkina,' she laughed.

Jolly, handsome, daring, not unduly intelligent. The very thing.

Skukin was a different kind of individual, but also striking. The world was chock-a-block with cynics, but you didn't meet such an honest person very often. The complete absence of dissimulation was a very powerful quality. In both women and men. But what intrigued her about Skukin was a certain inner coolness or, rather, stability, fixedness. That was it: fixedness. As if the man had an unshakable fulcrum that he could use to shift the world while remaining motionless himself. Only extreme egocentrics possessed this enviable quality.

And he was also handsome, in a restrained, un-Russian kind of way. Economical, elegant movements. Definitely intelligent. Clearly not a jolly blade. At first glance he appeared less attractive than 'Shaenka', but she could sense a concealed second level to him, and that was always enticing.

In the face of this competition, poor old 'Venerable Sergius' with his American diploma paled into complete insignificance.

As if he himself could sense this, immediately after their meal he said:

'Time to turn in. We sleep for two hours. Then we move on.'

He didn't give the young men a chance to regale a lady with conversation, although 'Shaenka' had kept casting genial glances at Mona and seemed not averse to spreading his tail feathers. 'The admiral's word is the sailor's law,' he said, sighing. Then he lay down with his elbow under his ear and started snuffling instantly.

Skukin arranged himself in the corpse position, with his hands crossed on his chest and his rucksack set under his head instead of a pillow. The Reverend Elder Sergius dozed off majestically, with his back slumped against a tree.

Since the jolly picnic had failed to materialise, Mona also settled down to rest: a little distance away from the men, in the launch. The sides of the boat cut her off from the earth, leaving only the sky up above her. As she closed her eyes, it was light blue. When she opened them – literally only a second later – it was already black. Night.

Mona had been woken up by the launch starting to sway on the waves.

'Have we been under way for long?' she asked in a voice hoarse with sleep.

They hissed at her: 'Ssssh.'

Someone told her – from the whisper she couldn't tell who: 'Quiet. At night sounds carry a long way on the river.'

'Are we already in Kozolupia?'

'Yes.'

She sat up to take a look, but at first she couldn't see anything apart from absolutely motionless blackness up above her and more blackness, swaying to and fro, down below. Little by little her eyes grew accustomed to the darkness and she was able to distinguish the dense grey strip of the nearby bank and the light grey ripples on the water. The boat was drifting with the current, slowly and soundlessly.

Someone was sitting in the bow in a motionless pose, with his elbows sticking out in a strange way. Skukin, Mona deduced from the figure. What was he doing? Ah, he was looking through binoculars. But what could anyone see in the darkness?

Suddenly Skukin flung up one hand.

'What is it?' whispered Kantorovich. He was sitting in the bottom of the launch, immediately in front of Mona, but she had only just spotted him now.

'Something glowing, I can't tell what,' Skukin replied.

The staff captain moved to sit with him.

'Let me have your miraculous goggles ... Yes, a light. In the middle of the river? Strange. Hey, old man, steer over towards that headland.'

The rudder creaked quietly.

Up ahead the river took a bend, and the launch set course for the bank where it protruded into the water. The bow nuzzled gently into sand and the men climbed out one by one, trying not to make any sound. Mona followed them.

Something crunched. Skukin was climbing a short, crooked tree.

'What's he doing?' Mona asked Father Sergius, who was standing in front of her.

'He has a pair of night-vision naval binoculars.'

She walked a little way along the bank and parted the branches.

There really was a light. The river narrowed greatly at this spot, down to forty metres, or even thirty, and right in the middle of it there was a yellowish cone blazing on something flat. It was impossible to make out anything more, and Mona went back.

'What's out there?' the staff captain asked, touching the heel of Skukin's boot.

'Don't bother me.'

Another two or three minutes went by before Skukin came down.

'Gentlemen, the situation is as follows. It's a ferry line and the ferry has been moved out to the centre. There are three men with rifles on it. There's a fire burning in a barrel, lighting up the water. It is impossible to sail past unnoticed.'

Kantorovich gave a quiet whistle.

'A cordon, fuck it! I beg your pardon, madam.'

'And that's not all,' Skukin continued imperturbably. 'Opposite it, under the trees on our bank, there's a machine-gun nest. I could make out sandbags, a gun barrel and two heads.'

'What are we going to do?' Kantorovich asked.

'Let's consider things from a different angle. Come on, Staff Captain.'

The two of them walked over to the water's edge, talking quietly about something.

'Civilians and the weaker sex are not invited to participate in the council of war,' Father Sergius remarked ironically. 'But let's see what the G-general Staff decides.'

'Yes, sir, Mr Lieutenant Colonel,' said Kantorovich, raising his voice slightly. He stepped into the thickets. And disappeared.

And Skukin came back to the boat, as imperturbably brisk as ever. 'A combat situation,' he declared. 'So I'm assuming command.'

'Where is he going?' Mona asked about the staff captain, and Father Sergius asked:

'What is the plan of action?'

Naturally, Skukin answered the man, not her.

'The Reds regard the Kozolupinsky Republic as an ally. Its motto is "Soviets without Yids and Communists". Therefore we shall continue on our way openly. I have identity papers as the deputy commander of the general command staff of a Red brigade. I'll tell them that I'm travelling downriver with dispatches. You, madam, will change your clothes – I have a spare uniform tunic in my rucksack. Take my cap and hide your hair under it. There are quite a lot of women serving with the Bolsheviks, but their heads are all shaved. You are simply a boatman' – that was to Father Sergius. 'When we've passed the cordon, we'll pick up Kantorovich. He'll make his way round on land. Is everything clear? The most important thing is: keep quiet. I'll do the talking.'

'But why isn't Kantorovich with us?' Mona asked. 'He has Soviet documents too.'

'Because he's Shaya Kantorovich,' the lieutenant colonel replied impatiently. 'As I already explained: the Kozolupinians are not fond of Jews.'

Father Sergius had a different question:

'What is our plan if they do detain us after all?'

There was no alarm in his voice, only curiosity.

Skukin replied even more harshly than he had to Mona.

'I repeat once again: this is a combat situation and I am in command here. A commander's orders are not discussed, but obeyed.' He looked at the glowing face of his watch. 'We'll give Kantorovich fifteen minutes – and forward. Take your places in the launch.'

They went back to the boat. Mona took off her shapeless 'robe' and blouse. In the darkness there was no need to worry about her virtue – the men wouldn't be able to see anything but a white blur. She pulled on Skukin's tunic, which was a bit tight on the bust. She stuffed her hair under the cap and it rose up a little – her hair was quite luxuriant. She secured the cap at both sides with hairpins to prevent it from falling off. It was a pity she couldn't take a look at herself in a mirror.

'It's time. Start up the motor, old man!' Skukin ordered in a loud voice. 'We're not hiding any longer.'

In the silence of the night the roar of the motor was deafening.

The launch sailed out into the middle of the river, leaving a track of white in its wake, rounded the dark mass of the headland and rushed confidently straight at the light.

Someone yelled from the ferry platform and waved his arms about.

'Cut the motor! Cut it! Come here!' Mona heard a voice say.

The boat's growling broke off and it slowed down as it approached the black rectangle.

'Moor the boat,' a rasping voice sodden with drink ordered from above them. 'Climb up one at a time.'

The first to go up was Skukin.

'Greetings, comrades. Are you Kozolupinians? Deputy Commander of the General Staff of the Fifty-Eighth Brigade Skukin. Here are my papers. I have my stenographer with me. We're on our way to Volchansk.'

He spoke very well. Confidently.

'Keep them covered, lads,' said the owner of the repulsive voice. 'Blast them at the slightest thing, shoot to kill.'

His face was no better than his voice: blue-grey and bloated, with an obnoxious smile on it. He was obviously in command here.

'Keep it a bit more polite, can't you?' Skukin protested. 'You're talking to a Red Army commander. We have a military alliance with your republic.'

'Uh-huh. And let's smooch a bit too.' The Kozolupinian chuckled and suddenly tore off Skukin's belt and holster. 'Our commune decided in full session that the Soviets are the working people's enemy and all you Reds should be wasted. Right, stand over at the side. Hey, you other two, come up here!'

Father Sergius said quietly behind Mona's back:

'The novel *War and Peace*, the Austerlitz defeat scene. The command's wise d-dispositions have misfired.'

A fine time for him to crack jokes, thought Mona. Her teeth were chattering.

She climbed up the rungs of the ladder on stiff legs, barely able to move. A gun barrel was jabbed straight into her chest.

'The dame's not too bad, big tits,' said the man in command. 'Don't worry, we won't do for you. You'll come in handy. Take her, lads.'

The second man grabbed Mona crudely by the elbow and shoved her towards Skukin. He was standing with his back to the rails, holding his hands in his pockets. The third member of the watch was standing beside him grinning, with his rifle lowered carelessly. His face was repulsive – it was more pleasant to look at the commander.

'Stop your swaggering, will you, Red-belly!' the man in command yelled at Skukin. 'Come on, get your hands up! You bastard, I won't tell you . . .'

Mona didn't understand what happened in the next second.

There was a loud crack, the pocket of the lieutenant colonel's breeches suddenly exploded, spitting out a little tongue of flame, and the man with the grey face doubled over without finishing what he was saying. The lieutenant colonel turned to the right, and then to the left, and his trouser leg spat out a vicious, crackling flame twice more. One watchman flung up his arms and tumbled into the river. The other cried out and dropped to his knees.

Then Skukin took his hands out of his pockets. His right hand was holding a small pistol. The lieutenant colonel struck the local commander on the top of his head with the butt of it, and the man collapsed into the water. The man on his knees went flying after him, propelled off the ferry by a kick.

Only two people were left up aloft now – Skukin and Mona, who was totally dumbfounded.

'Have you lost your mind?' Father Sergius shouted from the boat. 'What about the machine gun? Jump into the water! On the other side of the ferry! Quick!'

Mona dashed over to the rails, looked down into the black water and froze.

'Stay calm, madam. There's no need to jump anywhere,' Skukin said behind her.

She looked round.

The lieutenant colonel was standing there calmly, looking towards the shore – towards the very spot where the machine-gun nest was located.

'How are you doing, Kantorovich?' he shouted.

The riverbank replied.

'It's all done! Pick us up!'

'What do you mean, "us"?'

'Me and my new friend!' the staff captain replied cheerfully. 'A Hotchkiss, and two ammunition belts to go with it.'

Skukin jumped down into the launch.

'And don't you ever query the orders of your commanding officer again,' he admonished Father Sergius. 'Good dispositions make provision for all unexpected eventualities.'

The shame-faced old man said nothing in reply, and Mona gazed admiringly at the lieutenant colonel as she climbed down the ladder.

When all was said and done, the best men in the world were officers. At least when there was a war going on.

As if to fete the victor, the black vault of heaven suddenly parted, the stars peeped out, the moon started shining and the night suddenly resembled a picture by that sweet painter Kuindji.

'How did you manage to take a machine gun from two armed men?' Mona asked the staff captain when they put in to the riverbank. 'With no shooting and no noise?'

'With this. Snippety-snip,' he said, showing her a narrow, fearsome-looking knife. He wiped it on the grass and stuck it in his boot.

He set a metal thingamajig on a tripod in the boat, then got in, stretched and yawned.

Skukin reached into his boot too, only what he drew out was not a knife, but a small flute in a neat little case.

'No one minds, I hope? It helps me release the tension.'

No one did mind.

A minute later the southern Russian night became even more syrupy as a quiet, magical melody drifted out over the river. Skukin played quite magnificently, extracting icy-cool sounds of astounding precision, transparency and purity from his reed pipe.

Mona shivered as she listened. One of her travelling companions had just coolly slit two men's throats. The other had shot three men. Five lives had been broken off. Tolstoy and Dostoevsky could have written a great novel about each one of them, Leonid Andreev would have written a heart-rending novella. But there was a civil war going on, and everyone had grown used to such things. One killer was yawning, the other was making music with his eyes closed in ecstatic bliss. Like the boy Kai in *The Snow Queen*, who had a piece of ice instead of a heart.

The magical music roused an irresistible drowsiness in Mona, although it was less than an hour since she had woken up. No doubt it was the result of the shock.

She lay down in the bottom of the boat again, squeezed her eyes shut and started drifting down, down towards the soft, silty bottom, then pushed off from it – and surfaced into the morning. The terrible night might never have happened. Perhaps she had dreamed it?

The launch was hovering soundlessly in a grey haze, with smooth water below it, glinting with spots of light. The newborn sun was playing intricate light games with the mist. Instead of the flute, birds were singing – and their song was every bit as delightful.

This is primordial life, this is natural selection, Mona told herself. *Nature regrets nothing and repents for nothing. Someone wanted to gobble you up, you didn't let him and gobbled him up yourself. And for that the sun shines on you and the birds sing. No need to ponder over anything at all.*

And suddenly she had such a good, joyful, simple feeling. Of course, her travelling companions were not gallant knights, faithfully serving a fair lady, because they were not especially gallant and they quite definitely didn't serve her. But on the other hand, she felt safe with them.

I'm like Huckleberry Finn, sailing down the Mississippi, Mona thought.

Father Sergius was leaning against the rudder, writing something in a notebook. The officers were playing cards intently. A heap of Soviet banknotes lay on the bench between them.

'I'll see you, I think,' Skukin drawled. 'Aha! You were bluffing. I knew it.'

He pulled all the notes over to himself.

'A fat lot of good all that will do you with the Whites,' Kantorovich laughed. 'Why don't we play for flicks on the forehead, like we used to do in grammar school?'

'I was educated in the Corps of Pages. We didn't play for flicks. And money is money, it should be treated with respect.'

Nobody took any notice of Mona, and a different literary association occurred to her: *Three Men in a Boat (to Say Nothing of the Dog)*.

It would be good to wash her hair and tidy herself up – she really did look like some kind of stray mongrel . . .

The day passed by uneventfully. Well – almost.

They were not simply drifting with the current, but under sail, and at one point Father Sergius and Kantorovich also took up the oars. Rowed by four strong arms and with its sail unfurled, the boat ran along almost as quickly as when the motor was switched on.

Nonetheless, they used the motor to ride past the villages and hamlets, and just to be on the safe side the staff captain stretched out beside the machine gun.

However, nobody bothered the travellers. Either these parts were peaceful, or the muzzle of the Hotchkiss was an excellent substitute for a pass.

Mona kept glancing at Skukin all the time. The night before he had made a great impression on her.

A born leader. Cool, calculating and, most surprisingly of all, completely without any swagger. And what a musician! She liked everything about the lieutenant colonel now, even the fact that he had occupied himself with polishing his fingernails during the evening halt. Pushkin was right, quite definitely: 'One may become a man of business, and tend the beauty of one's nails.' *This Kai needs a Gerda, who will break the spell cast on his frozen heart*, she thought tenderly.

At that point Skukin looked up, caught her glance and said in his usual irritable voice:

'I know that tender look on a woman's face. It means: "I have identified the alpha male in the group and want a child from him". Cool down, madam. I am an alpha male, but I don't need a female.'

Mona flushed bright red at this insult, feeling ashamed (yes, yes, ashamed, because this smoke was not without fire) and hissed:

'You're not an alpha male, but an alpha queer! That's why you don't even need a female!'

And she walked away. She had never behaved like a lady with boors: she didn't consider it necessary.

It was good that the other two hadn't heard – they were cleaning the machine gun and talking about something.

Still seething, Mona walked over and listened for a while, but there was nothing interesting about the conversation.

They were discussing the next difficult area on their route that it would be best to pass through at night – the Green School Directorate. It recognised neither the Reds nor the Whites, and it had some outlandish customs. The ataman there was called the 'director' and his name was Zhovtogub.

She felt inclined to spend the remaining time until dark sitting here.

Mona's mood had been ruined, and she had stopped liking her travelling companions.

One was a boor, and quite possibly a member of the 'third sex' (that was a more cultured expression than the one she had used in the heat of the moment); another was an old man, and also not overly urbane; and the third one had a highly dubious sense of humour.

But on second thoughts it was worth taking a closer look at the third one, she told herself, glancing at the staff captain's broad shoulders and his arms, bared to the elbow.

He was really not too bad at all. Definitely more handsome than Skukin.

Mona's rage didn't last for long, because the river was aglow with the lazy gold of advancing evening, the young leaves were rustling, the baked fish smelled glorious, and that insolent ruffian Skukin would live to regret his behaviour.

On the whole, everything was not too bad at all. The second day of a hazardous journey was drawing to a close.

The Green School

During supper Mona sat apart from the others – facing the bushes, with her back to the group. She ate a quite delicious fish off a twig, thinking through her plan and finalising it.

The goal of the plan was to cease being a dog that no one ever mentioned and force the men to change their attitude to her.

To achieve that, she would have to:

Withdraw to a secluded spot in order to bathe and wash her hair.

Brush her hair out and arrange it. It had to be one of two options: either a 'bun' on the nape of her neck, with a back-combed fringe on her forehead, or a simple wave falling down over her shoulders (not very practical, but it looked even better that way).

Change her clothes. Take off the 'robe' – in this warm weather it was too hot anyway; reverse her skirt so that the correct, silk side was outwards; take the satin blouse that had been hidden away until she reached civilisation out of her sack.

Make an impressive reappearance in society.

Entice Kantorovich, treat Father Sergius as if he was still a fine figure of a man, ignore Skukin.

She tossed aside the skeleton of the fish and wiped her fingers on the grass. The three great heroes of legend didn't look at her, they were discussing masculine matters of some kind.

Watch out, you three little pigs. You're about to get a visit from a grey wolf with great big teeth – clickety-clack, Mona, the star of Petrograd's salons, thought with a predatory smile.

She grabbed her sack and slipped into the bushes – and ran straight into a man standing there completely motionless.

Before she could shriek, a rough hand squeezed her mouth shut. A pair of eyes squinted fiercely at her from only three inches away and a low voice whispered:

'Quiet now. Not a peep, or else.'

Then the voice spoke to someone else.

'Right then, my lads. Qui-i-etly does it.'

She sensed movement to the right and the left of her. Someone was advancing slowly, without rustling the grass or disturbing the branches.

Squinting left and then right, Mona made out two figures on her left and one on her right. They were wearing identical soldiers' blouses without shoulder straps and all had rifles.

The one holding his hand over her mouth – a middle-aged man with a drooping moustache – clicked his tongue and shook his head.

'Mind now, woman. Don't make any noise. If I get angry, you'll regret it. Blink if you understand.'

He said this so solemnly, so terrifyingly, that it never even occurred to Mona to disobey. She blinked.

Then the man with the drooping moustache took his hand away and grasped Mona firmly by the elbow. He was holding a Nagant revolver in his right hand.

'Now!' he shouted.

And all four of them went crashing headlong out into the clearing.

The three seated men only had time to look round. They saw the gun barrels trained on them and slowly raised their hands. All their faces assumed the same expression: frozen and intent, with only the eyes moving.

The commander let go of Mona's elbow and gave her a shove.

'Go over to them. Sit down.'

She ran from him to her companions, plumped down onto the ground and leaned against a male shoulder (it was the repulsive Skukin, but at this moment her resentment didn't matter).

At last she could take a look at the forest men.

The three with rifles were young and clean-shaven and they had green armbands on their left sleeves. They weren't holding their rifles just any old how, each of them was aiming at one of the seated men. The middle-aged man had an armband too, but it was a bit different, with a little white circle.

They were nothing at all like the men on the ferry the night before: they didn't look like bandits, but it was immediately clear that they were very dangerous. Especially the leader.

'They caught us very professionally,' Kantorovich whispered.

'Sit quiet!' the man with the moustache yelled. 'Don't lower your hands.'

Then he told his own men:

'I'll go and take a look at the boat. Keep your wits about you, lads. If anyone stirs a muscle – shoot.'

'Oho, what's this they have here!' he yelled from the launch. 'A Hotchkiss! And two ammunition belts!'

The soldiers turned their heads.

Seizing his opportunity, Skukin snatched his identity papers out of his breast pocket and flung them into the bushes.

'Listen to your orders,' he whispered rapidly. 'Each man for himself. We don't know each other. I asked you to give me a ride.'

Kantorovich got rid of his papers in exactly the same way.

The man with the moustache came back. In one hand he was holding the Hotchkiss, removed from its tripod, and in the other he had Father Sergius's large binoculars, which usually lay in the bow of the boat.

'Which side are you on? Who are you fighting for?'

'I don't fight for anyone, my dear man,' said Father Sergius. 'The binoculars are mine, I got them by bartering at a market. Useful things for sailing on a river. I'm a boatman.'

He didn't speak in his usual manner, but with a soft, southern Russian modulation. And he didn't stammer at all. Who could ever have suspected he had such great acting ability?

'The Hotchkiss is mine,' said Kantorovich, raising one hand higher. 'Don't hold it by the cooling jacket, mister, you'll bend it. I'm not fighting for anyone either. Not yet.'

'Then why would you want a machine gun?' the commander asked jovially.

'Because I'm a machine-gunner. And when I left the war, I took my gun with me. I'm wandering the world, looking out for a good position. Who are you? Do you need good machine-gunners? If we can agree terms, I'm yours.'

'Good machine-gunners are needed everywhere right now. And as for terms, we can agree those. Everyone likes it here at the Green School.'

Ah, so that's who they are, Mona realised. And she regretted that she hadn't listened more carefully to Father Sergius's recent conversation with Kantorovich. The only thing that had stuck in her memory was that the Green School Directorate was against the Reds and against the Whites. And that its ataman was called 'the School Director'. He had some funny kind of name.

'Well, and who are you?' the man with the moustache asked Skukin.

'A musician. From Moscow. There's nothing to eat there. I'm making my way down south.'

'And where's your instrument?'

The lieutenant colonel took out his flute.

'Shall I play something?'

He started playing a Russian folk song, the 'Kamarinskaya'.

'"I started dancing, stamped my foot, the hut started swaying and the door slammed shut",' the man with the moustache sang along, and slapped Skukin on the shoulder. 'Come and join us, musician. You'll earn good grub here.'

But he asked Mona a different kind of question:

'Who are you with, woman?'

Obviously in his world it was assumed that a woman couldn't be on her own.

'She's my daughter,' Father Sergius replied for her. 'We're from Belgorod, both of us. And the launch is mine. I don't know these two. I took them along for money, they're going my way.'

'And how come you've sailed so far from Belgorod?'

'We need to get to Lugansk. There's a mental hospital there. Some good people advised me to try it. My daughter's not right in the head. She's got demons.'

Everyone looked at Mona and she started blinking in surprise.

'She seems all right to look at.' Father Sergius sighed. 'But men drive her wild. When she's on heat, she flings herself at them. They say that the psychological doctors can give her a medicine for that ailment. So we set out.'

'She can fling herself at us, we don't mind,' said a freckle-faced soldier. 'Right, Uncle Semyon?'

And all of them laughed, including the commander.

'You shouldn't say that, son,' Father Sergius replied dejectedly. 'The Lord protect you from anything like that. When my Fedosya has a fit, she scratches a man's face and gnaws on his throat with her teeth. She almost tore one man's privates out by the roots. It's calamitous.'

Mona played along with him. She glanced at the freckle-faced lad's crotch and licked her lips. He backed away.

'Okay, we've heard you out,' the commander said when he stopped laughing. 'Now we'll take a look.'

And he started rummaging in the kitbags, taking his time and working thoroughly. He felt papers of some kind inside Kantorovich's lining and took them out.

'What sort of numbers are these?'

The codes, Mona guessed. The staff captain had said he stole them from the Reds.

'I don't have a damned clue. I picked them up for rolling cigarettes.'

The man with the moustache carried on rummaging. Suddenly he straightened up and punched Kantorovich in the face.

'And is this for rolling cigarettes too? You louse in gold shoulder straps!'

In his other hand he was holding an unfolded piece of cloth, with an enamelled medal glinting in it. Mona saw the white cross of an Officer's Order of St George.

The muzzle of a rifle was jammed against the staff captain's forehead. He sat there pale-faced, spitting out blood.

'Right, then,' the commander drawled, spotting Skukin's belt and holster and the case containing his maritime binoculars on the grass. 'And whose are these?'

'Mine,' said Kantorovich, who had nothing more to lose now. 'I'm an army man. And by the way, I never said that I wasn't an officer. I commanded a machine-gun company in the war.'

'Right, get up. And you too, the other one!' the fastidious snooper commanded.

He measured the belt against Kantorovich – it was too short: but it was a perfect fit for Skukin.

'Officers. Liars. Tie them up, lads.'

They secured the staff captain's and lieutenant colonel's hands behind their backs and frisked both of them. They discovered the little pistol in Skukin's breeches and the knife in Kantorovich's boot.

'It's your fault, you and your little trinkets!' Skukin told the staff captain angrily. 'Did you keep them even in the Red Army? You idiot! Because of your damned sentimentality . . .'

The commander punched him on the cheekbone.

'Shut up, Your Excellency! You can do your chatting later.'

He turned to Mona and Father Sergius, who were still sitting down.

'Let's sail on, daddy and daughter. Our doctors here in Greenfields are as good as any in Lugansk. They'll cure her.'

And he told his soldiers:

'We'll take them to the director, he can sort this out. These numbers mean something, lads. I saw some like them at the front, in the command HQ. They're called a "cipher".'

All of them climbed into the launch, which sank low in the water under their weight. They didn't talk because of the roaring of the motor. Mona looked in alarm at her bold knights, who had turned out to be not so very trusty after all.

Kantorovich's bloodied mouth was twitching angrily and Skukin was thinking intensely about something – no doubt trying to work out how he could wriggle his way out of this. Only Father Sergius looked imperturbable, and she had to admit that he was holding up very well. But then, he had less reason to be alarmed than the officers, and his hands weren't tied.

After they had travelled for about forty minutes using the motor, meaning they had probably gone about ten versts downstream, a village appeared on the right bank, some distance away from the river. It was quite large, with a hundred or so white-walled, wattle-and-daub houses, and the iron roofs of stone buildings and the five golden domes of a church glittering at its centre.

'There it is, our Greenfields. Maybe you'll stay here for ever,' the commander said ominously. 'We'll compost you. At least you'll be some use to the land as humus.'

Urged on by those words and the rifle muzzles at their backs, the prisoners climbed the steep path up the bluff from the landing stage.

At the top there was a large, open green meadow. A herdsman was driving a herd of fat cows with tautly dangling udders towards the houses, although there was still a long time to go until the evening – in late May the days are long.

Stretching into the distance for as far as the eye could see were ploughed fields, already covered with a haze of bright green. The gardens between the houses were white or violet with lilac. At the very edge of the village, on a vacant lot, youths wearing soldiers' blouses were being taught how to fight with bayonets. They were taking turns to run up, thrust a bayonet into a dummy with a scream, pull it out and go back into the line-up. A man with a moustache and good military bearing was in command. He also had an armband on his sleeve, with two little white circles on it.

'Where did you pick up the Hotchkiss, Semyon?' he shouted.

'Why, these officers here gave it to me. Are you thinking of having supper soon, Lieutenant?'

'I'll herd these little ones around for another half-hour or so, and then eat. Call round, Sergeant. Taisya's made borshch.'

'I will.'

They spoke amicably, like neighbours, as if there weren't any prisoners there, two of them walking along with their hands tied.

The village turned out to be prosperous. The houses were all neatly whitewashed, the fences were regular and even painted. Old men and women sitting on benches gazed at the strangers, but without any great curiosity. They were clearly a common sight.

The street led into a square with rows of market stalls, where brisk trading was being conducted, despite the imminent approach of evening.

There were even shops – a lot of them, about twenty. Mona ran her eyes over the signs. 'Meat', 'Bakery', 'Hardware', 'Groceries', 'Fabrics', 'Boots and Galoshes'. Even 'Books'! Why, there were more shops here than on half-dead Nevsky Prospect, now renamed 25 October Prospect.

The stone buildings surrounding the square also looked dapper – notwithstanding the general devastation throughout the whole of Russia. There was harmonious singing coming from the open windows of a long building with a sign that read: 'Four-Year People's

Academy' – a children's choir was practising there. The picture would have been entirely idyllic, if only the dominant colour in the crowd was not the pale green of peaked caps and soldiers' blouses.

The prisoners were led to a detached building with four columns and a wide flight of steps. 'District Administration', Mona read on the boring bureaucratic plaque. But higher up, immense, intricate letters painted directly on the plaster of the wall spelled out: DI-RECTOR'S OFFICES.

'Keep your eyes on them,' Semyon ordered the escorts and set off, running up the steps. 'I'll go and report to the director.'

After about five minutes, which seemed like an eternity to Mona, the door of the administration building started opening with a baleful creak, but then froze. Someone had been intending to come out, but had stopped.

'You think we should shoot them?' asked an imperious voice that was clearly audible from a distance. 'We'll take a look at them right away.'

Mona readied herself to see someone terrifying. But the man who emerged onto the porch was extremely placid, even boring in appearance. He was predominantly grey: greying hair in a round pudding-basin cut, a similarly coloured beard à la Chernyshevsky, and iron-rimmed spectacles. Under a mousy-grey jacket she could see a shirt with an embroidered Ukrainian collar, hanging outside his trousers. The man was holding a glass of tea in a metal holder. He didn't have a weapon.

'Good evening, lads,' he said, nodding to the escorts. 'Kolya, your neighbours are complaining about you. Come and see me afterwards. Saikin, have you read that book? How's your mother, Tisha? Has she recovered yet?'

All three youths greeted him politely, calling him 'Mr Director'. Each of them replied to what he had said, but Mona couldn't hear them – her heart was pounding too loudly. There was something frightening about this Chernyshevsky, about his gentle movements and his quiet voice that sounded like a teacher's. In kindergarten she had felt afraid of the formidable female director in exactly the same way.

The man walked down the steps unhurriedly. He was looking at the prisoners now. His eyes proved to be grey too, and probing.

Sergeant Semyon walked behind the director and pointed out each of them with his finger, explaining something in a low voice.

'Medals . . . Cipher . . . Madwoman,' Mona made out, and when she caught the ataman's searching glance on her, she jerked her head convulsively a couple of times.

'Mr Commander!' Kantorovich said loudly. 'Permit me to address you . . .'

He received a blow under the ribs from an escort's rifle butt and choked.

'You will speak when you are called up to the blackboard,' the director reproached him, shaking his head. 'No discipline, and he's an officer. Give him back his medals, Semyon. He came by them honestly. A brave man – you can tell that from his eyes. And dangerous. And the other one is not so simple either. Take them to Stepan Akimovich in the inspectorate. He can interrogate them about the ciphers and so forth. And you,' he said, turning to Father Sergius, 'come to my office, we'll talk. And bring your daughter along.'

The ataman was clearly not accustomed to objections. Having given his instructions, he turned round and walked back into the building.

The sergeant boasted to the escorts.

'I was right to bring the boatman to him. Did you hear? He's going to talk to him *himself*. I twigged straight off that there was more to the old man than meets the eye.'

Kantorovich and Skukin were led to the gates. Mona didn't say goodbye to them, she didn't even watch them go. She knew their fate was about to be decided.

In her agitated state she didn't really take in the interior of the administration building. She thought there were people sitting at desks, and a typewriter tapping away somewhere. Mona only looked at the director's back and rounded shoulders.

He pushed open a door, went in and beckoned for them to follow. 'Please come in.'

For Mona this sinister politeness was the most frightening thing of all.

They found themselves in a study that looked very much like a teacher's room. Nothing military – just bookshelves, and several notebooks on a desk. Even something like a class register with ruled-off columns, covered in neat handwriting.

The director sat down at the desk and indicated two chairs with his hand.

'Well, now, who are you? It is quite clear that you are not father and daughter. And you shouldn't lie about psychological illness either. We have an excellent psychoneurologist from Kharkov working in our hospital. He can check, if need be . . .'

'A psychoneurologist? In a village hospital?' Father Sergius exclaimed in surprise.

Mona squinted at him distrustfully. Was that all he wanted to ask about?

'Here at the Green School we have doctors of all varieties. They themselves come to us from the city. Because people here are well fed and life is calm.' The director wagged his finger. 'But, please, don't interrupt me. I haven't finished yet. So, you are not father and daughter, the woman is not psychotic, and you, naturally, are not any kind of boatman. Tell me the truth. I punish people for lying.'

'Punish' wasn't exactly the most menacing of words for wartime, but Mona shuddered.

But as Father Sergius looked at the ataman he didn't seem frightened at all, more curious, in fact.

'I mentioned the lady's demonic frenzy so that your soldiers would not pester her.'

'Our people don't rape. That offence carries third-degree punishment,' said the director, examining Father Sergius with equal interest. 'Listen, in thirty-five years of pedagogical work, I have learned to read people very well. And in you I sense an individual of quite exceptional magnitude . . .'

Mona started at Father Sergius in amazement. He was an impressive old man, of course, but could you really say he had 'exceptional magnitude'? Or had she failed to notice something about him?

'You are not, of course, a spy, as the lieutenant suspected,' the director continued. 'That's not your level. But then who are you?'

He finished his tea and suddenly – Mona cried out – flung the empty glass straight at Father Sergius's face. The glass was seized in mid-air.

The director laughed contentedly.

'I can see it – that incredible precision in every movement. Like a circus acrobat. Who are you?'

'An acrobat, among other things,' Father Sergius replied imperturbably.

'But apart from that?'

'A researcher. I'm on an ethnographical expedition. Studying Russian anarchism. From that point of view, I find your "republic" to be of great interest.'

Mona couldn't believe her ears. How was it possible to talk like that with a man who could give the order for you to be shot at any moment?

But the director didn't take offence.

'Let's introduce ourselves,' he said. 'Nikodim Lvovich Zhovtogub. Only what I have here is not – Lord forbid – a republic, but a school. The Green School. And concerning anarchism, this isn't the place you need to visit, you should go and see Nestor Ivanovich Makhno, in Gulyaypolye. Owing to his youth and inclination to romanticism, he is fond of the "Black Truth". But we here have the "Green Truth".'

'What is that, the "Green Truth"? Can you tell me?' Father Sergius asked, as if this was all perfectly ordinary small talk.

'With pleasure. I don't often have occasion to talk with an intelligent adult. The eternal problem of the pedagogue – you are always surrounded by children.'

Neither of them paid the slightest attention to Mona, and that suited her quite excellently. In general, she would have been glad to sneak out of this place, only she was afraid that any superfluous movement would remind the softly-spoken ataman of her presence. 'But first permit me to tell you about myself. To help you understand how the Green School came about . . . At the age of twenty, before I had even graduated from Kharkov University, I "went to the people", carrying the high ideals of liberty, equality and brotherhood to the "wild peasant".' Zhovtogub laughed. 'With the passage of time, after I had got to know life and the people a bit better, only one of the three ideals remained – the most important one:

brotherhood. Freedom and equality do not exist. They are urban chimeras, and our "Rassiya" is a peasant country. It is not black with factory smoke, but green with fields and forests. And the Russian Truth must also be green, a peasant truth. Simple and severe, but honest; not borrowed, but *our own*.'

Father Sergius listened very attentively.

'So what is it like?'

'For the peasant, the state is hostile and anarchy is dangerous. The foundation of peasant life is the family. And what are things like in a large peasant family? There is neither freedom nor equality, but there is brotherhood, that is, love. The father's word is law. A good father loves his children, but he doesn't spoil them, like city folks. And he teaches them, he teaches them constantly. How to plough and sow, how to improve the home, how to get along with the community. A peasant family is also a school. That is why our green community is called the "Green School".'

'So you regard the people as children?'

'In their broad mass – most certainly. Exceptions do occur, but they are very rare. I am the director of an elementary school and I teach my pupils the basic rudiments. I have a certain number of adult assistants who bear the exalted title of "teachers" and consti- tute our governing body – the Teachers' Council, of which I am the chairman.'

'Are the teachers elected?'

'That's the very last thing we need! The people are stupid, they would elect a bunch of loudmouths and tub-thumpers. As director of the school, I appoint the teachers. The most respected individuals, selected on merit. In the peasant family, respect for the individual is not a gift that everyone is granted at birth. Respect has to be earned. Who respects an infant that can only soil its nappies? First grow up, demonstrate your usefulness, earn a diploma in the school of life – and then lay claim to respect.'

At this point Father Sergius asked a question that made Mona squirm.

'But who appointed you as the school's director, Nikodim Lvo- vich? By what right do you decide who is worthy of respect and who is not?'

Once again, however, Zhovtogub did not take offence.

'I was appointed director of the Greenfields People's College thirty-five years ago – I founded it myself. And throughout those years all the local people here who are forty-five years old or less have completed my programme of study. They have been accustomed to doing as I say since they were children. We have been living under our own authority here since last autumn, when everything collapsed in Petrograd. And we live rather well. We sow grain, we hold weddings and we have established thirty new farmsteads – because more and more people are arriving all the time. There is famine and devastation on all sides, but my directorate has one and a half thousand square versts of perfect order. There is plenty of land, enough for everyone – we have requisitioned the large landowners' estates. According to the latest census in May, I have 11,483 souls. Almost half of them are male peasants in sound health of working age – labourers and defenders. Because of the war, there is a shortage of men everywhere, but we have many of them. Deserters come to us – from both the Whites and the Reds.'

'I noticed that there were a lot of men in soldiers' blouses in the street.'

'But of course! In times like these we have to be ready to defend ourselves. Under the order of things here, every man performs military duty one day a week. And so there are always eight hundred men under arms, and if need be I can declare a general mobilisation, and there will be seven times more. We have a lot of weapons and ammunition. Last November we went to Kupiansk, closed off the railway line and spent a week disarming German military trains. We have field artillery and even armoured cars. Just let anyone try sticking his nose in here! There have been some who wanted to try it and did try: Whites and Reds, and Cossacks from the neighbouring district. They have all regretted it. I have good soldiers and they defend the Green Truth stoutly. We have some former officers, but there is one iron rule: I don't take blue-bloods, their souls are corrupted. I only take the low-born who have advanced through the ranks.'

'Those little circles on the armbands – are they badges of rank?'

'Yes. One circle is a sergeant, two is a lieutenant, three is a captain, four is a colonel. No one is drilled senselessly, but discipline is better than in the tsar's Life Guards. We don't punish anyone without good reason, but if you have committed an offence, then you must take your stripes. As is only right and proper in a peasant family.'

'But how do you punish people?' Father Sergius asked, frowning slightly. 'You mentioned "third-level punishment". What is that?'

'You're an intelligent man. I don't need to explain to you that children can't be managed without punishment – or they'll be spoilt. Children must be praised for doing good things and thrashed for doing bad things. It's beneficial for them and a good lesson to others. Punishment has to be frightening. Because fear is an excellent educator. Life, the most important teacher of all, is frightening in general. And it punishes offenders severely. If the penalty is comprehensible and just, people will always approve of it. We have three levels of punishment. For petty offences and acts of mischief we put people in solitary confinement or scourge them with rods. For intermediate offences, we expel them from the school. And the third level of punishment, for grave crimes, is public execution. Let me explain with a specific example. In our school the drinking of wine is forbidden. Alcohol is prohibited. It is a mistake to think that in Russia people have always drunk and Russians can't live without vodka. That demon Ivan the Terrible introduced taverns in the sixteenth century to augment the revenue of the public purse and made the people drunkards. Well then, our punishment for drunkenness is first-level: scourging. For distilling vodka at home, the punishment is second-level: we send the man packing. For trading in alcohol, the punishment is death. And we set the offender's head on a pole to discourage others . . . Why are you frowning like that?' Zhovtogub laughed. 'It will be a long time yet before European sensibility takes root in our Russian hinterland. Let me tell you: the Green Truth is harsh – but it is the only thing that can save Russia.'

'And how do you envisage this salvation?'

'Quite simply. Everything real is simple in principle. Green Russia needs to unite, while Red Russia fights White Russia. A union of peasant republics – that is what we need. Let the industrial north live as it wishes. We don't need the Urals or Siberia either. And the foreign borderlands even less. We shall base our life on our black-earth agricultural region. We shall feed the whole of Russia and the whole of Europe with bread – not free of charge, naturally. We shall obtain whatever we need by barter or purchase. We shall teach our children the sciences and build a new, healthy society, based on brotherhood and justice. We already have a leader – Nestor Ivanovich Makhno, the people's hero. He has an army of twenty-five thousand. All that is needed is for Makhno to abandon his anarchist mumbo-jumbo and accept the Green Truth. Then the bat'ko and I will come to terms and others will reach out to us . . . So, tell me where you are really going, and why?' the director suddenly asked. 'After all, you haven't even told me your name yet, have you?'

'I'll tell you where I'm going,' Father Sergius replied after a brief pause. 'And I'll introduce myself. But not just at this moment – later. First I want to take a closer look at this green paradise of yours.'

'That's right. I'm the same myself, I don't like to rush things,' Zhovtogub said with a nod. 'Well then, stroll around and take a look.'

'But how is it that all your men are clean-shaven?' Father Sergius asked. 'Even Peter the Great couldn't achieve that.'

'Not all of them. Those who have demonstrated their maturity – commanders, master craftsmen and other respected individuals – can wear a moustache. And the most highly respected of all, the members of the Teachers' Council, wear beards.' Zhovtogub smiled as he tugged on his own small beard. 'It's the same as things are in life. As a man matures, the hair sprouts on his upper lip first, and then later all over his face.'

'Then you must have a b-barbershop?' said Father Sergius, asking another nonsensical question.

'We have three. Do you wish to have a shave?'

'And a haircut. I'm sick of going around looking like a porcupine.'

'Then here is some money for you. We print our own.'

Zhovtogub held out a few pieces of green paper and Father Sergius took them with a curious air. Then he got up.

'When you have seen enough, come back. I'll be waiting for you. And you, my beauty, stay and live here,' the director said to Mona when she also jumped up off her chair. 'We don't have enough young women, but we have a lot of bachelors, each one more handsome than the last.'

'Thank you,' she said politely. 'If it's all right, I'll take a walk and look around too. Perhaps someone will take my fancy.'

And she hurried after Father Sergius, in order not to be left behind.

The Spooker

In the square Father Sergius gave her some of the money.

'Get something to eat, and I'll go and get myself tidied up. We'll meet here in an hour.'

'What do you mean, "tidied up"?' Mona hissed. 'How can you? Our comrades are in a torture chamber somewhere in this "director-ate", they're being interrogated and then they'll probably be killed! We have to save them!'

'They are not my comrades. I don't like either of them. And don't worry, nothing will happen to them. Everything will work out splendidly,' the heartless old man declared indifferently. 'Well, you do as you wish, but I shall go and take a look at how well green practice corresponds to theory.'

He turned around and set off, leaving her all alone.

'Old cynic!' Mona shouted after him.

She didn't feel hungry at all. Firstly, because her nerves were too strained. And secondly, she had eaten her supper not long ago.

But she did buy some food after all – to give it to the two arrested men: some boiled potatoes and sausage. And at the same time, she asked the market woman where the inspectorate was.

'You walk past the church towards the sunset, my love, and you'll see the Spooker behind the fence, then turn sunwise from there.'

Mona didn't know what 'Spooker' and 'sunwise' meant, but she didn't say anything: it was all right, she would work it out.

She was in a decisive mood. Of course, she had got a really bad fright when she ran into those men with rifles in the bushes, and then she had really lost her courage with that quietly appalling 'di-rector', but that was only because she had let her guard down in male company. *I turned too womanish.* When life goes tearing off at a wild gallop, you had to stay firmly seated in the saddle and hold on tight to the reins – looking out for yourself. And that was something that Mona always did excellently.

When she reached the fence, she grabbed a little urchin running past by the sleeve.

'Child, where's the Spooker round here?'

'Over that way,' he said, waving in the direction of a piece of wasteland with crows circling densely above it, and went running off on his urchin's business.

Mona turned off the road, shielding her eyes against the crimson rays of the setting sun. There were about twenty poles standing on a smooth, well-trampled, open area, each with an earthenware pot on its top.

The croaking of the crows grew more and more deafening. 'Sunwise, turn sunwise from here,' Mona murmured. She reached the open area, looked round – and shrieked.

The things hanging on all the poles weren't pots – they were severed heads. The immense black birds were lazily pecking at them with their beaks.

Mona staggered and grabbed hold of a pole. Something clattered above her head – it was a skull's teeth chattering as it swayed.

Mona looked up and couldn't tear her paralysed eyes away again. Some heads had been stripped down to the bone, but others were quite fresh. There was a large board with an inscription under each one of them.

'I traded in moonshine', 'I'm a rapist', 'I'm a White spy', 'I'm a Red agitator', 'I had an abortion'.

The last head was especially terrifying: a clean-pecked skull with a sumptuous plait dangling down from it.

Mona shrieked again and dashed away from that place, stopping only when she ran out of breath.

'Fear is an excellent teacher' – she recalled what the director had said.

So the large village carried on with its life: working, trading, making merry, the women cooking food, the little children playing, and right there, just outside the fence, was the Spooker. Of course there would be good order in a school like that! You wouldn't get up to any mischief here . . .

Mona wanted to flee from this green paradise, to run as far away as possible. Anywhere at all would be better than this, even if people there were shooting guns and starving. Still not having recovered her wits, she turned into the open field, but stopped when she saw a white building with barred windows not far away.

And she also saw Kantorovich. His hands were tied together in front of him, and an armed escort was tugging on the rope. A second escort was walking behind, with his bayonet attached.

She went rushing towards them.

The staff captain noticed her and shook his head abruptly: Don't come close. His face was covered in blood and he had a blue bruise above his eyebrow.

And somehow the fear disappeared. Mona was sitting in the saddle of a furiously galloping horse, with a tight grip on the reins.

She flung aside the bundle of food and shouted in a shrill voice, like a peasant woman.

'You scum! You White bastard!'

And she dashed straight at Kantorovich.

'I'll scratch your foul eyes out!'

The leading escort grabbed her by the shoulders.

'What are you doing, woman?'

'He's an officer, I can tell from his ugly mug! The officers killed my husband!'

'Calm down. He's a dead man anyway. He put Akimich's jaw out at the interrogation. We're taking him to the ravine.'

Mona tore herself free, flung herself on the condemned man and started beating and shaking him.

They pulled her off.

'I told you: he'll get what he deserves. And they'll find another husband for you. Why not marry me, I'm a passionate man,' the escort said with a grin.

'I'll go with you,' Mona declared. 'I want to see you finish the viper off.'

'Come on, then,' he told her. 'Only don't you get in the way of a bullet.'

She fell in behind, every now and then shouting out curses – more or less the same all the time, since her stock of insulting phrases was not very extensive.

Now that the deed had been done, she suddenly felt very frightened again. Would Kantorovich manage it or not?

While she was shaking the staff captain, Mona had thrust her little 'carver' into his hand. Was it far to the ravine? Would Kantorovich have enough time, would he be adroit enough to cut through his bonds? And if he did, would he be able to deal with two armed men? The only thing Mona could do to help him was fling herself on the man at the back and grab him round the neck. How long would that delay him for? A couple of seconds at the most.

'Will you let me have one last smoke?' Kantorovich asked. 'I've got my own tobacco. You can take it afterwards.'

'You'll smoke in the ravine,' the one at the front replied indolently.

'I like to smoke while I walk. It's a habit from the trenches. You couldn't stand still there. The Austrians fired at the glow.'

'All right. Where's your pouch?'

'In my right pocket.'

The escort turned round and walked up to him. The other set his rifle butt on the ground and took out some matches.

Now! Mona thought, and readied herself to jump on the shoulders of the man at the back. The fear had disappeared again.

But she didn't need to jump.

Kantorovich kneed the first man in the crotch, then swung round and smashed his fist into the bridge of the second man's nose, knocking him down. The next instant the staff captain was holding a rifle in his hands. He swung it back to thrust the bayonet into the fallen man.

'Don't!' Mona shouted. 'Don't kill him!'

'Why not?' the staff captain asked in amazement. 'They were going to kill me, and they would have, if not for you.'

'Well, for my sake, then: don't.'

He sighed and shrugged but did as she said.

He tied up both of them with his own rope, after first cutting it in two, and strapped their feet together with their belts. Instead of gags, he stuffed their soft soldiers' caps into their mouths. The escorts looked absurd with their eyes bulging out of their heads and their caps sticking out of their mouths.

'We have to run for it!' Mona said.

He hung one rifle on his shoulder and gave her the other one.

'Do you know how to fire it? Let me cock it for you. Keep them covered. I'll be back soon.'

And he set off back towards the village.

She caught up with him.

'Where are you going? What for?'

'To get Skukin. And where's your old man?'

'Don't worry about him. He's absolutely fine.'

'Well, Skukin isn't fine at all. I have to get him out of there.'

'You're out of your mind!' Mona screamed in panic. 'Be thankful that you've escaped! We have to run for it!'

'How can I abandon my comrade?' Kantorovich asked in amazement. 'Skukin's an obnoxious piece of work, of course, but they'll top him. Now, don't you worry, my wonderful Fedosya. It will get dark soon, and there's only one clueless sentry on guard there. It's a pushover. We'll be back in the twinkling of an eye, before you can even miss me.'

The last ray of sunlight painted the staff captain's battered face magenta, and it suddenly seemed beautiful to Mona.

On a passionate impulse, she pulled Kantorovich towards her, put her arms round his neck and kissed him on the lips. They were swollen and salty from the blood. It must have been painful for the staff captain and he couldn't suppress a groan. Or perhaps he wasn't groaning from pain.

Mona felt herself squeezed in strong arms, teeth clashed against teeth, everything went dark and her heart started pounding, but it all ended too quickly.

He backed away, breathing heavily.

'You're an amazing woman,' he said in a dull voice. 'You saved my life. And you're very beautiful, I've only just noticed that. But . . . you shouldn't have anything to do with me. I lost the one I loved. And I can't . . . It will be two years soon, but I can't . . . I'm sorry.'

He's wonderful, thought Mona. *There aren't many men like that in the world.*

'I don't even know what your real name is,' she said.

'Alexei. Alexei Parisovich Romanov. I have a funny patronymic – Parisovich . . .'

'And I'm Mona. That is, actually I'm Elizaveta Anatolievna Turusova, but my friends call me Mona.'

And she asked another question, an important one.

'How old are you, Alexei Parisovich?'

'Twenty-seven. Ten minutes ago I was walking along, lamenting that I wouldn't live to see my twenty-eighth birthday.' He smiled, but his eyes were mournful. 'It would have been an idiotic way to die. Thank you, Elizaveta Anatolievna. For God's sake, forgive me for making myself out to be Joseph the Fair-Minded,' he added quickly, seeing her face turn gloomy. 'But I'm a cripple, an invalid.'

But that wasn't why Mona's face had turned gloomy.

'It's all right.' She sighed. 'You're too young for me in any case. Go and get your comrade, I'll wait. Only for God's sake be careful.'

And now this one has rejected me, she thought. Not boorishly of course, like Skukin, but beautifully, only it still feels bitter. I have to make myself look decent as soon as possible. The 'cripple' might start recovering at any moment.

The escorts were not just sitting quietly. They had squatted down with their backs to each other and were trying to untie the ropes.

Mona gave a warning whistle and picked up her rifle.

One of them started mumbling something menacingly and the peak of the cap in his mouth started shifting up and down.

'Just what kind of men are you?' Mona said to them. 'Aren't you disgusted by the way you live? Letting yourselves be scourged with rods. Someone else decides whether you can grow a moustache. You can't even drink a glass of wine.'

More mumbling.

'Stop mumbling and listen!' she shouted at them. 'I'm the teacher now. Do you see my pointer?'

And she showed them the bayonet. The mumbling stopped and the prisoners turned as good as gold. But Mona didn't feel like talking to them any more.

'It's a bad time right now. It's men's time. When the war ends, the women's time will begin, and everything will become normal again,' she said, not so much to them as to herself. She set the butt of the rifle on the ground, leaned on the barrel and started worrying: How was Romanov getting on, would he get into trouble?

She wasn't left to worry for long. Soon after darkness fell, two figures – one taller and one shorter – appeared on the road, moving rapidly. Even from a distance she could hear Skukin's peevish voice.

'And I tell you, it was really stupid not to finish off the sentry! He'll come round and raise the alarm.'

'Elizaveta Anatolievna wouldn't have approved,' Romanov replied, waving to Mona. 'Why don't you just tell me what our plans are, General Staff brain?'

'Good evening, madam,' the lieutenant colonel greeted her. His stand-offishness no longer irritated her; on the contrary it lifted her spirits.

'How glad I am to see you free!'

But the dry stick was no longer paying any attention to her.

'Plans? We have to get as far away from the village as possible, while there's still no moon. Only it's not clear which way to go. Those clodhoppers took my Swiss watch, and it has my compass on it.'

'Let's turn our back on Greenfields, and trust in God to lend strength to our legs,' Romanov suggested.

And that was what they did. But then, a few minutes later, Alexei (in her own mind Mona thought of him in that simple fashion, without a patronymic) turned off the road into the open field.

'That thing about "turning our backs on the village" was just for the guards,' he explained. 'In fact we need to find our way to the river. It must be somewhere in that direction, so we'll come across it sooner or later. Then we'll go back upstream to the landing stage and get into the launch.'

'I was going to suggest the same thing,' Skukin muttered, annoyed that he wasn't the one giving the orders.

They blundered on through pitch-darkness for about an hour, very probably moving in zigzags, but then they caught the scent of damp air ahead of them.

'Careful!' Romanov warned the others. 'There's a steep bluff here.'

He went down first, holding Mona by the hand. The lieutenant colonel overtook them.

Down below water splashed.

'Upstream is to the right. I wonder if it's far to the landing stage?'

It turned out to be quite a distance. Although, of course, it was easier walking on the river sand than on the grass. Mona was about to ask what had made the others think they needed to go upstream and not downstream, but just then the clouds turned silver, sad moonlight came pouring down from the sky and the boards of the landing stage glinted very close, only a hundred paces away. The launch was there too, swaying to and fro.

'To hell with the school! Lessons are cancelled. Freedom!' Romanov proclaimed, running out onto the gangway.

Then he suddenly stopped and dropped his rifle. He threw up his hands and took a step backwards.

A dark silhouette rose up above the boat and a familiar voice said:

'That was a long stroll, officers. I was already thinking I was wrong to expect you to come back to the launch.'

Sergeant Semyon! With a revolver in his hand.

The sand crunched behind them and several other men emerged from the dark mass of the bluff.

Romanov backed away as far as Mona and whispered:

'I jinxed us. I'm not going to live to see my twenty-eighth birthday after all . . .'

She started sobbing ignominiously, like a peasant woman. There is nothing more terrible than thinking you have been saved, only to discover that the worst nightmare is yet to come.

She didn't remember the walk back, she was looking down at her feet. There was a bayonet jammed against her back and she was afraid it would rip her open if she stumbled.

They were taken to a white building. Probably the same 'inspectorate' that Mona had seen just before sunset, but she couldn't make it out properly in the darkness. There they were separated and she was shoved into a little windowless cell that smelled of mouldy straw.

Mona was terribly tired, but when she felt that damp putrefaction under her feet, she decided not to sit down on it. She scraped a spot in the corner clear and told herself: *Well, this is definitely the end now. I only have until morning left to live.*

She could see it quite clearly, right there in front of her: a pole with a head stuck on it, the long auburn hair hanging down, the eyes pecked out by crows, and a sign below it. What would they write on it? 'I'm an enemy agent'? Ah, who cared anyway?

Oh God, how frightened she was!

And she remembered a story that her mother had told her many times.

About how, when she was a silly young fool, she had run off to the Turkish War and almost fallen into the hands of the Bashibazouks. They were ferocious and bloodthirsty and they cut people's heads off. But back then her mother had been rescued by a hero whom she had pined after for the rest of her life. When Mona grew up, her mother had told her: 'Never mind, it's quite normal to love two men: one you live with and grow old with, and another, with whom you are eternally young. We women have two natures in us. One needs a man like your father, the other needs a man like my Erast Fandorin. But there are no more Fandorins in the world. They were all left behind in the last century . . .'

Well, thought Mona, wrapping her arms round her shoulders. *No Fandorin is going to save me here, and there won't be anything else after this. Only pain and darkness, and then the pole and the crows.*

Imagining a rough beak plunging into her eye, she put her hands over her face and burst into tears.

Eek . . .

It was quite amazing that she could manage to fall asleep after thoughts like that.

She had a dream based on her mother's story. A terrible dream. A horseman in a shaggy sheepskin hat was galloping across an open field, and Mona knew that his name was Death. He was shouting gutturally in a language she couldn't understand, and there was something round dangling beside his saddle, but for a long time she couldn't make out what it was. Eventually she did: it was a dead head, tied to the pommel by its auburn hair.

Mona cried out and jerked upright abruptly, not immediately realising where she was.

There was a grey line running across the floor – light coming in through the crack of the door.

Morning.

The cell was dark and stifling, but Mona would have agreed to stay in it for ever. Just as long as the door never opened!

As if the malicious door had eavesdropped on her, it started creaking its hinges. Mona screwed up her eyes against the unbearable brightness. Shielding them with one hand, she made out a silhouette in a shaggy sheepskin cap in the doorway.

'Eat up, lady,' said the silhouette

An earthenware jug clinked against the floor and a large chunk of bread was set on top of it.

'If you need to go out, just hang on, they'll be taking you out soon.'

And the door closed.

Why did he say that? Mona wondered. *What did he mean by 'they'll take you out'? Surely not in order to shoot me? Then why bother to feed me?*

She answered her own question with a strange kind of detachment: *That's how they do things for some reason. They always give condemned prisoners breakfast and then, just before the execution, they let them have a smoke too.* 'They' meant 'people' and their world, to which she no longer thought of herself as belonging.

I won't eat, she thought. But the bread was freshly baked and smelled glorious, and there was milk straight from the cow frothing in the jug.

She ate and drank everything, and it was the most delicious breakfast of her entire life, more delicious than croissants with marmalade at the Astoria.

The door creaked again.

'Come out.'

Mona clenched her teeth and got up. She was amazed at what

a Spartan maid she was: her knees didn't give way and her heart wasn't racing.

But outside it was sunny, with the scent of a fresh wind, larks were singing joyfully out in the field, and her newly acquired calm abandoned her.

No! No! No! She refused to leave this world!

'Good morning, Elizaveta Anatolievna. Or not so very good . . .'

Romanov. He was squinting – no doubt he had only just been brought out too. Romanov was a brave fellow – he was smiling. *He's trying to cheer me up*, Mona realised, and she also made an attempt to smile.

Skukin was there as well, but he wasn't smiling and he didn't greet her.

'Six of them,' he said morosely, nodding at the guards. 'Why so many?'

Yes, there really were six men today, and all holding rifles at the ready.

Romanov whispered to the lieutenant colonel:

'When they come close to tie your hands, punch them in the teeth and try to take their rifles. I'll lash out too. Better to get a bullet in the chest, in a fight, than in the back of your head, on your knees.'

'A matter of taste,' Skukin replied sourly. 'Just look who's come to visit . . .'

Sergeant Semyon walked out of the building.

'Attach bayonets! You four – take this one. Lyokha and Sidor – take the other one.'

Two bayonets were thrust against Skukin's right and left sides. Romanov – no doubt as the more dangerous man – found himself surrounded by four bayonets.

'You won't start kicking up with me,' the sergeant said, and winked.

'Where are we going?' Romanov asked him. 'Not to the ravine again, surely? I'm sick of that.'

'To the director.'

They're not going to kill us now, Mona realised. *First there'll be a trial, or whatever they call it in the Green School. A 'faculty meeting'?*

They walked through the village slowly, because two of the

escorts were walking backwards with their bayonets held against Romanov's chest.

'They respect me,' said the staff captain. 'But you haven't earned their respect, Skukin.'

'I didn't attack my escorts, and I didn't punch an "inspector" in the face,' the lieutenant colonel replied. 'Actually, there's nothing to shoot me for.'

People they met gazed at the procession curiously. Urchins fell in behind them.

'What's the redhead done?' one of them shouted.

'She's a spy. They're going to shoot her.'

Eventually they reached the administration building.

The director was standing on the steps, talking to some city gentleman in a sandy-coloured summer suit and straw boater, with a decent travelling bag. But what was someone like that doing here?

They shook hands and the city gentleman turned round.

Mona caught a brief glimpse of a thin face with a black moustache. But she was looking at Director Zhovtogub.

The director walked down into the yard and approached her unhurriedly. His expression was reproachful.

'Fine travelling companions you have,' said Zhovtogub, shaking his head. 'They got up to all sorts of outrageous things. It could have ended badly.'

He turned towards the city gentleman, who had also come over. He raised his hand to wipe his tall forehead with a handkerchief. His neatly trimmed hair was grey, but his moustache was black, and his face was youthful. And strangely familiar. But Mona was still not looking at him.

'Holy mackerel,' Romanov muttered, 'it's our wandering pilgrim.'

Only now did Mona recognise Father Sergius. What a metamorphosis!

'Didn't I tell you everything would work out fine,' the miraculously transformed reverend father said angrily. 'At least nobody has been killed, or Nikodim Lvovich here wouldn't have let you go.'

'Are they letting us go?' Skukin asked quickly. 'But why?'

'Because the director holds Bat'ko Makhno in high regard. And I have a pass from M-Makhno's headquarters. For me, and for everyone with me.'

'I didn't know about that,' Mona babbled. 'You only told me about the letter.'

'Your confiscated possessions will be returned,' Zhovtogub declared. 'Everything apart from the machine gun. We'll find a good use for it. Fraternal greetings to Nestor Makhno and Aron Liberty. Convey my proposal to them. And be sure to say that they must not delay. Everything will be decided in the next few months.'

The director shook Father Sergius's hand once again and went back into the building.

'Listen, whatever you name really is!' exclaimed Skukin, still not satisfied, even with this. 'Why didn't you present your warrant immediately? They almost shot the staff captain yesterday. And me into the bargain.'

'The staff captain has only himself to blame. He shouldn't have battered the highly respected inspector S-Stepan Akimovich around the face. Nobody likes impolite people.'

Romanov remarked flippantly:

'Yes, if not for Elizaveta Anatolievna, I would already have migrated to the next cycle of reincarnation. Do you know that the Chinese and Japanese believe the soul lives many times?'

'I have heard something of the kind,' Father Sergius said, and looked at Mona. 'Elizaveta Anatolievna . . .?'

'Turusova. And you?'

He bowed, touching two fingers to his hat.

'Erast Petrovich Fandorin.'

'Eek!' Mona said in a quiet voice. And she repeated it again, even more quietly: 'Eek . . .'

She suddenly felt dizzy.

'Where did you get dolled up like that, Mr Fandorin?' asked Romanov, who hadn't noticed her reaction.

'At the m-market. City clothes are cheap here. No one buys them.'

'Haven't you abandoned the masquerade too soon? We still have to sail on farther down the river. You'll attract attention. And incidentally, if we're having a demasking, I hereby disavow Shaya Kantorovich. Alexei Romanov. I hope we shall be friends.'

'The masquerade will no longer be required. Zhovtogub has given me a document of safe passage for the next republic, that of Bat'ko Kovtun. After that comes White territory, where we will be received according to how we are dressed.'

'And what commission did the director give you for Bat'ko Makhno?' the lieutenant colonel enquired.

'He is dreaming of an alliance with the anarchists. I didn't want to upset him, but nothing will come of it. The "Black Truth" and the "Green Truth" are not merely different, they are opposites. One is a truth of freedom, the other is a truth of unfreedom . . . All right, gentlemen, let us return to our waterborne craft . . . And what about you, Elizaveta . . . Anatolievna?' he asked, glancing round at her and not immediately remembering her patronymic.

She nodded without speaking, absolutely dumbfounded.

Erast Petrovich Fandorin?

She said nothing all the way to the landing stage, or when the launch was already under way. She just kept looking at Fandorin, unable to tear her eyes away, and couldn't believe it.

She had heard that name all her life, ever since she was a child. For her it sounded like 'Sir Lancelot' or 'the Count of Monte Cristo' or 'Denis Davydov', the Russian soldier-poet. Something magnificent, ancient and entirely unreal.

And on the subject of 'ancient': how old was Fandorin? Her mother had said that he was a year or two younger than her. Did that mean he was sixty-two or sixty-three, then? Not old at all for a historical figure, but too old for . . .

For what? thought Mona, pulling herself up short.

It was her mother's fault. She was the one who had always spoken about Fandorin as her might-have-been lover. That was probably why Mona was looking at him in this way now: not as an old man of sixty, but as a man capable of arousing powerful and long-lasting love.

And to be quite honest, in his new guise, Erast Petrovich looked nothing at all like an old man. He was a handsome (perhaps even too handsome), elegant, middle-aged man, with imposing, prematurely grey hair.

Good God, Turusova, those words – 'elegant', 'imposing' – aren't even in your vocabulary, you always considered them vulgar, Mona told herself, but there was no getting around it, Fandorin was precisely that: elegant and imposing. Only there was nothing vulgar about him. Because vulgarity was when the sordid pretended to be the sublime, and Erast Petrovich was clearly not one of those who are given to pretending.

He was sitting in the stern, shaving his already ideally smooth cheeks with a cut-throat razor: the sharp blade flickered about like a dragonfly, while a little mirror gleamed in his left hand. His collar was unbuttoned and she could see his muscular neck. His sleeves were rolled up and his forearms were even more beautiful than Romanov's – slim but strong.

Catching her eye on him, Erast Petrovich smiled.

'I haven't shaved for a year. It feels good. And I'm sick and tired of being a wandering p-pilgrim . . .'

Her mother had said that Fandorin had a charming stammer, Mona suddenly recalled. There was absolutely no doubt about it. It really was him.

And she was astounded that she had failed to see the real 'Father Sergius' before. Could the only difference really be that he had shaved and changed his clothes? No, of course not. It was the power of a legend. A legend enveloped a man in a blinding radiance and he was magically transformed. One day before the war, when Mona saw an exhausted and rather crumpled-looking individual with dishevelled hair at the next table in a restaurant, she had said to the girl she was with: 'Look at that. I can't believe he's eating his steak with such a high and mighty air, as if he's deciding the fate of the world.' And her girlfriend had whispered: 'My God! It's Alexander Blok! In person! The poet!' Mona had taken another peek at him and seen the celestial gleam in his eyes, the inspired profile, the elegant curve of his slim fingers. *My God, Blok, how beautiful he is!*

Skukin kept pestering Erast Petrovich, asking him about the director and the directorate. What interested him most of all was the last thing that Zhovtogub had said – about the need to avoid delay, because everything would be decided in the next few months.

'What will be decided?'

'Who will win – the Whites or the Reds. In the director's opinion, a "third force" has a chance of success, as long as the outcome of that conflict has not yet been determined. Afterwards it will be too late.'

'The outcome has already been determined,' Skukin said confidently. 'The White cause is winning, it's obvious. In the east Admiral Kolchak has reached the Volga, in the west General Yudenich is advancing on Petrograd, my uncle's army will take Kharkov at any moment and turn directly towards Moscow from there. The only thing that the White armies lack is co-ordination of their activities. And precisely that was the subject of my graduation thesis at the academy: "The co-ordination of activities and assignment of responsibilities in war under conditions of coalition". I'm not angry with you any longer, Romanov,' he said, turning to the staff captain. 'You may be a wild man and a reckless adventurist, but thanks to you I've switched to the right side in good time.'

'Yes,' Romanov exclaimed sarcastically. 'What a tremendous stroke of luck for the White Army. Your graduation thesis will decide the fate of Russia.'

'Definitely,' said the lieutenant colonel, nodding. A sense of humour was not one of his strong points.

'Listen, skipper, is it far from here to Kharkov? If you go straight across the steppe?' the staff captain asked Fandorin.

'Forty or fifty versts.'

'Skukin, why don't we just make a beeline for the affray? We can't just go on sailing down the river while our people are fighting!'

The lieutenant colonel pondered for a moment.

'Hm. I suppose not. I'd definitely like to be involved in taking Kharkov. It's a major strategic point. There'll be promotions and decorations.'

And he demanded imperiously:

'Put in to the right bank!'

'How about you,' Romanov asked, looking at Mona.

She shifted her gaze away from Fandorin with an effort.

'What?'

'Miss Turusova needs to get to the sea,' Erast Petrovich replied for her. 'And so do I.'

'Really?' she exclaimed. 'But what about your excursion to Gulyaypolye?'

'I think I shan't go. I've already had enough with the Green School. I don't find a return to simple social manners attractive, whether according to the "Black Truth" or the "Green Truth". I'm in favour of more complex manners. I'm all for civilisation. If my country wishes to simplify itself, by all means, but count me out. I hope you won't mind if I keep you company as far as Rostov? I expect we can reach it in a week.'

'I won't mind,' Mona replied in a quiet voice.

The boat scraped on the bottom.

'Goodbye,' Skukin said with a nod. He grabbed his kitbag and jumped out onto the bank.

And he set off just like that, the dry stick, without even glancing back.

But Romanov lingered.

'Mona . . . You said I could call you that, didn't you . . . I desperately don't want to part from you. Believe me, if it were not for my duty . . .'

'It's quite all right,' she interrupted impatiently; she wanted to be left alone with Fandorin as soon as possible. 'I understand. An officer's duty. Take care, Alexei Parisovich.'

'You've taken offence.' He sighed. 'Give me time. Perhaps we shall meet again, and then . . .'

'No, no. I told you, you're too young for me.'

Romanov was far from stupid. He raised one eyebrow, darting a sideways glance at Fandorin, and his expression became quizzical.

Mona smiled and nodded. She was filled with ecstatic delight at life's unpredictability.

Romanov kissed her hand, bowed to Fandorin and trotted after Skukin.

'Why did he call you "Mona"?' Fandorin asked.

'My mother (her name is Varvara Andreevna) . . .' – Mona paused and smiled enigmatically – '. . . used to say when I was a child: "Why are you always smiling so enigmatically? Like the second coming of the Mona Lisa." And she nicknamed me Mona.'

'Mona, I wish you happiness!' Romanov called touchingly from the bank.

She waved without looking round.

Elizaveta the Third?

Actually, happiness had already arrived, and Mona was revelling in every minute of it.

A river, a boat and nobody superfluous. And it would be like that for a long time, for several whole days!

Of course, she had already fallen in love with him, she couldn't have done otherwise. This was a feeling that she had inherited, so to speak.

Fandorin sat at the rudder, entirely unaware, gazing sagaciously into the distance: he was probably thinking about the fate of Russia, or something of that kind. Mona kept glancing at him and smiling all the time. He was like a rabbit who didn't even suspect that the hungry python's supple body had already twined itself round him.

But serious thoughts occurred to her too.

One being that her entire previous life had been nothing more than an appetiser before the main dish. Real life was only just beginning now. And the important thing was not to hurry and spoil it all. There was time.

Yes, time there is, but I'm feeling hungry, the python whispered.

'Why do you keep laughing like that?' asked Fandorin, finally noticing her condition.

Mona recalled a phrase from her grammar-school past. She had admired it for seven years from the desk at the back of the room. Hanging above the blackboard was an inscription in calligraphic writing: 'The destiny of the young generation of Russians is to realise the aspirations of their forebears. *Tsar Nicholas II.*' Exactly – realise the aspirations of her forebears. What had not worked out for the mother forty years earlier would work out for the daughter.

People were funny in the nineteenth century. How could Mama

have been there beside him, in love with him, often alone with him, and still not achieve her goal? *There can only be one explanation*, Mona thought confidently. *This man was not preordained to be my father, but simply to be* mine.

'Tell me, do you believe in fate?' she asked. 'That every event has a meaning, that nothing ever happens by accident, and that your life has a definite, preordained plot to it?'

Erast Petrovich answered as if he had thought this question through a long time ago.

'There are a number of preordained plots. Many, in fact. But you yourself decide which of them your life will follow. That is called "karma". In principle, every person, no matter what path he might follow, has a chance of arriving at one and the same supreme point: of becoming a *bosatsu*, or bodhisattva – a being with a completely enlightened consciousness who is entirely free from the bonds of corporeality.'

'And do you also wish for that?'

'Of course. How could one not wish for it?'

The next question would be difficult. Mona plucked up her courage.

'And do you mean that you have already . . . liberated yourself from corporeality?'

'Alas, no,' Erast Petrovich declared sadly. 'Although that is strange. You see, I suffered . . . a long illness, when my consciousness slept and I had no sense of corporeality at all. It was possible to hope that it would never return. But nothing of the kind. I am still too young. But then, there is nothing to be surprised about. I still have a long time to wait for old age. I have not yet even attained the age of m-maturity, there is still six months to go.'

'The age of maturity?'

'Yes, for a man who lives his life correctly, maturity arrives at the age of sixty-four years. That is eight times eight – the time of phys-ical and intellectual perfection. The time when the most f-fruitful and enjoyable stage of life for a man is believed to commence: the movement from earthly to celestial perfection, to a wisdom that also consists of two eights, only not multiplied together, but observing an equilibrium: eighty-eight years.'

'I would really like to spend that pleasant stage with you,' Mona would have said, if she had been a fool. But she was intelligent and simply listened and nodded.

'The Japanese master who once taught me to control the will and the body used to say that he had only become a fully adequate human being at the age of sixty-four,' Fandorin continued. 'That is the so-called "age of the first perfection": the body and mind are completely developed, and the spirit's turn arrives. That takes two twelve-year cycles, after which the body and the mind lose their significance. Only the mature spirit remains.'

'And what is there after that, after the age of eighty-eight?'

'Nothing. The development comes to an end. The sage lives until such time as his interest in life fades away, and then departs. The Taoist elders possess the ability to halt their life in a single exhalation – at any moment that seems appropriate to them.'

'And I suppose their remains don't even decay after such a spiritual life?' Mona asked derisively: she very much disliked all this high-flown chinoiserie. It had obviously been invented exclusively for men. Any normal woman would find it disgusting to think of herself as an old woman without any mind or body, with nothing but her spirituality.

'No, they don't,' he replied seriously. 'They say – although, to be honest, I haven't seen it myself – that in secret crypts, to which only very few know the entrance, elders who have reached the ultimate state of enlightenment are preserved in an imperishable state for centuries, and supposedly even after death they are capable of exerting influence on people. It is perfectly possible. A great deal of spiritual energy accumulates in a man like that, and it is also subject to the law of conservation. In that respect metaphysics is in no way different from physics.'

Mona couldn't tell whether he was joking or not. She wrinkled up her brow and started doing the arithmetic.

How old would she be when he reached that infernal age of wisdom? Fifty-nine? Well, all right. It wouldn't happen for another twenty-five years, in 1944, may God help her. All the revolutions and wars in the world would have raged themselves to a standstill long before then, and perhaps Erast would have changed his mind about becoming a Taoist or a bodhisattva (what was the difference between them, by the way?).

However, it was time to divert this conversation into a more productive channel. Mona moved onto the attack.

'But I don't want to be liberated from corporeality,' she said with a wistful sigh, and performed an elementary female trick – hitching up her bust and stretching like a cat. 'I love my body.'

'And for good reason,' Fandorin murmured, looking away. But his glance had been the right kind, a man's glance. Mona was satisfied. Apparently, the rabbit had started to suspect something.

And now for a slight digression, so that he wouldn't become wary.

'I wanted to ask: where did you get that travelling bag from? And what's in it?'

'I bought it in Greenfields,' Erast Petrovich began explaining with obvious relief. 'It contains a change of underwear, two shirts, collars and toiletry articles. They have almost everything there – which is amazing these days. And I also bought something for you, on the assumption that you would want to change your clothes.'

'How sweet of you!' she exclaimed, intrigued. 'I'm so grateful to you! I'm sick and tired of going around like a beggar woman too!'

Of course, there was no need to mention her satin blouse and the fact that her skirt could be reversed to expose its decent side.

'Forgive me, I bought things according to my own taste.'

Fandorin took out a maroon dress with hideous pink roses.

'How charming!' Mona exclaimed in hypocritical delight.

But the shoes were not too bad. She tried them on and the fit was perfect.

'You guessed the size!'

'I didn't guess, I have a very precise eye.'

'I didn't think you'd had time to take such a good look at my feet,' she said merrily. 'But didn't you buy any underwear? Only stockings?'

He was embarrassed.

'The shop didn't have any lingerie. Apparently there's no demand for it from the local female inhabitants.'

'I shall have to put the dress on over my naked body,' Mona bleated like an innocent little lamb.

He started blinking again. No, he wasn't entirely a bodhisattva yet!

'Yes, yes, I'll look away.'

And he moved to sit on the bow, assuming the pose of a stone idol.

Mona stripped naked, stood up on the rear bench and flung her arms open wide in greeting – to the river, the sun, the air, the world.

She dived into the exquisitely cold water, turned a mermaid's somersault and swam after the launch.

Right, bayonets bared!

She cried out:

'Ai!'

Fandorin swung round abruptly.

'What?'

'Something slithered over my leg! Could there be water snakes here?'

'I don't know. Perhaps grass snakes.'

'A-a-a-ah!' she howled, and started beating her hands on the water. 'Pull me out of here! Quick! Close your eyes and pull me out!'

He obediently squeezed his eyes shut and pulled her out energetically, but gently.

Mona flung one leg over the stern, then the other, and kneeled down. She pretended that she couldn't keep her balance and flung her wet arms round Erast Petrovich's neck. His flushed face and closed eyes were very, very close, and she decided to put an end to all the Chinese ceremonial. He wasn't an adolescent and she wasn't a boarding-school girl.

She whispered:

'Kiss me. And don't think about anything.'

The eyes opened.

'But . . .' Fandorin murmured. 'Are you . . . sure?'

And Mona suddenly got the idea that this was all a dream. She really had been shot in the morning. And now her dead head was stuck up on a pole, revelling in its fantasies.

But so what? If this was a dream, so be it.

Mmm, what a kiss . . . And what a smell! Men always smelled not so very wonderful, but she could have squeezed this one into a little bottle to make 'Fandorin' eau de cologne, and then perfumed herself with it every morning. A certain female novelist had been right when she wrote: 'Let's learn love from the animals, they do not love with the eyes, but with the nose.'

She loved him with everything that was in her, there was no remainder left over. The river, the sun, the air and the world didn't interfere, they waited patiently. The moment went on and on.

Coming round after her blissful half-swoon, Mona did not allow herself to rest on her laurels. She had to build on her first success and move on. 'Erast was too complicated for me, little fool that I was,' her poor mother, the child of an innocent age, used to sigh. But only weak men could be too complicated. The stronger they were, the easier they were to manage.

Mona continued in an entirely intimate tone, because lovers were always the same age and he should realise that himself straight away and not dare to take a paternal attitude.

'You haven't liberated yourself from corporeality at all yet.'

'The *ki* energy was accumulating for t-too long,' he replied incomprehensibly.

Mona put her head on his shoulder and soon fell asleep. That bound even stronger bonds than passion did. The soldier serves even while he sleeps.

Through her sleep she heard the motor start, but she didn't wake up, because his shoulder hadn't gone anywhere. Somehow he must have managed to reach the lever without disturbing her. Mona kissed his biceps muscle (it would have been good if it was a bit softer) and fell sound asleep again.

The next time they made love together was under the stars, and the world of night was every bit as good as the world of day.

And it is also very good to talk in the dark.

'There's nothing left for me to do in Russia,' Erast Petrovich lamented, running his fingers through her loose hair. 'I tried for so many years to change the country's unfortunate karma somehow, to avert d-disaster, but I failed and I didn't avert the disaster. I won so many battles, but I lost the war. And now I'm leaving, because I don't know who to fight against. Against the land? Against the air?'

She listened, waiting patiently for him to start talking about the most important subject of all. It would be wrong for her to lead him on to that subject herself.

After indulging in male self-castigation and bemoaning the fate of Russia for a while, Fandorin finally asked the question that Mona had been waiting for with a fluttering heart.

'I'll take you to Rostov, and from there to Sebastopol. What then? Will you go to Switzerland, to join your parents?'

She hadn't told him about her mother yet – she had left that for later, when the initial joys would start to pall and it would be time to take the relationship to a new, more providential level. Let Fandorin also be filled with awe at the exalted design of destiny.

Right now it would have been more intelligent, of course, to be surprised and reply: 'Why, yes, I'll go to Switzerland, where else?' And let him ponder for a while whether he would like to be parted from her. After a day or two of this idyll, he himself would have suggested staying together, and she would have agreed with the air of doing him a great favour.

But now, under the starry sky, Mona didn't feel like being intelligent. And she said:

'I want to stay with you. I want to be where you are, and I couldn't care less about anything else.'

Fandorin began squirming, and she was frightened that she might have ruined everything. But he turned out to be concerned about something else.

'My friend Masa is waiting for me in Sebastopol. We have been inseparable for forty years, and I hope that we shall never part until we die. It would be difficult for you with him. He has always had a difficult character and he has only become worse with age. And you know, you are no soft v-velvet mitten yourself.'

'I love everything that you love,' she said meekly, recalling what Kitty said to Levin in *Anna Karenina*. 'So I shall love your Japanese too.'

But to herself she thought: *What fiddle-faddle*. In her hands she held levers of influence inaccessible to any friend. And she added ferociously:

'I love you as no one has ever loved anyone before!'

And then, instead of replying with equal passion or at least whispering uninventively 'I love you in the same way', he murmured something mysterious.

'Elizaveta the Th-Third? But that would really be too much . . .'

Mona sat up, took him by the throat with both hands and demanded that he explain immediately what those words meant.

He explained at great length and incoherently, several times attempting to hide away in his shell like a tortoise or thrust out his prickles like a hedgehog. But of course Mona didn't back off until she had found out everything.

Then she moved away and started thinking.

It was good that both of his wives had also been called 'Elizaveta'. It meant it was his – what was it called? – karma.

But it was bad that both marriages had ended so terribly. Although, would it have been better if they had been successful?

And in general, it was third time lucky. She had to give him what Elizaveta the First didn't get a chance to give him, and Elizaveta the Second couldn't or hadn't wanted to give him.

And in that very second Mona resolved with great ease a question over which mystical philosophers had racked their brains for centuries: how to incarnate the incorporeal and ensnare the impalpable.

And it was very simple.

Envelop the impalpable firmly, render a little particle of it captive to your own body, and nurture your complete possession from that tiny tot. Of course, she would have to reconsider her principles and change her attitude to the question of reproduction, but strict adherence to principle was the preserve of intelligent men and stupid women.

Concerned about the prolonged silence, he asked timorously, speaking with a pronounced stammer:

'I shouldn't have s-said that about Elizaveta the Th-Third. Have I ruined everything? What c-can I do to make you f-forgive me?'

Mona turned back towards him and stroked his cheek.

'I may be the third, but I am also the last. And I will forgive you on one condition. If you still have a little bit of *ki* energy left.'

The moment stopped

The next day they were sailing through the domain of a certain Ataman Kovtun. The war had passed through here only recently and the villages they encountered were of three kinds: deserted, male and female.

Mona turned away from the deserted, smoking ruins, not wishing to spoil her endless glorious moment. At the male villages men with guns came out onto the bank and ordered them to put in. Erast showed them the pass from the school director Zhovtogub, and the launch continued on its way. At the female villages – those where no one was waving guns about – Mona got out onto the bank. At one she bought food with the remaining Green School money, and at another she exchanged the idiotic floral dress for a quilted blanket – to make the bottom of the boat softer for lying on.

But closer to evening, someone shouted to them from under the willows hanging down over the water on the right bank.

'Lookee, a gent and a lady in a little boat! Hey, dope in the hat, row this way!'

There were three men there, watering their horses and brandishing carbines.

'Don't worry,' said Erast. 'I'll show them the piece of paper and we'll sail on.'

He steered the launch towards the bank.

'We're travelling on an errand for Director Zhovtogub. Here's our pass.'

One of them took the document, glanced at it carelessly and flung it down on the sand.

'We couldn't give a damn for your director. We're our own men. You, mamselle, jump over here to us. And you, take that jacket off. And the boots.'

Fandorin sighed, got up and took off his jacket.

'I'm sorry. It won't take long.'

Mona wasn't afraid. More interested.

Erast Petrovich jumped lightly over onto the bank, and no sooner did one foot touch the ground than the other described an arc through the air and struck the ruffian on the cheekbone. The ruffian dropped his carbine, and before he even had time to fall, Fandorin twisted round on his heel and slammed his elbow into another man's eye.

'Bravo!' Mona shouted. 'Encore!'

But there was no encore, because the third bandit (and beyond all doubt, they were common or garden bandits, since they were 'their own men') flung away his gun and took to his heels, dashing off through the bushes.

The injured men lay there quietly, but the one running away bawled:

'Lads! Lads!'

Somewhere, horses started whinnying. A lot of horses.

Erast picked up one of the carbines and jumped back into the boat.

'Let's not overstay our welcome,' he said. 'There are more lads here too.'

'Trrr, trrrrr, trrrrrrrrrr,' the motor growled.

The boat started picking up speed.

Soon the willows came to an end and an open field began.

Things in the field looked bad. There were horsemen hurtling along at a gallop, a machine-gun carriage throwing up dust and the air was filled with bandits' whistling.

The launch turned abruptly towards the other bank.

'On the water they'll mow us down with the machine gun,' Erast explained quickly. 'We have to get out and take cover. Into the bow.'

He took hold of her hand. The very moment the boat struck the bank, they both jumped. And they ran.

'Ta-ta-ta-ta-ta!' The sound rolled across the river.

Mona went tumbling headlong in the grass – Fandorin had jerked hard on her hand.

The air above them rustled.

'Can you crawl?'

'I haven't tried since I was two, but I'll remember how,' Mona replied. She wasn't afraid in the slightest. With him she wasn't afraid of anything, anything at all.

They started crawling. Around them grass crunched and fell, mowed down by bullets.

'So now they've left the b-bank,' Fandorin murmured, half-rising and looking round.

Mona took a look too.

There were men's heads jutting up out of the river. Each with an arm stretched out above it, clutching a rifle.

'How about running? We have to get to that hollow. The machine gun can't reach us there.'

'I'm a cyclist. You should see how strong my legs are.'

'I know. Three, four!'

They dashed off, holding hands. *Like when I was a kid*, Mona thought. And she also thought: *This moment is glorious all the same, even like this.*

They slithered down a shallow slope and switched to a fast walk.

'Where are we going?'

'Did you see the burial mound with an idol, a stone woman, out there in the field?'

Mona shook her head. She hadn't been looking forward, only down at her feet.

'That's where we'll go to ground. If they try to come at us there, so much the worse for them.'

They crawled out of the hollow and ran, hunched over, to the small hillock.

'Hide b-behind the idol, and don't stick your head out.'

But Mona, of course, did stick her head out.

Men were running across the field, strung out into a cordon. They looked ludicrously short, because the grass hid them up to the waist.

'Just like that other time,' said Mona.

'What "other time"?'

'When you and my mother bolted from the Bashibazouks. Do you remember Varya Suvorova? I'm her daughter.'

It would have been hard to imagine a more dramatic moment for this dramatic announcement.

Erast's black eyebrows curved up into perfect arches, but his jaw dropped rather inelegantly.

'What?' he gasped. 'That's impossible.'

Mona laughed. 'You can't escape from our family. We have long arms. And legs . . . Oi!'

A bullet had ricocheted off the stone hip of the female idol with a repulsive sound.

Erast forced Mona right down to the ground. He shook his head, unable to gather his wits.

'You are V-Varvara Andreevna's daughter? But . . . things like that d-don't happen.'

Mona was really delighted that he was so bewildered and babbling like that. The whistling of the bullets only lent greater poignancy to the scene.

'Agh, what a nuisance these b-blockheads are!' he said angrily, looking round at the gunfire.

'Mama told me the Turks galloped along and you took aim at them with a rifle. It's just the same for us now, isn't it?'

'It's better. There were more Bashibazouks, and my Winchester turned out not to be loaded. There are only ten of these, and this Mannlicher . . .' – he jerked back the bolt – '. . . has a full magazine. Please, I implore you, don't stick your head out.'

But he stuck his own head out. For a second. Took aim, fired – and hid again.

Someone yelled out in the field. Mona peeped out from underneath Fandorin. One of the bandits was whirling round on the spot, clutching his shoulder. Another shot rang out above her head and another bandit dropped his rifle and swayed, also clutching at his shoulder.

The others hid in the grass.

Erast waited, moving his rifle barrel about slightly.

A shot!

'Aaagh!' a deep bass voice howled. A man sprang up and went running away – once again clutching his shoulder.

'You're hitting them all in exactly the same place,' Mona told him.

'When the civil war started, I decided to stick to a firm principle: I only ever kill men who are obviously bad. Like that raftsman Stas. I don't know anything about these men. A wound is enough for them. An excellent opportunity for them to lie qu-quietly for a while and think about their lives.'

At that moment he was so magnificent with his idiotic principles that Mona couldn't contain herself. She jumped to her feet, embraced him and started kissing him.

'I love you so terribly, simply unbearably!'

'Wait . . .' he said. 'Really, not now . . . Because of you I didn't see where the one on the far right went to. In a round astrakhan cap, with a Mauser . . . What if he creeps up from the flank, where the stone woman doesn't cover us?'

'I'll protect you better than any stone woman. I'm a stone woman too,' Mona whispered passionately.

She hugged Erast against herself with all her might. And suddenly, as she glanced over his shoulder, she saw a head in a flat astrakhan hat and a slim gun barrel just sticking up out of the grass.

With a strength that she had never suspected she possessed, Mona swung Erast round and changed places with him.

Something hit her on the shoulder blade with a crunch, like a little hammer or a stick.

'Dar . . . ling,' Mona murmured into the rapidly thickening darkness.

And the glorious moment stopped.

THE WHITE TRUTH

It's hard dealing with cretins

On Merchants' Slope, Alexei stopped in front of the mirror-bright window of the new café 'Nord', as if in order to adjust his peaked cap, but actually in order to check whether he had a 'tail'. There was no one he could think of who could be tailing him, and no one who had any reason to do so, but as the saying had it: 'The foundation of good health is the prevention of illness'. When he set out to the secret meeting place, Romanov always followed the rules: he never travelled directly there in a cab and he checked periodically that he hadn't picked up any 'dust on his back' (as this problem was called in the professional jargon).

His back was in perfect order. There was no one staring hard at the modest captain, no one had squatted down abruptly to tie a shoelace, hidden behind a street lamp or frozen beside a wall, shielding himself with a newspaper. The usual street crowd in unsettled times: more men than women; more military personnel than civilians. Ever since the headquarters of the Volunteer Army had been moved to Kharkov, 'rear-line heroes' had poured in here from all over the place, because there were jobs to be had and food to be enjoyed. Arkasha Skukin, who claimed to know absolutely everything in the world, ranted that there were fifty per cent more staff officers, quartermasters, liaison officers and, in particular, individuals who were 'OPL' and 'RWH' ('on permanent leave' and 'restoring weak health') here than there were officers at the front.

Suddenly Romanov was on the alert: there was a patrol heading directly towards him – a Volunteer Army lieutenant in a peaked cap with a crimson crown and two privates with white armbands. A standard check, or . . .

'Captain, may I see your papers, please. In connection with a certain incident in Kharkov, special security measures have been introduced.'

'I know,' said Alexei, inwardly relaxing. 'I drew up the order myself. Here, by all means.'

He held out his warrant card and also a mandate signed by the head of counter-intelligence, Prince Kozlovsky, enjoining all members of the army and the civilian administration to render the bearer every possible assistance.

'Have any suspects been detained?' he asked in a stern, commanding tone of voice.

'I can't say. I've only just come on duty.' The lieutenant looked at the captain in dismay. 'How could it happen, Captain? I feel so terribly sorry for the children. They're all so terribly miserable as it is! Who could have done it? If only they'd give me those bastards for literally just five minutes. You're in counter-intelligence! Find them!'

'We're searching,' Romanov growled angrily, taking back his documents.

He made another halt to check his back again on Klochkovskaya Street beside the 'Information Board' with reports from the front and announcements from the army command. He didn't spot anything suspicious this time either, but his mood turned even more sour.

Firstly, the military news was lousy. General Mamontov's cavalry corps had run through the Reds' rear lines, captured the Liskinsky railway junction and joined up with General Shkuro's strike force. Seven thousand prisoners had been taken and, if the 'Bulletin' could be believed, half of them had joined the Volunteer Army. The Red front was about to collapse at any moment, and then the road to Moscow would be open. And at the same time, in the north-west, General Yudenich was already only a hundred and thirty kilometres from the second capital, Petrograd. And secondly, the talk among the small group of men reading the information was appalling. No official notification of the tragedy at the Kaledin Orphanage had been published yet, but the explosion yesterday evening had been heard right across Kharkov, and of course the rumours had spread instantly.

One man – he looked like a proletarian, in fact – said almost exactly the same thing as the Volunteer Army lieutenant: 'When they catch these Reds, they shouldn't hang them, but let the people have them. We'd tear them apart with our bare hands.'

Alexei moved away, thinking morosely that when the newspapers came out, the entire city would curse the underground fighters. The announcement wouldn't contain a single word about an assassination attempt against the commander-in-chief, it would say only that the Bolsheviks had blown up an orphanage. And there would be photographs of dead, mutilated children . . . *Agh, you bastard Zaenko, what the hell do you think you're doing?*

He had to stop for a while at a crossroads as a marching column passed by, yelling out the Volunteer Army hymn.

> For Holy Rus,
> Boldly into the fray we go
> Spilling our young blood
> In the fight against the foe . . .

And they really were all young. With intelligent, enthusiastic faces. No doubt a student levy. Our thanks to Comrade Zaenko again – he had really fouled things up when he commanded the local Cheka and 'purged' the exploiting classes. The intelligentsia and young students – everyone who really ought to be for the revolution – all now hated the Reds, and they would fight them to the death. And after yesterday's stupidity the influx of volunteers would only increase . . .

From Klochkovskaya Street he turned onto Ivanovskaya Street, walked through the courtyards and emerged exactly opposite the 'Commercial Reading Room'. He glanced round once again before he walked towards the door.

There was very little time. Kozlovsky had said: 'At a gallop, Alyosha, be there and back in a flash.' Alexei would have to spin him some kind of a yarn. Kozlovsky would curse him roundly, of course, but he wouldn't suspect anything. Captain Romanov enjoyed his superior's absolute trust.

On the one hand, of course, that was extremely convenient. On the other, it was morally oppressive. This damned mayhem. It had driven a wedge between people who were so close they couldn't possibly be any closer. Old comrades who had fought shoulder to shoulder right through the Great War and saved each other's lives more than once. Alexei constantly found himself wanting to avert his eyes when he looked into Lavr Kozlovsky's open, amicable face. After all, it was repellent – deceiving someone who trusted you unconditionally.

On the other hand, how could he possibly reject such incredible good fortune? When Romanov got through to the Whites in early June and discovered that Colonel Kozlovsky had just been appointed head of the Special Department of the Volunteer Army, he had immediately informed the centre that he knew him well. Orlov, of course, had immediately ordered him: 'Fall into the embraces of your dear friend, oh fortune's favourite!' And the colonel really had been so delighted to see Romanov that he almost smothered him in his embraces. He had taken Alexei on as his assistant. For the cause, that was a tremendous stroke of luck, but for Alexei it meant daily torment.

But that was all sloppy sentimentality – to hell with it, he could endure all that. It was just so stupid that the unwieldy 'Operation Nephew' had all been for nothing.

In May Alexei had been recalled to Moscow from the Tsaritsyno front, to the Revolutionary Military Soviet of the republic – Orlov was working there now, because in the Cheka the upper hand had been gained by people he didn't like and referred to as 'crass thickheads'.

'The army needs information about the enemy,' Orlov had said, 'but the cretins in Dzerzhinsky's department deal with absolutely anything except that. Locking people up, standing them against the wall – they're good at all that, but they can't set up a decent intelligence network in the Whites' rear! If the Chekists have organised underground cells, they spend their time on all sorts of stupid nonsense. They blow up warehouses, damn and blast them! But we don't need bombings, what we desperately require is precise operational information. So this is what I have for you, Alyosha . . .' – like Kozlovsky, he also called Romanov 'Alyosha' – '. . . we've been working on a cunning scheme. In your line of work. You see, the commander of the Volunteer Army, General Gai-Gaievsky, whom the European press calls "the White Hannibal", has a little nephew, and he, believe it or not, is serving in the Red Army . . .'

The plan had seemed too complex to Romanov – there were far too many 'ifs' of various kinds, but Orlov was a hundred per cent right: you couldn't fight a war without decent intelligence. Half the disasters and defeats were a result of the fact that the Whites had an excellent intelligence service, while the Reds had absolutely damn all. And so, even though the Red Army was ten times larger, it was a fight between a blind bear and a pack of small, vicious dogs: the bear merely spun round and round, waving his arms about, while they flung themselves at him and tore at him with their sharp teeth. The bear was now bleeding profusely and on the verge of collapse.

Anyway, he had agreed. And more to the point, everything had gone amazingly smoothly. Comrade Kandyba from the Special Section of the Eighth Army had played his role impeccably, thudding picturesquely to the ground when he was shot with a blank cartridge. After that incident the 'little nephew' had behaved in the only way that he possibly could, the bullets hadn't caught up with them, they had escaped the pursuit, and after that everything had worked out well. The army commander and uncle had greeted his relative with open arms, and he, in turn, had promised the comrade of his adventures a good spot – but then an even more desirable option had come up with Kozlovsky, and it turned out that he needn't have bothered about the escapade with Skukin. He had merely presented the Whites with an experienced general staff officer who, as a man without any political convictions, could just as well have served the Red Army, but was now in the enemy camp. Romanov had person-ally delivered a capable helper to the commander of the Volunteer Army. Now, that really was cretinous!

*

There was a notice hanging on the door of the reading room: 'The collected works of H. G. Wells have arrived. Because of excessive demand, lending of the volumes is <u>strictly</u> limited to three days. Any late returns will incur a fine. The discount for students and school pupils <u>does not apply</u>.' The underlinings were in red – so that Romanov would not walk by, but call in to see if there was any news. Today, however, Alexei would have called in even if there wasn't any news.

The reading room was an ideal venue for a secret meeting place. This form of commercial activity was very popular in a large university city that had been left without new books, so many people dropped in, including military men.

'Good afternoon, Mr Zuev. How's my order coming on?' Romanov asked, removing his peaked cap.

There were only two or three people in the hall and they were sitting a long way off, so they could hardly have overheard a conversation, but conspiracy is conspiracy.

The stoop-shouldered little man looked over the top of his blue spectacles and mumbled:

'Aha, it's you. Your books have arrived, but we'll only issue two of them to you now. New rules.'

After seven years in a cell, almost all of Ivan Maximovich Zuev's teeth had fallen out and his sight had deteriorated badly. He also walked with a stick, because of his rheumaticky knees. To look at, he was just a little old man who wouldn't hurt a fly. A retired teacher, or perhaps an accountant. But that impression was deceptive. Zuev was the head of the Revolutionary Military Soviet's Kharkov intelligence network, which was small, but intelligently and cautiously organised. Romanov, for instance, knew only Ivan Zuev himself and his daughter Nadya.

'Then let me choose. Where are the books?'

'Let's take a stroll to the repository, then. Nadya, stay here in the hall!'

A very young-looking woman came out – she seemed almost a child – with an unremarkable appearance: grey plait, grey dress, grey knitted shawl on her shoulders. A perfect little mouse. She simply nodded to Romanov (according to their cover story, they had never been introduced), but her glance was quizzical and demanding. Alexei inclined his head ever so slightly and Nadya Zueva brightened up.

He didn't know very much about her: she was nineteen years old and had been raised by her uncle, a Kharkov lawyer, because her parents had served hard labour in exile from 1905, and her mother never returned – she had died during a hunger strike. Nadya had really only got to know her father after she turned sixteen. Zuev used her as a courier and for coding and decoding work.

The corridor led deep into the building, into the Zuevs' apartment, and only when he reached it did Romanov start talking about business.

'Why the red underlining? Has a dispatch come in?'

Zuev thrust his hand in under the leather covering of a desk and pulled out a sheet of paper bearing a decoded message from the centre in Nadya's fine, girlish, grammar-school writing. Orlov urgently demanded news about General Mamontov's plans: in which direction would the cavalry corps that had shattered the Reds' lines of communication turn – to the north or the south?

'Write: HIGHNESS to AVIAN.' (It was Orlov who had thought up the conspiratorial alias 'Highness' for Alexei – because of his tsarist surname, and because without a pronoun its gender was indefinite, so it wasn't clear if it was a man or a woman.) 'According to information obtained from Cockroach . . .' (that was their designation for Kozlovsky) '. . . Mamontov's Cavalry Corps is turning back because their horses are tired.' Having answered the question from the centre, Romanov moved on to his own problem. 'Once again I earnestly request you to bring your influence to bear on our production partners. Yesterday an unsuccessful attempt on the life of the commander-in-chief was responsible for the deaths of pupils and teachers in an orphanage. This is a massive gift to White propaganda. Take measures in Moscow, otherwise I shall take them here myself. It is impossible to work like this.'

'Do you know what they did?' he complained to Zuev, no longer dictating. 'Do you know the details? Yesterday the commander-in-chief came to Kharkov and visited the orphanage for the children of officers who have been killed. A bomb placed under a table exploded. The directress of the orphanage, one governess and eight children were killed, another eleven were wounded and the others suffered blast injuries, but for some reason the general suddenly broke off the ceremony just a minute before the explosion, apologised and left the room. Only orphanage staff and pupils were killed, while he remained absolutely unharmed. Those idiots! They screw up everything they try to do! They've merely provided the Whites with a new intake of volunteers. And if the assassination had succeeded, that would have been even worse. Instead of Palliasse . . .' (that was what the White officers called the phlegmatic commander-in-chief of the Southern Russian forces among themselves) '. . . we would have got Gai-Gaievsky. He would have been ten times more dangerous! It's hard dealing with cretins!'

Zuev worked his toothless mouth.

'Mm, yes. They're only interested in making an impression in Moscow, they don't think about the cause. I know from my experience in the Party that the worst damage of all is done by your own side. Less energy was spent on fighting the Okhranka than on infighting with dear comrades in the Party. But are you certain the explosion was Zaenko's work?'

'No, you're right. Maybe the Whites blew themselves up!' Romanov replied caustically.

The worst thing of all was that even Orlov wouldn't be able to rein in the Chekists. Up there in Moscow two lines of strategy had collided. How should we regard our revolution? What are we fighting for – the victory of socialism in a single country or a global revolutionary conflagration, for the sake of which we are willing to burn Russia down? They were arguing and reviling each other, everyone trying to pull Lenin over onto their own side, and he was buying time – saying one thing to some people and something else to others. The military wanted victory over their enemies – they were soldiers, after all. For the Chekists, the more cracking and crunching, the better. That was why they were piling on the Red Terror. Why have any pity on our class enemies, if we have no pity on the whole of Russia?

Dzerzhinsky's people had their own cell in Kharkov, founded by the head of the city's Cheka, Comrade Zaenko, who had gone underground, and there was no concord, or even contact, between the two networks.

'That dog Zaenko has set all of Kharkov against him. You should have seen what happened here under Soviet power, Alexei, when someone was "liquidated" every day in the Black House.' Zuev sighed. 'I proposed excluding Zaenko twice at the Party Bureau. Nothing came of it. And the result was that we had to surrender Kharkov without a battle. The moment the Whites got close, there was an uprising. Zaenko's to blame for that. And now he's ruining things for us in the underground.'

'And he could be helping. We all serve the same cause!' Roma-nov grated his teeth in frustration. 'Even I, the deputy head of the Special Section, wasn't informed of the commander-in-chief's precise schedule, but they found out from somewhere that he was supposed to arrive at the orphanage at exactly twenty to eight. The timer was set for seven-fifty. That means Zaenko has his own source of information. Somewhere right at the top . . . And anoth-er thing . . .' – Alexei glanced at his watch, he had to hurry – '. . . Kozlovsky has sent for Greyhair again to ask for help. Do you re-member how quickly Greyhair exposed the men who carried out the special operation in August? Well, now he'll expose Zaenko himself in exactly the same way. I told you, he's a very dangerous man.'

'Perhaps that's all for the best?' Zuev remarked calmly, demon-strating quite starkly how deceptive his herbivorous appearance was. 'Your counter-intelligence operatives can liquidate our damned production partners. Then they'll stop getting under our feet. And Moscow won't have anyone else in Kharkov except us.'

Alexei was dumbstruck.

'Are you out of your mind? Whatever they may be like, they're our comrades, Bolsheviks.'

Zuev looked at him condescendingly.

'You haven't lived in the underground, young man. You don't know Bolshevik dialectics. Who is your comrade and who isn't is a situational question. Well, all right, if you want to protect Zaenko

– let's take out Greyhair. We know where he lives. He doesn't have any bodyguards . . .'

'I'll take you out,' Romanov growled gruffly, but he was disconcerted. He really did find it difficult getting a sound grip on Bolshevik dialectics.

Zuev drawled significantly:

'Mmm, yes, it is hard dealing with cretins. You're right about that . . . Okay, Nadya will encode your tearful petition and Operator will send it.'

He had a man in the army's signals operations centre (his code name was simply Operator), who used a Winston transmitter to send coded messages that flew through the airwaves at a speed of seventy words a minute, straight to the Khodinskaya radio station in Moscow.

Romanov was shown to the rear entrance by Nadya – not out of politeness, but for secrecy's sake: first she would glance out into the courtyard and make sure the way was clear.

In the corridor she asked in a whisper:

'Did you bring it?'

He didn't say anything.

'But you promised!'

'I did, I did . . .' Alexei stuck his hand in his pocket.

She held out her little hand demandingly; at the centre of the palm there was a round, pink spot. Alexei knew the story of that scar – Zuev had told him.

In the summer of 1917, when the Provisional Government was still in power, Zuev had started setting up an underground network. At that time the Bolsheviks were declared German spies and had started being arrested. Ivan Maximovich's daughter Nadya, whom he had not seen for many years, asked him to involve her in the work, but he refused – why get a child involved in adult games? And then she had said: 'I won't try to persuade you. I'll hold my hand over a flame until you agree.' She lit a candle and held her palm to the flame. He thought she would jerk it away after a second. But she didn't. And when he smelled burning flesh, he gave in. 'There's nothing to be done, her mother was just the same,'

Zuev had concluded his story proudly and sorrowfully.

'Give it to me!' Nadya demanded.

He took a bar of Eminem chocolate, her favourite, out of his pocket and put it on her palm.

'Better take this instead.'

The girl flushed bright red and hid her hand behind her back.

'Shame on you! You promised!'

'What do you want a Browning for? Who are you planning to shoot?'

'Myself! If they try to arrest me, I won't let them take me alive! I don't want them to torture me!'

Romanov glanced at his watch again. *Damn!*

'First of all, we don't torture anyone, Kozlovsky doesn't allow it,' he said absent-mindedly, moving towards the exit. 'And secondly, if they arrest you, then you'll end up with me, and I'll get you out of it. So eat your chocolate and stop thinking about this nonsense.'

'Why do you always talk seriously with my father, but only joke with me? Do you think I'm funny?'

Her voice trembled so agonisingly that Romanov had to stop. He turned round.

'I think you're an extremely beautiful young woman. And I joke because when I see you, it puts me in a good mood.'

She looked at him suspiciously – was he joking again? Alexei put on a very serious face and Nadya beamed.

'Don't bother to see me out. I'll check the yard myself. No offence taken?'

He held out his hand, and when Nadya held out hers, he couldn't resist – he raised it to his lips and kissed it directly on the scar.

'What are you doing?' she asked. She hadn't jerked her hand away from a burning candle, but she shied away now and almost fell.

When Romanov walked out, the smile lingered on his face for a while, but the expression of his eyes was already quite different, intent and focused.

Alexei was thinking through what he would say to Greyhair.

Clouded happiness

You ought to stick to writing about war and peace and not make clever-clever comments about things you don't have a clue about, Mona told the author. She had set out to reread *Anna Karenina,* but had been distracted immediately. That had been happening to her all the time just recently. *For you all happy families are the same, fancy that! You couldn't puzzle out your own wife, but you still blow smoke in your readers' eyes.*

Everyone's happiness was different. For instance, the kind that existed in Mona's family had probably never existed before anywhere. For the world to be collapsing all around them, with appalling news coming from all sides, each report worse than the one before; with starvation and pestilence and terror, and no way of knowing what would happen tomorrow – and yet, it was an immense happiness. Not unclouded, of course – in fact the sky was covered by black storm clouds, riven by lightning – but that only made the feeling of happiness even keener. And it had been like this for more than three months.

Well, of course, for the first month after she was wounded, things hadn't been so very cheerful – there was pain, and helplessness, and fever, but even so there was happiness. Because Mona had missed the very worst part, she had been unconscious. She had woken up in hospital, after the operation. She had opened her eyes, seen the gloomy face of her 'noble man' looking down at her and immediately smiled. And from that very second, life had started getting better, and there had been more and more and more happiness.

She had borrowed the expression 'noble man' from Masa. She didn't consider herself to be a 'noble lady', but the term could not possibly have suited Erast better. And that was what she called him: 'My noble man, stop combing your hair and come and have breakfast.'

Erast fussed over his parting for a long time and set his collars at precisely the right angle. He thought that with such a young wife he had to look immaculate. He was so funny!

On the other hand, it was a good thing that he was such a stickler for detail and cared so meticulously for his hairstyle – otherwise there would not have been any happiness. The bullet that passed straight through Mona had hit the steel comb in Erast's breast pocket. Afterwards the Japanese had scratched a hieroglyphic saying on the ruined comb and set it in a silver frame. The translation of the saying was: 'The seeker of beauty defeats death'.

First Mona had spent a month being happy, because Erast came to see her every day and because getting well was very enjoyable. Then she had been discharged and moved in with Erast, and that was genuine bliss. Living together under the same roof, sleeping in the same bed, waking up together. Of course, the apartment was appalling – on the outskirts of the city, with a tin-plate washbasin and a wooden-plank lavatory, which Mona called 'le privy', and she called their haven itself 'le hovel' because, as the Russian saying has it, life with your darling is heaven, even in a hovel.

In August the Kharkov branch of Crédit Lyonnais had opened, and Erast had managed to transfer the money from his American account to it (yes, yes, her 'noble man' had turned out to be rich as well). And then the happy family had moved into a deluxe two-room suite in the Metropole, a miraculous, world-class hotel that had opened shortly before the war. And there they had soft feather beds, hot water, a telephone in the apartment, an excellent restaurant and palms everywhere – like in the Garden of Eden.

Mona preferred not to leave that little island of normal life, especially after it became clear that the delay in her female cycle was not the result of her injury, as had previously been assumed. The finest obstetrician in the city, Professor Liebkind, had said that the traumatic start to the pregnancy might entail a high risk of miscarriage up until the twentieth week, and therefore she was prescribed as much peace and quiet as possible: every possible measure had to be taken to 'slacken the tonus of the womb'. Including lying in bed as much as she could (preferably on her back, and it would be good if her feet were raised), correct nutrition and avoiding anxiety at all costs.

Mona took immense pleasure in slackening the tonus of her womb. She read in bed, with her feet raised. When she grew tired of lying, she sat in an armchair, manicuring her nails and whistling. She drank tea with sour Antonovka apples, glancing out of the window from time to time with her eyes narrowed.

The world outside the window was not alluring in the slightest. Out there, unhappiness prevailed. Rat-grey marching columns extended along the street, wounded men were driven past, a dreary crowd hurried on its way to somewhere. War.

But Mona couldn't give a damn. There was only a month left until the hallowed bourn of the twentieth week, when, with Dr Liebkind's blessing, they would go to the Crimea, board a steamship and set sail for somewhere far, far away from the country of victorious rats. Happiness would become unclouded.

Mona's belly swelled, but not as fast as she would have liked, although she ate for two. Her belly was an important ally. Every time that her noble man grew tired of reading the newspapers and started striding morosely round the room, Mona stuck her belly out and complained of nausea, which she had never felt – the future mother's pregnancy did not cause her even the slightest unpleasantness. Her complaints made her noble man immediately take fright and forget about the world outside the window.

I have to hold out for another four weeks, and then I can relax, Mona told herself, sitting down in front of the mirror and taking pleasure in examining herself. Bags under her eyes – excellent. And what was this on her forehead – a new wrinkle? Magnificent! When would at least one grey hair appear? She wanted to look a bit older, to come a bit closer to Erast's age – the poor dear suffered so badly because he was thirty years older than her.

It was still too early for lunch. What could she busy herself with? Perhaps she might do a bit of sculpting?

She put on her working smock and walked out of the bedroom into the living room. Masa was sitting there, tracing a little brush across a sheet of paper. Two days earlier he had bought China ink, brushes and some special kind of paper in the Chinese quarter. And now he was drawing his squiggles, with little black dots on his forehead and the tip of his nose.

'Shall we do a bit of work?' Mona asked.

The Japanese got up and bowed respectfully.

He had appeared when she was still in the hospital, occasionally drifting off into oblivion. One day she had woken up and seen a large, round face with narrow eyes at the spot where Erast's face was usually located. She had thought it a dream, but it had turned out that her noble man had sent a telegram to summon his Sancho Panza from Sebastopol.

The Japanese saw that the patient had woken up and inclined his entire torso, without bending his neck (that was the way they bowed). He said:

'Masahiro Shibata. I hope you will grant me your love and favour.'

Mona had immediately granted both love and favour. She found him terribly amusing, even more so than Erast.

Masa lived in the hotel room next door but was almost always in their living room – and always without fail when Erast was absent.

Of course, Mona could have kept her noble man beside her continuously – it would not have been hard for a pregnant woman in a weak state of health – but it was a bad idea to keep a man like that shut away between four walls, he would start languishing. She had to deal with Erast differently, constantly inventing small, difficult errands for him, so that he was always kept busy with something and pondered less on the fate of the world.

First Mona's feet started feeling terribly cold, and socks made from the wool of a newborn lamb were required to warm them. Erast set out round the villages in the district in search of this Holy Grail, but it was not easy to find it, because hardly any sheep are bred in the Kharkov region and, as everyone knows, lambs are not born in the summer. Nonetheless, he had obtained the wool and Masa had knitted the socks. But at that point Mona's chilly fits had ended and she had started having fits of nervous anxiety. Only the very latest Swiss remedy could help, and Erast spent a week running around hospitals and pharmacies; he was even on the point of setting out for Constantinople, but that would have been excessive. Mona declared that she received perfectly adequate relief from an infusion of thyme.

A month ago she had felt a desire to sculpt – and after long searches her noble man had obtained some decent wax. And then a rather more difficult task had arisen – good colours, new ones all the time. Today, for instance, Erast had been commanded to obtain mandarin ochre, with which the artist was thinking of tinting her portrait of Masa.

As a matter of fact, in this way she had won the passionate gratitude of the Japanese, who at first had seemed to be jealous. But now they had become as thick as thieves, and Mona knew quite certainly that in any argument with her husband, Masa would be on her side. Dealing with men was easy, especially the strong ones. Be weak with them, ask their advice about everything and ask them to relate their previous heroic exploits. And another thing – a mere trifle, in fact: when Erast and Masa performed their idiotic *rensiu*, pounding each other with their fists or wooden sticks, she always cheered on the Japanese. Her husband was a little offended by this, but she could always console him in a thousand other ways.

In preparing to pose, Masa sat down near the window, where a big, round ball of wax was lying on a little table. He set his features in a redoubtable and haughty expression.

Mona took her subject's head by its prickly top and turned it as required.

'Do you want me to talk about something again?' the Japanese asked while she rubbed talc on her hands. Mona nodded: when he spoke, his face came to life.

'I have been thinking about our last conversation, mistress, and I would like to say this. You can't have a little girl. Just look at the master. How can he possibly have a daughter? It is unimaginable. He is too much a man.'

It was Masa's dream to be a mentor to a boy, because Fandorin understood nothing about children and would be certain to spoil his son.

'Look at me.' Mona palpated his short nose with her fingers, in order to discern its three-dimensional geometry. 'Only don't turn your head.'

He squinted sideways.

'But can I have a boy? Am I not too much a woman? Don't wrinkle up your forehead!'

Masa didn't like this idea. He started breathing heavily.

'Tell me something,' Mona instructed him, extruding the wax quickly through her fingers.

'What about?'

'About the women whom Erast has loved. How many have there been?'

She had been building up to this subject stealthily for a long time.

'No. The master will be angry.'

'Ah, what a pity,' said Mona, disappointed. 'I often think about this and start worrying. I have actually just felt a pang in my heart. I'm not asking out of jealousy. Who feels jealousy for the past? I simply want to learn to love him as well as possible. And for that I need to know about the women whom he has loved. What were they like, how did he love them?'

Her anxiety was always a fail-safe argument. The Japanese pondered and started bending down his fingers. They soon ran out and he started straightening them back up again.

'I mean love, not just any sort of tomfoolery.'

'Then it is easy. My master has loved three women very greatly. And another three greatly, but not very greatly.'

'First tell me about the three he loved very greatly.'

Masa sighed sadly.

'The first one was before my time. I cannot tell you anything about her. But she was very young, and it is unlikely that you could learn anything from her . . . Now the second – I knew her – was a genuine *sensei* of love, oh yes, but she was a *kitsune*-fox. And the third did not really exist.'

'How do you mean?'

'She was always playing some role or other, but she herself did not exist.'

'The women Erast loved very greatly were, first, a little girl, then a she-fox and then a dissembler?' Mona knitted her brows. This conversation was unpleasant, but dreadfully interesting. 'I suspected that he has been stupid in love.'

'Yes,' agreed Masa, 'hopelessly stupid. I was not fated to teach him this, although I tried. Thank God that he has fallen in love with you.'

Not that he really had a choice, thought Mona.

But Masa changed the risky subject:

'Have you decided where we will sail away to? The master will do as you wish, you know that.' His face became obsequious and his voice as sweet as honey. 'If we set sail for Japan, it will be the *momiji* season there now. There is nothing more beautiful in the world.'

She and Erast had been arguing about this for a long time, and Masa was right: it would be for her to decide. But she was still hesitating. Fandorin was trying to persuade her to choose America, because Europe was in the grip of serious and chronic illness. Masa, naturally, was agitating for his homeland, and Mona was seriously considering that possibility. She did not know much about the Land of the Rising Sun, but pictured it to herself as a beautiful little doll's house, and that image delighted her heart. And if all Japanese were like Masa . . .

There was a knock at the door. The hotel staff had long ago been taught not to present themselves without being summoned: it could only be Erast. With his old-fashioned punctiliousness, he didn't even enter his own apartment without knocking.

'You can't come in!' Mona shouted. 'We're not dressed!'

The Japanese snorted angrily. He didn't approve of such jokes. He walked quickly over to the door and opened it, but it was not Fandorin standing there, it was a tall military man.

Her heart skipped a beat.

Without giving any sign of her agitation, she said affably:

'My God, Staff Captain Romanov in person! We haven't seen you here for a long time. Please come in.'

The last time Romanov showed up, it had ended badly: Erast had broken free of his leash. Or rather, he had stretched it so far that she had been obliged to let him off it. Of course, that time the staff captain's superior, the gammy-legged Prince Kozlovsky had come with him. Perhaps there was no reason to be alarmed?

Mona held out her hand to be kissed.

'Where have all the little stars on your shoulder straps got to?'

'My superior has arranged a promotion to the next rank. I haven't received my new shoulder straps yet – they're in short supply, so I simply removed my stars. You are positively blooming, Elizaveta Anatolievna.'

He did not kiss her hand simply according to the formal rules of gallantry, but in a genuine fashion, with his lips, and he also gave her fingers a little squeeze. Men really were astounding creatures. They seemed to think that if you had permitted them some liberty ages and ages ago in a moment of weakness, it still meant something.

Mona took her hand away.

'Oh, come now, I am finding my condition hard to bear. Nausea, dizziness, no appetite.'

The captain exchanged bows with the Japanese, who, unlike Mona, was clearly glad to see their visitor. Masa had most pleasant memories of their adventures in August and now he was like Pavlov's dog when the lamp lit up in front of it.

'Is Erast Petrovich at home?' Romanov asked.

Her heart skipped a beat again. Her dark premonition had been confirmed.

'Why, there he is,' said Mona, pointing to the table.

The captain looked – and shrank back.

Standing at the centre of the table was her composition 'The Trophy of Herodias': Erast's head in a setting of asters, roses and chrysanthemums. Mona had sculpted it life-sized, diligently and lovingly. She had chosen and dyed the wig, glued on the moustache and eyelashes, traced the lines of the veins on the temples. A genuine feast for the eyes! Only the head's eyes were closed, because Mona had worked in secret, at night, when her husband was asleep. She had wanted it to be a surprise for him. It rather infuriated her that he was always so reserved and imperturbable, that he could never be astonished or thrown off balance by anything.

The surprise had been a glorious success.

One morning, they were in the bathroom together – Mona was sitting in the bath and he was shaving – and she had asked in a feeble voice: 'Darling, could you get me the lavender bath essence?' Her unsuspecting noble man had opened the dressing cabinet – and there was his own head. Mona laughed so hard at the hilarious expression that appeared on Fandorin's face, she almost suffered a miscarriage. That would have been stupid, of course. But now it was pleasant to recall the occasion. Even now she giggled.

The Japanese was also pleased by the captain's reaction.

'Beautifur, isn't it? I'll have one soon too. Even better. With grass eyes.'

Romanov tugged on the collar of his service jacket.

'Ooph. You lead a merry life. Unlike myself . . . Will Mr Fandorin be back soon?'

They replied in unison.

Mona: 'No, not soon.'

Masa: 'Yes, soon.'

The captain was at a loss.

'Will you permit me to use the telephone?'

He gave the operator the number and then asked someone, probably a duty officer, to connect him with 'the colonel'. The conversation was brief.

'Lavr, I'm at the Metropole. He's not here. No one knows when he will be. I'd better come back . . . Very well, I understand. I'll wait for as long as necessary.'

She had taken a terrible dislike to Colonel Kozlovsky from the very beginning. The first time he appeared, she and Erast were still living in their rented apartment. Kozlovsky had been brisk and to the point – which was why she had disliked him. He had spoken to her husband as if Erast were some kind of religious hierarch, saying that in 1914, when he was transferred from the Guards to the counter-intelligence department, he had taken special courses, on which he had studied Fandorin's operations during the Russo-Japanese War. 'It is an incredible stroke of good fortune that you happen to be in Kharkov, Your Excellency,' the obnoxious visitor had said. 'We need you very badly. I would regard it as an honour and a boon to serve under your leadership.' And that had been followed by all sorts of stuff about the White cause and the salvation of poor Russia from the Red plague. Mona had been on the point of collapsing in a faint to cut this dangerous conversation short, but Erast had interrupted the prince to say that his enemies were not the Reds, or the Greens, or even the Purples, but scoundrels of any kind, who could be of any colour, and enemies of the Fatherland. Under present circumstances, who should be considered enemies of the Fatherland was not obvious. To him personally, it seemed that all of the participants in this accursed bloodbath were to be considered scoundrels.

And Kozlovsky had left with nothing for his pains.

But in August he had put in another appearance – this time here, at the Metropole. 'You fight against scoundrels? Very well. Here is a loathsome atrocity worse than anything you could possibly imagine. No doubt you have already heard that yesterday on Ekaterinoslavskaya Street the military treasury car was robbed. Some degenerates flung grenades at the car in the middle of a crowded crossroads. Eleven bystanders were killed and about thirty people were injured. I have no experienced detectives, my only hope is that you will help.' He had shown Erast a photograph. Erast's face had turned to stone and his brows had knitted together – and Mona had realised that the situation was beyond saving, even by means of a faint. She had been obliged to unfasten the leash, and had spent the two days after that flouncing around the room, trying to persuade herself not to worry.

Surely it couldn't happen all over again?

She suddenly wanted very badly to throw Romanov out before her husband came back, but of course that was nonsense. The captain would simply wait in the foyer, and then she wouldn't even know the purpose of his visit.

'But what has happened, Alexei Parisovich?' Mona asked, taking a confidential grip on Romanov's elbow. 'You appear agitated.'

'You don't know yet? We've been on our feet all night long. An explosion at the orphanage. An attempt to assassinate the commander-in-chief. The prince wanted to come to see Mr Fandorin himself, but he is busy with the investigation. He sent me, with a package.'

Mona shuddered. The orphanage? That was trouble. Erast would break away again.

'Masa, please bring me my pills from the bathroom,' she said and, having sent the Japanese away, asked the captain peremptorily: 'What is in the package? Show me.'

Romanov hesitated.

'It contains photographs. Terrible ones . . .'

But he took the envelope out of his map-case anyway.

The first photograph, a large one, showed a group of children in identical uniforms, together with women wearing aprons with crosses on them – probably their governesses. The faces of eight of the boys and two of the women had been crossed out with a red pencil.

'Those are the ones who were killed,' Romanov explained. 'All the others were wounded or shell-shocked.'

The other photos were even worse: each of the dead separately.

'The prince ordered me to show all this to Erast Petrovich without fail.'

A damned psychologist, Mona thought spitefully. *He knows how to make an impression.*

'Dear Alexei,' she said in a soulful voice. 'I have a favour to ask of you, a very great one. You could simply tell Erast that your superior is asking for his help, and not show him the photos.'

'But Lavr ordered me to show him them without fail,' Romanov exclaimed, perplexed. 'How can I possibly not follow orders?'

'For my sake. For the sake of everything that we went through together . . . Do you remember?'

And she looked into his eyes tenderly, as if to say: 'I remember everything, how could I forget something like that?'

She wasn't expecting him to agree, but wonderful Romanov sighed and said:

'All right. Since you ask . . .'

And he hid the dangerous photographs away in the envelope, and the envelope in the map-case.

'Thank you,' she whispered, very pleased that the conversation had taken place without Masa being there.

Just then there was another knock at the door.

'There's no one in!' Mona responded merrily.

Erast walked in, looking sullen.

'Did you get the ochre?'

He took a little bottle out of his pocket.

'I hope it's the right k-kind.'

And then he stopped speaking for a moment, noticing Romanov standing by the wall.

'You?'

'Good health to you, Your Excellency,' the captain rapped out.

'What k-kind of "Excellency" am I to you?' Fandorin asked with a frown.

'An actual state counsellor, in military terms a major general. I am not here on a private visit, but on the colonel's orders. Yesterday evening an attempt was made on the life of the commander-in-chief. Not our army commander, but the actual chief,' Romanov added, not entirely trusting a civilian's knowledge of the military hierarchy. 'The prince urgently requests you to take part in the investigation.'

The promise given to Mona had been honestly kept. She thanked Romanov with a slight inclination of her head.

But then Masa, who had come back from the bathroom, interjected inopportunely:

'They exproded a bomb in the orphanage. We have to find out if any chirdren were hurt.'

'They were,' Erast replied sombrely. 'Eight boys were killed, and many were wounded. A monstrous abomination.'

So that's why he's so gloomy, Mona realised. *He already knows.*

'All right, Captain. Let's go straight away,' Fandorin said . . .

Living in the Yin World

. . . and looked at Mona apprehensively.

'Get a cab and wait for me in f-front of the hotel,' Erast Petrovich added.

Romanov saluted and walked out of the room. Mona lowered her eyes and said nothing. That was the worst thing of all – her silence.

'Children were killed there. And even more terrible – some have been mutilated. They were wretched enough already, after l-losing their parents. And the people who did this are strolling around on the loose and God only kn-knows what else they will get up to . . .'

Mona didn't say anything.

'I promise that I won't get drawn into anything risky. And that I will try to deal with everything as quickly as possible . . .'

She finally looked at him, with an expression of sad reproach.

'You promised, didn't you? Can you really not wait for a while? There's only a month left.' She sighed. 'All right. I can see that you won't be able to sit still. But on one condition.'

'Any condition that you like!' Fandorin exclaimed hastily.

'That you will tell me everything. Without holding anything back. With all the details.'

'I give you my word.'

'And that you will take Masa with you again.'

'No. We agreed: one condition, not two!' Erast Petrovich brandished his fist at the Japanese, who had leapt up out of his chair, as if to say: You keep quiet!

'You are in your fifth month. The doctor says that is the most hazardous period. I will not leave you unattended for a single m-minute. *Masa, o-negai da kara! Tanomu dzo!*'

Masa groaned and accepted his fate. Fandorin did not often ask him to do something in that tone of voice.

'Take care now, you gave me your word.' Erast Petrovich's wife drew him close and then pushed him away. 'That's all, now scram. And remember: if anything happens to you – you will kill both of us, me and the child.'

In the carriage Romanov tried to strike up a conversation about the job, but Fandorin just looked away and didn't listen to him.

He was thinking about the Yin World.

Of course, Erast Petrovich had known for a long time that there was no 'human world', just as there was no abstract human being. There was man and there was woman. They were constituted differently, they lived differently, they were interested in different things and they were guided in their behaviour by different ethical and aesthetic norms. In many respects the Yang World and the Yin World were opposites. Fandorin himself had always lived in the Male World, he had made an excellent study of it and attained one of the highest possible degrees in its system of co-ordinates.

The Yang World was subordinate to reason and subservient to the will, it was firm and clear, a place in which 'yes' meant 'yes', and 'no' meant 'no', and where in general the difference between Good and Evil was always clear.

But a little more than four months earlier, at the whim, or possibly through the mercy, of karma, Erast Petrovich had suddenly made the transition to the Yin World. It had happened during those terrible hours when the gun carriage taken from the bandits was hurtling across the steppe towards a large city with genuine hospitals, while wounded Mona tossed about, unconscious, on an armful of hay. Fandorin had sworn to himself then that if she survived – oh, if only she survived! – he would never leave her.

A miracle happened. Mona did survive. And Erast Petrovich was not accustomed to breaking his oaths. And so it happened that a master of Yang found himself in an alien world, with the status of a mystified and helpless apprentice.

Objectively speaking, the female world is incomparably superior to the male one. It is both kinder and more selfless, both more beautiful and more *alive*. The apologists of bushido assert that the true goal of a man is to die well. If that is so, the true purpose of a woman is to live well. It is no fortuitous circumstance that men are at their most adroit in taking away life, but women make a gift of life. It is not easy for a man to exist in the Yin World. Never before had Fandorin felt so weak and uncertain, never before had he found himself in a state of constant fear. What if something should happen to Mona? Or – a fear that was utterly and completely unfamiliar – to *him*? After all, she was right, that would mean that he would condemn both his wife and his unborn child to death.

The ancient sage was right: the noble man should not acquire a family. And if you have acquired one – then cease to live by the rules of the noble man, you are no longer alone in the world. But Erast Petrovich did not know how people lived by other rules and did not even want to think about it.

His only hope lay in eight times eight. Soon, in January 1920, he would reach the age of sixty-four, the age of maturity. In theory, at that age the gap between Yin and Yang should start narrowing, since one arrived at the next pair of eights, the age of eighty-eight, as no longer either a man or a woman, but a Consummated Human Being. And, in addition, the child would be born in February and there would be three of them. *That is when I shall start thinking about different rules*, Fandorin thought, and calmed down slightly, even allowing himself to dream a little. It would be good if they had a little girl. One just like Mona. At least Masa wouldn't try to butt in with his views on upbringing.

'We're here,' said Romanov, and Erast Petrovich returned to reality.

'At the station?' he asked in surprise. 'Why not the counterintelligence unit?'

'The prince is with the commander. He told me to bring you straight to the meeting.'

Gai-Gaievsky was known as a man who did not like to stay in the rear and constantly dashed from one of the various sectors of the front to another. The army's field headquarters were located in a train. The general had a reputation as a genius of modern railway war: he flung military units impetuously from flank to flank at breakneck pace, across hundred of kilometres, like chess pieces, making adroit use of armoured trains, and his flying maintenance crews were capable of restoring damaged tracks with lightning speed. For his swiftness and unpredictability (and probably also because his surname was too long), the European newspapers called the commander of the Volunteer Army 'the White Hannibal'.

'Well then, I'll take a l-look at this Hannibal of yours,' Fandorin said sceptically, recalling a different White general, from a quite different time. It was hardly likely that the new hero would be able to eclipse that old one.

Vladimir Zenonovich Gai-Gaievsky really did look utterly unheroic. Sitting at the head of a long table covered with maps in the saloon carriage was a fat, flabby elderly man with a crimson nose and an extinct *papyrosa* in the corner of his mouth. Small, swollen eyes blinked drowsily behind a pince-nez. The slovenly black uniform tunic with faded shoulder straps hung on him baggily, with a sprinkling of ash on its front, and an unfinished glass of tea trembled in his pudgy hand.

But it was precisely this unpicturesque appearance that made an impression on Fandorin. A military commander who did not consider it necessary to act out his greatness must be very sure of himself. It was said of Gai-Gaievsky that, when necessary, he had led the ranks into the attack in person and had been wounded eleven times. Before the war with Germany, Gai-Gaievsky's career had not gone well, he was not good at serving in the army in peacetime. Despite holding a diploma from the Joint Staff Academy, in 1914 he was still only a lieutenant colonel and had been preparing to leave the army when he reached retirement age. But at the front he had made rapid headway and finished the war as commander of the Guards Corps. In 1918 this paunchy, ageing man had made his way south from Petrograd and joined a volunteer regiment as a private, with no expectations of high-ranking posts. Now, a year and a half later, he was leading the most important of the White armies towards Moscow. The front-line soldiers adored Gai-Gaievsky, admiring their commander most of all not for his bravery (who wasn't brave these days?) but for his legendary capacity as a drinker. Rumour had it that the general put away three bottles of cognac a day and was always slightly tipsy, but never drunk. It was also said that he was constantly losing and dropping things, that without his adjutants he was like a child without his nanny – and for some reason this trait also aroused the soldiers' particular affection. In spite of all that, the butter-fingered general's army worked like clockwork.

'Ah' – that was all Gai-Gaievsky said at the sight of Erast Petrovich (Romanov had stayed outside the door). 'Tea?'

'N-no, thank you,' Fandorin said with a brief shake of his head, giving the other men at the meeting only a very brief glance, because he knew both of them.

One was Colonel Kozlovsky, the head of counter-intelligence: a thin, creased face with a nervous tick and a long cockroach moustache. The other was Skukin, who had recently been promoted to colonel. He served his relative as an aide-de-camp and rumour had it that he possessed greater influence than all the other members of the command staff taken together.

Kozlovsky smiled at Fandorin in obvious relief. Skukin nodded drily, demonstrating what an important individual he was now. Since they had last seen each other in late May, Arkady Skukin really had changed very greatly. His impeccable bearing, uniform and coiffure seemed in some way to compensate for his uncle's unkempt appearance.

Another officer, a captain, appeared quietly, without knocking, from the inside of the carriage, where the commander's private quarters must be located. Dressed in the same black Volunteer Army uniform as the general, he was trim and dashing. His brilliantined parting glittered and his brand-new aiguillettes gleamed. Without asking permission, he removed the glass from Gai-Gaievsky's hand and topped it up with dark brown liquid from a flask, which made it clear that it wasn't actually tea at all. *So the talk of cognac is not just rumour*, Erast Petrovich realised.

'Makoltsev, were you summoned?' Skukin hissed hostilely through his teeth. 'What kind of impudence is that! And you ought to stop, Uncle. It's still morning!'

One of Fandorin's eyebrows rose slightly – he found the manners in this company extraordinary. However, to judge from the other men's reactions, this scene was quite usual. Kozlovsky merely tugged impatiently on his moustache, while the adjutant did not seem offended in the least and the general boomed in a conciliatory tone of voice:

'Oh, come on, Arkady. I was just going to call Pavel, and here he is already. Intuition. And I can't stop. I'm like a petrol trolley: I won't start without a top-up.'

And he took a drink, relishing it with an unctuous laugh.

'What are you hanging about here for, cup-bearer?' Skukin asked the captain in the same angry voice. 'Your job's done, now off you go.'

But the general took his adjutant's part.

'Don't give Pavel orders. Where I go, he goes. Who followed me under fire from the Red machine guns the day before yesterday? Who picked up my favourite cigarette case when I dropped it? You, Arkasha, stayed back at headquarters.'

'And it's pointless for you to put yourself in the line of fire, Uncle. If you're killed, then who will lead the army against Moscow?'

Erast Petrovich cleared his throat.

'Gentlemen, I was told that the matter on which I was summoned is urgent.'

Kozlovsky glanced at him gratefully.

'Permission to continue, Vladimir Zenonovich? . . . Well then, the commander-in-chief's train arrived in Kharkov at precisely sixteen hundred hours – we all know how punctual His Excellency is. A conference was held in the headquarters saloon until half past five.

In addition to the commander-in-chief and Your Excellency, your personal assistants were also present: the commander-in-chief's Colonel Schroeder and your . . .' He nodded in Skukin's direction. 'Then an award ceremony for officers who had distinguished themselves was held at the station. It had to be interrupted halfway through, since the commander-in-chief had a stomach upset . . .'

'During the meeting he ran to the privy twice,' Gai-Gaievsky put in. 'He ate too much sauerkraut. I told him: "It's because you're a teetotaller, Anton Ivanovich. Wash it down with vodka or, even better, cognac, and everything will be just fine."'

The prince waited politely for a moment in case the commander said something else and then continued.

'Next on the schedule was a visit to the Kaledin Orphanage. The commander-in-chief arrived there at seven-forty, as planned. He gave a brief talk to the children and their governesses and started handing out treats. They were lying on a table that was covered with a long tablecloth. As later emerged, a bomb with a timing mechanism had been placed under that very table. Very soon the commander-in-chief apologised and hurried out of the room – he had suffered another spasm – and literally a minute after that there was a thunderous explosion. The fatalities included . . .' – Kozlovsky glanced at a sheet of paper – '. . . Ilya Sapozhnikov, eight years of age; Boris von Minich, nine years of age; Nikolai Beletsky, nine years of age; Konstantin Leshschenko, nine years of age; Pyotr Milovanov, eleven years of age; Alexander Stein, ten years of age; Semyon Koltsov, nine years of age; and Kornei Ranz-Zass, six years of age – he is the son of Colonel Ranz-Zass, who was killed two weeks ago at Kursk. He had only just joined the army. The boy was younger than the regulation age, but . . .' The prince became embarrassed and didn't finish.

'Yes, I gave the instructions, the innocent blood is on my hands.' The general crossed himself and took a gulp. 'I thought: how will a little kid like that get on, with no father and no mother? And it turns out that I signed the boy's death warrant. Two women were also killed, I think?'

'Precisely so. The head of the orphanage, Nekritova, and the governess Baroness Lande, the widow of a Volunteer Army officer.

She was pregnant, and they say she was very much hoping to have a son . . .'

A heavy silence descended.

'What measures have you taken since yesterday?' asked Erast Petrovich, who was not constrained by the army line of command. He felt very sorry for the victims, but grief had always roused Fandorin to action.

'Intensified patrols. Expert evaluation of the fragments of the explosive device. Questioning of the entire staff of the orphanage, to establish if there were any outsiders.'

Fandorin frowned.

'Patrols will not be any help. Nor will the type of explosive device. And, of course, no outsiders were noticed – otherwise you would have managed without me. Tell me, Colonel, did the schedule of the commander-in-chief's movements that you mentioned exist in written form? Who had access to it?'

Kozlovsky took offence.

'Who do you take me for? I'm a professional, in previous times I was an adviser on the security of His Majesty the Emperor! All appropriate security measures were taken. The commander-in-chief's planned movements were known only to me – and to Vladimir Zenonovich, to whom I reported the previous day.'

The general nodded. 'All other personnel were only informed within the limits of their own authority. The station master concerning what would happen there. The commander of the convoy concerning the route, but not the precise time.'

Fandorin pondered briefly.

'Why did the m-malefactors choose the orphanage specifically? Surely they must have realised that children would be killed, and that would provoke universal indignation?'

'I think it was easier to plant a bomb there. It never even occurred to anyone that the Bolsheviks would dare to blow up children. Almost all the security guards were left outside.'

'But s-surely the hall was examined in advance?'

'Naturally it was, and in the most scrupulous fashion. Half an hour before the event. I told you,' said Kozlovsky, addressing the commander, 'it's some kind of devil's work. Permission to smoke,

Your Excellency? My head's as heavy as lead.'

Gai-Gaievsky gave a sign to his adjutant, and he clicked his cigarette lighter. The prince lit up a *papyrosa*, puffing his sunken cheeks in and out.

'There's no devil's work involved here. And moreover, it will not be difficult to pick up the trail,' said Fandorin. 'It is obvious that the organiser or organisers of the bombing received precise information from someone f-familiar with the schedule. We should search from that side. So, who apart from you and the commander could have known the schedule? Your assistant Captain Romanov, for instance?'

'No, he was not in the city. He was on an operation in the Zmiyevsk district, where he destroyed a Red partisans' arms depot. I reported on that to Your Excellency. My deputy, Lieutenant Colonel Cherepov, was only in charge of security, he didn't know the schedule, so there couldn't have been any leak on that side.'

'How about on your side?' Erast Petrovich asked the general. 'Did you tell anyone where the commander-in-chief would be and when?'

At a loss, Gai-Gaievsky looked at his nephew.

'Did I tell anyone?'

'Me,' the colonel replied. 'You asked my advice on whether to arrange supper at the orphanage, because with women and children present there would be a cosy, domestic atmosphere. Captain Makoltsev was present at the conversation.'

Amazingly enough, the adjutant had disappeared as silently as he had appeared. A minute earlier he had been standing by the wall, but now, when everyone looked, he wasn't there.

'. . . He said there was no need for a supper. There had been a message from the commander-in-chief's headquarters staff that no banquets were to be arranged. You actually laughed, remember? You said: "The laggard is sulking because I pinched Wrangel's armoured train, the 'Dobrynya'. Well, fine."'

'Yes, yes, that's how it was,' the general confirmed. 'But how about Anton Ivanovich's lucky star, eh? Diarrhoea saved his life. Something very similar happened to me in Galicia in 1916, when they poured aviation spirit into my hot punch . . .'

And he told a vivid but unappetising story that made Kozlovsky laugh and Skukin frown. As for Fandorin, he didn't even listen – he just waited for the end, so that he could ask the next question.

'And who in the orphanage knew the time of the commander-in-chief's arrival?'

'Only the directress, Nekritova. Of course, she could have told someone who was involved in the preparations for the meeting. But we questioned the survivors, and no one admitted to it,' Kozlovsky replied.

'There is nothing else that I need to know. Your Excellency, g-gentlemen . . .'

Erast Petrovich got up and walked out, followed by an outraged stare from Colonel Skukin: how could anyone leave like that, without asking the commander's permission?

But Fandorin didn't have any commanders in this world.

'Consequently, there are only three leads,' he said, summing up his story for his wife and Masa in the hotel apartment. 'The first is Gai-Gaievsky's entourage. Skukin is not loose-tongued, but there is also Captain Makoltsev, a rather slippery individual. The second is the commander-in-chief's entourage. After all, someone there also knew the route and schedule of his superior's movements. The third lead is the s-slenderest – the orphanage. Two of the female staff were killed, and one is unconscious. It will not be easy to establish whether they let anything slip to any suspicious characters about the general's arrival.'

Then Fandorin started talking about the victims. He mentioned each boy by name (Erast Petrovich's memory was superb) and did not forget to mention Baroness Lande's heartbreaking story.

Mona's eyes started gleaming. She sniffed and said angrily:

'That's enough playing on my pity. Damn you. You can have your leave pass. Do what has to be done. But this time there will be two conditions.'

'What are they?' Fandorin asked too quickly, feeling the world of Yin drawing him imperiously towards itself.

'The first one is the same. Masa will help you.'

'No, he will st-stay with you!'

The Japanese declared with a dignified air:

'I am not an item of furniture. I have waited for a rong time.' When he was agitated, he still confused 'l' and 'r'. 'Do you know who is to brame for those poor chirdren and unfortunate women being kirred? We are.'

'And j-just why is that?' Fandorin asked in surprise.

'When we were rooking for the bad men who tossed grenades in a city street, we picked up the trair of the Red underground very quickry. But you decrared that we would only catch the men who were guirty of kirring bystanders. We caught two *akunins*, gave them a chance to offer resistance, and then kirred them without a qualm. And you didn't want to go any farther than that. You said: "We are not taking part in the civir war." But now the very peopur we reft arone then – the Chekist Zaenko's men – have carried out another bombing. So who erse is to brame, if not us? You know the raw of the samurai; either correct your mistake or srit your belly open.'

'Don't mention the belly like that,' Mona told him. 'Erast, you didn't mention that you killed someone that time. I thought you simply arrested them.'

'Some people are too loose-tongued,' Erast Petrovich growled. But he knew the Japanese was right: the bombing must certainly have been carried out by the Chekist butcher Zaenko's men, and he could easily have been neutralised back in August.

'And some peopur are too narrow-minded!' Masa snapped back. 'Or have you forgotten that a genuine investigation is never conducted arong only one line? You deal with the source of the leak in the command staffs, and I'll work from the side of the Red underground. That will make things go more quickly.'

'And Mona will stay in the hotel alone? Shame on you. I thought you were a r-responsible individual.'

'Mona will not stay in the hotel,' his wife interrupted. 'You haven't listened to my second condition yet. That's what it's about. I am feeling much better and I need some fresh air. Don't say anything. This is not a point for discussion.'

Zaya and Shusha

Alexei opened his eyes and jerked upright.

The phone was ringing. His watch said half past seven.

Romanov had been at work until very late at night and only got back to his room at the Hotel Switzerland just before dawn. It was a lousy, 'three-star' hotel, with nothing Swiss about it, but he had a telephone in his room. His job couldn't be done without round-the-clock communications.

It was Lavr Kozlovsky.

'Disaster, Alyosha. An act of sabotage twelve versts outside the city. The "Dobrynya" has been blown up. Get dressed and shoot over to the department.'

'I didn't get undressed. I'll be there right away,' Romanov replied, bewildered.

The 'Dobrynya' was the best armoured train in the entire White army. With the impudence of a gipsy horse-thief, Gai-Gaievsky had stolen the massive war machine from the Caucasian Army of Baron Wrangel, intending to relocate it to Oryol, where the Reds had gone on the counter-attack. If the 'Dobrynya' didn't stop them with its 152-millimetre guns, the entire situation on the front could change.

The colonel was already waiting outside the entrance to the building of the Special Department of the Volunteer Army – that was the official name of the army's counter-intelligence section. Previously, under the Reds, the Cheka had been located here and Comrade Zaenko had seared the exploiting classes with the sizzling iron brand of the Red Terror. The people of the city had dubbed the terrible place 'the Black House', because those who ended up there never came back out alive.

Counterintelligence had occupied the former Chekist lair because the accommodation was very convenient. The façade of the three-storey building overlooked the street, and the courtyard, enclosed by a high stone wall, overlooked a ravine, into which in Zaenko's time executed prisoners had been thrown. The only change Kozlovsky had made was to order the walls to be painted white, so that the former spine-chilling name would be forgotten. The prince said that the population should regard the counter-intelligence services as their protector, not as a terrifying bogeyman. 'We're the Whites, we should dress in white robes,' he liked to say. 'That's the only way we'll win.'

'Damn it, my boot's gaping wide open,' he said to the captain in place of a greeting, pointing angrily at his lame foot. His face was crumpled, his eyelids were red, and his mouth reeked of stale alcohol. The department's dusty Ford was snorting beside him.

'I'll have to change into my dress boots. Let's go, Alyosha. I'll tell you everything on the way.'

Kozlovsky lived a mere stone's throw away, you only had to cross Sumskaya Street and walk through the courtyards. He rented a former porter's lodge in an apartment building. It was a tiny little flat, but it had a separate entrance. Lavr Kozlovsky was indifferent to conveniences, he slept in snatches and usually in his office. In any case, his pay would not have been enough for more comfortable accommodation. Officers were poorly paid. The commander-in-chief said that the knights of the White Cause should be ascetics, and he set an example himself, going about in a patched tunic that people said his wife washed. Of course, not many members of the command in the rear followed this exalted example; they almost all had lucrative deals of some kind going on. It was ancient knowledge that Mother Russia could not be cured of bribery and corruption by example alone.

But Colonel Kozlovsky was one of the few who believed in principles. The 'dress' boots that he changed into proved to be little better than the ones that had given up the ghost. As he listened to the prince's story, Romanov suddenly thought that his White superior was remarkably similar to his Red one, Orlov. For him too, nothing existed but an idea.

'More treason, no doubt about it!' the prince said, baring his metal teeth angrily.

In 1917 he had been beaten almost to death by revolutionary soldiers – simply for being an officer. After that his path had been clear: flight to the south, a volunteer regiment, the Ice March southwards from Rostov.

'The schedule of movement was only known in the army command, and someone let it slip or, even worse, is spying for the Reds. We're not working well enough, Alyosha. It's my fault! I've withdrawn too far into reconnaissance and landed all the counter-intelligence work on you. I promise I won't do that any more.'

You poor devil, Alexei thought, *no matter how good a professional you are, you won't get anywhere if your right-hand man is one of the enemy.*

The results of the Volunteer Army's counter-intelligence work were strange. It did an excellent job of unmasking Ukrainian agents, nimbly caught Makhno's scouts and the ordinary bandits, but simply couldn't eradicate the Red underground. Romanov had been obliged to resort to all sorts of subterfuges in order to disguise this all-too-obvious fact. For instance, two days earlier in the Zmiyevsk district, when he destroyed an underground arms depot belonging to Bat'ko Makhno's 'Revolutionary Rebel Army', he had reported that the weapons belonged to the Reds.

'Why are you pulling that ugly face?' the prince asked.

'You reek like a wine barrel,' said Romanov, forcing himself to smile. 'Not a member of the Riurik dynasty, but Chelkash.'

'Who's that – Chelkash?'

'A character out of Maxim Gorky's work.'

'Ah, I've heard of him. A bastard. It's not wine that I smell of, but cognac. Because I was drinking cognac half the night with Gai-Gaievsky and his adjutant – what's he called? – Makoltsev. Although I'm a Guardsman and familiar with the subject, I can't drink as much as they do. I got tired and started pleading for beddy-byes. And then Skukin appears and says: "They've blown up the 'Dobrynya.'" The general starts yelling at me: "You're doing a lousy job in counter-intelligence! The Red underground has become totally brazen, and all you want to do is knock back cognac!" How about that, eh? He almost forces it into me, and then reproaches me! And that dog Skukin just had to tell tales too. "You're working like a cissy," he says. "You have to brand them with red-hot iron, organise raids and public hangings, use every means possible to beat confessions out of suspects, even stick needles under their nails." And the commander joined in with him: "I don't care what means the counter-intelligence service uses, I demand results." Well, I exploded. I said: "Don't you try to teach me my job, Your Excellency, I know more about it than you do. A counter-intelligence agent isn't a butcher, but a surgeon. He doesn't work with filthy hands and an axe." And he told me: "If a surgeon works badly, they send him packing!" Anyway, we had words . . .' The prince sighed. 'It's bad, but Gai-Gaievsky is right. If we make a mess of this operation, we should be sent packing.' He stamped his boots. 'That's it, I'm ready. Let's go.'

At the site of the anticipated wreck, twelve versts along the railway line, the armoured train was standing unharmed. The locomotive was panting angrily and a crowd of soldiers had gathered beside the tracks. The prince resolutely forced his way into it and emerged five minutes later, looking pleased.

'It's not all that terrible. The explosion occurred too soon, the train was travelling at low speed and had time to brake. Twenty metres farther on, and it would have gone tumbling down the embankment, but we were lucky.'

Alexei had also not wasted any time and had already got to the bottom of what had happened. The ham-fisted saboteurs had either suffered a fit of nerves or they didn't know their job very well: they had merely torn up the rails pointlessly. The repair brigade would restore movement in two hours, and the formidable armoured train would go dashing off towards the front. The Red counter-offensive was doomed.

'Cretins' – Romanov muttered the little word that had been slipping off his lips so often just recently. 'A total cock-up . . .'

Just then the prince gave him another lousy piece of news.

'We had another stroke of luck too. A quarter of an hour after the explosion a Cossack patrol stopped two factory hands one verst from here – simply in order to check their documents. One of them tried to make a run for it. The Cossacks cut him down. Under his jacket they found a coil of safety fuse. He obviously took along more than enough and couldn't bring himself to discard the excess. The second man was taken alive. Shall we have a talk with our client?'

Romanov nodded. *God, and they managed to get caught too. One with fuse cord wrapped round his pot belly! Fucking amateurs.*

The arrested man was standing to one side, between two escorts. Middle-aged, with a sallow face gashed open by a whip.

'I'm the good guy, you're the bad guy,' the colonel whispered, and shouted: 'Bring this man to my car!'

They sat him between themselves, on the back seat. Kozlovsky started working on him immediately.

'I'm the head of the Special Section, which means I know a thing or two about people. I can see that the leader was the one who ran off, and you didn't even resist. Don't get down in the dumps, man. Wait a while before you kiss your life goodbye. The armoured train is undamaged, no one has been killed or hurt. According to martial law, you should get the noose anyway, but I don't like unnecessary deaths. I'm Kozlovsky. You've probably heard about me?' Without waiting for a reply, he went on: 'Too many people are dying anyway, and all of them ours, Russians. So if a man's not a sworn enemy of ours, I won't let him be executed. Especially if he has a family and children.'

The prisoner stared straight ahead without blinking his wide-set, light-coloured eyes. Alexei knew this Russian type very well, as hard as flint. He used to have a non-commissioned officer exactly like this in his operations group – he had been killed in 1916.

'Nothing to say, you shit?' Romanov roared, exploding exactly as the uncomplicated scenario required. 'Why are you casting pearls in front of this swine, Colonel? Hand him over to Cherepov, let him rake his guts out!'

'Keep calm, Captain. Hand him straight over to Cherepov? Let me talk to the man first.'

Cossack Lieutenant Colonel Cherepov, who had recently been appointed deputy head of department by order of army headquarters (Romanov was listed only as an assistant), was a Kuban Cossack officer from the 'Shkuryntsi' – General Shkuro's White partisans. Kozlovsky didn't involve his deputy in investigations, keeping him for so-called 'combat functions': arrests, seizing positions, actions against the Green and Red rebels. 'Fearsome of face and pasty of brain' was how he described Cherepov. The lieutenant colonel's appearance was terrifying, and sometimes he was invited to an interrogation to terrify a stubborn prisoner. It worked with the timid ones. But this prisoner wasn't timid. No matter how hard Lavr tried to ingratiate himself with him or Alexei tried to intimidate him, he kept his mouth shut as tight as a clam.

Even Cherepov was no help, when the prince summoned him as soon as they reached the department.

The lieutenant colonel appeared in the interrogation room,

looking like death: lanky and bony, with a black eyepatch on his face – his eye had been put out by a Red bullet. He leaned down over the motionless, silent Red partisan, drilling into him with his fearsome single eye for about thirty seconds.

'Colonel, just leave me alone with this piece of meat. Go and have lunch. Come back in an hour or so – and you'll have a tender, bloody steak.'

He always said that. Usually it worked. But this time the prisoner didn't even raise his head.

'Clearly I shall have to,' the prince lamented. And he addressed the prisoner reproachfully: 'Why do you force me to resort to extreme measures? You simply leave me no choice. Go to your cell and wait.'

When the two of them were left alone, Romanov said:

'A tough nut. Even Cherepov won't gnaw him open.'

'I won't let anyone be gnawed, this isn't a menagerie. There's a more effective means.'

'Which?'

'He's a sound man, the dependable kind. With a highly developed sense of responsibility. Let's see which is stronger.'

'What do you mean?'

'You've become unobservant, Alyosha. Did you see the white strip on his ring finger? That's from a wedding ring. The ring itself was taken by the Cossacks, of course. We have to look for his family. Let him have a meeting with his wife and children – if he has any. And let him decide to whom he owes the greater loyalty – his own kin or the International.'

'But how will we find his family if he won't even tell us his name?' Romanov asked, although he already knew the answer – he was no novice.

'He's wearing a railway jacket. That means he works or he used to work in the traffic department. Now I'll go and report to the commander that the "Dobrynya" is fine, and then we'll take our Mucius Scaevola round the railway offices and workshops. Perhaps someone will recognise him.'

That was exactly what Romanov would have done himself. And the colonel was talking good sense: stern men of this type were capable not only of hate, but also of love. A woman's tears, let alone the tears of children, had a greater effect on them than any torture.

'All right. I'll go with him and ask some questions.'

'Why you? It's a simple job, purely technical. I'll send Spirin. You'd better go home and catch up on your sleep. You probably won't get a chance tonight . . . Have you heard anything from Greyhair about that bombing?'

'Nothing yet . . . You're right. I'll go and get some sleep, while the boss is feeling kind.'

But it went without saying that this was no time for sleep.

Twenty minutes later Romanov knocked on the door of Zuev's flat. Nadezhda opened it and started blinking.

'You? Why didn't you come through the reading room?'

'There's no time. Is your father at home? Call him.'

But the young woman didn't go anywhere.

'Why did you kiss my hand last time?' she asked in a hostile tone of voice.

'What?' he exclaimed in surprise, not immediately recalling the incident.

'If you were kissing me like a child, that's really quite insufferable! I'm not a little girl. And if . . .' Nadya lost her train of thought. 'And if . . . if you weren't kissing me like a child, that's insulting.'

Instead of replying, Alexei gave her a quick hug and kissed her again quickly, on her hot cheek. He took hold of her shoulders, moved her aside and walked in.

'There's no time, Nadya, no time. It's an emergency. Bring your father, quickly.'

She flushed but stopped trying to settle the matter and ran into the apartment.

Zuev listened to his story calmly.

'I already told you: let the Whites solve the problem of Zaenko for us. The Chekists cause nothing but harm anyway. First they failed to kill the commander-in-chief and only turned the whole of Kharkov against us. Now they've blundered with the armoured train, and Kozlovsky will start harassing the railway workers, and I've got a very good cell there. If that's smashed, we'll be left with no information about the redeployment of troops. So let counter-intelligence take our production partners and leave our people alone.'

'Zaenko's a cretin, but they'll be taking our comrades, Bolsheviks like you and me. If you could have seen the man who's under arrest now, you wouldn't talk like that. I came to you because I have an idea. I need a helper. A simple job, anyone can manage it, as long as he's efficient and not a coward. I'll do all the basic work myself.'

'I won't give you anyone,' Zuev snapped. 'It's more expedient for the cause if the second underground network ceases to exist. Then the Whites will decide that the Red organisation has been crushed, and we can carry on with our work calmly, without any interference.'

Alexei became furious.

'You can't reduce everything to expediency! Men aren't chips of wood.'

'Dialectics, Romanov, Bolshevik dialectics. Get it into your head: men aren't good or bad, they're divided into "ours" and "not-ours". Ours are the ones who are useful. The ones who are harmful aren't ours. And I don't intend to risk ours for the sake of those who are not ours. That's all. The conversation's over.'

'Some day the Party will decide that you have also ceased to be useful and throw you on the rubbish heap!'

But Zuev could not be broken down.

'Then that will be where I belong.'

'Ah, to hell with you!'

Alexei walked out and slammed the door. He tried to work out if he could pull off his scheme on his own – no, it wouldn't work.

In the courtyard Nadya overtook him. During the conversation she had stood behind her father, without opening her mouth once, but now she started jabbering rapidly.

'My father's wrong. You said anyone could manage it. That means I can. I'm efficient and I'm not a coward. And I might not be very big, but I'm very strong.'

She showed him her clenched fist. Her lips were pursed tightly too.

Romanov suddenly recalled the young ladies in the Women's Battalion of Death. They were all exactly like this, although they were fighting for something quite different.

'No great strength will be required,' he said, coughing to clear his throat – he was afraid that his voice would tremble.

Second Lieutenant Spirin was a brute, a butcher, Alexei didn't feel sorry about bumping off someone like that. Or the second escort, Sergeant Major Kononenko, either. He was simply an executioner, who hired himself out for money to hang condemned men. But there was a question about the third man, the driver, whom Alexei didn't know, and therefore didn't want to kill. That was why he needed the kerchief.

Romanov stood in a gateway on a quiet street into which the counter-intelligence car had to turn on its way to the railway depot. He was wearing a jacket and a long, tight-fitting coat, with a cap pulled down over his eyes. When the familiar Ford trundled round the corner, he tied the kerchief over his face.

The street was empty, with only a trolley loaded with bottles of sunflower-seed oil standing on the pavement. The urchin selling it was shouting in a ringing voice: 'Refined oil for them as wants it! Refined oil for them as wants it!'

The car picked up a bit more speed and drove past the gateway. The trolley suddenly toppled over abruptly, the jars scattered across the road with a crash and yellow liquid flooded over the cobblestones of the roadway. The car braked sharply.

Clever girl! Right on time!

There were four men in the Ford. In front, at the wheel, was a man with a moustache. Spirin was sitting beside him and behind them were the prisoner and Kononenko – following instructions, he was holding his revolver at the ready. Romanov began with the sergeant major, setting the revolver on the folded elbow of his left arm and taking aim at the fat nape of the man's neck. It wasn't a difficult shot, a motionless target from about twenty metres.

The window shattered and Kononenko's head banged into the back of the front seat. The prisoner's head disappeared. Good for him, he had ducked. The second lieutenant only had time to turn his head. The second bullet struck him in the middle of his face.

Without lowering his Nagant, Alexei walked quickly over to the car and shouted at the driver in a hoarse, disguised voice:

'Right, get out!'

The reply was a shot. And worst of all – not at the attacker.

The driver was acting according to instructions, and they prescribed that in the case of an attempt to free the prisoner, the first thing that must be done was to shoot him.

Cursing himself for his benighted sloppy sentimentality – *Ah, how can I kill a man I don't know?* – Romanov emptied his entire cylinder. The windscreen disintegrated in pieces and the driver didn't have time to fire again.

The prisoner was lying hunched up on the floor, breathing noisily.

'Where are you hit, comrade?'

'In the belly . . .'

The first thing I've heard him say, thought Romanov.

'Just a moment. Hang on.'

He dragged the heavy driver out onto the roadway and got in behind the steering wheel, but the dead Spirin tumbled onto him from the right and Alexei couldn't shove him out while he was sitting down.

The door was opened from the other side. Nadya was there – blazing eyes under a boy's peaked cap, a thin little neck in an open collar. Without saying a word, she grabbed the dead body by the shoulder and started tugging on it.

'I told you: push over the trolley and scram!' Romanov barked at her.

She didn't reply, just carried on tugging at the corpse. Her arms really were surprisingly strong. The second lieutenant finally tumbled out onto the roadway.

People were sticking their heads out of windows and shouting. Somewhere nearby a whistle sounded.

Alexei snapped briskly:

'Squeeze in behind somehow. Try to stop the blood. Just plug the wound with something. And shake him, keep shaking him so that he doesn't lose consciousness.'

He made a sharp turn to avoid cutting the tyres on shards of glass and skidding on the cobblestones. The steering wheel was slippery with blood.

He stepped on the gas, accelerated and battered the remains of the windscreen with his elbow – better to have no windscreen at all than one with bullet holes in it.

It was a risk, a desperate risk, but what could be done about it? He couldn't abandon the wounded man.

He drove to Great Panasovskaya Street through the side streets and lanes. Of course, it wasn't very close to Zuev's apartment, but at least they could go through the courtyards.

'Can you walk, comrade? You have to,' said Alexei, looking round. 'What's your name?'

'I can,' the wounded man replied through his teeth. 'I'm Terenty . . . Nazarov.'

'We'll hold you up from both sides, as if you were drunk. If we meet anyone, sing or swear.'

The wounded man immediately cursed obscenely and then carried on swearing non-stop. Nadya winced in sympathy and stroked him on the shoulder.

Nazarov fell silent only after the doctor (their own man, from Zuev's underground network) gave him an injection of morphine. Then he went limp and hung his head.

Meanwhile Zuev was upbraiding Romanov in a ferocious whisper:

'Look what you've done! You've blown the rendezvous! Out of snivelling sentimentality. Now we'll have to move out of here. And we won't be able to warn all our people quickly that the reading room has been blown. I'm not working with you any more, Romanov. We're parting company.'

'Then you're parting company with me too,' said Nadya, turning pale. 'Alexei acted like a comrade, like a Bolshevik. I never thought that I would feel . . . ashamed of you.'

The old man shuddered, and Romanov thought: *He's not such a man of iron after all.*

'Take a look at Nazarov, Ivan Maximovich. This man will never betray anyone. And I didn't rescue him out of sentimentality, but for the good of the cause. Through him I'll find Zaenko and try to agree terms with him. We've been acting separately for too long.'

The devil only knew what affected him more – Romanov's logic or his daughter's gaze – but Zuev gestured hopelessly and growled:

'Well, beware. If anything happens – you'll be responsible . . .'

He went to see the doctor out. And Nazarov suddenly jerked upright, raised his head and started talking rapidly – no doubt it was the effect of the narcotic.

'Eh, we didn't blow up the armoured train. We did everything the way it was written on the paper, only we must have cut the fuse too short, it went off too soon!'

He squinted at Romanov, who was standing with his back to the window, which meant the man couldn't see him clearly.

'Why don't you take off your kerchief, comrade? Your voice sounds familiar to me.'

'I mustn't show my face.'

Nazarov would have recognised the captain from counter-intelligence, and that wasn't a good idea. Alexei made his voice even deeper.

'Are you from Zaenko's organisation?'

'First you tell me who you are,' the wounded man said warily.

'An underground group of the Revolutionary Military Soviet. I'm Alexei, and this is Comrade Nadezhda. So are you with Zaenko?'

The man nodded.

'I need to meet with him. We've been fighting separately for too long. Look at how you knew when and where to ambush the armoured train, only you blundered with the fuse, but we've got a good explosives man. Together we're twice as strong.'

Nazarov didn't say anything, and it would be wrong to hurry him. Let him think for a while.

'Can you take me to where I say? I can't stay here with you in any case. And I heard the gaffer cursing and swearing.'

'We'll take you. You only have to get as far as a cab. You can pretend to be drunk again. And I really will give you some vodka. The doctor said if you were in pain, to pour a glass into you. Afterwards he can come to wherever he's needed.'

'We've got our own doctor. But vodka's the right stuff,' Nazarov said with a smile. 'Only better pour two glasses into me.'

He didn't give any answer about a meeting with Zaenko.

*

That evening, after darkness fell, Romanov dropped in again. He had barely managed to get away from work – so intense was the mayhem stirred up by the underground agents' attack on the counterintelligence section's car. Alexei himself was in charge of combing the area where the abandoned Ford had been found, and he had taken care to make sure the reading room was left alone. The two of them got into the cab. Instead of the kerchief, Romanov had wrapped a bandage round his cheek, raised his collar and pulled down the peak of his cap, but Nazarov didn't really peer at him that hard, and it was already dark anyway.

They drove out past the Kholodnogorskoe Cemetery, into a district of workers' barracks buildings.

'We'll get out here,' Nazarov told the driver.

But after that they walked for a long time, weaving about. The wounded man asked to take a rest twice.

The third time they halted was right in the middle of a plot of wasteland.

'That's it. I'll go on from here myself. Be seeing you, comrade.'

'What about Zaenko?'

In the darkness Alexei couldn't see Nazarov's face, only the gleaming of his eyes.

'The gaffer there has a phone. What's the number?'

Alexei told him.

'Wait for a message. From Terenty.'

He hobbled on painfully. And in his own mind, Romanov continued his argument with Zuev. How was it possible to spurn men like Terenty Nazarov? Then what was it all for?

The next evening Alexei was called to the phone at work.

'Captain Romanov, this is the Commercial Reading Room,' a girlish voice said drily. 'A book by Schlichter has arrived for you.'

That was a prearranged signal.

'Excellent, young lady. I'll drop in straight away.' And he explained to Kozlovsky: 'They've got hold of a reference work on composing random ciphers for me. I've been waiting for it a long time. I told you I was intending to change our entire coding system, the present one is outdated.'

The prince muttered 'uh-huh' without looking up from his operations report. Tonight he had to go to see the commander – to drink cognac and report on progress in investigating both bombings. The first case was at a standstill, the second was a total dead end, and Kozlovsky was in a gloomy mood.

'My father's not here,' Nadya told him anxiously. 'I'm alone. There was a phone call. An unfamiliar voice. They said: "Greetings to Alexei from Terenty. Terenty isn't feeling well and would like Alexei to visit him. At midnight, beside the pumping station in Karpovsky Park." I wrote it down word for word.'

At midnight Karpovsky Park was deserted and quiet. A good spot, judiciously chosen. Anyone could be heard from a distance.

It was half past nine now.

'I'll go home and change into plain clothes. I can't go in uniform.'

'Wait. I have to have a word with you. I've been wanting to for a long time, but either my father's here or there's no time . . .' Nadya frowned in determined fashion, but her forehead was too smooth and it wrinkled up unconvincingly. 'Never kiss me again. Never!'

She brushed away an angry teardrop.

'All right,' Alexei replied very seriously. 'I won't do it again. You have my word.'

'Aren't you going to ask why?'

'Why do I need to ask? It's clear enough. You don't like it. You've proved that you're not a little girl, but a comrade-in-arms. So that's how I'll treat you.'

To his amazement, Nadya flew into an even greater fury.

'You don't understand a thing. I do like it. I like it a lot!' Now she was looking at him almost with hatred. 'I have to think about what's most important, the main thing, the great cause, and all day and night I'm wondering like an idiot: What did he mean when he said this or that, why did he look at me in that way, or why didn't he look at me? Yesterday I sat down in front of the mirror and sat there for an hour and a half without even realising it. And I should have been encoding messages . . . You kissed me on the palm of my hand, and it was like an electric shock. You kissed me on the cheek and it stayed hot right through the day and the night. It's unbearable, it's shameful! Please, don't torment me.'

At this point Romanov did what he had been longing to do: he hugged the young woman against his chest and started kissing her wet, salty face.

'I didn't ask you to . . . This wasn't what I meant at all . . . I'll die on the spot . . .'

And she started trembling so hard that he took fright and released her. He had begun trembling too, and he felt a sharp pang in his chest.

Alexei grabbed at the spot.

'What is it? What's wrong with you?' Nadya cried. 'Are you feeling unwell? Oh, your eyes are wet . . .'

'I don't know,' Romanov murmured inanely. 'I thought it would never . . .'

He had thought that it would never happen to him again. That his chest would never tighten again like this, and the world would never shrink to the size of a woman's face again. He thought he had been killed in 1917, in that accursed trench, and now he was merely walking the earth as a phantom called by the same name.

'I . . . I have to . . . change my clothes . . .' he muttered, leaning against the wall.

Nadya also turned limp and sank down feebly onto a chair.

'Yes . . . yes. You go. And I'll sit for a while. Somehow my legs . . . This is terrible.'

And even later, on his way to the important meeting, Alexei was still in a kind of daze. His head was filled with thoughts about the wrong things.

About how the soul was like water. When frost strikes, it turns as cold and hard as stone. It seems as if it will always be that way, as if the winter will never end. But then spring arrives and the stone thaws, oozing out a drop, and then the moisture floods out and starts warming up in the hot rays of the sun.

Nadya was right, this was terrible. Because there was a war going on, and in a war you had to devote all your strength to it, otherwise you wouldn't win. That was how he had lived until this moment, it was the only reason he had survived. Although it hadn't really been all that important whether he survived or not. For a phantom to die was no great loss. But now he would want to live. He already wanted to. And that meant he would be afraid, not only for himself, but for Nadezhda. That name, meaning 'hope' . . . it was dangerous. Romanov shivered, seeming to hear it for the first time.

Distracted by these confused, anxious thoughts, Alexei forgot to keep looking round and didn't even remember crossing the river and the railway tracks (the South Station was not far away), then walking up the incline of the tree-lined avenue to the low pedestal of the water tower.

A figure detached itself from the wall. Romanov's fingers clutched the handle of the revolver in his pocket, but he saw from the silhouette that it was a woman with her hands lowered and no weapon in sight.

A romantic assignation with a beautiful female stranger, Romanov thought. He was no longer tormented by his exalted suffering, his professional skills had been called into play: hearing, night vision, intuition.

So, is there anyone else here?

There didn't seem to be anyone in the bushes on the left, or on the right. But he thought he saw something stirring over there in the black shadow on the right side of the tower.

'It's me, Alexei,' he said in a loud voice. 'Are you from Terenty?'

The woman replied in a song-song voice.

'You halt. Arms this way.'

She demonstrated: Hold your arms out to the side.

A Chinese woman? Original. Although they do say that Zaenko's Cheka has a Chinese squad that carries out sentences.

Romanov stopped and posed in the form of a cross.

The woman moved closer. She really was Chinese. He couldn't make out her face properly, but the eyes were slanting. Slender, only up to Alexei's chest.

The woman frisked Romanov very adroitly, as well as any experienced undercover agent, and she took not only his Nagant, but also the Browning from under his armpit (the one that Nadya had asked for and not received).

'Oho, erotic massage!' Alexei joked when the light hand groped at him from below.

Turning towards the tower, the frail-looking woman announced, half-speaking and half-singing:

'Zaye, me check him.'

Aha, so 'Zaya' is here after all, Romanov thought in relief. His mood immediately improved although, of course, this operetta performance made him feel angry. The Mikado's son Nanki-Poo and the beautiful Yum-Yum in the town of Titipu.

Under the tower a match scraped and the little light grew bigger – someone had lit a kerosene lantern.

'Right, come over here. I'll take look at you. We'll have a banter,' Alexei heard a low, not particularly friendly voice say.

He walked over.

A miner's lamp standing on a step lit up the man sitting there with reddish light. He had broad shoulders and his long arms were resting lazily on his knees. The unshaven face turned towards Romanov was a quivering mass of black shadows.

Alexei squatted down on his haunches in order to be on the same level as Zaenko and get a better look at him.

The head of the city Cheka had a face that was classic Lombroso – the 'born killer' type, a broad, flat face with protruding cheekbones, simian eyebrow ridges, a goitrous throat and a dark, intense gaze. In short, a handsome specimen.

A thought flashed through Romanov's mind: the revolution had two faces, like the god Janus. One was chaste and pensive, like Nadya's. The other was like Zaenko's. Sometimes the revolution showed one face, and sometimes it showed the other.

'And where have you been all this time, you Revolutionary Military Soviet heroes, hiding away so there's neither sight nor sound of you?' Zaenko asked spitefully.

'We work well, that's why you never hear about us,' Romanov replied in the same tone of voice. 'You're the ones who create all the flash, bang and thunder, you cack-handed bomb-flingers.'

But he had shown his teeth, and that was enough. He hadn't come here to quarrel. So after that he spoke in a different, more judicious tone.

'Listen, Comrade Zaenko, you and I are not in Moscow, like our bosses. We have no time for quarrelling. We walk the razor's edge, just like you do. Let's help each other. You have things that we don't. And vice versa.'

'Right, so what do you have? Boast a bit,' said Zaenko, narrowing his eyes.

'We have communications with Moscow. I can't tell you how they work, but things get there the same day. We'll share. We have our own explosives men, better than yours. If you co-ordinated your actions with us, you could rely on . . .'

'Your woman can co-ordinate her actions when she's . . .' Zaenko interrupted crudely. 'Bloody new commanders.'

Romanov restrained himself and continued in a calm voice.

'We have our own sources of information. In counter-intelligence. And you have yours, in the army command, right?'

No answer.

'That's how you found out about the orphanage and the armoured train, right? Let's exchange information.'

Zaenko blinked, but still didn't answer.

'All right, shall I go first? There's a very serious man trying to find you and expose you. And you can be certain that he will find you.'

'Kozlovsky, you mean?' Zaenko asked with a wry grimace. 'I know that already. A cunning bastard, Terenty told me about him. There are three of them there in counter-intelligence: the lame colonel, one-eyed Cherepov and Captain Romanov. Nazarov says the captain and the Cossack are numbskulls, but the lame man's sharp, slithers up on you like a snake. Never mind, we'll draw his teeth. And you Revmilsovs can clear off back to where you came from. We don't need you slobbery goody-goodies. Right, Shusha?'

'Hao, Zaye,' the Chinese woman replied from behind him.

Well then, I'll talk with you in a different style, Romanov decided. *I'll give you 'slobbery goody-goody'. You don't understand friendly talk, only one argument works with types like you – force.*

He got up, grabbed the Chekist by the neck with one hand and easily lifted him up so that they were eye to eye.

'Listen, Zaya, I'm going to smash your brains out against this wall. And I'll arrange things with Nazarov. He's not such a cretin as you are . . .'

He drew back his fist, but something struck him on the elbow – it didn't seem painful at all, but his arm suddenly went numb and started dangling limply.

Alexei swung round. The Chinese woman Shusha had shrunk, becoming even shorter – she seemed to have turned all spiky and sunk down, so that she looked like a spider. She bared her teeth and hissed, then touched his other arm just as lightly – and it suddenly lost all feeling too. Romanov stood there as if he was tied up with rope, unable to understand what was wrong with him.

Zaenko swung him round towards himself.

'Thought you'd snarl at me, did you? At me? You snot-nosed amateur!'

He rammed his knee into Romanov's crotch. Alexei felt that all right and he doubled over with a scream. A powerful blow to the ear sent him flying to the ground and then he received a kick to the ribs.

'I'm dealing with you simply, Russian-style,' said Zaenko, looking down on him. 'But if you get under my feet – I'll hand you over to Shusha here. She'll work you over Chinese-style. And you'll squeal like a piglet. Lie here in the cold, Revmilsov, and think a bit. Shusha, take his legs away.'

The toe of a little foot tapped briefly against one of Romanov's knees, then the other. Now all four of his limbs had been disabled.

Zaenko spat fruitily on the lying man.

'Give him back his pop-guns. We don't want what isn't ours.'

The Nagant and the Browning were dropped on the ground. The weapons were lying right in front of Alexei's nose, but he couldn't pick them up.

It took a long time for the paralysed nerves to start thawing out and Romanov got chilled to the marrow – the October night was cruelly cold. Two hours went by before his arms started stirring – then at least he was able to crawl to the steps on his elbows. An hour later his legs recovered slightly, but Alexei shambled through the park like an old man, barely even moving.

Eventually he returned to his normal self and strode rapidly to his 'dressing room' – as a secluded spot for changing your appearance was called in the professional jargon. Romanov had a little wooden shed for this purpose, in a dead-end courtyard not far from the hotel. There Alexei transformed himself back into a dashing officer and hid his plain clothes outfit under a stack of wood.

As he walked into the dimly lit foyer of the undistinguished Hotel Switzerland, he thought morosely: *I screwed things up. I tried to build a relationship with our production partners, but I only ruined everything. It was a lousy night. I'll just collapse into bed and sleep, tomorrow will be a new day.*

But the night wasn't over yet.

A private, first-class – one of theirs, from counter-intelligence – jumped up off a chair as he approached.

'Your Honour, I came to get you!' he shouted out, forgetting to salute in his agitation. 'The colonel has been killed!'

'What!' Romanov gasped. 'When? Where?'

'Near his apartment, in the gateway. A bullet to the back of the head. Less than an hour ago. I came to get you immediately, but you weren't here . . .'

Ah, Lavr, Lavr . . .

Romanov grated his teeth. Those cretins, those bastard cretins! They had decided to 'pull his teeth', and they had done it. Immediately.

So he had inadvertently got his comrade killed . . .

For the second time that night tears sprang to Alexei's eyes. He couldn't even remember the last time he had cried before this . . . His heart had thawed out, but it had grown weak.

Amusing anthropology

It turned out that, even without realising it, in her Garden of Eden she had missed the great world outside. It was noisy, dirty and ugly, but Mona found herself enjoying breathing in the smell of petrol, and even of horse dung.

Of course, Erast had refused to agree for a long time. He had fumed and argued, and threatened to summon Professor Liebkind immediately, but eventually he had capitulated. Mona knew which arguments would work with her husband.

'The worst thing of all for the child is when I'm in a nervous state. That's why the doctor told me not to go outside. But sitting in here with nothing to do, I shall simply go insane from anxiety. Why can't you understand that I need to busy myself with something? It will calm me down, and I shall feel glad being of help to you. And then, what kind of strain is it – a short journey in a comfortable automobile and a cosy conversation between two women?'

Eventually they had come to an agreement.

Erast would deal with the sources of the information leaks. Masa would take on the more dangerous task of coming at the business from the side of the Red underground, and the future mother would try to find out whether anyone could have let something slip about the time of the commander-in-chief's visit to the orphanage.

The day after this difficult conversation Fandorin had left for Taganrog – he had decided to start with the commander-in-chief's command staff. Masa had simply disappeared early in the morning, and Mona had enjoyed a delicious breakfast in the restaurant, changed some dollars in reception, dropped into the neighbouring arcade and taken her time choosing an appropriate outfit: a black dress, black coat and black hat. And she had also bought some wonderful half-boots with silver rivets that she was quite unable to resist. The banknotes were funny, with the black and orange ribbon of the Order of St George and the Tsar Bell in the Kremlin: they were known as 'jingle bells'.

She got changed and felt very pleased with how she looked in the elegant mourning outfit. It was a pity that she hadn't found a veil in the shop, but that would probably have been overdoing it. She called the receptionist to have the car made ready. And she set out.

But at the Kaledin Orphanage Mona's exuberance instantly evaporated. She cried for a while in front of the board with photographs of those who had been killed and regretted that she had not brought flowers.

Then she started weeping even more miserably when a governess led her past a group of children in their uniforms, half of whom had their ears bandaged up as a consequence of blast injuries. The others were undoubtedly newcomers. Fathers were killed at the front every day and in the rear mothers were mown down by typhoid, so there was a constant influx of officers' orphans. *If the command of the White Army took as much care of the families of common soldiers*, thought Mona, *then the civil war would be over already.*

She asked in the outer office about seeing the new directress and was told that Mrs Makarova was in a lesson, and she would have to wait.

Mona took a seat outside the glass-walled office, and when a tall, severe-looking woman walked in, she waited a while before following her. Before they talked, she had to work out just what this Makarova was like.

For this Mona had a Method. Every time before she made a portrait, she looked at the person for a long time in order to get a feeling for their essence and their inner vibration, and to *become them*. The key to this process was very simple: you had to genuinely fall in love with the subject of investigation, and for that you had to get inside their skin and see the world through their eyes. Only after that had been achieved would a portrait come alive. The best thing of all, naturally, was to palpate the subject's face but unfortunately, in the case of Mrs Makarova, that was impossible, so Mona had to focus on observation.

The directress sat at her desk, dealing with her own business and not even suspecting that an invader had crept in under her skin. But for Mona it really was as if she had migrated into the other person's body. She felt the weight of a bust that she had never possessed and the pressure of a close-fitting bodice, the coarse, square shoes pinched her, and the pince-nez slid down off her nose. *I'm short of sleep, my right side aches, I knead it gently with my hand . . . Bitter folds beside my mouth – I'm lonely. I have nothing but my work, but it is very important and necessary work. I am a very important individual. I am not liked, I know that, but I am respected. And I don't want your love! What would I need it for? But you do not dare disrespect me!*

. . . I think that's clear.

She got up and knocked.

'Come in.'

She went in.

Mona talked with the directress in a way designed to evoke the natural sympathy of such a complex individual: in a restrained, dignified manner, to the point and without any emotionality – God forbid!

She said that she was a professional artist and could give the children lessons in drawing and sculpture – that was very good for orphans, she had read that in a pedagogical magazine. She did not need a salary, because she had been left means by her husband.

'You are in mourning. A widow?' asked Makarova, still wary at this point.

Mona sighed sadly and did not reply, as if she did not wish to add to the orphanage directress's already heavy burden with her own sad story. Makarova liked that. Mona was still partly her, and seemed to be seeing herself through the other woman's eyes: a modest, sweet lady with a firm but uncomplicated character, someone who could be relied on.

'I would take you on, despite your lack of experience, we could certainly do with art lessons, but I think you are in a delicate condition, are you not?' Mrs Makarova asked with an amicable smile, and that was already a success, because the directress obviously did not smile very often.

'I have heard that your colleague who was killed, Baroness Lande, was also pregnant,' Mona said calmly, without any pathos. 'I am only in the fifth month and I feel well. I think that three or four lessons a week would not fatigue me.'

In the directress's glance Mona read: 'She is like me. At last I shall have someone to talk to.' But out loud Makarova said something different.

'But I don't have authority to hire new teachers, you see. I have been appointed on a temporary basis.'

'Take me on a temporary basis too. And in any case, your decision will certainly be confirmed.'

'How do you know that?'

'I'm an artist. I read people and can even see into the future a little.' Mona pretended to be hesitating about whether to continue or not, but she did anyway: '. . . And another thing. Pardon my directness, but I am plain-spoken by nature. Don't punish yourself. You are not to blame.'

The other woman started.

'For what?'

'For the fact that you had a terrible relationship with the previous directress and she was killed.'

'How . . . How do you know about our relationship?' Makarova asked in a sterner tone of voice. 'Did somebody tell you?'

'No, but it is not hard to work it out. You were not at the ceremony where the outstanding members of staff were presented to the commander-in-chief. So the late Nekritova must have disliked you.'

'But because of that she saved my life! If I had been in the hall . . .' Makarova shuddered. 'Nekritova's head was torn off. And the blast wave threw Masha Lande against a glass cupboard, there were shards stuck all over her body . . . It was dreadful!'

Mona remained sympathetically silent.

'And after all, nobody knew why they had to be in the assembly hall at half past seven, did they?' Makarova continued in an agitated voice. 'The directress hadn't told anyone, she liked to spring surprises. Neither the governesses nor the children had the slightest idea that the commander-in-chief himself would arrive.'

'Nobody but Nekritova knew? Not a single soul?' Mona exclaimed disappointedly. She had been hoping so much that she would come across a lead and could go back to Erast with a trophy!

'We guessed that some kind of event was in the offing. At six o'clock a Cossack officer arrived with some soldiers, a tall, severe man with a patch over his eye . . . I saw him inspect the hall and place two sentries in front of the door so that no one would be allowed in. But it never entered anyone's head that the commander-in-chief himself was about to arrive. I tell you, only Lydia Nekritova herself knew, God rest her soul . . .' Makarova crossed herself.

'And did you get a good look at the sentries?'

The directress was surprised.

'Yes. One had a forelock, and the other had a ginger moustache. But why did you ask?'

Mona pressed her hand against her chest and put on a pained expression.

'I suddenly feel sick for some reason. I'm so sorry. I seem to have jinxed everything by saying I felt well.'

There was no point in staying here any longer. She had found out everything that she needed to know.

A day later Mona met her noble man when he returned from Taganrog empty-handed, although he called it 'a reduction in the number of theories'. In the entourage of His Excellency the detailed schedule of the visit was known only to the senior adjutant, Colonel A. Schroeder. He swore that he had not informed a single living soul about the time of the visit to the orphanage, and Fandorin judged that the officer's word could be trusted: he was a serious, responsible man.

'The spy or b-blabbermouth is here in Kharkov,' Erast Petrovich said in a preoccupied tone of voice. 'I suspected counter-intelligence, but my initial theory was not confirmed . . . Has Captain Romanov paid another visit since the last time?'

'No. And I haven't seen Masa since yesterday morning either.'

Her husband didn't even ask about her visit to the orphanage, only about how she was feeling. That was a little galling.

And when he declared – more to himself than to her: 'I suppose I'll start with the command staff of the Volunteer Army,' Mona remarked innocently:

'If I were you, I'd start with counter-intelligence.'

'B-But why?'

And then she told him about the one-eyed officer who had inspected the assembly hall before the explosion and positioned two sentries there.

It was the finest possible compliment that Erast didn't praise her or express admiration, but immediately sank his teeth into the news, like a wolf grabbing his prey. And he started asking her advice.

'E-excell-ent,' he drawled with a predatory smile. 'How shall we find out who exactly was standing on guard? Should we entrust that task to Colonel Kozlovsky? By the way, it's strange that none of his men met me at the station. I had to take a cab, although I sent off a telegram from Taganrog.'

'Perhaps it's too soon to talk to the colonel?' said Mona, leading him gently towards the decision that she had already taken. She was really enjoying the role of Vasilisa the Wise with Ivan Tsarevich. 'If we could somehow gather together in one place the entire complement of the . . . what do they call it – an escort guard half-squadron?' (In actual fact she had already established that in counter-intelligence the security of top brass was indeed handled by an escort guard half-squadron and it was under the command of Cossack Lieutenant Colonel Cherepov, the one-eyed officer.) 'Probably more than one Cossack has a forelock, and I expect more than one of them has a ginger moustache too, but I could bring in Mrs Makarova, she could take a look at them without being seen – from a window, say – and point out the ones we want.'

And once again Fandorin didn't say: 'What a clever girl you are!' or something else patronising, but simply started rubbing his hands together enthusiastically.

'Excellent! Let's go to the counter-intelligence department. We'll have a talk with Kozlovsky and decide there and then whether to let the colonel in on the plan of action or simply ask him to convene the escort guard on some pretext or other. If you decide it would be better not to, give me a signal. Let's say, s-scratch your eyebrow.'

Mona had to struggle with all her might to prevent her lips slowly extending into a happy smile. He had started talking about her and himself in the plural: 'we'll have a talk', 'we'll decide'! He trusted her opinion! They were working together. That was far better for her pregnancy than lying in bed with her feet raised.

'Yes, I think so,' she agreed pensively. 'And while they're getting the half-squadron together, I'll go and get Makarova. They'll give me a car, won't they?'

'Something has happened here.'

Erast frowned.

There were saddled horses standing in front of the house with white walls. A car shot off in the direction of the centre with its horn wailing and its tyres squealing. An officer ran out onto the steps, holding down his sword, and then another two military men came darting out and shot off as fast as they could run in different directions.

Fandorin let his cabby go and presented his pass, signed by Kozlovsky, to the officer of the guard.

'Not valid,' the lieutenant replied. And when Mona asked him to call Captain Romanov, he narrowed his eyes suspiciously and said nothing at all.

Strange goings-on indeed!

'Let's go to army HQ,' said Erast, taking her by the elbow. 'We need to understand what's going on. No one here will tell us.'

'No need to go anywhere, army HQ is already here,' said Mona, jerking her chin to one side. A long black Packard pulled up at the pavement and Skukin climbed out of it.

He touched a gloved hand to the peak of his cap.

'Ah, Mr Fandorin. Madam . . .'

'What's going on here, Colonel? Why did they not let us in to see Prince Kozlovsky?'

'He's dead,' Skukin replied curtly.

'My God! Who killed him?' Mona exclaimed.

It was a stupid question, of course, womanish. It was obviously the Reds. The impolite Skukin didn't even bother to reply and turned to Fandorin.

'Another blow by the underground. The commander had hoped that you would help us to eradicate it, but clearly in vain. The new head of the Special Section, Cossack Lieutenant Colonel Cherepov, can decide whether he needs your help.'

Mona expected Erast to erupt, but he asked calmly:

'And where is Captain Romanov?'

'He has been relieved of his duties and placed under guard. After all, someone informed the Reds where Kozlovsky lived and which way he came home from work. One of our own people. And Romanov was friends with the dead man. And strangely enough, he didn't spend the night at home. They are trying to establish where he was . . . So have you discovered anything about the bombing?'

'One or two things,' Erast replied quietly, and Skukin's behaviour immediately changed.

'Then why didn't you inform me immediately? Let's go inside, and you can tell me.' The colonel squinted irritably at Mona. 'But is your wife's presence absolutely necessary?'

He bears grudges and hasn't forgotten about 'alpha-queer', Mona thought, and smiled sweetly when Fandorin snapped:

'As you will soon see – it is.'

'Very well. Please come in, madam.'

She smiled even more agreeably. Since the most important person, the one who was taking decisions here, was Skukin, it was only right to apply the Method to him.

And Mona forced herself to love Arkady Sergeevich. It proved to be very easy. Not because Skukin was particularly lovable, but because he loved himself so very much and demonstrated this with every movement he made: 'Look at how well set up and articulate I am, I am the centre of the universe, it revolves around me. No, even that's not right – I am the one who spins it and whips it on.' Mona distinctly heard the cold, clear sound of a flute. *Under Nicholas I, the Flogger, soldiers were probably herded on their way to a scourging with rods to the sound of that music.*

Skukin's mood was also transmitted to Mona: exhilaration, preparedness, taut nerves.

The colonel called over the officer of the guard.

'Where is Cherepov?'

'Questioning the residents of the building where Count Kozlovsky lodged. The colonel was shot in the gateway. Someone might have seen something from a window,' the lieutenant reported.

Meanwhile Erast and Mona talked in whispers.

'Cherepov won't listen to me.'

'Then we'll have to explain everything to Skukin. He won't agree to work blind,' she said confidently.

Her husband nodded.

'Arkady Sergeevich, one m-minute. There's something I must tell you . . .'

Skukin listened, and his internal flute started whistling an accelerated march (Mona could almost hear it). He grasped everything at the first hint, without needing to ask questions or demand details.

'A man with a ginger moustache and one with a forelock? Excellent! We'll smoke the little darlings out right away. Let's go to see Cherepov, Erast Petrovich. I'll order him to assemble the half-squadron, but I won't explain anything to him. And you, Eliza-veta Anatolievna, please get into my car and bring the directress of the orphanage as quickly as possible.'

He remembers my first name and patronymic, he says 'please'. Well, that's more like it.

Now that the goal had been achieved, Mona immediately stopped loving him. He really was disgusting after all, this Skukin. Cold and slippery as an eel.

'Duty officer! Escort Mrs Fandorin to my car! And you know what – just to be on the safe side, go with her. Bring back the lady Mrs Fandorin will indicate to you . . . Right. Where's Cherepov?'

'On the second floor, Colonel. That's where the interrogation room is.'

Skukin and Fandorin walked towards the stairs and Mona and the lieutenant set off towards the exit, but suddenly there was a loud howl from somewhere upstairs, followed by a resounding crash. And then everything went quiet again.

Mona stopped, of course.

Skukin threw back his head and shouted:

'What's the matter?'

An officer ran down the stairs.

'A detainee has attacked Lieutenant Colonel Cherepov!'

Everybody went dashing up to the second floor. And Mona too, of course. *Who was this prisoner? What if it was Romanov?*

A man with a terrifying, bony face and a black patch over one eye came walking towards them along the second-floor corridor. His other eye was glistening and he was rubbing it with an immense fist. His sleeves were rolled up to the elbow and his massive, hairy, sinewy arms were like a ship's mooring ropes.

'I'm sorry, Colonel,' he said in an embarrassed voice. 'I was questioning a resident of Kozlovsky's building. A certain Salnikov, a bank clerk. I pressured him a little bit. Well, the usual kind of thing: "Confess, you bastard, we know everything." I say that to all of them. Well, he started yelling and he attacked me . . . So I thumped him good and hard. I miscalculated the blow and caught him on the temple . . . he's not breathing . . .'

Skukin winced, moved the one-eyed man aside and glanced in through the open door. Mona gasped when she saw the pair of unnaturally twisted legs lying on the floor.

'At least we know who tipped off the killer,' Cherepov boomed. 'Otherwise why would he have gone for me?'

'You killed a man who could have given us a lead?' Fandorin asked mistrustfully.

'As I said, I miscalculated the strength of the blow. He caught me by surprise.'

'And why are your sl-sleeves rolled up? Did you have time to roll them up while Salnikov was attacking you?'

Cherepov gave Erast a furious look.

'My sleeves are rolled up so they won't get spattered with blood. I don't mollycoddle prisoners, there's no time for that. Instead of "good morning", I give them a backhander – and they turn smooth as silk in a trice. After that they don't beat about the bush, they answer.'

'You beat the witnesses? All the residents of the building, one after another?' Erast glared at the officer in disgusted amazement. 'Just to make them "as smooth as silk"? The women too?'

'A slap on the cheek's enough for a wench,' Cherepov muttered, glancing round at Skukin as if seeking protection. The Cossack lieutenant colonel apparently didn't really understand who this annoying, grey-haired gentleman was and why he was acting so affronted. What if he was some kind of high-up?

The colonel said imperiously:

'You are out of touch with the facts of the moment, Erast Petrovich. Yes, the lieutenant colonel is a tough man. Even cruel. I'm sure that in present circumstances that is exactly the kind of man we need as head of the Special Section. One who knows how to instil fear. We must act like the Tatar-Mongols, using calculated cruelty as the most effective means of propaganda. Rumours of the terrible punishments awaiting anyone who dared to resist spread far and wide, and cities surrendered to Genghis Khan of their own accord. Paralysing terror – that is what will lead us to victory. And when we are victorious, this ramshackle country will have to be squeezed tight in a fist of steel that will not be relaxed for a long time to come. Until a population that has gone crazy recovers its reason. Our orators love to pontificate about the "the White Truth". That's nonsense. The real truth is a quite different colour.'

'Which c-colour is that?'

Mona could see that Erast was genuinely interested, and she immediately recalled that he had questioned the 'director' of the Green School with exactly the same curiosity.

'Brown. The colour of shit – I beg your pardon, madam.' Skukin spoke calmly and confidently, no doubt expounding something that he had thought through a long time ago. 'Foul-smelling and, to put it mildly, unappetising, but honest. The truth is that any state, and ours in particular, is only maintained by fear and coercion. Men are divided into those who take decisions and those who carry them out, even if they don't want to. Because they're afraid to disobey. Russia tottered and began falling to pieces when a weak and foolish tsar started playing at freedom in 1905. Everyone whose prescribed lot was to hold their tongues immediately started babbling incessantly. The common herd that was supposed to gather together only when ordered to do so was immediately transformed into a hunting pack. And who is any better off because of that? No one. In the Russia that we shall rebuild on the site of this conflagration, everything will be different.'

'How?' Fandorin asked curtly.

'Things will be firm and solid, and for the herd – terrifying. First we shall hang the Reds, Purples and Pale Pinks in all the squares and at all the crossroads. And they will hang there for a long time, until they decompose. Like the Streltsy under Peter the Great. We shall send all those who grumble and find fault to special camps, where they will die or be re-educated. We shall have a strong, ubiquitous secret police, the very name of which will be enough to set people trembling in fear. And to lead this organisation we shall need men like Cherepov. Not men like the late Kozlovsky.'

The Cossack lieutenant colonel, who had already been listening to Skukin with approval, nodded his head twice emphatically.

'A fine head of secret p-police you have. The moment a lead appeared, he snapped off the thread with his own hand.'

'He'll restore it in the same way as he snapped it off. Thanks to

Elizaveta Anatolievna a new chance has emerged for us to get a grip on the underground from the other side. And you know what? Perhaps we'll manage without the directress and take a simpler approach.' Skukin turned to Cherepov. 'Do you remember who you put on sentry duty at the door of the assembly hall just before the commander-in-chief arrived at the orphanage?'

Cherepov knitted his brows.

'A couple of men who came to hand . . . Sorry, I can't recall. The escort guard half-squadron was only established just recently. I know them all by name, but I don't know the faces so well. Why do you ask?'

Skukin sighed.

'Then we can't manage without a witness identification after all. Go and get the directress of the orphanage, Elizaveta Anatolievna. And you, Cherepov, assemble the half-squadron in the courtyard. Every single man. One of those sentries, or perhaps both of them, planted that bomb in the hall. The directress will point out the blackguards to us, and then we shall decide whether to arrest them immediately or put them under surveillance.'

'They couldn't be Filimonov and Tesliuk, could they?' Cherepov asked hesitantly. 'You see, two Cossacks went missing from the barracks yesterday evening. I thought they'd just gone absent without leave, on a bender . . .'

'One with red hair, the other with a black forelock?' Mona asked quickly.

'Yes, I think so . . . Hang on . . . hang on . . . Those *are* the two I set to guard the hall! Definitely!'

Skukin swore roundly, this time forgetting to apologise to the lady.

'Elizaveta and I will be g-going,' Erast said impassively. 'There's nothing more for us to do here. You can sort out your "secret police" yourself. The only thing is . . . Cherepov, did you find out where Captain Romanov was during the night?'

'He says he was with a lover. But he won't give the name, he cites the honour of an officer. I don't trust him, Colonel. He used to serve in the Red Army.'

'So did I, as a matter of fact,' Skukin reminded him austerely.

'And together with Romanov. He's a brave, enterprising officer. And unlike you, an experienced counter-intelligence agent. Let the captain go. He'll be your deputy.'

'Yes, sir.'

'Well, we haven't managed to arrest the enemy, but at least the men have been identified and we know who to look for. The credit for that is yours, madam.' Skukin touched his hand to the peak of his cap and Mona inclined her head ceremoniously. 'And now, with your permission, Cherepov and I will put together a plan for tracking down the criminals.'

'What are you thinking about?' Mona asked her gloomy husband when they walked out into the street.

'If the White Army starts fighting according to the Tatar-Mongol method, it will win. But in what way is a Brown Russia better than a Red one? It's probably worse . . .'

It can be sky-blue pink for all I care, as long as we're not in it, thought Mona. *The farther away from this privy, with its Shĭt Truth, the better.*

And suddenly she smiled, because she had been visited by one of those epiphanies known by the beautiful Japanese word 'satori'.

They shouldn't go to America, or to Japan. Those places weren't far enough away. New Zealand – that was where they should go. Mona had read about that distant, blessed land in the magazine *Niva* before the revolution. The true fairy-tale kingdom was there. The month of May all the year round, no predatory beasts, no reptiles, no bloodsucking insects, nothing but green meadows with white sheep, transparent lakes, blue mountains and people who are quiet, calm and neighbourly.

'Have you been to New Zealand?'

'Yes,' replied her amazing husband, who had been everywhere in the world, and he started blinking his blue eyes. 'Why d-do you ask?'

'Is it good there? Is it really the best climate on earth?'

'It is very boring there. Nothing ever happens. What does New Zealand have to do with anything?'

Boring – that was exactly what was required. If there was one thing that was certain, it was that Mona had had quite enough adventures for a lifetime.

'It is true that it's like the velvet season in Yalta all year round?' she asked innocently, because the ground for a conversation about New Zealand needed to be laid well in advance.

'I s-suppose so. What are you getting at?'

'At the idea that perhaps we should move to Yalta. It's more agreeable there. You can see that I'm feeling quite splendid. If we have already established who bombed the orphanage, hasn't your promise to Gai-Gaievsky already been kept?'

'Probably, yes . . .' her husband replied.

Mona heard a note of regret in his voice and decided definitely: *To Yalta, and as soon as possible. A quiet town in the rear, with no temptations.*

'Excellent. We'll wait for Masa to get back, and then go.'

In Port Arthur

Masahiro Shibata had passed these two October days in exquisite serenity, like the white heron in the classic verse:

> Above the mountains
> Of Hakone in autumn
> A white heron soars.

And then the sky had been riven by lightning, making the world terrible, but even more beautiful.

But all in due order, in due order, following the movement of the brush.

Before Masa set out on his solitary hunt, the mistress had asked him where he was thinking of starting.

'I shall wait for *satori*,' Masa had replied. 'There is nothing else I can rely on.'

But he had been striking a pose, in order to produce a greater effect later. In actual fact, he knew perfectly well where to start. At the same place where he and the master had left off in August.

At that time, while investigating the case of the villainous bombing in a city street, they had rapidly established that the killers had been assisted by Chinese street traders hawking all sorts of bric-a-brac. They always plied their trade at crossroads, and had passed the message along the chain that the treasury car was approaching the site of the attack.

There were many Chinese in Kharkov. They had poured in during the world war, when the armaments plants had been evacuated from Poland and a large amount of manpower was required – all the local men having gone into the army. On the outskirts of the city an entire neighbourhood of two or three thousand people had sprung up, all of them babbling in a melodious language that normal people couldn't understand.

After the revolution, when the factories came to a standstill, many of the Orientals had left, but many of them had stayed. The Chekist Zaenko had an entire Chinese squad in his garrison, and they mercilessly exterminated enemies of the Soviet authorities in the name of the Third International. The street hawkers who had helped the subversives were almost certainly from that squad.

Colonel Kozlovsky's agents had no hope of finding them, all Chinese looked the same to Russians, and in any case, outsiders could never infiltrate this milieu.

'But it's a different matter for you,' Fandorin said.

'I never expected to hear you say that,' Masa replied, offended at first. 'Only ignorant *akahige* can confuse a Japanese with a Chinese. For the Chinese, we are the same kind of foreigners as white people.'

But the master had replied by quoting a koan:

'A thinking head is like a head of cabbage.'

Masa had started thinking and, of course, he had come up with something. It had been excellent work, pleasant to recall. Masa had not had so much fun for a very long time.

He had passed himself off as a natural-born Chinese who had been taken to Yokohama as a child, and had almost forgotten his native language there. 'Almost' – because in his youthful bandit days Masa had learned to chat a little with the Shanghai smugglers in their southern dialect, and many years later, during the investigation of the sensational 'Siamese Twins Case', he had worked for three months as a bouncer in San Francisco's Chinatown and learned to make himself more or less understood in the northern dialect, which is called Mandarin. An easy language, not like Russian.

The 'Yokohama Chinaman' had rapidly settled in among the yellow-skinned residents of Kharkov and found one of them who was connected with the Red underground network. From that point it had been no problem at all to find the bombers. Those bad men had paid in full for their villainy, but the master had ordered Masa not to touch his Chinese acquaintance, since he had not spilt any blood. It was this Cheng that the Japanese had now set off to see. He was a third-rate kind of man – a *xiaoren* in Chinese – but in the Celestial Empire, as in the Land of the Rising Sun, a debt of gratitude was regarded as sacred.

The next day Masa sought out Cheng, who had changed his place of residence but, the ancestors be praised, remained in Kharkov.

Masa's old acquaintance was quite astonished to see his unexpected visitor.

'Ma Sha? What happened to you? And how did you find me?'

Masa had selected Chinese hieroglyphs that would be read to sound like his genuine name 馬厦.

'What do you mean, what happened to me?' he asked, choosing to ignore the second question. 'I warned you to run for it, and I went into hiding too. But one good turn deserves another. Remember, you told me you would put me in touch with your *laoda*, but I didn't want to do it. Now I do. Take me to the *laoda*, and I'll be one of you.'

Cheng was not particularly bright, there was no need for any great subtlety with him. 'Laoda' means 'chief' or 'commander'. Masa probably expressed himself clumsily in Chinese, something like 'me warn you go run and me hide too', but Cheng understood him.

'Why have you changed your mind?' he asked after a pause.

'For the Whites we are half-people. They call me *slanty-eyed* . . .' – Masa pronounced that word in Russian – 'I'm for the International now. For the Reds. You take me to the *laoda* and I'll tell my story myself.'

'I could do that before, but not now. It's called *secrecy*. I can't bring strangers. I'll have a word with the *laoda* about you.'

'So the *laoda* can refuse or start checking me for a long time? That would be right, if you didn't know me. But you do know me. I've already been checked. Take me straight to the *laoda*!'

'I can't. We have strict rules. Bringing outsiders is forbidden.'

'Ah, shame on you . . .' Masa made the gesture with which the Shanghai smugglers expressed contempt: he waggled his little finger. 'When I saved your life, I wasn't an outsider. All right then, I'll go away, and may you be ashamed for ten thousand years.'

To refuse a request from someone to whom you are indebted means to lose face completely. No even half-decent Chinese could act like that. And neither could Cheng.

'All right,' he said with a sigh, tomorrow's *xīng qī sān*. You come with me.'

'What's tomorrow?' Masa asked, not understanding immediately. 'Ah, Wednesday.'

'The *laoda* gathers us together on Wednesdays. They give us our weekly wages and assignments.'

'They pay you wages?' Masa asked.

Cheng puffed out his chest.

'And sometimes there are bonuses. Last week they gave me a new jacket, because I counted the trucks with White soldiers on the road well. And I'm taking a very great risk if I bring you without permission. I'm doing you a great favour, a very great one. If the *laoda* gets furious, it will be terrible.'

'I'll explain everything to him,' Masa promised. 'I'm very useful. The *laoda* will understand that straight away, he'll even reward you.'

Cheng giggled. 'Not he, but she.'

'Your *laoda* is a woman?'

'Yes, but not a simple one. She is called Shusha-tunji.' He wrote the name Shu-Sha 舒莎 on a sheet of paper. 'Shusha-tunji was a bodyguard in Beijing, in the Forbidden City, she guarded Her Majesty the Empress. And now she guards Zaye-tunji himself! Have you heard of him?'

'Who has not heard of him?' Masa said respectfully, realising that they were talking about Zaenko. 'Take me to Shusha-tunji. Then we will be even.'

On Wednesday evening they set out for 'Port Arthur', as the conglomeration of rough wooden-board sheds where the workers from the closed ammunition factory lived was known in the city. The slum neighbourhood had a lousy reputation and local people didn't go there. The place smelled of roasted garlic, rotting garbage and washed laundry, and there was even a sweet whiff of opium coming from somewhere – Buddha only knew where the Chinese got it from in these impoverished times.

Cheng became more and more nervous with every step they took: he made several attempts to talk his companion out of his plan, and at the door he stopped dead, rooted to the spot, but Masa took him by the scruff of his neck and shoved him into the wooden hut.

About ten men were sitting at a table, under a kerosene lamp hanging from the ceiling. Sitting at the end of the table, on a chair with a high back, was a woman. Face like a nun's – dispassionate. Age indeterminate. Hair cut short. Lacklustre eyes. A long cigarette holder in her hand, with a *papyrosa* burning in it. A black jacket with an upright collar.

When trying to understand the nature of any particular woman, Masa always imagined what she would be like in a moment of passion – tenderly yielding, like a roe deer; exigently clinging, like an octopus; or lavishly generous, like a luscious watermelon. But it was quite impossible to imagine Shusha in a man's embrace, and that was a very bad sign. Masa became wary.

Bowing, he greeted the honourable company.

'*Da jia hao!*'

They all looked at the stranger, but no one even nodded. The expression on all of their faces (some young and some not so young, but not a single one that was old) was exactly the same, and Masa did not like it: that was the way people usually look at a fly that has flown in before they swat it.

Cheng began speaking in a trembling voice, so quickly that Masa didn't understand half of what he said, only the general meaning, which was that this was the Ma Sha who had saved him from White counter-intelligence in August, Shusha must remember that, and Ma Sha was from Shanghai, but he had lived in Japan since his childhood. He implored me to bring him here. He wants to be with us . . .

Cheng grew confused and fell silent. Masa bowed again with his hands folded together in front of him in the Chinese fashion.

The faces turned towards their leader – what would she say?

Well trained, like little monkeys in a circus, thought Masa. He was still looking only at Shusha; the others were obviously of no importance.

The woman took the *papyrosa* out of the cigarette holder and carefully set it down in an ashtray.

Quietly, very quietly (everyone craned their necks to hear), she said:

'Comrade Cheng, didn't I tell you not to bring outsiders?'

'He's not an outsider, I explained that . . . He saved me. He is for the International, he wants to fight with us against the White devils.'

'I decide who is an outsider and who isn't, and an order is an order. You know what happens if you disobey an order, don't you?'

Shusha took something out of a little box and put it in her mouth. Probably a cinnamon or mint lozenge. The Chinese liked them.

'So, what is the penalty for disobeying an order?' she repeated through clenched teeth.

Cheng started trembling.

'Hear me out, honourable Comrade Shusha,' said Masa, 'and you will see that I am not an outsider.'

The woman raised the empty cigarette holder to her lips; there was a quiet sound and Cheng clutched at his throat, with his eyes bulging out of their sockets. The men sitting there squirmed.

Cheng wheezed for a few seconds and dropped his hands. His eyes had glazed over. As rigid as a stick, he toppled to the floor with a thud. There was a needle sticking out of his neck, at one side of his Adam's apple.

Ah, that's why the cigarette holder is so long, Masa realised. *The Japanese ninjas also have such a weapon – a pipe for spitting out poisoned thorns. It's called a* 'fukiya'. *I know about that, I learned it. But what astounding accuracy! To hit the artery from that distance!* Masa couldn't have done that. Only if he trained very seriously.

He fixed his eyes on the Chinese woman again, even more attentively, and noted the incredible thriftiness of her movements, or rather, their complete absence. After killing a man with only a slight tensing of her lips, Shusha froze. Something glinted in the fingers of her left hand. Another needle.

Masa coughed and his neck suddenly started itching, right beside his Adam's apple.

They said that all the imperial bodyguards held the highest possible ranking in their art. It was called 'living stone' because, when there was no danger, the stone was dead, it did not attract any attention to itself or betray its presence in any way. But at the slightest threat to the individual under protection the stone came to life.

Without taking his eyes off the needle, Masa prepared to spin round and jump if necessary.

The woman's lips started moving, but apart from that she remained as stonily immobile as ever.

'Now I will speak with you, stranger. You are old. You are not a genuine Chinese, you do not even bow correctly. Nobody apart from the *bendan* Cheng knows you. What good are you to me? If you do not give me a good answer, you will follow your worthless friend and depart for *ushuishi*.'

Masa did not know the word *ushuishi*, but he doubted that it signified anything good.

'I am not old. And I am very useful. I can beat all your men on my own.'

She smiled very slightly and put the needle away in a box. That was already good.

'Beat me. I will sit and use only my left hand.'

She stood up and lifted the heavy chair with her fingers like a feather. Carried it to an empty spot. Sat down. Hooked her feet round the chair's legs. Put her right hand behind her back.

What a face she has, Masa thought. *Like dense mist, through which the soul cannot be seen at all. Nothing at all can be seen.*

'With one hand?' He laughed politely. 'I suppose you are joking?'

'If you beat me, you will live. If not, you will die.'

The men sitting at the table started whispering quietly but animatedly, conspiring about something among themselves. Masa guessed what it was. The Chinese loved to make a wager. Apparently no one could be found to bet on the stranger.

Well, now I'll give you the Sino-Japanese War, Masa thought. *Like in the twenty-seventh year of the Meiji Era, when your hordes thought they would crush our little army like a mosquito, and then fled for their lives.*

Without any build-up, he darted forward and started employing the technique of *hi-no-hyo* ('fiery hail') – that is when short blows shower down from all directions.

Not one blow reached its target. His fists always struck against the fluttering palm, and as soon as Masa relaxed the pressure for a split second, the palm slapped him painfully on the tip of his nose. Blood started to flow.

Infuriated, he doubled the frequency of his blows, but the Chinese woman's single hand easily beat them off. He tried swinging his knee in from the left, and it was met by an iron elbow.

Masa was so focused on that cursed, ubiquitous, impregnable hand that he saw nothing else. So an unexpected attack from the other side caught him by surprise. Shusha struck him on the temple from the right, and the fight was over.

When Masa surfaced out of rippling blackness, he discovered that he was lying on the floor with a little foot in a leather slipper thrust against his chest. From below Shusha appeared huge, towering up almost to the ceiling. And from this angle her face was like the radiant moon.

The first thought that came into his still not entirely clear head was: *Buddha Amida, what a woman! I've never seen one like her.*

'You said you would fight with only your left hand,' he reproached her. 'That is unfair.'

'The only reason you are alive is that my left hand alone was not enough. I have not encountered such a serious opponent for a very long time.'

The ripples retreated completely and Masa saw that there was no one in the room apart from them.

'Where is everybody?'

'I sent them away. I want to get to know you a bit better. Tell me what you came here for. Only do not lie and say that you wish to fight for the International. You are too cunning and too old for that.'

'I am not old!'

How old is she? Thirty? Forty? Fifty? Forty would be good, the very best age for a woman. But even if she's older, that's all right too.

He glanced at the foot pressing down on his chest. Thank

goodness, it was normal, not bandaged. But then, they wouldn't have taken her into the bodyguards otherwise.

'You fight for the International yourself. Why can't I?'

'I have my own reason.'

'For helping the Bolsheviks? What is it?'

'I'll tell you. Why should I conceal it? You will either get up as one of us, and then we will be together. Or you will not get up, and then you will not tell anyone anything. I help the Bolshevik Zaye, even though he is a stupid barbarian, because in Moscow he has influential . . .'

Masa could not make out the last word, but he guessed it was 'superiors' or 'patrons'.

'The Bolsheviks will be victorious in this war. And when they make the entire country of Eluósi Red, they will want to make the surrounding countries Red too. That is what the "International" is. Then I shall go back to China as a commissar from Red Moscow. And my time will come.'

A great woman with great ideas, Masa thought in rapturous admiration. *I have never met one like that before. I wonder if her legs are straight. I can't see under the trousers. But I could forgive such a great woman even that.*

He even liked the fact that she was standing over him like this, pressing down on his chest.

'I am being more open with you than I ever am with anyone else,' said Shusha, 'because I see that you are a serious and fearless man.'

Flattered, Masa shifted his eyebrows, in order to appear even more serious and fearless.

'You be open with me too,' she continued. 'I know how to cause pain, I was taught that very well, but I know that I won't get anything out of you with pain. If you don't want to tell the truth – you won't. But bear in mind that it is impossible to deceive me. In the Forbidden City we were taught an indispensable art for a good bodyguard: how to see falsehood in the eyes. The eyes of a man who is planning a hostile act are always deceitful. Look into my eyes, Ma Sha, and answer me. If I see even a trace of falsehood, I shall crush your heart.'

The foot increased its pressure and Masa's heart started fluttering, only not from fear, but from a very intense and even rather pleasant sensation for which there was no name.

'I shall tell you the truth. I came here in order to get to Zaye-tunji.'

The narrow eyes narrowed even farther: it was like a faint shadow slipping across the face of the moon.

'What do you want with him?'

'Not I. My *laoda*.'

'Who is he?'

'He is the one who in August found and punished the men who killed many peaceful civilians in the street in the summer. My master is a *junzi* . . .' (in Chinese that meant 'a noble man') 'and his goals are always noble. He is a great detective and a master of the Japanese school of martial arts, ninjutsu.'

'What school?'

Masa raised her trouser leg and wrote the hieroglyphs 忍術 on her skin with his finger. The skin was smooth and cool. He wanted to kiss it, but he didn't.

'Ah, *rensiu*, I have heard many interesting things about it. Is your *laoda* Chinese or Japanese?'

'Russian.'

The slim eyebrows trembled very slightly. This was undoubtedly a sign of extreme astonishment. Little by little Masa was learning to read her face of stone.

'I did not know that there were *junzi* and masters of *zhenshu* among the Russians . . .' Shusha sighed very gently. 'What am I to do with you, Ma Sha? I can kill you, but then your *laoda* will send someone else, whom I do not know. Or start taking revenge for you himself . . .'

How intelligent she is, thought Masa. *It is a pity that I am lying and she is standing. It would be better if we were both lying.*

'And for some reason I do not wish to kill you,' she said pensively. 'That is very strange. Usually I enjoy killing.'

'That is because karma has brought us together. Karma sent me because your time of solitude has come to an end . . .'

'. . . I was certain that my time of solitude would never come to an end.'

She took her foot off his chest, turned away and wrapped her arms round her shoulders. Masa was moved by this unexpected womanly gesture and her defenceless back.

Jumping lightly to his feet, he barely managed to restrain the impulse to embrace her and said with poignant feeling:

'. . . But karma has led me to you because my *laoda* no longer needs me. I have served him faithfully and loyally for many years, because he pursued a great goal: he punished Evil. But soon I shall be free and alone, I shall be left with no meaning in my life, because my master is withdrawing from the world and renouncing his great goal. But you have one. It does not matter to me what it is. It is enough that it is great. And if you wish, I will serve you.'

Shusha swung round rapidly. Her eyes were wet and tears immediately sprang to Masa's eyes too.

Plum blossom on a withered branch

For a minute or so Masa actually hesitated, Mona-san was so tremendously delighted to see him. When he knocked on the door of the deluxe apartment in the morning, she even gave a shriek of joy. And she embraced him and kissed him too.

'Since yesterday evening I haven't been able to think of anything else, I've just been wishing you'd get back soon!'

Perhaps I won't be the odd man out, thought Masa, suddenly doubtful. *The mistress loves me sincerely. I wasn't really serious when I said that about raising their son, I only said it to please her, but what if? What if?* And once again his eyes were dimmed by the tears that were so close to the surface all the time now.

But after that Mona had turned to Fandorin and said:

'He's come back! We can go to Yalta.'

And Masa realised that she hadn't been happy to see him, but because his return brought her happiness nearer. But he wasn't offended in the least by the realisation. Women, that is, *ordinary* women, had their own truth of life, and it was worthy of respect. Well then, that meant that the decision taken during the night, on the spur of the moment, was correct. It had been *satori*, and *satori* never deceived.

'Perhaps we can first listen to what Masa has been d-doing for these three days. I think he has something worth telling.'

The master knitted his eyebrows. He had sensed something – he knew his vassal too well.

'Yes, I do have something worth telling,' Masa declared solemnly.

And he told them everything that had happened. At first only the events. And then he moved on to the feelings.

'. . . I never thought it would happen to me. You know how many women I have had, master.' And he clarified that, because he was grateful to every one of them. 'Five hundred and sixty-seven, if I don't count that excessively high-strung Brazilian woman, who died of passion before I had finished the job, and that perfidious Venetian woman, who tried to thrust a stiletto into the back of my head at the most inappropriate moment. She died too,' he explained to Mona-san, in case she hadn't understood that. 'After all, I shall be sixty next year, and then suddenly – a great miracle! As if plum blossom has appeared on a branch that withered long ago! I've never met a woman like her in my life! I'm sure there isn't another one like her. She's like the green mamba that almost bit me twenty years ago on the Congo river, just as deadly and beautiful!'

'She beat you with just her left hand? Th-that's incredible,' said Fandorin, shaking his head. The emotional outpourings had not made the slightest impression on him. Concerning those, the master merely said: 'You simply needed a woman who is stronger than you. And you thought you liked fat women, you smart aleck.'

'Not just her left hand, but a little bit with her right hand too. And I assure you that you wouldn't have coped with this imperial bodyguard either,' Masa replied with dignity to the first half of this cold-hearted tirade. He ignored the second half as insulting and started talking exclusively to the mistress.

Now *she* listened properly – gasping, pressing her hands to her chest and dabbing at her eyes with a handkerchief.

'I spoke to Shusha about my love for a long time. At first she was angry and wanted to beat me, and she did strike me once, very painfully. But I gathered together all the beautiful Chinese words that I know. I said that I would be with her to the end of my days. That I would be her servant and fulfil all her whims. That I would make her the happiest Chinese woman in the world. And all the time I was looking at her, and the master knows how I can look at women. She began listening. Then she started thinking. Then she agreed . . .'

'This is a remarkable love story!' Mona-san sobbed. 'Almost like ours. Isn't it, Erast?'

The master remained sullenly silent.

The difficult moment was drawing nearer. Masa summoned up his courage and turned to Fandorin.

'Will you . . . release me, master?'

'How can I not release you? You're the one who started this c-circus with a "master" and a "vassal" in the first place. It's for you to decide when it will all end. But I can see there's something you're not telling us.'

The next stage of the conversation was equally difficult.

'A tigress grows up a tigress because she is the daughter of a tiger and was raised in a band of tigers. Shusha is a bodyguard from the Forbidden City. She was chosen for that fate as a child, she was raised by the fighting eunuchs of the palace, stern and cruel men. She lives by internal rules which can appear monstrous. It will take a lot more time for Shusha to change under my influence . . .'

'Keep it short,' the master requested.

'I said that I wanted Zaenko, because he is a villain, and if I am dear to her, she must hand him over to me as a sign of her love . . .'

Masa faltered.

'And what did she say? Did she refuse?'

'No, she agreed . . . But she said that I must also prove my love. One *laoda* in exchange for another.'

'What?' asked Mona-san, who hadn't understood.

'That I must kill my master, and then Shusha will trust me,' Masa explained to her.

Mona-san shrieked, but Fandorin remarked coolly:

'In essence a quite logical counterproposal. The two of you could make an interesting c-couple.'

'Of course, I'm not going to kill the master,' Masa explained to the frightened mistress. 'I'll simply *say* that I have killed him. And that little lie can remain on my conscience.'

'Little?' asked Fandorin, insulted.

But Mona-san babbled:

'She won't take your word for it!'

'She will take mine. I shall be very convincing. Only release me without any bitterness, master. And wish me happiness.'

This request was declared with true feeling, through tears, which Masa was not ashamed of at all, for many centuries ago it had been written:

> Dew on the green leaves
> Of a bristly burdock plant.
> Tears of a soldier.

Instead of being moved and embracing his old friend, the master asked absent-mindedly:

'And which empress did she serve – Cixi-taiho or Longyu-taiho?'

'I didn't ask. What difference does it make? Shusha said she left the service of the palace eight years ago.'

'Then it was the Empress Lungyu, because Cixi died in 1908. I see.'

'What do you see? You're just spinning things out, because you don't want to release me!' Masa exclaimed angrily. 'You haven't answered my question!'

'Of course, g-go. And I also wish you happiness.'

And he turned away – no doubt to conceal his moist eyes. But Mona embraced Masa and whispered tenderly:

'I am very excited for you. And I'm longing to see the woman who has had such an effect on you.'

'You can't see her yet. First I have to re-educate her . . .' He lowered his voice – he didn't want the master to hear this, but he could say it to Mona-san. 'I am already too old to spend the years I have left on conquering China. What do I want with China? I want to be happy in love, as you and the master are happy. With me Shusha will change. Perhaps we will also have a child. After all, she is still young, she's only thirty-three. Love and motherhood work miracles. And when it happens, we will seek you out. And we shall be together again.'

345

Mona-san sobbed. And he cried too, wiping his cheeks with his sleeve.

Masa walked to the appointed place with a soaring stride and the little wings of a colourful butterfly fluttering in his chest. *This is what love is*, he thought. *Just look what it's really like. Completely different from what I imagined.*

Shusha had told him to walk from the goods station along the rusty rails of the abandoned branch line as far as the track patrolman's cabin.

And there was the little cabin with peeling paint and a gaping hole instead of a window. Masa still had fifty metres to go to reach it when he spotted Shusha. She was sitting under a bush with her long cigarette holder, puffing out smoke.

Lending his face a severe expression, because one had to be restrained with women, Masa stopped.

'I have kept my promise. Have you kept yours?'

She got to her feet. The corners of her mouth shifted noticeably away from each other. Shusha was smiling!

'I will take you to Zaye-tunji and you can do what you like with him. But first I must make sure.'

'In future, when you get to know me better, you will learn to take my word for things,' Masa said strictly. 'Here, look.'

He took off his rucksack and loosened the string. 'This is my *laoda*'s head. I loved him very much, but I love you more.'

Shusha glanced into the bag.

'A genuine *junzi*. Beautiful even in death.'

She stretched her lips out even farther – that was probably a peal of laughter – and smacked Masa on the top of his head with her open palm, seemingly not hard, but he tumbled over onto his back. His ears were ringing and there were bright, rainbow-coloured circles spinning in front of his eyes.

'And you are a genuine *bendan*. Goodbye, you have amused me greatly with your funny Chinese and your stupidity.'

She dropped her *papyrosa*, stuck a needle in her mouth and raised the cigarette holder.

Masa could have rolled off to the side, because the blow had

346

knocked him off his feet, but not stunned him. But he didn't want to. What was life good for, if it treated you like this?

'Bitch,' he said to Shusha in Russian. There was no time to compose a deathbed haiku.

Instead of making a spitting sound, the pipe roared like thunder. A little black circle appeared precisely at the centre of the Chinese woman's forehead, her head jerked back abruptly and her body collapsed into the grass.

Masa sat up in astonishment. The master was walking along the rails with a smoking revolver in his hand.

'You've completely gone to pieces,' he said reproachfully. 'You didn't even notice me following you. For shame.'

But Masa was not delighted at all. He put his hands over his face and started sobbing and shuddering.

'She didn't love me, I was wrong . . . But I . . . I fell in love with her. I thought we would be together. Like you and the mistress. I thought we would have a child too. I thought you could have a girl, and we could have a boy, and when they grew up . . .'

He couldn't go on.

The master took his weeping friend by the scruff of the neck and dragged him roughly over to the corpse.

'Well, children wouldn't be very likely.'

'What are you doing?' Masa shouted in horror, seeing Fandorin pulling off the dead woman's trousers.

'Take a look. This is no woman. Your Shusha is a eunuch.'

Masa looked at the exposed spot, batting his eyelids.

'When I ascertained that the object of your affections served in the bodyguard of Empress Longyu, I realised it straight away. If we had been talking about Cixi, now that's a different matter. The old empress ruled for herself and was famous for her cantankerous disposition and disrespect for traditions. She could easily have surrounded herself with female bodyguards. But Lungyu had no power at all and not for anything would she have dared to break the rules of the Forbidden City. Did you really not know that the personal apartments of the sovereigns there could only be guarded by eunuchs? You need to read more books.'

'If you guessed that Shusha was deceiving me, why didn't you tell me?' asked Masa, pressing on his temples. Instead of disappearing, the rainbow-coloured circles only started spinning faster. 'That's cruel. I've never felt so humiliated in my life . . .'

'You wouldn't have believed me. Love's like that.' The master patted Masa on the back of his head. 'You poor fellow. It must be hard for you, seeing Mona and me.'

Stooped over, as if he had aged a hundred years, Masa struggled to his feet.

'I am very ashamed, master,' he said in a lifeless voice. 'I thought only you were made foolish by love. But you have never been such a great fool as I have. Forgive me. I have spoiled everything. Now we shall never find the villain Zaenko. Shusha has warned him, of course.'

Fandorin flicked him on the forehead.

'Hey, snap out of it. You know me, don't you? When have I ever broken the thread of a trail? Would I have killed this monstrosity if Zaenko wasn't already in our hands?'

'Eh?' asked Masa, which was, of course, terribly impolite.

'While you were billing and cooing here, I looked around carefully, and I spotted flashes of light from the window of the cabin. There's someone watching from there with binoculars. Who do you think Shusha would arrange this p-performance for? Zaenko came along to enjoy watching the death of the man who punished the bomb-throwers. Now our comrade Chekist is sitting quietly, waiting for us to go away. Go and get him. You need to cheer yourself up a bit.'

The circles immediately stopped spinning.

'I'm feeling a lot better already,' said Masa.

A cure for toothache

The fate of the revolution hung by a thread. The steel jaws of the White armies were closing on the throat of the Republic, which was on the point of bleeding to death, but the Bolshevik Romanov was looking out of the window and thinking about love.

The day before Nadya had told him: 'You don't understand. It's not you, it's me. A man is capable of loving *something* more than *someone*. It doesn't work like that for a woman.' Alexei was angry. They were alone together at last, but Nadya had thrust her little fist into his chest, turned her face away and kept saying the same thing, over and over again.

'Can you put that a bit more clearly?' he had asked.

'Yes I can. If we do this, then you'll block out the rest of the world for me, and I'll only be able to think about you and live for you. But I mustn't abandon the revolution just now. Without any one of us, even tiny little me, it could go under. Let's wait until the victory's won. Then I'll be able to be yours completely, through and through.'

Alexei had stopped hugging her, folded his arms across his chest and laughed. 'Beautiful words. But in reality you're just a little girl who wants to do it, but is afraid. You came to my room, then got frightened, and now, as a good, well brought-up little girl is supposed to do, you're packaging your fear in bright, shiny wrapping paper.' He really had got terribly angry. Because he wanted Nadya so badly that his knees were trembling. He had deliberately said things to offend her. So she had just flared up and run out. And now, instead of thinking about the great cause, Romanov was staring out of the window at the rainy street and telling himself: *Nadya's right. It's no time for love in Russia right now. In Russia it's never the right time for love.*

Take his first love: puerile and stupid as it was, it didn't seem that way at the time, and it had been shattered by the war.

His second, deceptive love was a chimera spawned by war.

His third love had quite simply been killed by the war . . .

He squeezed his eyes shut and drove away the terrible memory of that field of death. He hadn't been able to do that before, but now it was almost effortless.

His love for Nadya was his last love. There wouldn't be another, the lizard wouldn't grow its tail back again. *Wait for the victory? But when we are victorious – if we are victorious – yet another Russian Plague will emerge, and it will be more important than love and incompatible with it . . .*

He shook his head. *That's enough whinging, Comrade Romanov. First let's win the victory, then we'll see what's what.*

And he finally started thinking about the state of affairs. To employ a cultured expression, it was shitty. What the little girl had said was true: the Soviet Republic was on the brink of destruction.

General Yudenich had already reached Tsarskoe Selo, and the fall of Petrograd, the cradle of the revolution, was expected any day now. Gai-Gaievsky's army was approaching Tula and the Red front there was faltering and bending out of shape. Alexei knew it would soon be shattered to smithereens – a troop train had just been dispatched from Novorossiisk with brand-new English tanks, ideally adapted for manoeuvre warfare. The armoured monsters would cut down the Red cavalry with their machine guns and crush the emaciated workers' infantry under their caterpillar tracks. And then, in only two or three dashes, they would be rolling through the defenceless rear towards Moscow . . .

The most appalling thing was that Romanov couldn't do anything about it. He no longer had access to any secret information. The new chief had released him from arrest but didn't let him get near any serious work. He had given Alexei a useless assignment: sit in the hotel without going out anywhere and compile a staff schedule for the All-Russian Department of Security (what the Special Section would be transformed into after Moscow was taken). Captain Romanov was effectively under house arrest, which meant that the intelligence network of the Revolutionary Military Soviet was paralysed.

The only hope was that the second underground would remain active and effective. Of the two Cossacks who had disappeared, only Filimonov had been found – in the River Lolan, with a bullet in the back of his head. The other, Tesliuk, had vanished without trace. He was definitely one of Zaenko's men, and they had a good source of information at army headquarters. Zaenko was a repulsive bastard and Lavr Kozlovsky's murderer, but apart from the Chekists, Romanov had no one he could count on.

And in the meantime there were wholesale arrests in the city. Trade union activists were being rounded up in the factories, workshops and railway depots. The entire editorial staff of the only liberal newspaper, *Voice of the South*, had been arrested, and on the streets anyone who looked even slightly suspicious was picked up.

The Special Section had become known as the 'Black House'

again, because the howls of prisoners under interrogation poured out of the windows and the courtyard resounded to the rumble of shots. In the market square a team of carpenters was hastily cobbling together a gallows. Skukin's plan for ruling through terror was being put into effect.

He had to act through Skukin – that was the decision Romanov came to after racking his brains good and hard.

No more moping away in 'house arrest'. He had to go to the section, without waiting to be called in, and kick up such a stink with Cherepov that it would be impossible for them to work together. At the first stage, at the very beginning, Skukin had offered to get his comrade-in-arms a place on the command staff. He had said emphatically: 'I need men I can trust.' Now Alexei had to go to him and say: 'Right, make it this way and that way, Arkasha, and I'm yours. Take me under your wing, I'll serve you like the Japanese serves Fandorin. At a turbulent time like this, being at HQ is far more useful than being in counter-intelligence.'

Feeling more cheerful now, Romanov put on his greatcoat and peaked cap, then picked up his shoulder belt. Forward!

As always just recently there was uproar in front of the Special Section, with men running up the steps into the building and others dashing out of it. A truck, bristling with bayonets that made it look like a hedgehog, drove out of the gates with its engine growling. A cavalryman went galloping off towards the centre at a furious pace. The uproar had grown even worse since the last time Alexei was here.

'What's all the hurly-burly about, Misha?' he asked the duty officer.

'You mean you haven't heard yet?' the lieutenant asked, his face twitching in agitation. 'They've arrested Zaenko! He's lying over there, the bastard. Fandorin's Japanese has only just dragged him in. The boss is at army HQ. They've just phoned him.'

'Lying?' Romanov asked, swinging round. He saw backs packed tightly together in the corridor. Everybody was looking down at something. 'Dead?'

'Alive. Go on over and take a look.' The lieutenant chuckled.

Alexei pushed his way through the men.

The Japanese was sitting on a bench in a motionless pose, with the palms of his hands planted on his knees, staring solemnly into space. Lying on the floor under his feet was a man completely entangled in ropes, as if he had been stuffed into a string shopping bag. There were even ropes across his face, and a piece of wood sticking out from between his teeth, tied in place at both ends with a shoelace. The prisoner's eyes were goggling ferociously, with the whites glinting. They settled on Alexei and narrowed in hate. The man had recognised him.

Like the captured wolf in the scene from War and Peace, Romanov thought.

'How did you manage it, Mr Shibata?' he asked.

'Very simply. He fired, I jumped. When I jump, it's very hard to hit me, he didn't hit me. Then he ran out of cartridges. Then I struck him on the ear, with this foot.'

He pointed to his shoe, from which the lace was missing.

'And why did you put the piece of wood in his mouth?'

'So he wouldn't bite his tongue out. He's a very serious *akunin*, capable of anything at all. After I had knocked him down and grabbed him by the throat, he bit me on the arm.'

The Japanese showed Alexei his wrist with tooth marks on it.

'A serious what?' Romanov asked, feverishly thinking what he ought to do. He could quite happily have finished off this brute Zaenko with his own bare hands – but there was the Chekist underground, and there was the situation at the front . . .

'That's a long story,' Masa said, and got up. 'Now you've come, I can go. I'm handing this bad man over to you. Do whatever you like with him. The master told me to tell you that this is the end of his participation in the war between the Whites and the Reds. The promise that he made to you and your superiors has been kept. I'll leave the shoelace.'

The Japanese bowed ceremoniously and the men parted to let him through.

'Take out the gag,' Romanov ordered. 'No, I'll do it myself . . .'

He leaned right down to the man on the floor and whispered:

'Keep calm. I'll think of something.'

The other man, barely able to speak, hissed:

'Decided to get even, Judas? I'll take you to the next world with me . . .'

'Make way, make way!' a loud voice said.

Cherepov had arrived. Empty space immediately appeared on all sides – the Cossack lieutenant colonel's own subordinates were afraid of him.

'Well, Dzerzhinsky's hawk, flown back to the nest, have you?' Cherepov chuckled ominously. 'You used to run the show around here, now you'll gnaw on the other end of the carrot.'

'Yes, I'm Dzerzhinsky's hawk,' Zaenko answered from down on the floor. 'And your captain here is Trotsky's crow' – he jerked his head in Alexei's direction.

'You're all bluster, my dear enemy.' Cherepov leaned down and hit Zaenko with a short, powerful punch in the face. The prisoner went quiet. 'Right, then. Take him to the operating theatre. He'll soon start singing a different tune. Get him ready, Kalmykov.'

The prisoner was seized by the arms and legs and dragged up the stairs. Sergeant Major Kalmykov, the lieutenant colonel's orderly, walked in front.

'What operating theatre is that?' Romanov asked.

Things are bad, he thought. *Zaenko will come round and start shouting about Trotsky again. And eventually Cherepov will start listening to him.*

The beaming chief didn't even recall that he had forbidden his assistant to leave the hotel.

'While you've been writing your dissertation, Captain, one or two things have changed around here. Do you remember Kozlovsky used to have a card-index room on the second floor? Well, I've installed a new interrogation room in there. So we can do our job properly. We'll go up now and you'll see it for yourself. Only I'll just phone Colonel Skukin. He can inform the commander that we've actually caught Zaenko.'

It's already 'we've caught', and soon it will be 'I caught', Alexei thought perfunctorily, but Cherepov's ambition was the last thing that concerned him right now.

The former card-index room was unrecognisable. The shelves of little boxes had disappeared. The Chekist was lying in the middle of the empty room, stretched out completely naked in the form of a letter 'X' on a carpenter's bench. His wrists and ankles were secured with straps, his mouth was taped shut with sticking plaster and his eyes were shifting about frenziedly. Kalmykov, wearing a leather apron, was standing nearby, setting out carpentry tools on a little table.

Humming a little tune, the lieutenant colonel also put on an apron and sleeve protectors, without hurrying at all and pointedly ignoring the prisoner. He walked over to a low cabinet where an elegant gramophone with a glittering lacquer horn was standing and started selecting a record.

'I like a bit of comfort when I'm working,' he explained to Alexei.

'Why is he naked?'

'I always reduce patients to the natural state. Remember rule number one: the subject under interrogation must feel like a naked piece of meat. That rids him of any ambitions and inclines him to be sincere.'

'. . . And what's the plaster for? He won't be able to answer!'

'At the initial stage that's not necessary. A man starts lying and wheedling, hoping to talk his way out of it somehow. Or he remains haughtily silent and doesn't want to speak. The beef needs to be well tenderised first. That way all the bellowing gets finished with. Let the meat beg and beseech: stop, I'll tell you everything! But we won't stop that soon. Rule number two: the opportunity for the subject under interrogation to provide an honest confession must not be a free offer, but a reward that has to be earned. In the long run this tactic will save time.'

The lieutenant colonel put on the fashionable Russian romance 'Happiness is Over'.

'The music provides a background. All the bellowing and growling will begin now . . . Right, then, to start with, a gentle clean-up.'

Humming along to the record – 'Happiness is o-ver, it was all a drea-eam, my heart is yearning, my heart is aching' – he took a piece of emery paper and scraped it along the bound man's shin with a crunch. Blood immediately started oozing out.

'Mmmmmm!'

The plaster on Zaenko's mouth swelled up.

Cherepov laughed.

'How about that for second-voice harmony?' He patted the prisoner on the belly. 'Right, to be going on with I'll outline the subject of the forthcoming conversation. You're going to tell me who's in your gang, every last one of them. And where I can grab each one. Then you'll tell me the most important thing: who is your spy in Army HQ. But we're in no hurry. You have a large programme of events ahead of you. I haven't even run the rasp over you yet.'

The prisoner started bellowing again.

'What's that?' Cherepov asked in feigned surprise. 'Want to start chatting already? What about the rasp? You're upsetting me. Well, all right, then . . .'

He ripped off the plaster at one side and Zaenko uttered a savoury obscenity.

'That's my boy,' the lieutenant colonel exclaimed with a nod of approval, returning the plaster to its previous position. 'That makes things more interesting. I'll think I'll skip the stage with the rasp. Kalmykov, hand me over that little vice.'

Romanov's fingers were poised on his holster.

The first bullet for Cherepov, he calculated. *The second for Kalmykov. I'll have to finish off Zaenko with the third. There's no way I can save him, but at least they won't be able to torture him. And then, in all the confusion and toing and froing, try to get away myself . . .*

'And blow your cover? Leave the Republic with no intelligence network at all at this fateful hour? Just because you're such a delicate cissy?' a stern voice enquired. Alexei had no answer to that. His fingers started trembling and sweat broke out on his forehead.

Cherepov and the sergeant major leaned down over their victim and there was a quiet clanging sound. Zaenko started arching up and thrashing about. The holster seemed to unbutton itself . . .

Then the door opened with a crash.

'So this is the famous Red Rocambole!' a handsome, dapper captain with aiguillettes exclaimed merrily. 'Khariton, the commander sent me to see you.'

Alexei recognised Gai-Gaievsky's adjutant with that pseudo-Scottish kind of name – Makoltsev. It was curious that he addressed Cherepov in such a familiar fashion.

'Pavel!' the counter-intelligence chief exclaimed, delighted to see his visitor. 'Skukin has already reported to His Excellency!'

Makoltsev winked.

'General Gai-Gaievsky ordered me to bring you to him immediately. Prepare your chest for a medal and your throat for cognac.'

'I wanted to disembowel the client first and then report about everything . . .'

The lieutenant colonel pointed to Zaenko, stretched out on the bench.

'A superior's orders are not discussed, but what? Correct: they are obeyed. Come on, come on, Khariton. His Excellency's adjutant Pavel Andreevich Makoltsev has come to get you in person. In the general's Delaunay-Belleville.'

'One moment, I'll just put my uniform tunic on,' said Cherepov, beginning to bustle.

'Come as you are, in the apron, like a butcher,' the adjutant declared with a grin, casting a glance at the sergeant major and giving Alexei a casual nod.

'That's it, let's go,' said the chief, fastening his buttons. 'Kalmykov, put this one in the Icebox. And you, Romanov, keep away from him. I'll interrogate him myself.'

He walked up to the bench and stroked Zaenko on the cheek.

'See you soon, sweetheart. Wait for me.'

When he heard the Icebox mentioned, Romanov realised what he had to do.

The Icebox was a cellar located in the middle of the courtyard. In former times it had been used for storing ice and under the Chekists it had been used for executions. At that time there had been a gate in the stone wall encircling the courtyard, and bodies were dumped into the ravine through it. Unfortunately, Kozlovsky had ordered that exit to be bricked up, thereby fencing himself off symbolically from the appalling Bolshevik past, otherwise Alexei's task would have been simpler.

The plan that had instantly come to mind was this.

Since Cherepov had been taken off to drink cognac, he wouldn't return until the middle of the night. Romanov had to wait until it was dark, eliminate the sentry guarding the Icebox and get Zaenko over the wall. He would need a ladder, but there was one in the garage, he could get that.

Risky, but feasible.

At seven o'clock, just before he went home, Romanov, as the senior officer, checked the guards. He also dropped into the courtyard and yelled at the sentry, finding fault with his poorly shaved cheeks, then sent him to the guardhouse. Because of the prisoner's exceptional importance, he set Sergeant Major Kalmykov himself to guard the Icebox. (The idea was to combine business with pleasure: if he had to waste someone, then let it be a real creep.) He said goodnight to the duty officer, signed the register, gave orders that he should be phoned if anything came up and walked out into a fine drizzle.

At that time of day in October, and especially in weather like this, it was almost completely dark, but to be on the safe side Alexei decided to wait two hours – to make sure that the last members of staff had left.

And he had to pay a visit to his hotel room in any case. Zaenko couldn't go running through the city stark naked, could he?

Romanov stuffed some civilian clothes and shoes from his 'clandestine' wardrobe into a sack. He also put in a flask of vodka – the prisoner must be frozen stiff in that cellar.

Alexei returned to the mansion in complete darkness, which seemed even thicker in spots that weren't reached by the light of the infrequent street lamps. He crept along the wall and looked round, then climbed in through the window of the ground-floor lavatory (he had deliberately left the catch open before leaving). Treading silently, he walked through the quiet, empty corridors to the back entrance. Opening the door slightly, he glanced out into the courtyard and waited for a moment.

He couldn't see a thing.

That damned old soldier Kalmykov wasn't striding to and fro, or smoking, or making the slightest sound.

Romanov stepped outside, without trying to conceal himself, and lit up a *papyrosa*, standing so that the sergeant major would see who it was, but if someone happened to glance out of a window, his face wouldn't be visible.

He set off indolently towards the Icebox, waving his right hand. It was holding a knife, with the blade upwards.

He called quietly.

'Hey, sentry! Are you asleep, Kalmykov?'

No answer. Had he really gone to sleep? That would simplify things greatly.

The sergeant major was sitting on the ground with his head slumped over onto his shoulder. The door of the Icebox was ajar.

Alexei quickly squatted down and touched Kalmykov on the shoulder – the sergeant major tumbled over limply. The entire front of his tunic was wet. Blood! Not yet cold.

There was no one in the cellar. How could this have happened? And where had Zaenko got to? He couldn't have sprouted wings and flown away!

The mystery was solved when Romanov ran over to the wall. There was a rope ladder hanging down from the top of it.

Someone had acted very simply. They had climbed over into the yard from the other side, killed the sentry and left by the same route, with the prisoner. Someone who knew exactly where to look. They had left the ladder because it wasn't needed any more.

Alexei also made use of it, in order not to risk going through the building again. And to get back to the hotel as quickly as possible. When the phone rang in his room, he had to be right there on the spot and answer in a sleepy voice.

After scrambling through the tangled thickets of the ravine, he set off at a run along the street.

He had to admit that the Chekist organisation worked better than the Revolutionary Military Soviet's one, which, to be quite honest, had got completely bogged down. Maybe competition wasn't such a bad thing after all. And to do Zaenko justice, he might be a really bad bastard, but he was a tough customer.

And suddenly Romanov was struck by an idea, a very interesting one. He promised himself to put it into effect tomorrow.

He flew into his room, panting for breath. Without turning on the light, he stopped in front of the phone: had they called or hadn't they?

'I thought you weren't going to come,' the darkness whispered.

A small, slim shadow got up off the bed.

'Just don't speak. Don't say anything . . .'

In the morning he shaved in front of the mirror and sang the romance that had got stuck in his head, about happiness that had ended and everything being a dream, only not plaintively, but cheerfully. Alexei had once had a fine voice, which disappeared after he was wounded in the throat, but he still had his musical ear.

Nadya had left half an hour ago. When she left she had told him: 'That's it, Romanov. The damage has been done. I love you more than the revolution.' And she had laughed quietly.

He had replied seriously: 'Well, I love only you. The revolution is just work. And there's nothing to love it for. We need to get it over with as soon as possible and forget about it.'

No one had called from counter-intelligence during the night. When they discovered the dead sergeant major, they must have reported to Cherepov, and he must have forbidden them to inform his assistant. He was hoping he could catch the escaped prisoner himself before the trail turned cold. Well, there wasn't much chance of that.

'Monastery Lane,' Romanov told his cabby.

The street where General Gai-Gaievsky's headquarters was located, in the mansion of the Assembly of the Nobility.

Alexei halted outside Skukin's office. He could hear the limpid sounds of a flute coming from inside. That meant the colonel was alone and immersed in complicated deliberations of some kind. Skukin had told Romanov that music helped him arrange his thoughts in strict harmony.

Now I'll sing, and you'll accompany me, Romanov said to himself, chuckling, and knocked in an agitated, demanding manner.

'I've only just found out!' he shouted from the threshold. 'Fandorin and his Japanese brought us Zaenko on a plate and Cherepov let the Chekist escape! And what's more, he didn't even tell me, his deputy, anything about it! I only just found out, here in the orderly room. Do you think that's right?'

Everyone at headquarters really was talking about the 'emsit' (emergency situation) during the night. This new word, which had appeared during the war with Germany on the crest of a wave of general enthusiasm for abbreviations, had become one of the most frequently used words in Russia, and wits had even suggested re-naming the country 'Emsitland', because Russia itself was one big emergency situation.

'I didn't know that Zaenko was arrested by Fandorin,' Skukin said with a frown. 'Cherepov said . . .'

'Arkady, counter-intelligence is an absolute mess!' Romanov inter-rupted. 'And it isn't even Cherepov who's to blame! It isn't an idiot's fault that he's an idiot. The one to blame is the one who installed the idiot in a responsible position! Why did you do that? Just because he's personally loyal to you? You're an intelligent man. You could be called a management genius. Surely you know that loyalty alone isn't enough for counter-intelligence work? Tell me, would you let a cack-handed surgeon perform your operation just because he adores you?'

The colonel was taken aback by Romanov's onslaught. This was exactly the right way to talk to him, alternating verbal assault with flattery.

'Listen, you know me very well, we've been through all sorts of scrapes together,' said Alexei, changing tack to amiability. 'Remem-ber how I shot Comrade Kandyba to save you? How I went back to get you at the Green School? How the two of us fought our way through to our side at Kharkov? I'm the one who's personally loyal to you, not that cretin Cherepov! Because I realised a long time ago that you're a high-flyer. Let's fly together. As the professional pilots say, you're the lead and I'm the wingman. Send Cherepov packing, let him command punitive detachments. And put me in counter-in-telligence. I'm a professional!'

Skukin listened as he was supposed to do, with his eyes narrowed.

'So I can trust you?' he said slowly. 'Completely? In everything?'

'Think of me as your flute,' Romanov replied solemnly. 'I'll play the tune that you blow.'

The colonel walked over to the door, which his agitated visitor had not closed completely, and slammed it firmly.

'What's your assessment of the situation in the leadership of the White movement? I don't ask Cherepov questions like that, he doesn't think in such categories. You're a different matter. And I have to understand how you think. Answer with absolute candour, keep nothing back.'

This is the examination that will decide everything, Alexei realised.

'With absolute candour? By all means. Our leadership is mediocre. The commander-in-chief is weak. A hopeless general, a hopeless administrator and an absolute blockhead in politics. With an army such as he has, advancing on Moscow, he acknowledged the supremacy of Admiral Kolchak, although the Reds are beating the shit out of him! What kind of stupidity is that? And as for your uncle, as far as military operations are concerned, of course, he's a soaring eagle, but he doesn't have a clue about civil administration. I'm sorry, but he needs a good nanny.'

The smile of satisfaction that appeared on Skukin's dry lips made it clear that the examination had been passed with flying colours. The next question confirmed that.

'What actions would you take if you were in charge of the Special Section? A concrete assignment: how would you find Zaenko and wipe out the Red underground?'

Romanov had his answer ready in advance.

'Firstly, I'd find the spy whom Cherepov overlooked and who helped Zaenko to escape. He's one of ours. Secondly . . .'

The telephone rang demandingly.

'Skukin,' the colonel said into the receiver, then whispered to Alexei: 'Cherepov. Talk of the devil.'

Then he listened for a long time, growing more and more animated.

'Right . . . right . . . right . . .' he said, and every 'right' was more expressive than the one before it. 'How did you find out? I see . . . How do you mean – he shot himself? . . . Well, that's just excellent! Of course. Keep up the good work.' But he concluded strictly: 'Only be careful, Cherepov, this is your last chance to redeem yourself. There won't be another.'

The colonel hung up and said:

'You abuse him, but he's smoked out a Bolshevik safe house.'

'Zaenko's?'

'It's not clear yet. He got a call in his office at dawn. An unidentified person informed him in a whisper that there was a Bolshevik intelligence network centre in the Commercial Reading Room on Ivanovskaya Street.'

Alexei's heart skipped a beat.

'He sent a detail to the address. There was an old man there. They didn't take him alive, though, he shot himself. But Cherepov had enough wits to leave an ambush. And an hour ago a little bird flew into it, a young girl. She tried to run for it, but they caught her. She didn't have anything to shoot herself with, thank God. Now Cherepov will go to work on her, the way only he knows how . . . Hey, where are you going?'

A dreary October rain had set in and he couldn't find a cab. Passersby gaped out from under their umbrellas at the officer holding down his sabre as he bounded wildly through the puddles.

Romanov didn't know what he was going to do, he wasn't even thinking about that. He had to get there in time, in time!

Finally the familiar building swam out from round the corner. In the damp it wasn't black or white, but grey.

Suddenly a window shattered on the second floor. A white, almost unnaturally slim little figure, completely covered in shards of glass, came flying out of it, tumbled over in the air and landed on the cobblestones of the roadway with a dull thud. Somewhere in the distance a woman started shrieking hysterically, the sentry ran down off the steps and someone leaned out of the window above Romanov: Alexei thought it was Cherepov in his leather apron, but he was looking down, not up.

His legs carried on running out of sheer inertia, as if they had a will of their own.

Nadezhda was lying face down, exactly as she had been in the morning, when he was admiring her before waking her up: naked, with her hair scattered in all directions.

'Captain?' a coarse voice howled from above him. 'Take a look to see if she's alive or not. Shit! Would you believe it, she broke free, took a run and flung herself head first at the window . . .'

Romanov automatically squatted down and felt for the pulse on her neck. The neck was warm. But there was no pulse.

It was strange, but Alexei didn't feel anything.

Even after that he remained stonily impassive. He stood there watching as they carried her away. Watched the thin little arm dangling. Listened to the lieutenant colonel trying to make excuses and cursing.

Romanov wasn't thinking about anything at all. His breathing was regular, his heart was beating steadily, even more slowly than usual. At the same time it was aching, but in a feeble sort of way, like a toothache that hasn't got into its stride yet. Who said that, about a toothache in the heart? He had read it somewhere. Ah, Maxim Gorky.

The pain in his heart was a mere trifle. Alexei knew how to get rid of it. He simply needed to be left alone with Cherepov. And that was why he not only nodded to his superior, but even answered a few questions, and at the end he said:

'Let's discuss how to report to Colonel Skukin, just the two of us.'

'Yes, yes,' Cherepov said with a nod, glancing at the staff members crowding round from all sides. 'Come on.'

Soon now, soon now, hold out just a little bit longer, Romanov coaxed himself on the stairs, looking at the broad back and the tie strings of the apron on the neck.

In the office the first thing Cherepov did was take a bottle of vodka out of the desk and splash some into a glass.

'You're glad, I suppose?' he said in a hoarse voice. 'Think I don't know where you went running off to this morning? I know. Skukin called me just as soon as you went running to him to muscle in on my success. Me and Arkady Skukin are like that.' He set two fingers together. 'We've got so many bonds of all kinds, no one can come between us. And this business won't set us at odds either. So don't go building up any illusions . . . Hey, what are you doing with my Browning?'

He'd spotted Romanov picking up the holster.

Without saying a word, Alexei released the safety catch, aimed the barrel at his superior, who had backed away, and shot him in his single gaping eye. He cast a curious glance at the red blotch that had appeared on the wallpaper. It was made up of separate dots of different sizes. Beautiful.

Leaning down over the fallen man, he thrust the pistol into his nerveless fingers.

The toothache in his heart immediately disappeared, and suddenly it was obvious that his heart was never, ever going to ache again. No matter what happened.

'Hey, this way!' Romanov yelled desperately, turning towards the door. 'It's an emergency, the chief's shot himself!'

His Excellency's adjutant

'I show.'

Mona-san covered the master's three jacks with a royal flush. With his two pairs, Masa had prudently passed.

'And he boasted that he always wins and we would be bored!'

Laughing rapaciously, the winner raked the heap of green pieces of paper towards herself.

'Incredible,' Fandorin declared. 'The third time in a row! Fortune has abandoned me for you. How w-well I understand her.'

They were playing for dollars, of which there were fifteen hundred left from the American credit transfer. Mona-san had suggested dividing them in half and playing poker. She was constantly thinking up new amusements. It was obvious why: to distract the master from dangerous thoughts.

'You'll both be my kept men, ponces,' the mistress laughed. 'You'll do whatever I tell you to.'

'I already do whatever you tell me to,' said Fandorin, inclining his head meekly, for which he was kissed.

Watching the lovebirds billing and cooing was delightful, but Masa was thinking sad thoughts.

How cruelly karma had mocked him! To fall in love on the threshold of old age – and with whom? Not with a beautiful, sunny lady, like the master, but with a gelding! What an appalling disgrace! A fine connoisseur of women . . . It wasn't a matter of the humiliation, though, but the fact that after so many years of service the faithful vassal had almost abandoned his master. Frivolously, for the spectral chimera of personal happiness!

If Masa had not lost the greater part of his Japanese nature in his long years of life abroad, he would have committed *seppuku* out of shame.

His entire previous road had been as straight and clear as the blade of a sword with the hieroglyph 'Fidelity' engraved on it. But now there was no more point in baring the steel, now it would rust in its scabbard. The master had an intelligent, strong-willed companion who would make her husband what she wanted him to be, and that should not be resisted, because he would be happy with her. A couple like that had no need of a faithful vassal, their own fidelity would be enough.

Ah, if only Mona-san would agree to go to Japan! Then at least Masa's life would complete its circle and conclude where it began. But to insist on that would be egotistical. He had to be honest: Japanese people would not like the mistress. She was too independent for a woman, too conspicuous with her red hair, too tall, she laughed too loudly. Like Harionna from the island of Shikoku – the witch who snared men with her hair that was as sharp as needles.

After the next deal Masa turned up his cards. His prospects in life were as good as this hopeless combination: ace, king, queen, eight and six. He set the king and queen aside, in order not to break up the family, and discarded the rest. But his draw brought a valuable surprise – another three kings. Four of a kind!

And his mood immediately improved. It was a hint from on high: never, ever lose heart.

'I double,' Masa said, and smiled rakishly, like a man with a poor card trying to bluff.

Fandorin immediately quit, he was completely disenchanted with his luck, but the mistress took the bait and raised the stakes even higher.

'I double,' Masa repeated. And then again – 'I double . . .'

This is the answer to the question of what the happy couple needs me for, he thought joyfully. *The master doesn't know how to manage money, and the mistress has all the hallmarks of a terrible spendthrift. I shall deal with the money. Now I'll take all the dollars and prove to the mistress (the master already knows) how skilfully I can direct finances.*

'I go all in,' Mona declared, and laughed exultantly, because Masa had nothing to match her with.

But she had rejoiced too soon.

'Master, lend me what you have left,' he said.

Fandorin nodded absent-mindedly; his thoughts were soaring somewhere far away.

'I'm probably done for,' Masa said dejectedly. Inwardly, gloating laughter tickled his *hara*, it felt very pleasant. 'Show me what you have, mistress.'

'No, you first.'

There was a knock at the door. Ah, what bad timing!

Masa went to open up.

It was Colonel Skukin and Captain Romanov. The former was brisk, as always, the latter was unusually lethargic. He always smiled, but this time he merely nodded. And his eyes were like a corpse's – glassy.

'May we?' the colonel asked. 'Captain, follow me!'

'Yes, sir.'

Strange, Romanov had never behaved like a subordinate before.

'I'll get straight to the point,' Skukin began energetically, after sitting down on the chair that was offered. 'Erast Petrovich, I'm appealing to you as an old acquaintance, hoping for your understanding and help. But naturally, you have already guessed that this is not a social visit. Permit me to introduce Captain Romanov in his new capacity of acting head of the Special Section. Cossack Lieutenant Colonel Cherepov has shot himself.'

The mistress gave a quiet cry – not exactly of distress, more of surprise.

'He was an unfortunate choice for such a responsible position,' Skukin said with a sigh. 'It was one fiasco after another. You and your Japanese caught the Chekist Zaenko – Cherepov let him get away. Last night somebody phoned Cherepov and whispered to him the address of a Bolshevik meeting place. Counter-intelligence captured a girl alive there, and she would have told us everything. But Cherepov managed to let her slip through his fingers. And, to judge from the coded messages found there, it was more than just a meeting place, it was the centre of the entire underground network. After failures like that, I'd probably have shot myself too.'

'You'll never shoot yourself,' the mistress said in a hostile voice. 'And Cherepov wasn't the kind of man to lay hands on himself.'

'You didn't know him very well,' the changed Romanov responded in a flat voice. Probably he had turned so pompous because of his new position. 'I'll spare you the details, but believe me: Cherepov was psychologically abnormal.'

'Yes,' Skukin said with a nod. 'People who knew him for a long time said he changed greatly after he was wounded in the head.'

'What do you want from Erast Petrovich?' Mona-san asked in the same hostile manner.

Obviously realising who took the decisions here, the colonel focused on her.

'Dear Elizaveta Anatolievna, the decisive moment of the war is approaching. The fate of Russia will be decided in the next few days. Out there . . .' – he pointed vaguely at the wall – '. . . at Tula.'

'And what does that have to do with Erast Petrovich?'

'An enemy spy network is operating under our very noses. Its leader Zaenko is at liberty. And he has an informer with access to headquarters' secrets. The man who informed the underground activists about the commander-in-chief's visit to the orphanage. The one who arranged the murder of Colonel Kozlovsky. The one who organised Zaenko's escape. But anyway, that's all ancient history. Right now, there's something else that troubles me more. The success of our offensive depends on a train carrying new English tanks reaching the front. They are the lance with which we shall break through the defences of the Reds and pierce through their rear lines all the way to Moscow.'

'What kind of new tanks?' asked Masa, who took a great interest in technical progress.

'Twelve Whippets. An excellent fighting machine. Fourteen tonnes, four machine guns, strong armour, a forty-five-horsepower engine, it can surmount almost any obstacles in its path, and its fuel range is a hundred and thirty kilometres. Can you picture it?'

'But is Erast Petrovich really a tank soldier?' the mistress asked sarcastically.

'The tank soldiers are English,' Skukin explained to her. He was one of those people who don't understand sarcasm. 'The help we need from Mr Fandorin is of a different kind. The schedule of the special train's movements is top secret but, after all, someone informed Zaenko's saboteurs of the movements of the armoured train "Dobrynya". If the tanks don't reach the front, victory might escape our grasp. Help us to neutralise the underground network, Erast Petrovich. The outcome of the war depends on it!'

Mona-san glanced at the master significantly and he, of course, replied:

'What does your war have to do with me?'

'Let's go, Arkady. I told you, it's pointless,' Captain Romanov said sombrely.

The colonel stood up reluctantly.

'In case you should happen to change your mind . . .' He put a folded piece of paper on the table. 'This is a warrant signed by the commander, ordering all members of all units and all departments to afford Actual State Counsellor Fandorin every possible assistance. Think, Erast Petrovich. I implore you. On behalf of General Gai-Gaievsky and on my own behalf.'

And the officers left.

'Something has happened to Romanov. Something very bad,' the mistress said.

'We know what. His best f-friend Prince Kozlovsky was murdered.'

Mona-san shook her head doubtfully, but said no more about it and picked up her cards.

'Shall we show? All the money is at stake.'

Masa imperturbably laid out three kings, then acted panic-stricken when she laid out three aces in exactly the same way. Then he threw down the fourth king on top of the others, and gasped when the fourth ace plopped down on top of it – the same one that Masa had recently discarded.

'You lose, son of the Mikado!' the mistress laughed, raking up all the money.

She's cheating, and I didn't notice a thing, Masa thought admiringly. *Oh, what deft hands she has!*

But the mistress glanced anxiously at Fandorin, who was clicking his rosary beads intently, wrinkled up her nose and sighed.

'All right, Erast, I know that manner of yours. What's on your mind?'

'I've j-just realised my mistake. I only followed one lead, but there are two. There are two Red undergrounds in the city, possibly not even connected with each other! No wonder things didn't quite fit together. I'm f-familiar with this kind of situation. Under the old regime the Okhranka and the gendarmes competed in exactly the same way. Sometimes they even helped terrorists kill their competitors in the other department! So that's the significance of the anonymous phone call! Look, Masa. Here's Zaenko's organisation, with its own informer. And this is the other organisation, with its c-centre in the reading room . . .'

He started drawing little circles and lines on a sheet of paper, but caught his wife's gaze on him and broke off.

'I'm not feeling well,' the mistress said in a weak voice. 'I have a sinking sensation in the pit of my stomach and cramping lower down. Dearest, make the infusion that the doctor gave us, quickly . . .'

The master dashed into the bathroom, and Mona-san said in a quiet voice:

'Masa, what can I do? I can see that he wants to carry the investigation right through to the end. I spoke to Professor Liebkind this morning. He is categorically opposed to my travelling anywhere by train. There's too much jolting and – God forbid – there could be emergency braking. He told me to wait for another two weeks. But two weeks is a very long time. Erast will eat his heart out from inactivity, and I'll eat my heart out watching his torment. What's to be done?'

'If you want to leave, we will leave,' Masa replied, happy that she was asking his advice. 'I'll buy feather mattresses at the market and lay them everywhere in the compartment, and you won't feel any jolting. But in your place, first I would let the master finish the case, it's a simple job, he'll crack it like a nut and then the master won't feel that he is not free in his actions. Men don't like that.'

Mona-san stroked his hand gratefully, and at that point Fandorin came back with a glass in his hand.

'It's all right, the spasms have eased off,' the mistress said cheerfully. 'Damn you, you noble man. I know what's eating at you. You want to find the villain who informed Zaenko about the orphanage. Well, find him, then. Let him pay for the deaths of those children. Will twenty-four hours be enough for you?'

'Yes,' Fandorin replied immediately. 'I already know how to search for him. It's very s-simple.'

'But Masa should go with you. For my peace of mind. Don't worry, I won't leave the apartment at all. I need to pack for the journey. Why are you just sitting there? You have twenty-three hours and fifty-nine minutes left.'

The master set off towards the hallstand with a dignified but very rapid stride.

'Are we going to the telephone exchange?' Masa asked when they walked out into the street and turned towards the Nikolaevsky Cathedral.

'Naturally, wh-where else?'

'It's strange that Romanov-kun didn't pick up this obvious trail.'

The master didn't reply to that.

Because of the emergency situation, the Kharkov municipal switchboard had been militarised, and instead of telephone ladies, it was manned by army signallers. Fandorin showed his warrant to the officer in command and requested that he gather together the entire night shift: fortunately the barracks was close by. Masa would have done the same thing: try to find the anonymous informant. There aren't many calls at dawn, and the operator must certainly recall a request for one to the counter-intelligence department.

And so it turned out.

In response to Fandorin's question, an elderly soldier immediately raised his hand.

'Yes, sir, there was a call like that. I put it through.'

'Where was the call made from? Do you remember?'

'Yes, sir. From army headquarters.'

Fandorin gave his assistant a significant look and the two of them took the witness to one side.

'What kind of man was it? Try to describe him,' the master said gently. 'When you hear a voice in the receiver, you must picture to yourself the person calling. All telephone operators do that, to avoid being bored.'

'I couldn't say. To avoid being bored, I always think about sausage. I'm extremely fond of sausage,' the soldier explained. 'A voice like any other: "Connect me with the Special Section, brother, and make it quick." And he gave me a three-digit extension, I don't remember it. He wanted to get straight through to the Party.'

A man used to commanding, Masa realised.

'Can you recall the p-precise time of the call?'

'Probably a quarter past four. Or half past.'

'Good man. Here, take this, for s-sausage.'

The master gave the soldier a banknote.

'Why are you looking so pleased?' Masa asked. 'We didn't find out very much. It was already clear anyway that the spy is in army headquarters. There are a hundred or two hundred people there. How can we tell which one of them called?'

'There are far fewer people on duty at night. That is one. The call is not likely to have been made from a phone for general use – the risk of s-someone overhearing is too great. That is two. Which means the man who called the Special Section has his own phone. And thirdly, the man who called is known in counter-intelligence.'

'Because he spoke in a whisper?'

'Not only because of that. He gave the operator Cherepov's internal number instead of simply calling the Special Section and g-giving the extension to the duty officer there.'

'So we won't need twenty-four hours. Let's go to army headquarters to search for the spy, master.'

'This is a full list of staff members who are on duty at the time you indicated,' Skukin said as he came back into the office. 'I checked, eighteen men (the names are underlined) have access to a telephone. Five of them, indicated with a tick, could have spoken freely without any risk. Well, I hope my uncle doesn't count. At three o'clock in the morning he let me go off to sleep, while he stayed in the office. The other four are Adjutant Makoltsev – in the reception office; the head of the courier service, Captain Rzheshevsky; the duty officer in the garage, Lieutenant Stube; and the head of the commander's escort, Cossack Sub-Captain Popenko. Could any of them really be a member of the Red underground? It's hard to believe.'

'Let's not draw any conclusions prematurely,' the master replied evasively. 'I'll t-talk to each one of them. But first of all, with your permission, I'll simply stroll round headquarters and get my bearings.'

The large, beautiful building, in which the flower of the Kharkov nobility once used to gather on solemn occasions, was now, during the day, full of military men, assiduously dealing with their military business, and they were a delight to behold. Masa liked it when people made an effort.

Some were sitting down, writing or typing, some were drawing beautiful diagrams with coloured pencils, some were walking somewhere quickly with their spurs jingling pleasantly, and some were yelling hoarsely into telephones. And they were all smoking, so that bluish smoke swayed under the ceilings, like the mist in the *tanka* about the valley of Musashi:

> Blue mist
> Over the Musashi valley.
> Huddling into the ground,
> The diligent peasants
> Do not admire the beauty.

People glanced at the two civilians strolling round headquarters with some surprise, but without any suspicion. If they were there, they had a right to be.

Listening to the telephone conversations and fragments of discussions, Masa soon realised that everything circled around three main subjects: the situation on the northern front (where things were going quite well), the movements of the 'special' (that was the train with the English tanks) and a surprise offensive by Makhno's partisan army (it had been thought that the bat'ko was defeated, but he had suddenly struck at the White army from the rear).

The master, of course, took an interest in the train. He spoke with the head of the railway traffic service, after first presenting his magical document. That proved to be insufficient and the department head checked with Colonel Skukin by phone before he started answering questions.

The patrols had been augmented at every station, he said. Cavalry units were patrolling every track on the route. A final refuelling stop had been arranged at Chuguev, but the precise time was not known even to the traffic service. To prevent sabotage the schedule of movement was *spo-rad-ic*, with the train sometimes hurtling along at full speed and sometimes making unexpected stops. The periodicity was controlled by special coded telegrams from the commander.

Fandorin thanked him politely, and once they were out of the office he said to Masa:

'Skukin's right. In the large areas there isn't a single phone from which you could call counter-intelligence without attracting attention. So the circle of suspects remains unchanged.'

'Who shall we start with?'

The master was surprised.

'Are you still asking? Naturally, with Captain Makoltsev. He knows everything that the commander knows, and probably even more. That is one. The adjutant entered the general's office when the details of the commander-in-chief's visit to the orphanage were being discussed. That is t-two. He was in the counter-intelligence department shortly before Zaenko's escape. That is three. And, of course, he is informed about the timetables of secret trains. Very probably he is the one who takes the instructions to be coded. That is four.'

The captain was not in the reception office. The duty officer said that Makoltsev had left in a car half an hour earlier, and he had driven himself. He had said he wasn't feeling well.

'Does he live far away?' Fandorin asked.

'No, in the Hotel Paris.'

'Then why the car? That's only five minutes' walk away.'

'I couldn't say. He must have been feeling really unwell. He was looking a bit . . . strange,' the officer recalled after thinking for a moment. 'The captain is always cheerful and smiling, but this time he was gloomy and pale. I hope to God it's not typhoid.'

'To the hotel!' the master snapped to Masa. 'Quickly!'

But Makoltsev wasn't in his room. And in addition the receptionist said the captain had not put in an appearance since morning.

They walked upstairs and opened the door with a picklock.

'Are we going to make a search?' Masa asked. 'If he's a spy, he must have a secret hiding place. I take the right side, and you the left?'

Fandorin stood at the desk, leaning over an open notepad.

'Wait with th-the search. A page has been torn out here.' He held the notepad up to his eyes. 'Recently. Now, then . . .'

He went into the bathroom, sprinkled a layer of tooth powder on the paper and cautiously blew it off.

Looking over the master's shoulder, Masa saw letters appear in the fine indentations.

'Rostov 03.15. Alexandrovsk – indecipherable. Yu . . . Ah, Yuzovka 11.30. Lugansk – indecipherable,' Fandorin read out slowly. 'Chuguev 18.15.'

'What is it, master?'

'Stations on the southern line. And, apparently, arrival times. No, more likely departure times, since the rate of movement is uneven, with stops of d-different lengths . . .' He looked at his watch and murmured: 'Ah, so that's why . . .'

'What?'

'Why Makoltsev needed a car. To get to Chuguev. It's half past five now. The c-captain must already be approaching the station. We have to hurry.'

And he dashed to the door, after grabbing a pair of field binoculars off the desk. Masa, of course, was close behind.

'Does the adjutant want to blow up the train?'

'Probably not blow it up. There isn't any time to lay a charge, and it doesn't l-look as if he has any accomplices. Makoltsev wants to derail the train. I don't know how. But he's a very bold and enterprising individual.'

'And where are we hurrying to?'

'Back to headquarters. I saw an excellent Harley with a s-sidecar in the courtyard.'

'Are we going to this Chu . . . Chuguev? But what for? We just have to phone the officer of the guard at the station, so he can arrest the spy.'

'I don't want them to arrest this v-villain,' Fandorin replied in a quiet voice, and Masa didn't ask any more questions.

The master wants to settle accounts with this akunin *for the deaths of the children and women. A very correct decision.*

They were already on the grounds of the headquarters building. Another two minutes were spent on obtaining the motorcycle with the help of the warrant.

'It's eleven minutes to six now. We won't be in time. The train will set out before we reach the station. Maybe we should call after all?'

'To hell with the train!' the master growled. 'That's not our fight. For me it's all the same as the War of the Red and White Roses. I don't know which side in the war is right. Our job is not to let the s-scoundrel get away. So hold on tight.'

They hurtled out through the gates with a roar and a rumble. The motorbike sped up to eighty kilometres an hour, hopping like a frog on the cobblestones and leaping like a tiger on the bumps. Masa clung to the sides of the sidecar with both hands, otherwise he could have gone flying out.

'Good!' he shouted. 'Remember how we rode round Baku?'

'Eh?' asked Fandorin, who hadn't heard.

Masa tried to repeat the question, but an especially sprightly bound made him bite his tongue. Nothing more was said for the rest of the way.

The master drove the powerful machine so well that if this had been motocross, he would probably have won first prize, but he didn't drive all the way to Chuguev. The motorcycle braked sharply with a mile still to go.

'What's wrong?' Masa asked, then understood when he heard shooting in the distance.

They were too late.

The Harley turned off the road and bounced up the slope of a shallow hill, round the railway line which curved on the far side.

From the top there was a view of the station, with its tangle of main lines and side tracks. A train picking up speed: a powerful locomotive with a string of flat wagons behind it, covered with tarpaulins. It was definitely the 'special'.

'Binoculars!' the master shouted, standing up on the saddle to get a better view.

But Masa didn't give them to him – he wanted to take a look himself.

In the little circles he could see soldiers shooting as they ran along, and opening their mouths soundlessly. Then two little black figures separated from the locomotive, one after the other, jumping from the moving train and tumbling down the embankment.

'He's seized the locomotive!' Masa shouted. 'Made the engine driver and stoker jump out! But what does he want to do? Steal the tanks?'

'No. The train has turned into a dead end. Makoltsev must have switched the points in advance.'

Masa moved the binoculars along the line that the train was hurtling down and saw that it broke off in about five hundred metres, running straight into an embankment.

The train was rushing along at full throttle, getting faster all the time.

'A genuine *akunin*,' Masa said approvingly, 'with a black but brave heart. Now he'll die very beautifully.'

And he prepared himself for a picturesque spectacle, training the lenses on the site of the inevitable crash.

'Oooh!' he exclaimed rapturously when the black torpedo of the locomotive smashed through the barrier, slamming into the ramp of earth and flinging up its rear, then overturned, thudding down with its wheels in the air, and rolled a bit farther. The flat wagons humped up into a zigzag, crashing into each other and scattering right and left. The heavy carcasses of the tanks flew off them and bounced like matchboxes. Turrets, caterpillar tracks and other metal objects were sent flying.

And what rumbling and crashing there was! As if Raijin, the god of thunder, had struck all ten thousand of his celestial drums at once!

'There won't be any tank breakthrough,' the master said, sitting back down at the handlebars. 'The chances of the Red and White

Roses are evening out. Get in the sidecar. Let's go.'

'Where to?' Masa asked. 'The captain has punished himself. And I think I'll recite a funeral prayer for him. He died like a warrior.'

'When you look through binoculars, you lose sight of the overall p-picture. Ten seconds before the crash, Makoltsev jumped down the slope. So let's kill him first. And then recite a prayer.'

The motorbike rushed down the slope and a minute later they were beside the smashed 'special' and Masa saw the mangled tanks, shattered flat wagons and torn-up sleepers from close up.

'There he is!' cried the master, jerking his chin forward and to the right.

Over there a man in an officer's double-breasted jacket was lying a few dozen paces from the last, hopelessly deformed tank.

Masa ran up to him and saw that he was unconscious, but alive. The captain had a purple bruise on his cheek, his eyes were closed and his lips were tightly compressed.

'Bring him round,' the master ordered. 'In a few minutes the soldiers will come running up, and we need t-to have a word with him. Something here doesn't add up . . .'

'I agree,' Masa said with a nod. 'A villain who calmly kills children wouldn't risk his own life like this.'

He pressed on an energy point below the *akunin*'s shoulder blade. If the man wasn't dead, he would wake up.

The adjutant opened his eyes immediately. He blinked a couple of times, moved his head this way and that, and smiled.

'Ah, the Pinkertons . . . I couldn't care less. The job's done. I won't answer any questions.'

He tried to get up and groaned. He seemed to have broken ribs, and possibly more than that.

'I have only one question,' said Fandorin. 'You won't have to betray anyone. As a reward for an honest reply you'll receive a revolver with a single c-cartridge.'

Makoltsev smiled again.

'Bolsheviks don't shoot themselves. But I'm curious. What's the question?'

'Didn't you feel sorry for them? Not at all?'

The Red spy was surprised.

'For whom?'

'Ilya Sapozhnikov, eight years old; Borya Minich, nine years old; Kolya Beletski, nine years old; Kostya Leshschenko, nine years old; Petya Milovanov, eleven years old; Sasha Stein, ten years old; Senya Koltsov, nine years old and Kornei Ranz-Zass, six years old.'

'My God, and who are they?'

'The boys who were killed at the orphanage. When your underground tried to blow up the c-commander-in-chief.'

'That wasn't us. Why would we kill Palliasse? So that instead of an old deadhead the White army would be commanded by that sharp-toothed wolf Gai-Gaievsky? We're not idiots.'

'Then who d-did it? The other underground, the one you gave away to Cherepov?'

The captain frowned.

'You mind your own business. I only agreed to answer one question.'

'With your permission, I also have one question,' said Masa, bowing to the *akunin*. 'If General Gai-Gaievsky is such a dangerous enemy, why didn't you kill him? It was very easy to do.'

'They kept asking me that all the time . . . never mind who,' Makoltsev answered with a sigh. 'I couldn't make myself do it. I like the old drunk.'

Masa spoke to the master in Japanese.

'This is a sincere man. Everything he says is true.'

'I can see that. Let's leave. We'll leave him one final minute to crawl away. If he manages it, that's his good luck.'

'This man will manage it,' Masa said confidently and bowed to the Red samurai once again in farewell.

They walked away.

The adjutant shouted after them.

'Hey, Pinkertons, where are you going?'

But he received no answer, because Masa and Fandorin were talking.

'Reds and Whites, like the Taira clan and the Minamoto clan. Implacable enemies, but on both sides there are black scoundrels and white knights,' said Masa.

'It's always like that in war. You don't choose between Good and

Evil. Only which rose you're fighting for, and if the smell of a rose makes you feel sick, you keep clear.'

'That's the most difficult thing, keeping clear,' Masa remarked sadly.

And he concluded in his own mind: *The noble man, born for action, doesn't know how to do that. And you won't manage it either, master.*

Two small tasks – one small and one little

'Pavel . . . I mean Makoltsev went insane. There is no other explanation,' Gai-Gaievsky said mournfully after listening to the story. 'It's a pity you let him get away, Mr Fandorin. I would very, very much like to look into his eyes . . . No, it's absolutely incredible. I regarded him . . . as a son. We talked about so many things, we spent time under fire together.' He shrugged in bewilderment. 'I'm sixty already, and it turns out that I don't understand people at all.'

'Which I have told you more than once, Uncle,' Skukin immediately put in.

Erast Petrovich said nothing. He still didn't understand why he had been invited to see the commander, and so insistently and urgently. Skukin had already been informed of the previous days' events in Chuguev (with the exception of certain details that the colonel didn't need to know about). So what had Fandorin been summoned for? To relate the same story again?

'Uncle, didn't I try to impress on you that you ought to get rid of Makoltsev? God knows how many setbacks on the front have occurred because of that spy,' said Skukin, pressing his point.

'I thought that you were simply envious, Arkady, because I spent more time with him than with you. But you're a teetotaller, and always whining about work, and sometimes a man has to relax . . .'

'Look where relaxing has got you. Congratulations.'

Gai-Gaievsky frowned stubbornly.

'Anyway, I'm still certain Pavel went crazy.'

'No, Your Excellency,' said Fandorin, who was getting fed up with this family squabble. 'Makoltsev was a Red agent. The attempt to blow up the armoured train and Zaenko's escape were undoubtedly your adjutant's work.'

'And you've forgotten the attempt on the commander-in-chief's life,' Skukin added. 'Makoltsev informed the underground of the schedule for the visit, and two Red underground agents, who had insinuated themselves into the Special Department's half-squadron, planted the bomb.'

'Yes, yes, you reported about that,' said His Excellency, nodding. 'Afterwards one of them was found dead, and the other disappeared.'

'No doubt the second one was the leader and he did away with his assistant in order to cover his tracks. The Reds live by the laws of wolves, Uncle.'

The commander seemed to have found a reason to be angry with his nephew.

'If you hadn't persuaded me to appoint that fool Cherepov as head of counter-intelligence, we would have exposed the enemy network sooner. My tanks would have been safe and sound, and our victory wouldn't still be hanging in the balance!'

He turned to Fandorin, who had raised one eyebrow – the news that Cherepov had been made counter-intelligence chief at Skukin's insistence had come as a surprise to him.

'In fact, that's what I want to talk to you about, Erast Petrovich,' the general continued. 'Without the tank spearhead the offensive could peter out. There aren't enough men, and the flanks are over-extended. And that's only half the problem. I believe in my soldiers. If they're not impeded, they'll tear through the front of those lousy Red divisions. But that's just the point, they are being impeded. No later than tomorrow I shall have to withdraw large forces from the front line to plug a hole in the rear. Have you heard about the offensive by Makhno's hordes?'

'Yes, the newspapers write that the Insurrectionary Army is pressing hard from the east,' said Fandorin, inclining his head. Military events did not greatly interest him, and just at the moment he was preoccupied with other thoughts. His fingers slipped into his pocket and felt for his jade rosary. As usual, touching the cold, smooth beads accelerated the process of deduction.

'The papers do not write even a tenth part of the truth! In some miraculous fashion, Makhno, whom we had driven to the very edge of the Ukraine, has assembled new hordes and swept aside our covering force, and now he's bowling across the steppe on his machine-gun carriages, heading straight for Taganrog. They've already taken Melitopol and Berdyansk. If we don't redeploy at least two divisions to that sector, there'll be a catastrophe! And without those two divisions, I can't break through the Red front!'

'Why do I need to know all this?' Erast Petrovich asked frostily.

The commander looked at the colonel.

'Arkady says you could stop Bat'ko Makhno . . .'

It was said uncertainly. Apparently Gai-Gaievsky himself was not completely convinced of the possibility.

But Skukin butted into the conversation again.

'The bat'ko's main adviser and ideologue is the anarchist Aron Liberty. They say that he is the supreme authority for Makhno. I remember how the document from him saved us all in the Green School. You are closely acquainted with Liberty. He will listen to your opinion. Makhno hates both the Whites and the Reds, but for Liberty the main enemy is Bolshevism. We know that a few days ago at the Congress of Peasant Delegates, Liberty declared that the Insurrectionary Army must fight against the dictatorship of the proletariat and the communists. And when the Red command sent their emissaries to Makhno, Liberty persuaded the bat'ko to send them packing. If you were to speak to your acquaintance and explain to him that by fighting against us the anarchists are helping the Reds . . . if we could agree a truce and joint operations . . . The Reds have an undefended flank facing Makhno, just as we do. The bat'ko could slice through it like a knife through butter. And we are prepared to provide him with weapons, ammunition, uniforms, medical supplies . . .'

Fandorin winced and got up.

'Don't w-waste your energy. My participation in this war is over.'

Almost over, he added to himself, and walked out. He was feeling apprehensive. There was another difficult conversation with his wife in the offing.

Masa was waiting for Fandorin in the lobby of the Metropole. From the stiff, cheerful smile on his face, it was clear immediately that something was wrong. The Japanese even began by saying:

'Master, just don't be alarmed . . .'

And Erast Petrovich immediately felt so alarmed that his hands started trembling, although they didn't usually shake, even when he lifted two-hundred-pound weights.

'What's wrong with her?' he shouted.

'The mistress started feeling a pain. Just here,' said Masa, demonstrating. 'I called Liebkind-*sensei*. He said he couldn't come right away. I told him that if he didn't come in a quarter of an hour, I would come to him. And I told him what I would do to him. The *sensei* has arrived. Now he's saving the mistress and the child. I left them, so that the *sensei* wouldn't be afraid. When a doctor is afraid, he can make a mistake.'

'You d-did the right thing. Come on, we'll wait in the drawing room.'

They ran up the stairs, entered the apartment quietly and scurried about restlessly in the room for a while: Erast Petrovich strode to and fro along one wall and the Japanese did the same along another. Occasionally they heard quiet moans from behind the closed door. Every time it happened, they both froze on the spot and glanced at each other in panic.

Eventually the professor emerged from the bedroom.

'It's a good thing you called me immediately,' he said to Fandorin, without looking at Masa. 'Isthmic cervical insufficiency is a dangerous thing.'

'What is that?' Erast Petrovich asked with a sinking heart. The diagnosis sounded frightening.

'A constant readiness of the neck of the womb to open spontaneously,' the obstetrician explained rather obscurely. 'Don't worry, I have inserted a pessary ring. But for the next two weeks, please be sure to observe a regime of strict bed rest, so no travelling or moving home. And, naturally, no agitation, even over the very smallest thing.'

Only now did he cast a sideways glance at the Japanese, who had stayed behind Fandorin's back.

'My dear sir, would you really have ... mmmm ... done what you threatened to do?'

'It was unforgivable of me,' Masa said with a low bow.

'Phenomenal,' Liebkind murmured. 'You know, Mr Fandorin, from now on my fees are doubled.'

'Yes, yes,' Erast Petrovich agreed hastily. He wanted to get to his wife as soon as possible.

Mona was lying in bed, looking pale but perfectly calm, even cheerful.

'The child of such restless parents can't sit still either,' she said. 'But he's not going anywhere now. Well, two weeks it is, then. I'll teach you to play canasta. Of course, you haven't got any money left, you'll have to borrow to play. And I want to practise my English a bit too. But right now I'm famished. Masa, order some lunch from the restaurant. You know what I like.'

She ate heartily, chattering briskly all the time, but before dessert she sighed and asked:

'What is it, Erast? I know that look. What's eating you?'

'Nothing,' Fandorin lied. 'I just got overanxious.'

After that she reclined in an armchair and he read aloud the latest Conan Doyle collection: *His Last Bow. The War Service of Sherlock Holmes*. Mona repeated unfamiliar words in a whisper. Suddenly she reached out her hand and closed the book.

'You're giving off vibrations. Tell the truth, or else I shall start getting agitated, and I mustn't.'

He had to confess.

'I have two tasks remaining. One is small and the other is positively l-little.'

The future mother's brows drew together menacingly.

'Again?'

'No, no, nothing risky. Simply two c-conversations that are essential for my peace of mind. The only thing is that one of them will require me to leave Kharkov for a day or so.'

'To go where?'

'Taganrog.'

'To the commander-in-chief's headquarters?' Mona asked, calming down. She wasn't frightened by a journey deep into the rear. 'All right. Go. And stop vibrating.'

'I'll relieve my soul of a burden and return in a state of total serenity, like the Buddha,' Erast Petrovich promised.

He was already feeling tremendously relieved. As the ancient maxim put it: 'He who does not punish evil is no better than the one who does evil.' And in the Buddhist hell, a rock weighing a hundred *kame* was hung on a sinner for failing to fulfil his moral duty. It would be pleasant to feel that juggernaut slipping off his soul.

The following day Erast Petrovich sat in front of a general and a colonel once again, but the former was more staid than the constantly tipsy Gai-Gaievsky, and the latter was incomparably more imposing than the slender Skukin. The conversation was taking place in the headquarters carriage of the commander-in-chief of the Armed Forces of Southern Russia.

'A conspiracy?' the general echoed, toying with his small, professorial beard, and cast a dubious glance at his adjutant. 'That's hard to believe. To be honest, I thought we were meeting about a quite different matter.'

'Listen to what Mr Fandorin has to say, Anton Ivanovich,' said the colonel. 'Believe me, it is no less important.'

From this exchange of barely comprehensible remarks, Erast Petrovich guessed that the lightning speed with which the adjutant had taken him to his superior was not accounted for only by the news that he had brought, there was also some other reason. Afanasy Ivanovich Schroeder (the same officer whom Fandorin had previously travelled to see concerning the bombing) had welcomed his visitor from Kharkov delightedly, like a dear relative – before Fandorin even had a chance to spell out the essence of his business.

The mystery will undoubtedly be resolved in its own good time, Erast Petrovich told himself, and continued speaking about the most important thing.

'Precisely so, Your Excellency, a conspiracy. At its head is the officer for special assignments serving the commander of the Volunteer Army, Colonel Skukin. The idea is to turn Gai-Gaievsky into a military dictator. This requires him to be elevated to c-command-er-in-chief before the fall of Moscow. The only obstacle to this is you. And therefore Skukin and his accomplice, Cossack Lieutenant Colonel Cherepov, organised an attempt on your life during the visit to the Kaledin orphanage. You survived by a miracle, but children and women were killed.'

'General Gai-Gaievsky has set his sights on my job? He tried to kill me? I don't believe it,' the commander-in chief snapped. 'I've known that man since the war with Japan. He is not like that.'

'*He* is not like that, and he doesn't have the slightest idea about the conspiracy. The entire plot was masterminded by his nephew, Colonel Skukin. What happened at the orphanage? Immediately before your arrival Cherepov, while supposedly inspecting the as-sembly hall, placed a time bomb under the table. The two sentries he set in front of the door guaranteed that no one would go in and no one would disrupt the plan. Subsequently Cherepov eliminated both of these witnesses, in order to divert suspicion onto them . . . When the assassination attempt failed, the conspirators evidently decided to wait for their next opportunity. And for that Skukin had to instal his man as the head of the Special Section, which, among other things, is responsible for the security of important individuals. Cherepov himself shot the former head of the section, Prince Ko-zlovsky, following which Skukin had his protégé appointed to fill the position . . .'

'How do you know this?' the general asked angrily. 'Did you see the lieutenant colonel commit murder?'

'No, but after Gai-Gaievsky said in my presence yesterday that his nephew had persuaded him to appoint Cherepov to replace Kozlovsky, I put the facts together. And immediately after that I questioned the murdered man's neighbours. The lieutenant colo-nel interrogated them aggressively to find out if anyone had seen anything suspicious from a window. One of these people, a certain Salnikov, supposedly flung himself at Cherepov and tried to punch him in the course of the interrogation. During my talk with the res-idents yesterday, I established the following. The deceased Salnikov had told at least two neighbours that on that night he was smoking at the window and saw two officers in the gateway. He couldn't make out their faces, but they were both tall and thin. One, wearing a Kuban Cossack sheepskin hat, was walking slightly behind the other. And he shot the man in front in the b-back of the head.'

'Cherepov is a Kuban Cossack and he is tall and thin,' Schroeder put in.

'I believe that with that man as ch-chief of the Special Section, Your Excellency would not have returned alive from your next visit to the Volunteer Army.'

The commander-in-chief blinked his red, weary eyes indignantly.

'And these are White officers! It's monstrous . . .'

The collar of his crumpled tunic was soiled and there was grey stubble on his cheeks. Standing at one side, right beside an unfolded map, was a plate with a half-eaten meat rissole. In the corner of the room the edge of a camp bed jutted out from behind a screen. The general apparently ate and slept without leaving this room, in which the threads of the administration of the White armies converged.

'I considered it my duty to inform you about Colonel Skukin's conspiracy because, although I am not a supporter of the Whites, I quite certainly do not want Russia to become B-brown,' said Fandorin, mentally adding to himself: *And in addition, there's that rock weighing a hundred* kame.

Erast Petrovich would gladly have settled accounts with the cold-blooded killer of children in person, but the promise he had given Mona prevented him.

'What is this Brown Russia that you speak of?' the general asked.

Unable to gather his wits, he groaned without waiting for an answer:

'My God, organising a conspiracy at a time like this! And above all, for what?'

Schroeder cleared his throat.

'Anton Ivanovich, what will your orders be?'

The commander-in-chief heaved a sigh.

'Arrest Skukin. Relieve Gai-Gaievsky of his command. Conduct a thoroughgoing investigation. But naturally not right now, with such a tense situation at the front. In the week ahead, everything will be resolved, and then the guilty parties will answer for their crimes. For the time being, give no sign. The last thing we want at such a moment is to paralyse the administration of the Volunteer Army.'

He shook his head bitterly.

'Erast Petrovich, the only thing I dream of is to fulfil my mission, liberate Moscow from the Bolshevik dictatorship and retire from it all. I don't want any power. God forbid! I have a young wife and a little daughter. I want to live with them at my estate and never command anyone again, never fight wars with anyone or decide other people's fate . . .'

When he heard about the young wife and little daughter, Fandorin glanced at the commander-in-chief with curiosity and sympathy. He recalled what people said about the general. He had got married for the first time very late, to the young daughter of an army colleague, and he tried to spend every free moment in the bosom of his family.

'God knows, I didn't aspire to this position. But if the Lord has laid this heavy cross on me, weak and incapable as I am, I must bear it honestly. We are all crusaders. We must save exhausted Russia from destruction.'

'Why are you saying this to me?' Erast Petrovich asked, guessing that there was a reason for these soulful outpourings. 'You are an extremely busy man and you wouldn't waste your time to no purpose.'

The commander-in-chief gave him a searching look.

'The information you have communicated about the conspiracy is undoubtedly important, and I am grateful to you for the investigation that you have carried out. But there is an immeasurably more important matter in which you could help me. I know what General Gai-Gaievsky asked you to do yesterday, he told me about it in detail on the telephone. That is why I received you immediately, ahead of the queue. The advance detachments of Makhno's army are already only a hundred versts away from my headquarters. I have to take an immediate decision to redeploy forces from the front. By doing so I shall almost certainly let a definite victory over the Reds slip through my fingers. If you could go to Makhno and persuade him to halt his offensive . . .'

The general raised his hand, seeing that Fandorin was about to interrupt him.

'Let me finish. I understand now why you refused Gai-Gaievsky. Why bring scoundrels like Skukin to power? You can, of course, refuse me as well. Shrink from making a choice. But when a man could have saved someone and he didn't, that is also a choice. One that remains with him for the rest of his life. And after all, we are talking about saving an entire country, tens of millions of people. We Whites are no angels, we are flesh of the flesh of old Russia, with all its imperfections and vices, but also with its natural strength, beauty and history. Bolshevik power comes from Satan. It will turn Russia into a hell, into one great concentration camp.'

'Exactly what C-Colonel Skukin intends to do.'

'Now, thanks to you, he won't do that. I said just now that I dream about retirement. But I will only allow myself to retire from active service when I have completed my sacred mission. I have no illusions concerning my own gifts. I do not possess the iron will of Admiral Kolchak, the indomitable energy of Baron Wrangel or the military genius of Gai-Gaievsky, but in the onerous choice facing Russia today, I am the least of all evils. If only because I am firmly determined not to be an evil. And when I take Moscow – if I take it – there will not be any firing squads or gallows. I shall declare an amnesty throughout Russia, I shall pursue a policy of national reconciliation. Because it is not really a question of Lenin and Trotsky. The revolution was spawned by social injustice. And I shall correct it. At least, I shall honestly attempt to do so. White Russia is not a saintly, faultless Russia, but it is Russia, in which white is white and black is black, and in the struggle between them the power will be on the side of white. That is what the White Truth is.'

Fandorin said nothing. Anton Ivanovich's arguments had hit home. Especially the one about a refusal to act also being a choice. The commander-in-chief probably had no idea that he had precisely repeated an ancient Zen paradox: 'Inaction is equivalent to action, but action is not equivalent to inaction.'

'I can see what kind of man you are,' the general continued in a quiet voice. 'And it is obvious to me that you cannot just wash your hands of everything, leaving your homeland to be destroyed, and after it has been destroyed, to burn in the flames of hell. Even if I am mistaken in you . . . A man, unlike a country, chooses his own hell. That is all that I wanted to say to you. And now please pardon me. I have a difficult situation at the front and an even more difficult situation in the rear.'

Erast Petrovich left the saloon carriage pale-faced, very much frightened that Mona would not forgive him for this.

All the more gladly, therefore, did Fandorin seize on the opportunity to postpone the inevitable. There was still the second task that he had told his wife about. The little one.

When he got back to Kharkov on the night train, naturally Erast Petrovich first of all called into army headquarters to discuss the details of his forthcoming trip, but immediately after that he went to the Special Section.

Romanov received Erast Petrovich in his office and enquired politely about the purpose of this unexpected visit. The captain's gaze was lacklustre and his cheeks were sunken.

'Alexei Parisovich, you are a Red spy,' said Fandorin, not asking but stating a fact.

Romanov's eyes came alive and narrowed.

'Is this a joke?'

'I've known it for a long time. Since the day we m-met. Remember back then, in the boat, after your flight from the Reds, you shook the spent cartridge cases out of your cylinder and one bounced under my feet. I picked it up and saw that the neck was elongated. You had been firing blanks. Which meant that the entire story of your flight had been staged. I decided it was none of my business and kept my m-mouth shut . . .'

Romanov listened warily. He had strong nerves.

'When the bombing took place at the orphanage, you were the first person I suspected, but you turned out to have an alibi. Kozlovsky informed me that you were not in Kharkov. And I left you in peace again, because I was taking no part in the C-Civil War.'

'And has something changed now?' the captain asked in a quiet voice.

'Yes. I have made a choice. In two days I am setting out on an assignment which will probably determine the outcome of the war.'

'To Makhno? Don't be surprised that I'm so well informed. I'm Skukin's henchman now, he tells me everything.'

Erast Petrovich nodded approvingly. He liked the fact that the young man had not started wheedling or lost his composure and – most importantly of all – was not taking up his time unnecessarily.

'I find you rather likeable and do n-not wish to destroy you. You have two hours to go into hiding. Before I leave I shall send a note to Gai-Gaievsky, informing him of everything. So I advise you to disappear immediately.'

He got up, regarding the conversation as over, but the captain got up too.

'Are you going to attempt to kill me?' Fandorin asked, slightly surprised. 'I don't recommend it.'

'No, I know that nut is too hard for me to crack . . . It was clear to me that sooner or later you would make a choice. I hoped it would be a different one . . . You're an intelligent man. Surely you must understand that the real Russia is with us, and not with them?'

'With Comrade Zaenko? With streets befouled with spittle, defiled churches, trampled culture?'

'And what if that is the real Russia? If the Russia that you like was invented by Pushkin and Turgenev? But the real Russia is Stenka Razin and Emelyan Pugachev? Do you really know your own people? Of course, you can herd them back into the basements and bunkhouses, you can chain them up. But to do that, you will have to spill a great deal of blood. Arkady Skukin is right about that. The Whites won't create the land of Pushkin and Turgenev. Wouldn't it be better to stop deceiving ourselves? To accept that Russia is not a flower bed, but a dungheap? Not to cover our noses with scented handkerchiefs, but to take a firm grasp of our spades, without being afraid of the filth? And then perhaps in a hundred years the country will be transformed into a flower garden.'

'Skukin is an opportunist adventurer and a *xiaoren*. He will not be allowed to control the destiny of Russia, and your allegory is inept. Filth is to be feared. In fact, it's the only thing that is to be feared. If you stop intellectualising, trying to be correct, and simply listen to your inmost feelings, an inner voice will always explain to you what is right and what isn't . . . But then, it's your karma.'

And Fandorin walked out.

I'M NOT SAYING GOODBYE

. . . And we surface out of that impenetrably black passage through the building, onto the sun-drenched street.

You squeeze your eyes shut so tightly against the bright light.

'Where are we?' you ask, and I remember that you don't know Moscow very well.

'On Nikolskaya Street. To the left, just two minutes away, is Red Square. See how adroitly I have led you out here? This is my city. I know every nook and cranny in it. Let's go!

I am filled with a vigorous strength, a reverberating lightness. I feel – no, not young, I feel *complete*.

The man who many years ago taught me to master my own body called morality a dangerous barrier, dividing the flesh from the spirit. 'Morality always prescribes setting someone else's interests above your own, but the body is always guided only by what is best for it,' he taught. 'You do not wish to renounce the pernicious division bisecting your identity, preventing Yin and Yang from uniting, and so you will never become complete.'

My contemptible *sensei* was a monster, we regarded each other in the same manner: with respectful curiosity and at the same time with contempt. He called me 'my semi-pupil', I called him 'my semi-teacher'. I wouldn't be surprised if he is still alive today and can still easily run up a wall to the first floor and jump from the fourth. But my semi-*sensei* was mistaken. I did achieve completeness. Thanks to you. I would very much like to tell you about this, but I don't dare to. You are still angry.

Nikolskaya Street is full of people, all moving in the same

direction – slowly, no one is hurrying. The faces are cheerful, but not boisterously cheerful, they seem turned inward, and no one is shouting, no one is laughing. It is not that kind of day.

We stop beside the small Kazan Cathedral, from where we can see the Kremlin and Red Square, but there are too many people there. The crowd is moving towards St Basil's Cathedral. Everyone is looking around without speaking.

Along the front of the long Merchants' Row building stands a line of scaffolds, with hessian sacks hanging from them. There is a sign on each one. From where I am standing, I can read the three closest ones: 'Vladimir Ulyanov. Dictator', 'Lev Bronstein. I shot hostages', 'Felix Dzerzhinsky. Chief executioner'. The Streltsy executed by Peter once dangled here in exactly the same way. But now there are sacks stuffed with straw. The execution is symbolic. The commander-in-chief has kept his word.

I say:

'Listen, since a general amnesty has been declared, perhaps you can finally forgive me too? How long can you carry on punishing me? After all, everything turned out well in the end.'

You sigh.

'All right, then. Since it's the kind of day when everybody is forgiven . . . You're a scurvy oath-breaker, but all right. It was obviously my karma, to become involved with a "noble man". And after all, I do understand. You had no choice. I remember what you said: "It only seems to the noble man that he has a choice."'

'There is a choice. One can simply stop being a noble man. And now it's over. I shall simply be a man and a husband. I shall live only for you – and for our daughter.'

I nod at your bulging coat.

'For our son,' you correct me. 'I want a boy, and it will be a boy. But your amnesty is only declared on one condition. You must tell me about your trip. From the moment after your meeting in Taganrog when you decided in such a cowardly fashion that you wouldn't explain yourself to me, but leave surreptitiously. I only know that you sent a telegram to Masa and he, the treacherous Judas, went to meet you, without saying a word to me. What happened after that? Tell me, with absolutely every detail.'

And I start telling you.

The platform at the far side of Kharkov's Southern Station, reserved for the requirements of the headquarters of the Volunteer Army, was guarded by special patrols. The commander's train usually stood there. And I was supposed to set out from there too.

When they let Masa through onto the platform, I explained to him where I was going and why. I asked him to tell you some reassuring lie. I gave him a note about Romanov, which was to be handed to General Gai-Gaievsky. I didn't tell him about Skukin, because then Masa could easily have settled accounts with the villain in his own way, and that didn't figure in my plans. Let the villain be judged by a court martial. And it would have been hard to explain. Skukin was there with me all the time. He had been charged with organising my journey.

'If I don't return before the time set by Professor Liebkind, or if danger of any kind should arise, take Elizaveta to the Crimea,' I told Masa. 'Wait for me there for two weeks. On no account for any longer. Then go to Switzerland.'

'And shall we expect you there?'

'Yes, exactly.'

Something glimmered in Masa's eyes, and I suddenly felt a terrible desire to hug him. I can imagine how badly that would have frightened him. Instead of that I feinted with my right hand and slapped him on the forehead with my left.

'*Atari!* I win again.'

That was an old game of ours: one of us would strike an unexpected blow, and the other one had to deflect it.

'And never once honestly!' said Masa.

I could see that he desperately wanted to go with me, but he understood that he had to take care of you.

And then a lanky officer in a black leather jacket walked up to Skukin and reported something to him in a low voice.

'Erast Petrovich, the motor trolley is ready. You can be on your way,' Skukin said.

'All right, it's time.'

I nodded to Masa, he bowed to me, and we parted.

General Gai-Gaievsky, a railway enthusiast, had an entire trans-port fleet at the station, from a heavy armoured train for visiting the front with his entire command staff to individual locomotive-car-riages and light handcars for short journeys in the rear. I had chosen the smallest of them – a simple cabin with an automobile engine.

'Are you sure that you don't need anyone to accompany you? Not even a driver?' Skukin asked, not for the first time.

'I'm sure,' I replied, not looking at the colonel. I have always been disgusted by men with that kind of mentality.

Suddenly, a little distance ahead, I noticed a very strange scene for a high-security facility.

There was a railcar standing there: a tramline car adapted to travel on railway tracks – yet another vehicle from Gai-Gaievsky's collection. Boys in blue uniform coats, carrying identical briefcases, were climbing up the steps and each of them was seated in his place by two women.

'You know how the commander and I feel about the children at the Kaledin Orphanage. He has given orders to evacuate the or-phans to the Crimea,' Skukin explained, catching my glance. 'It's warmer there. Don't worry, they'll set off in a moment and the line will be free.'

I turned away again; the word 'orphans' had made me shudder. And I promised myself that I would have a talk with the colonel about the Kaledin Orphanage. When that was possible.

The man in leather came over again.

'Colonel, I've checked the motor of the railcar,' he said with a slight Caucasian accent, leaning down respectfully to little Skukin. 'It's very badly worn, but even if it cuts out, a push will get it started again. Even the children will be able to manage that. The carriage is very light.'

'Just as long as the railcar doesn't get stuck before the fork in the line, or it could delay Mr Fandorin. Erast Petrovich, this is Lieutenant Revazov, a special railway detachment engineer. I hope the trolley is in better shape, Lieutenant.'

'The trolley is perfectly fine,' said the engineer, saluting.

The children had already clambered into their carriage, and the governesses had also climbed up. Grating its wheels, the railcar set off. The boys in blue started chattering and waving their arms about, although no one was seeing them off.

I waved to them as they left. The colonel and the lieutenant didn't even look round.

'Right, then, the way is clear,' Skukin said energetically. 'For the first eleven versts, simply follow them. But immediately after the bridge over the river the line will divide. Your branch goes off to the right, to . . .'

'I know the route,' I interrupted. 'Lieutenant, explain to me how to drive the trolley.'

Businesslike and emphatically severe, the engineer climbed up into the cabin first.

'I've been told that you drive an automobile? The principle is the same, only for obvious reasons there's no steering wheel. Movement along the rails is very smooth, the resistance is minimal, so once you've picked up speed, only rev the engine very slightly. On a long descent, in order to save fuel, you can turn the engine off altogether.' He pointed downwards. 'That's the accelerator, that's the brake. Bear in mind that the braking distance is very long; at a speed of sixty versts an hour, it's at least two hundred metres. And so for emergency stopping, this lever here has been provided. It should only be used in an absolute emergency – the vehicle could fly off the rails, and you won't put it back again without outside help.'

'Pull it up, with a jerk?' I asked, testing the stiffness of the emergency brake lever.

'Not now,' the engineer shouted angrily, grabbing hold of my arm firmly.

Then he muttered:

'I'm sorry. It's not that easy to move it back . . . What else do you need to know? There's a spare canister at the back. But you'll only need it if you use the heater. At a steady pace it consumes very little petrol. Any questions?'

I didn't have any questions. The controls were elementary.

Skukin dismissed the lieutenant and blessed me with the sign of the cross.

'Go with God.'

'Are you really a believer?' I asked. Individuals of that kind are not usually inclined to mysticism.

'No, but in this particular case I can't manage without God's help,' he said assuredly, and his voice actually trembled.

Ah, yes, I had forgotten that among the Skukins you can find true believers – who believe that God exists for them personally.

Well, I thought, *soon you'll need your god very badly.*

Pretending not to notice the outstretched hand, I got into the driving seat and switched on the engine, which started up very easily.

The trolley rapidly picked up speed. It flew along like a racing yacht under a good ocean wind – smoothly and lightly. The station buildings flew past, followed by the long outskirts of the city.

I pondered the route.

Drive as far as Lozovaya, then turn towards Ekaterinoslav, which I will never reach, of course, it is already held by Makhno's men. They will stop me before I get there. That will probably happen in about three hours. It's the riskiest moment – probably the only risky moment: they might not stop me, but simply riddle the trolley with a burst of fire from a machine-gun cart. Then I'll have to jump off while the trolley's moving, but that's child's play.

As soon as I show them the pass signed by Aron Liberty, all the dangers will be over, and thank God for that. I'm not hankering after any adventures. I want to spend the best age of my life with my wife and daughter. Or, okay, my son, although the men of the Fandorin line are very unlucky with their fathers. My great-grandfather disappeared at the Battle of Borodino, before my grandfather was born. And my own male parent, whose ne'er-do-well soul is unlikely to have entered the kingdom of heaven, can hardly be called a father.

I started thinking about what kind of father I would be, and I forgot about Aron Liberty, Bat'ko Makhno and the war.

The trolley described an arc round a low hill and straight after the turn it ran out onto a railway bridge across a river.

Immediately after that, about a hundred metres from me, the familiar railcar was barely crawling along. There were little blue figures clinging to its back and sides.

It got stuck after all, they're pushing it.

That picture reminded me of something. Something from the

distant past. This had happened before: boys in blue uniforms and a spectre of disaster hovering over them.

But no disaster could occur this time.

I couldn't brake in the usual fashion – I would have crashed into the carriage and crushed the children – but there was still the emergency brake.

And I yanked it up towards myself with all my might . . .

'Why have you stopped speaking? What happened?' you ask.

I've stopped speaking because someone is calling me. Very insistently. I look round.

'I'll finish telling you later. I have to go. They're calling me. Can't you hear?'

'I can't hear anything,' you say. 'I'll go with you. Please!'

'Don't be silly,' I say with a smile. 'Wait here. I won't be long. Look at the festivities, and the people. I'll be back soon, before you even know I've gone. Right, I'm not saying goodbye.'

AND NOW FOR THE WEATHER . . .

The weather was marvellous again. Waking up, Mona opened her eyes and immediately closed them again – the sunshine had hit her right in the pupil, a precision shot. She tried to hide away in sleep again, in order to spend a little more time with the person she could see only in a dream now. But she couldn't. The worst thing of all was that she could never remember the content of her nocturnal visions. Something important happened in them. But what?

She had to get up. For some time now Mona had hated clear weather. It was much better when she woke up and the sky was in mourning, weeping rain, and the wind was howling. That was good. She felt in harmony with the world. If you have a bitter, chilly greyness inside you and you're surrounded by 'a May day, birthday of the heart', nature seems like a traitor. Especially if it's not even May at all, but October.

The cursed month of October again, but autumn just won't start in this place, the endless Indian summer drags on and on and every day is paradise, with the tranquil blue Alps and the indifferent golden lake. Alien, meaningless, postcard beauty.

Mona didn't like Switzerland, she called it a 'porter's lodge'. *Life in a porter's lodge, under the stairs, that's what your Geneva is like.* But there was nothing to be done about it, a child needs a grandmother. Especially if the child's mother is a cuckoo, who just sings 'cuckoo' from morning to night, 'cuckoo, cuckoo', and only about herself. 'Cuckoo, cuckoo'.

Mona said: 'What a person meant to you is determined by the size of the hole that's left in you. Sometimes the hole is so immensely huge that it sucks you in completely.' Masa replied: 'Are you talking about *Kuu*, about the Void?' And he drew the hieroglyph. 空. 'Everyone emerged from it, everyone will return to it. But why hurry, mistress? And in addition there is the sense of duty. You are not alone.'

What's true is true. If Mona were alone, she would probably still be stuck in Sebastopol, hoping for a miracle. But her mother had come rushing to the Crimea and carried her off, as swollen and quivery as a jellyfish, 'to give birth in normal conditions'.

'I'm a wetched movver,' Mona said with a sigh, standing in the bathroom and looking at herself in the mirror. There was a toothbrush sticking out of her mouth. Her face was lacklustre and dull.

Little Alexander Fandorin also lived here, in Geneva, with his grandmother and grandfather. Mona went to visit her son. When she felt that she was capable of smiling. Because when someone is not yet two years old, you have to smile at him. Or at least not blubber when he looks up at you with his sweet eyes, and they're as blue as . . .

I won't go again today, Mona realised, and sighed. *I'd better get back into bed. Until the weather improves.*

She turned off the tap and heard a knock at the door. Delicate but insistent. And it had clearly been going on for a long time. Masa.

'Just a moment!' Mona responded, slowly putting on her dressing gown.

'I've brought you some bread buns and a newspaper, mistress,' the Japanese said. He looked unusual today. And the fact that he had brought a newspaper was strange too. Mona never looked at newspapers. She had no interest at all in the news.

'Here, look.'

A headline on the front page: '*L'arrivée de la délégation Soviétique*'. Mona ran her eye over the lines of compact print without any interest.

'A mission from Red Moscow has arrived in Lausanne with the goal of obtaining for Russia the status of a plenipotentiary participant in the forthcoming international conference on the Black Sea straits. This is the first official initiative by Bolshevik diplomacy since . . .'

She didn't read any more.

'What do I want this for?'

Masa thrust his finger at the very last line: Do you see?

'Do you know where they're staying?' Mona asked after a long pause. She didn't feel like crawling back into bed any more.

'At the Beau Rivage Hotel.'

The windows of the deluxe corner suite in Lausanne's best hotel overlooked the esplanade and the lake. It was one of the most famous views in the world, but the well set-up military man in a field jacket with crimson trimming that sat on him magnificently was not paying any attention to the marvellous *belle vue*. He was sitting at the writing desk and writing quickly on a sheet of paper in amazingly neat handwriting.

'Yes?' he said, raising his head with its ideal parting.

His assistant entered with a squeak of lacquered boots. A tall man with dark hair, as trim as his chief.

'Comrade Corps Commander, there's a lady to see you.' And after a brief pause, he added significantly: 'She gave her name as Mrs Fandorin.'

The military leader of the delegation puckered one eyelid slightly and pensively rubbed the medal in the red calico rosette.

'Oh, really?'

He got up and walked over to the window.

'Shall I say you're not receiving visitors?'

'No, why? Only . . .'

The corcom shuffled his fingers vaguely, but the assistant understood.

'Naturally. If she refuses to submit to a search, I won't admit her.'

But the visitor didn't refuse. While the dark-haired man frisked her slowly and thoroughly in the next room, she stood motionless, with a blank expression on her face. When she was told: 'You can go in,' she entered just as dispassionately.

The medal-bearer greeted her with extreme politeness, inclining his head and clicking his heels.

'Elizaveta Anatolievna, what brings you here?'

Mona inspected him attentively, as if she was listening to something.

'What can I do for you?' he asked. 'You know that I'm an official personage, one of the leaders of the Soviet delegation, and you, I presume, are a White émigré.'

There is caution and there is curiosity, Mona determined, quite clearly hearing the sound of a flute. And something else. Joyful agitation. *He's glad to see me. But it's not male interest. No. More likely triumph.*

'Hello, Arkady Sergeevich, I simply wanted to find out where Alexei Parisovich Romanov is. I only know that in the autumn of 1919 he defected to the Reds. Perhaps you have come across him?'

'Romanov serves in the GPU. You know what that is, don't you? We sometimes see each other when work requires it. And what is the reason, if I may ask, for your interest in Comrade Romanov?'

Jolly flames flickered in Skukin's eyes. *He's enjoying the situation*, Mona realised. *Why?*

'You know the reason,' she replied in a quiet voice.

'If it is what I think it is, then Romanov has nothing to do with it.' And now Skukin even smiled as well. 'Would you like me to tell you how it all happened? Please, do sit down.'

He indicated an armchair in front of the writing desk with a gallant gesture. They both sat down. Mona with a straight back and her hands folded on her knees. Skukin casually, with one leg crossed over the other. She looked at him expectantly.

'Head of counter-intelligence Romanov came to see me at army headquarters. With some most unpleasant news and a most interesting proposal. The news was that I was going to be arrested, court-martialled, and undoubtedly shot. Captain Romanov had just had a conversation with your husband and, being an intelligent man, he drew the appropriate conclusions from the discussion. Mr Fandorin had hinted to him that my song was sung and Romanov deduced the rest for himself. At that time he was already participating in my . . . project,' said Skukin, fluttering his fingers indefinitely. 'Let's call it that. And so, in connection with the changed circumstances, Romanov suggested that I should close my project and join his.'

'I don't understand,' said Mona. 'What projects are you talking about?'

'It's not important. Romanov told me: "The White cause is hanging by a thread, and you can cut that thread. Don't let Fandorin reach Bat'ko Makhno, and our side will accept you as a hero and the saviour of the revolution." Naturally, I agreed. What choice did I have? It was a matter of mere minutes, but I managed it.' Skukin shook his head in admiration of himself. 'Romanov only wanted me to arrest your husband and detain him for two or three days. In that time Makhno would have reached central headquarters, and the commander-in-chief would have had to re-deploy troops from the front. But, bearing in mind your husband's phenomenal talents, I found a more radical solution for the problem. What if he didn't allow himself to be arrested? Or fled? Oh no. I saw Mr Fandorin off on his way with full honours, put him in an excellent carriage and sent him straight to heaven. Strictly speaking, Erast Petrovich transported himself there, with his own hand.'

He gestured as if he was pulling some kind of lever, and laughed.

'First there was a hero, and then there wasn't. There was nothing left, absolutely nothing. Five poods of dynamite is no joke.'

That day there was an explosion of some kind on the railway, Mona recalled. *The newspapers wrote about another failed bombing by the Reds, saying that children from the orphanage had suffered concussion again, but fortunately no one had been seriously hurt.*

Fortunately.

She squeezed her eyes shut, but only for an instant. Skukin started talking again, and Mona forced herself to listen.

'After the successful operation, I judiciously disappeared from Kharkov. And a week later I was already in Moscow. This Order of the Red Banner was presented to me in person by the chairman of the Revolutionary Military Soviet. The Soviet authorities appreciate services rendered, and the new Russia needs decisive men with dialectical thinking. Do you see the three pips?' Skukin touched a patch on his sleeve. 'A corps commander. That's like a lieutenant general before. I always knew that I would be a general, and the Kharkov incident became my Toulon.'

That's why he's so pleased, Mona realised. *He's savouring the greatest triumph of his life again.*

'That's with reference to our old discussion about an alpha male,' Skukin said, and winked.

So apparently there was another reason for his frankness. Erast had said that *xiaorens*, 'petty people', never forgot their grudges.

'If you are going to sob or shower me with curses, then not too loudly please. This is a respectable hotel,' the triumphant warrior continued. 'Or are we going to view the film *The Oriental Widow's Appalling Revenge*?'

'What can I, a solitary, weak woman, do to you?' Mona asked quietly. 'And anyway, your assistant searched me so thoroughly.'

'By the way, he was also acquainted with your husband. Only on nodding terms, though. Hey, Revazov!'

The assistant must have been standing right by the door – it opened immediately.

'Show Mrs Fandorin out. I have to work on some papers.'

Without saying anything more to Skukin, but keeping her eyes fixed on the assistant's sullen face, Mona slowly walked out of the room.

With the same somnambulistic gait she walked out onto the sun-drenched esplanade. She looked round at the windows. One was wide open and the pure sounds of a flute were flowing out of it. Corps Commander Skukin was indulging in sweet reminiscences.

Mona moved a bit farther away and sat down on a bench, where she waited until Masa arrived.

'You were right, and I was wrong. It's not Romanov, it's Skukin,' she said, looking at the mountains beyond the lake. 'The corner window on the first floor.'

The Japanese nodded without speaking, put on his straw boater and got up.

'. . . Wait. There's another one there. He also has something to do with it. I don't know exactly what, but when I looked into his eyes, I heard a fingernail scraping on glass.'

'I'll think about the second one,' said Masa, bowing his head. 'Go to the station, mistress. It will start raining soon. You'll get soaked.'

'I'll sit here for a while. I don't seem to have any strength at all,' she said, inwardly repeating the same phrase over and over to herself. *There is nothing left, absolutely nothing.*

The corps commander played through to the end of Haydn's 'Serenade' and started on Bach's 'Joke', which was an even better match for his excellent mood. He walked over to the open window and started admiring the spot of sunlight hopping about on the end of his instrument.

From the creak, he realised that Revazov had walked up to him and was waiting patiently. He took his lips off the mouthpiece and, without turning round, asked:

'What?'

His assistant stood beside him and started looking into the distance. As a man from the Caucasus, he liked mountains.

'I wouldn't dismiss that woman too easily. I didn't like the way she looked at me. You yourself always say: "God helps those who help themselves." The GPU has quite a good intelligence network in Switzerland. They'll find her and do what's necessary.'

'That's what I was intending to do. This meeting brought me pleasure, and pleasure should be paid for. Arrange it.'

Corps Commander Skukin half-closed his eyelids, but then he heard a sound beside him, and squinted sideways.

It was Revazov, who had grunted hoarsely. He grabbed his throat with one hand and pulled out a little needle, stared at it in astonishment, pointed down at something with his finger, without saying anything, and slumped chest-down onto the windowsill.

Mechanically following the line of the pointing finger, Skukin saw a narrow-eyed gentleman in a check suit on the esplanade below the window. The Oriental was holding a pipe to his mouth, so he and Skukin were like a duet of flautists.

Something pricked the bridge of the corps commander's nose. His eyes squinted towards each other and glared indignantly at the needle that had appeared out of nowhere.

Down below on the esplanade, Masa raised his straw boater and bowed. He didn't wait for the dying man to collapse. Skukin was still swaying on his heels with his mouth gaping open as the Japanese walked away, looking at the lake.

The surface had been dulled by ripples and a fine spray of water had started swirling above it. The sky rapidly turned grey and cold rain started trickling down, quickly growing heavier.

Masa took no notice of the slanting raindrops. He felt sad and calm.

Everything's right, he thought. *The mistress will be pleased. And it's a good thing that summer has finally ended. Now she'll stop lying in bed for days at a time, turning her face away from the sun. She'll take back her son. She'll live. She doesn't need me any more. Neither does he. What can I teach a European boy? I'm sixty-two years old and I don't know anything, I can't do anything. Apart from killing bad men, whose karma would catch up with them without me. I've had enough, I'm fed up.*

How did the venerable Muzen's final tercet put it?

> Over and over
> I have sung the same sutra!
> It's time for a change.